20/1/04

DISCARD

40P.

The stains, badly treated corners,
dots and circles are not my doing.
This is a great story.

But the way that some people
treat library books is beyond
the pale!

EJR July 2023

The Triumph

ALSO AVAILABLE BY CHRISTOPHER NICOLE

The Sun Rises
The Sun and The Dragon
The Sun on Fire
Black Majesty
The High Country
The Happy Valley
Pearl of the Orient
Dragon's Blood
The Regiment
The Command

THE TRIUMPH

Christopher Nicole

C

CENTURY

LONDON SYDNEY AUCKLAND JOHANNESBURG

First published in Great Britain in 1989
by Century Hutchinson Ltd
Brookmount House, 62–65 Chandos Place
London WC2N 4NW

Century Hutchinson (South Africa) Pty Ltd
PO Box 337, Bergvlei 2012, South Africa

Century Hutchinson (Australia) Pty Ltd
20 Alfred Street, Milsons Point, Sydney, NSW 2061, Australia

Century Hutchinson (NZ) Ltd
P O Box 40–086, Glenfield, Auckland 10, New Zealand

British Library Cataloguing in Publication Data
Nicole, Christopher, 1930–
The Triumph.
I. Title
823′.914 [F]

ISBN 0–7126–2959–9

Typeset by Deltatype, Ellesmere Port
Printed and bound in Great Britain by
Mackays of Chatham PLC, Chatham, Kent

Contents

Prologue

1985

'Well, old boy, nervous?' demanded Lieutenant Wilson.

'No reason for him to be,' remarked Lieutenant Manly-Smith.

'No reason at all,' agreed Lieutenant Murdoch Mackinder.

Because there wasn't. If he had only joined the Royal Western Dragoon Guards from Sandhurst a month previously, and was therefore by a long way the junior subaltern, Murdoch had still felt he was coming home when he had first put on his uniform. His father was actually colonel of the regiment. There had always been a Mackinder serving with the Westerns, for more than a hundred years. All his life he had known that he would one day take his place in this distinguished company; this night, his first regimental dinner, would merely establish that place for all to see.

The banqueting room of the Savoy Hotel glowed with light, and gleamed with the regimental silver and crystal. There were four long tables: a head, and three legs leading away from it. The room was draped with flags and battle honours, and a huge replica of the regimental badge, a flash of yellow lightning against an azure sky, was mounted above the centre of the head table. Beneath the badge was a painting. Murdoch Mackinder had stared at its copy often enough; it hung in his great-grandfather's study, in the family home of Broad Acres in Somerset. Now he gazed at it again, seeking inspiration for the evening: if there was no reason for a Mackinder to be nervous in these surroundings, it was difficult not to be, on such a night. The painting depicted a dusty plain on the Indian sub-continent, with a bright sun glaring from a blue sky. Milling around the

1

edges of the picture were a vast number of turbaned warriors, armed with spears and muskets. Approaching them, at the gallop, were two squadrons of horsemen, dressed in sky-blue uniforms with burnished brass helmets; they charged sword in hand, although carbines hung from their saddle holsters: they were the Royal Western Dragoon Guards at the most famous moment in their history. It had happened in 1843, during the conquest of Sind by Sir Charles Napier, when a reconnoitring force of the dragoons, commanded by their adjutant, Major Ian Mackinder, had been led into a trap by their guides, and surrounded by a huge force of Baluchis. The dragoons had been summoned to surrender, but Major Mackinder had refused, and after leading the regiment in prayer, had charged right through the enemy ranks and made his escape with the loss of only thirty men.

That Ian Mackinder had been his great-great-great-great-grandfather, Murdoch reflected, and from that moment the Royal Western Dragoons had become almost a family concern.

There had been famous moments before 1843. And even more, since. The regiment had actually been raised in 1685 to combat Monmouth's Rebellion. The Somerset land-owner who had summoned his tenants to defend their king and country had been one Sir Thomas Lord, and thus the dragoons had early been known as the Lord's Own. A hundred and twenty-five years of service later, when battle honours gained in North America and on the continent had earned them the crown on their badge, they had found themselves in the Iberian Peninsula, under Wellington. There, in the course of those to and fro campaigns, they had taken on their own unique personality.

Hitherto, like nearly all British regiments, the dragoons had worn scarlet tunics. But over a year of toiling across the Spanish and Portuguese mountains without relief had reduced them to rags, and, there being insufficient scarlet cloth available to re-equip them, the then colonel had received permission from the great duke to use whatever could be obtained. Thus they had for the first time worn their famous sky-blue jackets with the yellow facings, and sky-blue britches with the yellow stripe, which they had retained ever since; their nickname had promptly been changed to Heaven's Own, behind which sobriquet they had proudly charged their enemies on innumerable occasions.

Usually with a Mackinder in front. If the regiment had missed the Crimea, it had won fresh laurels in India, in the Boer War, and in both the World Wars, as well as a host of minor campaigns in various parts of the far-flung Empire, as it had then been. The battle honours had become legion, and to Sedgemoor and Blenheim, Malplaquet and Dettingen, Vimiero and Vittoria, Hyderabad and Kabul, the Modder River and Mafeking, Le Cateau and Amiens, Kut and Waziristan, Alamein and Caen, had finally been added the Falklands. In the course of time khaki had replaced sky-blue, except on ceremonial occasions, steel helmets had replaced the brass, and finally, berets had replaced the steel as their horses had been replaced by tanks. But tonight history again strode the stage. The room was filling up now, with officers of every age and rank, many retired, veterans of the famous campaigns of the past – and every man wore sky-blue and had a sword at his side, while their burnished helmets accumulated on the table against the wall.

And now, the moment of the evening was approaching. The regimental Sergeant-Major, standing by the open door leading into the vestibule, had come to attention. 'Colonel Mackinder, sir! General Mackinder, sir!' He drew a long breath. 'General Mackinder, sir!'

Every man present came to attention, to watch the three men entering the room. They too wore sky-blue uniforms. The first, tall and powerfully built, with the craggy features which Murdoch Mackinder had inherited, was Colonel Ian Mackinder, his father and the present commanding officer of the regiment. In his middle forties, he had in fact just been gazetted brigadier, but had not yet handed over his command. Once in the room, he paused, to allow his two companions to join him. The leader of these was a man of

3

over seventy, but still standing as straight as anyone present, even if he moved slowly because of some arthritis. Major General (retired) Sir Fergus Mackinder, VC, KCMG, DSO, and a host of other decorations, had in his time been colonel of the regiment and led it to glory. There were many men here tonight who had actually served under him.

But only Fergus himself had ever served under the third man who now entered the room, while there was an almost audible drawing of breath from the assembled company. For they were looking at the most famous Western Dragoon, and the most famous Mackinder, of them all, and realizing that Lieutenant-General (retired) Sir Murdoch Mackinder, VC, KCMG, DSO and bar, Légion d'honneur, whose campaign medals began with South Africa and went right through the Second World War, was now one hundred and four years old. Yet he had never missed a regimental dinner since his first, as an eighteen-year-old subaltern in 1899. And gazing at the tall, spare, upright figure it was difficult to feel he would ever do so. The blue eyes were as coolly piercing as at any time when they had gazed at an enemy, and if he moved as slowly as his son, he yet did so without the aid of any stick.

Men hurried forward to be introduced, or remembered. Sir Murdoch Mackinder had a word and a smile for them all, as he gradually made his way to the head of the table: as colonel in chief he occupied the seat of honour.

Lieutenant Murdoch Mackinder waited for him, heart pounding. He had worshipped this old man, after whom he had been named, ever since he had been old enough to recognize him; it was not possible to imagine life, or the regiment, without him. He had listened to his great-grandfather's reminiscences, dreamed of emulating him . . . of being given the opportunity, in this limited modern world. And now Sir Murdoch was smiling at him. 'Murdoch,' he said. 'Proud. Proud.'

'Thank you, sir,' Murdoch said. He had nearly called him 'Grandpa', and remembered just in time. He was in uniform.

4

'Proud,' Sir Murdoch said again, glancing at Ian Mackinder. 'Eh?'

'Oh, indeed, sir,' the Colonel agreed. 'I think we should get started, Lieutenant Mackinder. The General mustn't be late.'

'Or all the nurses go into a tizzy,' Sir Murdoch said with a smile. 'I wish Lee were still here to tell them where to go. But your father's right, boy. Let's get started.'

'Yes, sir.' Murdoch withdrew to his seat at the foot of the centre leg, where he remained standing while all the officers took their places.

The Sergeant-Major stood at Murdoch's side, the regimental colour, furled, resting against his shoulder. 'Gentlemen,' he said, when the rustling had ceased. 'The regimental prayer.'

Every officer stood to attention, and then, with a single movement, drew his sword and pointed it at the ceiling. There were a good seventy men present, and the gleaming blades held above the sky-blue jackets truly enabled Murdoch to take a glimpse back through history, as far even as that famous day in Pakistan, when the first Ian Mackinder had summoned his men to battle, in the words it was now his duty, as the junior subaltern, to repeat.

'Mr Mackinder, sir,' the Sergeant-Major said.

Murdoch took a long breath, and spoke in a loud, clear voice: 'May the great God of battle, who has guided the fate of this famous regiment on many a hard-fought field, and never failed to lead it to distinction, grant that on this day, faced as we are with a host of enemies of our Queen and our Country, every man will do his duty, so that should we fail in our ordained task, it will yet be said of us, they were the Royal Western Dragoon Guards, who fought and died according to the ancient valour of their regiment and their blood.'

He paused for a moment, and then added, 'Gentlemen, there is your enemy.'

The swords were sheathed with a deafening rasp, and there was a burst of applause, as the Sergeant-Major saluted and withdrew, and orderlies moved forward to relieve the

5

diners of their weapons and stack them against the wall. The officers then sat down, but Sir Murdoch Mackinder remained standing. 'That was well said, Mr Mackinder. Well said. The regiment is proud of you.'

He sat down in turn, and the waiters immediately began serving the soup. 'A great day,' Sir Murdoch remarked to Ian Mackinder, on his right. 'The last of the brood, eh?'

'Up to now,' the Colonel grinned.

'Oh, indeed, up to now,' Sir Murdoch agreed. 'We've only had our doubts about the continuation of the line once. Eh, Fergus?'

The Major-General, on Sir Murdoch's left, nodded. 'Just once,' he agreed. 'Just once. But then, I think we had our doubts about the continuation of anything, even Britain, when we got back from Dunkirk.'

PART ONE

DEFEAT

1
England, 1940

Rain swept across the Somerset moors, lashed into the houses of Bath, formed puddles in the arcades of the Crescent, pattered on the stained-glass windows of the Abbey Church of St Peter and St Paul. The weather was unseasonable. Not only was it June, and the threshold of summer, but it had been one of the finest springs in living memory, and the weathermen were forecasting that the sunshine would last.

That was a sombre thought to those who had been clawed back from the beaches of Dunkirk and death or captivity, and who knew that only a few miles across the English Channel a mighty, victorious army was poised to spring at the throats of an almost unarmed people.

But the weather suited the occasion. For not every British soldier had been evacuated from the burning seaport. 'Colonel Ian Mackinder died,' the Bishop said, 'as we would have expected a bearer of such a famous name to die. But more, he died as a British soldier. As we may all have to die, one of these fine days, in defending the world against a monstrous and hideous tyranny. His name will not be forgotten.'

The memorial service closed with the singing of 'Onward, Christian Soldiers'. As the stirring cadences of the hymn rose into the gothic arches above them, Lieutenant-General Sir Murdoch Mackinder, VC, KCMG, DSO and bar, Légion d'honneur, glanced to his left at what remained of his family; he had only been released from hospital the previous day, officially recovered from the wounds he had suffered at his son's side as they had waited, waist deep in the sea, to be taken off. He had been the lucky one, and lucky not to know that Ian had been dying, as he had

9

continued calmly to give orders and reassure his men. But then, he should not have been there at all. At fifty-nine he was considered too old for a field command. He had bent a few rules, and all but paid for it. Not for the first time, he thought. Nor, he told himself grimly, for the last, as long as he was even reasonably fit.

His younger son, Captain Fergus Mackinder, at thirty a veteran of eleven years' service which included action on the North West Frontier of India, had been even luckier, in that he had escaped without a scratch. Yet had they both watched their comrades, as well as their son and brother, die. Perhaps even worse, they had watched the regiment die, its tanks destroyed to prevent them from falling into the hands of the enemy. Those were days they would not forget.

Between them stood the Mackinder women.

Lee Mackinder's face was composed. It was a pertly pretty face, and if her short, slender body seemed dwarfed by the tall men and women to either side of her, she was yet well aware of being the link that kept them, she would say, civilized human beings. Lady Mackinder was in her middle fifties, and had been the wife of Murdoch Mackinder for more than thirty years. She had anticipated suffering bereavement too often to be overcome by it now, even if she could never have supposed the first member of her family she would mourn would be her eldest son. And, as an American, she was perhaps more aware of the futility of war than those whose passions were too closely caught up in the continuing rivalry between Britain and Germany.

She had done her weeping in private. So had her daughter Helen, to whom Ian Mackinder had always been a dominating eldest brother. Helen's eyes too were dry today. But Annaliese Mackinder wept openly and loudly. Her marriage to Ian had lasted, in real terms, only six days, before he had had to accompany the regiment to France. Just long enough for her to become pregnant. She had been giving birth, prematurely, at almost the precise moment that her husband had been dying, and in the month when her mother and father had also died. Annaliese, who had

10

fled her native Germany to escape the Nazis, had fled her parents and family as well, as they had been staunch supporters of Adolf Hitler. Yet she could not help but mourn them, just as she could not help but be aware that her eldest brother, Paul von Reger, was a colonel in that tremendous force across the Channel. Her grief was perhaps accentuated by fear. All England would perish if the Germans successfully invaded. But those who had fled Germany would suffer most.

Murdoch looked to his other side, at Retired Sergeant-Major Yeald and his two grandsons, standing on the far side of the aisle. Bert Yeald was an old friend as well as comrade in arms; they had first served together in South Africa as very young men, forty-one years before. But the two boys were even closer to the family, although the eldest, named Bert after his grandfather, wore the battledress of a corporal in the Royal Western Dragoon Guards. Their ill-fated parents had been more than friends to the Mackinders. And this memorial service was equally for Jennifer Manly-Smith, who had also died on active service. Carrying with her, Murdoch thought with a sigh, many secrets.

Lee heard the check in his voice, and looked up at him, quickly and anxiously. He gave her a reassuring smile, and a moment later the hymn was finished.

They shook hands with the Bishop, and hurried beneath umbrellas for the waiting cars. 'You'll come up and see us, Sergeant-Major,' Murdoch said. 'Bring the boys.'

'Thank you, General.'

'We need to talk, about things,' Lee said.

'Yes, my lady,' Yeald agreed.

Murdoch wondered what he was thinking. Certainly in part that the boys did present a problem. Ralph Manly-Smith had been in every way an officer and a gentleman, who had gone from Winchester to Sandhurst and thence into the regiment with an expectation of a long and famous career. That he had got the daughter of his own sergeant-major pregnant had been a disaster: that he had then insisted upon marrying Jennifer Yeald had at least proved him to be a man. Murdoch and Lee had supported that

11

decision, and Murdoch had done everything in his power to smooth Ralph's path, taking him to India as his ADC when he had been appointed to the command of the North West Frontier back in 1924. Ralph had reciprocated with the utmost loyalty – and that loyalty had cost him his life.

By then, Jennifer Manly-Smith, whatever her background, had become accepted as an officer's wife. But on the death of her husband she had chosen to return to keep house for her widowed father, and become again a sergeant-major's daughter. There had been no public school education for young Bert or little Joey. Nor had she been prepared to accept any help from the Mackinders. But her loyalty to the regiment had never faltered. Bert had joined it as a boy soldier, Joey would certainly follow him the moment he was old enough. As Jennifer herself had volunteered for the ATS the moment recruiting had begun. And followed her husband into a heroine's grave.

All of that would be going through Sergeant-Major Yeald's mind. But they were his grandchildren. And he was unaware of the other, deeper ties, that might make Murdoch wish to take more of an interest in the two boys. Now he saluted, and hurried them off to his old Austin Seven, while the Mackinders squeezed into the Daimler. Murdoch drove himself, Lee beisde him. Fergus, Helen and Annaliese sat in the back with Philippa Mackinder, Murdoch's older sister, a large woman who even in her sixties exercised her horses every morning and was usually both loud and jolly.

But today even Philippa was subdued. 'It was a nice service,' she said into her handkerchief. 'What a pity Harry couldn't be here.'

'Yes,' Murdoch agreed, giving Lee an anxious glance. Philippa had never been the most tactful of women. Harry Mackinder, the youngest of Murdoch's and Lee's four children, had chosen to emigrate to his mother's homeland and become an American citizen as he had pursued a literary career. That decision, against joining the British Army like every other male Mackinder, had been a blow. An even greater blow had been Harry's refusal to hurry into khaki the previous September, his apparent opinion that there were faults on both sides of the Anglo-German quarrel. Redeemingly, word had arrived only the previous month that he had joined up – the United States Marines. But America was not yet in the war, and no one knew if she would ever be. Harry's place had been here, standing shoulder to shoulder with his brothers, or at least with his parents when it came to mourning one of them. Murdoch's hands curled into fists as he guided the car through the puddles and out on to the country lane that led back to the village; Lee, appreciating his mood as he had hers, rested her hand on his for just a moment, comfortingly.

Annaliese burst into a fresh outbreak of weeping, discarding hat and veil to dab at her eyes, and Helen put her arm round her shoulders.

'Drop me off at the depot, will you please, Dad,' Fergus said.

'Oh, Fergus, you're not going back to work today,' his mother complained.

'Must,' Fergus said. 'We're taking in new recruits all day and every day.'

'Any word on armour?' Murdoch asked.

'It's promised,' Fergus said. 'But if the Germans come before we're ready, why, we'll just have to trot out our horses again.'

No one laughed at his attempt at humour; the subject was too serious. But Murdoch pulled off the road and into the gateway of the regimental depot, just a few miles outside the town. This place was as much a home to him as Broad Acres. As a boy of eighteen – the same age as Bert Yeald, he thought with a start of surprise – he had reported for duty here in the spring of 1899. His father had recently died, and he had been very aware of being the last Mackinder, and carrying all of that already considerable weight of family history on his shoulders.

It was a source of some pleasure to him that he had just about doubled that weight for his descendants – however much it might have proved too heavy for Harry to bear. When he had joined the regiment, it had been about to set off for South Africa, not suspecting that within a year they would be involved in one of the toughest wars ever undertaken by the British Army. That war had brought him fame in the shape of the Victoria Cross, and censorship for his affair with the Boer girl, Margriet Voorlandt, which had very nearly ended his career. But that was a long time ago, and since then he had ridden to fame and fortune time and again. Britain's most famous fighting soldier, was what the newspapers called him. Thus the sentry on the gate came to attention a little more smartly than usual as he discerned who was behind the wheel of the car. He would be telling his mates when he went off duty, 'The General came by today.' To a Royal Western Dragoon, there was only one general in the entire British Army.

Fergus saluted as he got out, khaki uniform darkening with the continuing spatter of rain, and Murdoch drove on. The village was three miles further into the country, and beyond the village lay Broad Acres, the Mackinder family home now for some hundred years, an old ivy-covered but most comfortable house, surrounded by several acres of sprawling garden and meadow sliding down the hillside beyond. Retrievers barked and frolicked as the car drew to a halt on the gravel outside the front door; if, like the intelligent beasts they were, they shared the family grief, they could not resist welcoming their beloved master with every possible display of affection. Especially when their master had been away for so long. Murdoch submitted to being licked and gnawed while the women went inside.

'I think you should take two aspirins and go to bed, Liese,' Lee suggested.

'But little Ian needs his feed.' Tears rolled down the beautiful cheeks, and the German girl's golden hair, usually immaculately coiffed and curled, was dishevelled.

'Well, as soon as you've done that. I'll come with you.'

Philippa hurried off to get changed – she hated wearing dresses – but Helen remained in the hallway as Murdoch came in. 'I suppose I should be getting back too.' She wore the dark blue uniform of a Wave, having just resumed duty at the Admiralty after the birth of her baby. Her husband was at sea as navigating lieutenant on a cruiser – where, no one knew.

'Surely you can spend the night,' Murdoch said, hanging up his cap and Sam Browne belts and thrusting his swagger stick into the stand. 'Robbins, I think a double scotch. What are you drinking, Helen?'

'A pink gin,' Helen said, and followed her father into the drawing room, where a fire blazed in the grate to dispel some of the damp. 'Well,' she said, 'I promised Aunt Rosemary and the girls . . .'

'They can wait another day.' Murdoch looked at the door as Lee entered immediately in front of the butler and his tray.

'I'll have one of those too, Robbins,' she said, and took a sip of Murdoch's. 'Brrr.'

'How is she?'

'Probably acting. Or at least forcing it. I mean, she's been like this now for the entire month. For God's sake, she's twenty-five years old, not fifteen. You're going to have to have a word with her, Murdoch.'

'Me?' he asked in alarm.

'Well, you know she looks on you as a father.'

'Um,' Murdoch said. Annaliese had always looked on him as something more than that. She was Margriet von Reger's daughter in every possible way, however much she and her mother might have quarrelled over their differing attitudes to Nazism. And Murdoch had never been sure how much Margriet had told her children about South Africa, and how much she regretted the chance of fortune which had left her married to the German, von Reger, instead of the Englishman, Mackinder. That Annaliese had chosen to flee to the Mackinder household when her opposition to Nazidom had endangered her life certainly suggested she had known she would be welcomed. But he had never felt she had intended to marry one of the Mackinder sons. That too had been a chance of fortune. So, as Lee had remarked with her usual acute sense of observation, the girl was probably forcing her grief. As well as being afraid of what would happen next.

15

Something about which he had no idea, except that as a Mackinder widow Broad Acres was her home for as long as she wanted.

'I'll take her up a drink,' Helen decided. 'Of gin.'

'She's feeding,' Lee protested.

'One drink isn't going to hurt that little bruiser. And it may do her some good. Anyway, I bet you two have a lot to talk about.'

She hurried for the butler's pantry, closing the doors behind her. Murdoch and Lee looked at each other. They had not in fact had much time together since his last leave, at Christmas. A few visits in hospital, and last night . . . but last night they had just wanted to lie in each other's arms. They certainly had not talked.

Now she raised her glass. 'Welcome home.'

He understood that she meant more than in a purely physical sense, took her into his arms and kissed her.

'I didn't have a chance to look, before,' she said. 'Where exactly is this one?'

'A bit of a tear up the right side. Not really serious, but I lost too much blood, they said. At my age. Ha.'

'At your age,' Lee repeated, severely. 'How many wounds is that? Thirteen? Your body is just about held together by stitches. Promise me it's done, Murdoch. You were sent to Holland as head of a mission, not to get involved in any fighting. I'm surprised you haven't been cashiered.'

He grinned, and kissed her again. 'I probably would have been, if Chamberlain was still PM.'

'And you think Winston is going to employ you.'

'He already has. As soon as I'm fully fit again.'

'Murdoch! You're fifty-nine.'

'A desk job.'

She was suspicious. 'Where?'

'In Whitehall. We'll use the flat. I'll come home to you every night.'

'And what will you be doing?'

'I'm afraid I can't tell you, right now. It's very hush-hush.'

'But you'll be staying in London.'

'That's right.'

'Well, that's something, I guess.'

'Although you'll have to let me fight if the Jerries do land. I think we'll all have to do a bit of that.'

'Will they, Murdoch? Can they?'

'I'm sure they *can*. As to whether they *will*, that depends on how sensible they are. Because I'll tell you something: even if we don't have any armour to speak of, if they land, they are going to get beat.'

She shivered. 'I wish I could believe that. After what happened in Belgium and France . . .'

'We didn't know what was going to hit us. We do now. And even then we shouldn't have lost like that. What was lacking in too many of the French generals was the will to fight. Where we were allowed to take on those fellows, even when outnumbered, we proved we were as good as they. We'll beat them, Lee. I give you my word.'

'We must,' she said fiercely. 'For Ian.' And then glanced at him. 'Murdoch . . . I'm sorry about Jennie.'

'I know.' She had told him that before. 'I'm sorry too, Lee. About so many things.'

She put her arms round his neck. 'So it's us, now.'

'Again.'

'And for always. We have a lot to do,' she said.

'Tanks,' Fergus announced, standing in the centre of the drawing room and slapping his hands together. 'Crusaders. Great big beautiful things. Sixty of them. Arriving tomorrow.'

He was jubilant. So was Murdoch. 'And then?'

'We're allowed a week to familiarize, then it's Norfolk. Jerry's expected every day.'

'Well, he'd better hurry,' Murdoch said. The french windows stood open, and the August sunshine was flooding across the room. The forecasts had again been proved accurate, and there was not a cloud to mar the deep blue. Down in Somerset they had seen little of the actual fighting which was filling the air to their east and south, although

17

there had been German bombers overhead from time to time making for the industrial areas of South Wales, but the news was grim enough, with the RAF holding on by, it seemed, the skin of their teeth. 'I'm off in two days' time, too.'

'To London? It's fairly grim up there.'

'So I've heard. I've tried to persuade your mother to stay down here until things ease up, but she's dead set on coming with me. So's Liese. She's to get Ian's medal, you see.'

'Hey, I may be there too. I'm to get the Military Cross.'

'Are you?' Murdoch slapped him on the shoulder. 'Best congratulations.'

'Actually, I think they're giving them to every officer who survived Dunkirk.' Fergus brooded at the rhodo-dendrons, his ebullience suddenly faded. 'It must be pretty damn near unique, both father and son getting the VC.'

'Not unique,' Murdoch said. 'Lord Roberts and his son both got the Cross.' He sighed. 'And young Fred's was posthumous too.'

'I'd like to make it a threesome, for us,' Fergus said.

'For God's sake don't try. You're the very last Mack-inder, Fergus.'

'What about Harry? And little Ian?'

'Harry's in the United States Army, not ours. And little Ian . . . well, we don't have any idea how he's going to turn out, do we?'

'Because Liese is his mother?'

'Perhaps. She's really not one of us.'

'Was Mom when you married her?'

Murdoch considered. 'No. But she was pretty tough. And, well . . . she fitted in.'

'Meaning Mom never sunbathed in the altogether.' Fergus flushed. 'Oh, don't bother, Dad. I've never joined Liese. But everyone knows she does it, even the staff.'

'Quite. Not really the sort of thing one would expect from a widow, is it?'

Fergus gazed at his father for several seconds, as though there was something he wanted to say, then obviously changed his mind. 'By the way, I forgot to tell you, I've also been promoted major.' He looked at the three stars on his shoulder straps, then up, somewhat enviously, at the crown and crossed swords on his father's. 'I haven't had a chance to change these, yet. Only heard this morning.'

'Well, that's tremendous, Fergus. Another step on the ladder. We'll open a bottle of bubbly. Have you told your mother?'

'Not yet.'

'Then it's going to be a celebration lunch. Wilkinson got the colonelcy, did he?'

'Well . . . he has six months' seniority.'

'Quite. But . . . you're staying with the regiment?'

'Oh, yes.'

'Then does that mean what I think it means?'

'I would say so. I'm certainly going to be adjutant.'

'Which means you'll certainly get the regiment, when Wilkinson moves up.'

'I hope so.'

Murdoch shook his hand. 'You will. You're a Mackinder. Oh, my very best congratulations.'

They drank Fergus's health time and again, and the women kissed him, time and again. Even Annaliese was smiling today. When she smiled she was truly beautiful. But then, Fergus thought, she was truly beautiful under any circumstances, and her magnificent rich yellow hair and suntanned complexion were admirably set off by her black gown.

He wondered what his father would have said if he had told him what was really on his mind? He hadn't taken the risk, partly because of Father's expressed disapproval of the girl, and partly because he hadn't been absolutely sure whether, in the eyes of the world, seeking to marry one's dead brother's wife would be outrageous or noble. But it couldn't be outrageous. Hadn't Henry VIII married his dead brother's widow?

Of course it was too soon. Ian had only been dead two months. And there must be no suspicion in anyone's mind that he was acting out of pity, or out of a desire to give little

Ian a father. Because neither of those was true. He was in love with Annaliese. He had been for years. If he had never done anything about it, that had been because he had always looked on the girl as almost a second sister. She had fled Germany in 1937, when she had been still rather immature. In the intervening years he had watched her grow, and laugh, and live ebulliently, happy to be under the aegis of the family she had always loved more than her own. He had seen enough of her, in bathing costumes and dressing gowns as well as smart frocks and evening dress, to know that she was everything he wanted in a woman. And he had thought of her, sunbathing down beyond the trees, and been tempted, so very often, to wander down there, as if by accident.

But Ian had acted first. The prerogative of an elder brother, perhaps. But had Ian loved her? He had married her to save her being sent, as an enemy alien, to an internment camp: as the wife of a serving British officer she was sacrosanct. That had been a most noble gesture. But had it been inspired by love?

Even more important, had Annaliese really loved Ian? Or had she sought the nearest port in the storm which had so suddenly blown up around her?

Then there was her past. Ian had touched on it, briefly, in France, when she had already been his wife. It had been brother to brother confidence, and Fergus had never been sure if Ian had told him everything. But Ian had known Annaliese in Germany in the early thirties, when she had been a teenager and he had been there as ADC to his father. Annaliese had taken him to various parties thrown by the new society of the Third Reich, and Ian had been shocked. No doubt about that. Just as he had been shocked when Annaliese had told him that she and her family bathed in the nude together on their summer vacations. No doubt Ian had been shocked to discover she was continuing the habit in England, even if in strict privacy. Ian had been something of a stuffed shirt. Fergus found the concept of a family sharing such intimacy most exciting – especially if Annaliese's sisters had looked anything like her.

But then there had been the business of her escape from Germany. The Regers had lived almost due south of Berlin. Annaliese had left the house, by herself and on foot, with only a small satchel and no money, and had made her way to England, just like that. It had taken her several weeks. How did a young girl live for several weeks, when she was in any event a fugitive, and when it was necessary to cross frontiers and enter Britain, without a passport? Father had, according to Ian, never had any doubts about the only possible way she had managed that, and for that reason had tried to talk Ian out of marrying her. For all his disapproval of many things about her, Father obviously loved Annaliese himself, as a daughter, and as the daughter of his first love, but that hadn't blinded him to the fact that her morals weren't those of a Mackinder, however much he might respect her courage and determination.

Ian had been unable to make up his mind whether Father had been right or not.

But even if she had prostituted herself across Europe, that did not interest him, Fergus reminded himself. Except to make her even more exciting. He would in any event be marrying another man's relict. If she was the relict of half a dozen living men as well, that couldn't possibly alter the length of long slender leg, the swell of breast, larger than ever as she was feeding, the curve of buttock, the smoothness of complexion, which made him dream of her every night.

If only he knew what Father would say.

But for God's sake, he told himself as he smiled at her across the table, I am all but thirty years old, and I am second-in-command of the Royal Western Dragoon Guards. I should be able to make my own decisions.

'I'm sorry I haven't been able to see more of you, these last couple of months,' Fergus told Annaliese as they strolled in the garden after lunch.

'You have been busy,' she agreed. 'Getting ready to beat Hitler.'

'Will you be glad about that? If we manage to do it?'

She stopped walking, turned to face him. 'You must do it. He is evil. Everything he stands for is evil.'

'Your brother fights for him.'

Annaliese hugged herself. 'Paul is evil too.'

Fergus was silent for a few minutes; the conversation had taken an unexpected turn. Annaliese continued on her walk, and he hurriedly caught her up. 'What I wanted to say was . . . well . . . I have to go with the regiment, of course, to the other side of the country. But there's a chance I'll see you in town, next week. And then there'll be leave, from time to time. Perhaps, when I come back . . . when . . .' Hell, he thought, if only he could just come out and say it. 'Well, in another couple of months, when . . . well . . .'

She stopped walking, and gazed at him. 'I will still be here, Fergus. In a couple of months.'

They stood on the porch to wave Fergus out of sight as he returned to the depot. 'Ian would be proud of him,' Lee said, and went inside. Today her eyes were damp.

Annaliese held Murdoch's hand. 'Sit with me, Uncle Murdoch.'

Murdoch allowed himself to be led to the porch settee. He was very relieved at the rapidity with which the girl had recovered her old spirits, but he was equally aware that her old spirits encompassed a great many attitudes of which not everyone would approve. Least of all himself. So he sat down rather apprehensively.

Annaliese sat beside him. 'Fergus nearly proposed to me, after lunch,' she announced, without preamble.

Murdoch was so surprised he did not immediately reply.

Annaliese glanced at him. 'I think he is going to, when next he has leave from the regiment. What should I do?'

'Fergus? But . . . he's your brother-in-law.'

'Does that matter? Now that his brother is dead?'

Murdoch glanced at her in turn. 'I suppose it doesn't.'

'So tell me what I must do when he asks.'

'My dear Liese, how can I tell you that? If you love him, well . . .'

'I am sure I could love him, Uncle Murdoch. He is Ian's

22

brother, and he is your son. But . . . do you want me to do that?'

'It has nothing to do with me.'

'Yes, it has,' she insisted. 'Murdoch . . .' she held his hands. 'You loved my mother.'

'That was a very long time ago.'

'But you loved her. More than you ever loved Aunt Lee.'

'No,' Murdoch said. 'I loved your mother in a different way to Lee.'

'More,' she insisted. 'And I look exactly like her, everyone has always said. Is that true?'

He made no effort to free himself, for the moment; he knew she had to get what was on her mind into the open – and he then had to react. It was a crisis he had seen looming for years; he simply had not expected it today. But his reaction would have to be a severe one, and he regretted that. Not that he intended to shirk it; Murdoch Mackinder had never shirked any duty, no matter how unpleasant, in his life. 'I would say you are even more beautiful, Liese.'

'My mother loved you.'

'Up to a point.'

'I love you beyond that point.'

'Now, Liese, you are being absurd. I am old enough to be your grandfather.'

'What is age? It is a system of accounting invented by man for his own convenience. I have known some men of thirty who are children, and others who have been old, old men.'

Murdoch wondered if she was thinking of Fergus, and in that case, in which class she placed him?

'While you are as handsome and attractive now as the day I first met you. Do you remember that day, in 1924, when you and Auntie Lee came to Germany to visit with us?'

'You were nine years old.'

'And I fell in love with you then. I winked at you. Do you remember?'

'I remember. I wondered if I shouldn't paddle your backside.'

'I wish you had. Uncle Murdoch, Murdoch, I have never loved anyone else.'

'Now really, Liese . . .'

'It is true. I married your son because that was as near to you as I could get. As you would let me get. But I loved you. Now your other son wishes to have me. I will give myself to him if you wish it. Just to be near you. But will you not take me for yourself, just once?' She stared at him, her face very close to his. 'No one will ever know. I am always here. You are here. Aunt Lee goes out quite often and Aunt Philippa is always riding her horses. No one would ever know if you came to my room tomorrow morning.'

Her eyes were unblinking, but slowly seeming to become opaque as she gazed into his. Not many people had looked into Sir Murdoch Mackinder's eyes when they wore that expression, and lived to remember it.

'You are obscene,' he said, speaking as softly as she had done. 'Yes, I loved your mother. And I love you . . . as her daughter. I have taken you in and given you a home. I was very happy when you married Ian. When he was killed, my heart bled at least as much for you as for him. When I stand beside you as you receive his Victoria Cross, next week, I shall be the proudest man on earth. And no one could have been kinder to you than your Aunt Lee. I know you have had a very hard life, Liese, and I respect the courage with which you have faced that life. I hope you will never lose that. But if you ever speak to me like this again, or make any suggestion like this again, I am going to throw you out on to the street. Understand that.'

Her fingers relaxed and slid away from him. She stood up, facing him, her face cold. 'And Fergus?'

'That must be your decision, not mine. But if you marry him, Liese, you will love him and be his wife. Because if you ever let him down, you will have to answer to me.'

She gazed at him for a moment longer, then turned with a swirl of her skirt, and walked away.

The best part of Annaliese's day was after the ten o'clock morning feed. Then she could hand little Ian back to his nanny, put on a bathing suit and a bathrobe, and walk away from the house and down the hill to a stand of trees, perhaps

24

a quarter of a mile from the house. On the far side of these trees, which acted as a wall, she looked down into the valley, a long slope of green grass studded with little copses. Beyond the boundary fence of Broad Acres there were sheep grazing, and the shepherd could often be seen – but he was a long way away. Within the boundaries she was completely alone. Even Philippa carefully avoided the trees when it was known that Mrs Mackinder was sunbathing. Once hidden by the trees Annaliese could spread her bathrobe on the ground, lay her bathing costume beside it, and lie on her back with her eyes closed.

It was not a pastime the British seemed to believe in, which, she was sure, accounted for their pale complexions and the prevalence of colds and coughs. When, before the war, the Mackinders had taken her to the seaside, even on a boiling hot summer's day like today, she had been amazed to see the amount of clothes everyone was wearing, the way the men would merely roll their trousers up to the knee, and would place knotted handkerchiefs on their heads the moment the sun grew too warm, while to take a shirt off was apparently indecent. The women were no more free with themselves.

Annaliese had been brought up to believe that the sun is the source of all life and strength, and that the nude human body is the only truly beautiful one of God's creations. From her earliest years, in the grim days after the First World War, Papa and Mama had set off for the river whenever they could, camping, swimming, and lying in the sun, with all of their numerous children, and not a bathing suit between them. Out of those days in the sun, encouraged for the whole nation by the Hitler regime, had come the bronzed, beautiful, brutal, beastly and unbeatable soldiers who wore the swastika.

No doubt a lot of evil had come out of it too. Evil she had been happy to escape. But she had never had it proven that the two were actually connected.

As nude sunbathing was not accepted in England, she had made this little nook her very own from her first days here. No one had offered any comment, taking their lead from the mistress of the house. Perhaps they did sunbathe nude in the States. More likely Lee was trying to be as understanding as she could. Thus a pattern had been allowed to build, and her daily retirement here had become an accepted part of the summer day's routine.

Always by herself. The other women of the house would have been shocked had she suggested they might enjoy themselves by accompanying her. And during her so brief honeymoon with Ian it had already been late September and a little chilly. Until yesterday it had never occurred to her that Fergus, who was even more stolid than his brother, might be interested. Now Ian was dead. And Murdoch was angry with her. Well, she was angry with Murdoch. She had not been so angry with anyone since she had been angry enough to flee Germany. She had offered herself to him, without reservations. And he would have liked to take her. She was certain of that. But he was so hidebound in his concept of what constituted a British officer and a gentleman that he could not bend.

Almost she felt like running away again. She had no doubt that she could survive. She had proved that before, with her beauty and her confidence . . . and her appeal. Men could not resist her. But then, she could not resist men.

The problem was little Ian, and Broad Acres. She had never been so comfortable anywhere before; she would not find its like again. And she was a mother. What a millstone to have tied around her neck, at the very moment when more than ever she needed to be free! So she would marry Fergus, at least partly to spite old Murdoch. But God, she thought, if Fergus was as inhibited in bed as his brother had been . . . She wondered what Fergus's reaction would be were she to invite him to sunbathe with her?

The crunching of feet upon the earth made her sit up with a start, looking to left and right. No one should have been here. In fact, this morning, there was no possibility of anyone being here, as both Lee and Murdoch were out, Fergus was at the depot preparing to leave, and Philippa had gone to a cattle market in the village. Down here in

Somerset it was really very difficult to realize there was a war on at all, if one ignored the ridiculous Local Defence Volunteers with their armbands and their pikes drilling with great solemnity on the village green.

But there was someone just on the other side of the trees, and coming round them. Annaliese stretched out her hand to pick up the bathing suit, then let it fall again. Whoever it was would get a pleasant surprise.

The feet stopped, and she gazed at the battle-dressed and heavily booted figure of Bert Manly-Smith. Whose face was slowly turning crimson. 'Oh, Mrs Mackinder,' he gasped. 'Oh, gosh!' He turned and appeared about to run.

'Why, Albert,' Annaliese said. 'Don't go rushing off.'

Bert hesitated, carefully staring into the trees. 'I had no idea, Mrs Mackinder,' he said.

'Why should you, have any idea?'

'I came up to say goodbye,' he explained. 'The regiment moves out tomorrow. But General and Lady Mackinder are out. The butler said I could wait. And when I asked if anyone was in, he said you were, Mrs Mackinder, in the garden. He didn't say anything else. So when he left me by myself . . .'

'You came looking for me,' Annaliese said with some satisfaction, and lay down again, her hands beneath her head, consciously copying the pose of the naked Maja. 'I think that was very nice of you, Albert.'

'Thank you, Mrs Mackinder. Well . . .'

'You can't just rush off like that, Albert. You came to say goodbye. Come and sit down.'

'Oh, Mrs Mackinder, I couldn't do that!'

'Why not? I have invited you to.'

'Yes, but . . . well . . .'

'Have you never seen a naked woman before, Albert?'

Bert swallowed.

Annaliese turned her head and smiled at him. 'I'm sure you have. You're a soldier. You were in France. What did you do on your nights off?'

Slowly Bert approached her and sat on the grass beside her. Now he could not stop himself looking at her, his gaze drifting up and down her legs, hovering at her pubes, moving up again to her breasts. This must be the luckiest day of his life, Annaliese thought. But then, was it not perhaps the luckiest day of hers, in the mood she was in? This boy was only eighteen years old, big and strong and undoubtedly virile. He would have a working man's approach to sex, which was presumably earthy and masculine.

Of course, he *was* working class, really, even if his father had apparently been an officer and a gentleman like the Mackinders. He was also an ordinary soldier. But then, she didn't want to marry him. She wanted to marry Fergus, and remain at Broad Acres. Indeed, married to Fergus, she would one day, when Murdoch and Lee were dead, inherit Broad Acres. That had always been a dream. Now, after Murdoch's rejection of her, it would add an extra pleasure: she doubted that eventuality had occurred to the old man.

But before all of those things happened, she just had to have a tumble from someone who wouldn't be afraid where he put his hands . . . or anything else. And there was absolutely no risk of anyone finding out. Not from Bert Manly-Smith. He would do anything rather than upset the Mackinders.

Annaliese turned on her side, facing him, rested her head on her hand, and allowed her legs to drift apart. Bert's head jerked. 'If you came looking for me,' Annaliese said. 'It must be because you wanted to see me, about something.'

'I . . .' he licked his lips. 'I think you are very beautiful, Mrs Mackinder.'

Annaliese smiled. 'That's very nice of you, Albert.' She stretched out her other hand, rested it on his battledress trouser leg, and then slid it up towards his groin. 'I think you are very beautiful too. Aren't we going to be beautiful, together?'

'Murdoch.' Winston Churchill rose and shook hands as Murdoch entered the office of Ten Downing Street. 'You know Spears.'

'Indeed.' Murdoch shook hands with the Prime

Minister's military aide, Major General Sir Edward Spears.

'Fit again, I see,' Churchill said. 'How was the investiture?'

'Like an investiture. But they were very kind to Annaliese.'

'Unique, presenting a German with the Victoria Cross. You don't mind my saying that?'

'Not at all,' Murdoch agreed. 'I'm sure it is unique. But it was won by a British colonel.'

'Quite. Sit down.'

Murdoch seated himself, as did the other two men. 'When did they start bombing London?' he asked. It was his first visit to the capital since being wounded.

'Two nights ago. They say it is in reprisal for our raids on Berlin. But it's at least partly because our fighters have been giving their bombers a succession of bloody noses when they've attacked our airfields by day.'

Murdoch nodded. 'I listened to your speech about never was so much owed to so few. Stirring words.'

'Words cost nothing,' Churchill growled. 'It's beating the Nazis that counts.'

'Just tell me how. When I look at that damage out there, it really makes me angry.'

'London can take it.' Churchill grinned. 'And we're knocking down a few houses in Berlin. Now, beating the Nazis. Right this minute, our problem is how to get at the bastards. Oh, we will return to the continent in force one of these days, but it is going to take some time, until we have re-equipped our army, and raised it to sufficient strength. Our best hope is for them to come here, then we can kill a lot of them at one go. But I suspect Mr Hitler isn't quite that stupid. So we have to keep ourselves occupied by doing what damage we can in Europe, by all the means we can discover.'

'What about the Italians? We could have a go at them.'

'They aren't doing much to trouble us, at the moment. Just a shot or two on the borders of Egypt and Somaliland, and the occasional naval clash in the Mediterranean. I'd rather leave them be, until and unless they start something.

I've a notion they aren't really keen on being in the war at all. No, it's Hitler and his gang we have to topple, by making life as uncomfortable as possible for them. Here's where you come in, Murdoch. I can't give you a command, by service rules.' He gave another grim smile. 'And even if I could, you'd have nobody to fight. So I want you to create your own command. There are in this country a large number of refugees from the fighting forces of the countries overrun by Hitler. We have Czechs and Poles, French and Belgians, Norwegians and Dutch, all looking for the opportunity to hit back at the Nazis. We are giving them that opportunity as fast as we can. Already we have a Czech fighter squadron, and a Polish one, fighting with the RAF. We are forming a Polish brigade in the army. That fellow de Gaulle is promising to recruit an entire French army. But amongst all of these people there are quite a few men, and women, who would be of enormous value to us were they to return to their homes. I want you to find those people, Murdoch, and put them to work. Organize your own staff, and use whatever nationalities you have to. Let me have reports on your progress, and when you are ready to start operations. I would like that to be as soon as possible.'

'These people who are sent home. What am I to tell them to do?'

'Anything and everything that will help defeat Nazism. Information, sabotage, downright assassination. We are fighting for survival, Murdoch. There can be no holds barred.'

'How will I get them there?'

'By whatever means is most convenient. Parachute or boat. Or you can infiltrate them in through Sweden or the Balkans.'

'Any limit on numbers?'

'The more the better.'

Murdoch considered for a moment. 'You realize that we could be sending a good number of people to a particularly nasty death?'

'Yes,' Churchill said. 'That's why I chose you for the job. You are a fighting soldier. You've never shirked sending men into battle.'

'With respect, Winston, I have always *led* them into battle, before.'

'Unfortunately, all good things come to an end. I know it's a grim assignment. But if any man can make it work, you can. So pick your agents carefully. Make sure they are trustworthy. They will also need some training. Spears here will give you the details on that. But Murdoch, remember . . . haste is imperative. Every day Hitler grows stronger. Hopefully, from now on, so will we. But he has an enormous head start. We have to chip away at that.'

Murdoch nodded. 'You'll have your secret army, Prime Minister. Just as soon as I can raise it.' He stood up, saluted. 'Starting today.'

'Murdoch,' Lee said. 'Murdoch, wake up.'

Murdoch opened his eyes, listened to the wail of the siren. 'Christ,' he muttered. 'Every God damn night.'

Lee was already out of bed, pulling on her dressing gown. Now she held his out for him. 'Let's hurry.'

Already they could hear the crump-crump of explosions in the distance and the sharper replies of the anti-aircraft batteries. They switched off the lights and followed the beam of Murdoch's torch down the stairs, joined now by the various other residents of the block of flats; this fortunately had its own deep cellars which had been reinforced for use as an air-raid shelter, and so there was no necessity to go out on to the street. Indeed, so used had everyone become to retreating to the cellars over the past fortnight of constant bombardment that each family now had its own little floor space; Lee, with her passion for organization, had brought down two camp cots and these were always made up, so she and Murdoch merely got back beneath another set of blankets, while she poured them cups of tea – only recently put on the ration list – from her Thermos and waited for the others to settle and the vast dormitory to be still.

Now the noise of the explosions was much closer, and occasionally the whole building would shake. 'There goes another picture,' Lee said.

Her calmness was magnificent. He had never doubted her courage, and their joint experiences on the North West Frontier in the late twenties had proved it was more than merely a passive acceptance of danger. But he couldn't bear to think of her harmed. 'By the law of averages,' he said, speaking in a low voice to avoid being overheard by their immediate neighbours, who were only a few feet away, 'one day this building is going to take a direct hit. Why don't you go back down to Somerset?'

'Then who'd look after you?'

'Do I need looking after?'

'Every man needs looking after. And you more than most. I'm not going to chance any other little ATS driver moving in.' She reached across to squeeze his hand. 'Forget I said that. But I do worry about you. You're working too hard.'

'So is everybody else.'

'I've never seen you looking so strained. It's the new job, isn't it?'

'I imagine so.'

'Care to share?'

'I'd love to share, my darling girl. But I can't. It is absolutely top secret.'

'And grim,' she suggested.

Murdoch finished his tea and lay down. 'Grim.'

'For you?'

'Not physically. But for the people I'm commanding, it very well could be. Very grim.'

This time she leaned across to kiss him. 'With you as the boss, they'll manage.'

The all clear went some three hours later, but they stayed in the cellar until daybreak, then found their way upstairs again. Amazingly, only one picture had indeed fallen off the wall in the lounge, but when they drew the blackout curtains the sight was horrifying. A huge pall of smoke lay over the stricken city, and there were damaged buildings in every direction, while across the morning seeped the sound of sirens and bells, and of people too, shouting and wailing.

'I'll get breakfast,' Lee said.

Murdoch shaved, heard the doorbell, and then Lee's excited voice. 'Fergus! Oh, boy, Fergus. Where'd you spring from?'

'The fens, I suppose. Where's Dad?'

'Right here.' Murdoch stood in the doorway. 'When did you arrive?'

Fergus grinned at them. 'I was supposed to get here last night, for a twenty-four-hour pass. But all the trains were out. So I hitch-hiked. Now I'm down to eight hours. God, what a mess this town is in. Broken water mains, shattered houses, fires burning everywhere . . .'

'Last night was a heavy raid,' Murdoch acknowledged.

'And we still have water.' Lee had returned to the kitchen. 'Eggs on their way.'

'How are things on the beaches?' Murdoch asked.

'They don't change. Not a German in sight, save those washed up by the tide. But Dad, I have the most tremendous news.'

'Tell us?'

They sat at the breakfast table in the kitchen. 'Two days ago the Italians invaded Egypt. Did you know about that?'

'It hadn't reached me yet. And you call that good news?'

'Well, for the Westerns. Seems General Wavell has called for reinforcements. So we're elected.'

Lee came in from the kitchen, frying pan in hand. 'You're going to Egypt to fight the Italians?'

'That's it. Gosh, it'll be great to be fighting someone.'

Lee looked at Murdoch, who shrugged. Fergus had to get back into the war some time. 'Last time around they were on our side. The PM has a notion a lot of them may wish they still were. Shouldn't be too rough.'

'But he'll be in the desert . . . ugh.'

'You fought in the desert, Dad. In the last show. What was it like?'

'As your mother says, ugh. But it should be good tank country. Lots of open space.'

'I can hardly wait.'

'Men,' Lee said sadly, serving. 'Just remember there's nobody else in the cupboard at home.'

'Yes,' Fergus said, suddenly serious. 'I've been thinking about that.'

Lee and Murdoch looked at each other again. He had not confided any of Annaliese's behaviour to her, but she was an observant woman, and had obviously formed her own ideas on both the slight stiffness between her husband and her daughter-in-law, when they had attended the investiture, and equally, the increasing warmth between Annaliese and Fergus before he had left.

'So?' she now asked.

Fergus was embarrassed, as usual. 'The fact is . . . we're embarking from Plymouth, and we're driving down there in our own tanks and transport, so the regiment is returning to the depot for one night on its way. I rather thought I'd stop by at Broad Acres.'

'Why not?' Lee asked, and allowed him a cue. 'I'm sure Philippa and Annaliese will be pleased to see you. It must be very boring for them down there; they don't even have any air raids to worry about.'

'Yes. I . . . ah . . . there's something I'd like to talk to you about.'

'I thought you were doing that,' Murdoch remarked.

'Yes. Well . . . the fact is, as you say, Mom, I am the last male Mackinder . . . at least on this side of the Atlantic.'

'I didn't actually mean that,' Lee pointed out. 'I meant of your generation. We still have little Ian.'

'That's exactly it,' Fergus said eagerly. 'I think he should have a father.'

They gazed at him, and he flushed. 'It's not illegal.'

'Have you spoken to her?' Lee asked.

'Well . . . in a manner of speaking. I didn't actually come out and ask her, if that's what you mean. I mean, I haven't seen her since last month, and Ian was only dead two months . . .'

'He's only been dead three months now,' Murdoch said quietly.

'I know. Believe me. And I wouldn't dream of it now, if we weren't being sent overseas.'

'You mean you want to make her a widow twice over as

rapidly as possible,' Lee said, with a rare touch of bitterness.

'Of course not, Mom. I'm not going to die. Anyway, I don't propose to marry her until the war is over. That would be too much. But if it's all right with you, I'd like to ask her now. Become engaged.' He looked from face to face.

'Mightn't it be better, if you don't mean to marry until after the war, not even to become engaged until then?' Murdoch asked, still speaking very quietly.

'Well . . . if I don't put a ring on her finger, she might go and marry someone else.'

'And you love her,' Lee said.

'Oh, yes,' Fergus said. 'Oh, yes.'

There could be no doubting that he did.

'And she loves you?' Murdoch asked.

'Well . . . I think she might. There's only one way to find out.'

'Well, then . . .' Lee looked at Murdoch again. 'Will you be able to let us know what she says?'

'Maybe you should go down with him,' Murdoch suggested.

'I don't think he'll want me butting in. Just let us know, Fergus. And if it works, congratulations.'

The bombers returned that night, long after Fergus had left to rejoin the regiment, and Lee and Murdoch sat in their cots together and listened to the rumbling crashes. 'I think he's going to be safer in Egypt than we are in London,' Murdoch said. 'Fighting the Italians.'

'Um,' she replied. 'And is he going to be safe down at Broad Acres?'

He turned his head to look at her. 'She's what he wants. And I suspect he's what she wants.'

'I never wanted her as a daughter-in-law,' Lee said.

'I know. But . . .'

'I've got her. So I may as well lie back and enjoy it,' Lee agreed. 'Twice. God, I hope she never lets him down. Because if she does . . .'

'I'll say amen to that.' Because Murdoch knew that Lee could be quite as ruthless as himself, when aroused.

35

2

Egypt, 1940

'Come along there, look lively,' snapped Corporal Albert Manly-Smith at his tank crew, as the hoists were adjusted to crane the huge vehicle on board the troopship. Theirs was one of the last of the sixty to be loaded, and he was determined his men should be as smart as all those before.

The Crusaders were not easy vehicles to load. If not so heavy as the 'Matildas', as the huge twenty-six ton infantry tanks were nicknamed, they were still considerably larger than the Ts with which the regiment had been equipped before the war, and more strongly armoured as well. But they were no better armed, carrying only a two-pounder gun. Even so he, and everyone else, was itching actually to use them against the enemy.

And to leave England again? It was an exciting prospect, to be sailing for Egypt, especially just as the English summer was drawing to a close. Bert had heard his mother speak of serving in exotic overseas climes, but he himself could only just remember India, as a very small boy, before Father had been killed charging the Mahsuds, and they had all come home. To a very different life, that of the village shop Grandpa had bought after his retirement from the regiment, where Ma had served behind the counter, and he had himself worked on the paper round. Then he and Ma had joined up, almost together. There had been no question but that he would join the Royal Westerns. Even had Father not been an officer, Grandpa had been the RSM.

If Father had lived, Bert thought, he himself might have gone to Sandhurst, and also been an officer. Oddly, he had never regretted that, until this summer. But then, he hadn't really known how to live, until this summer.

The hoist tightened, and the tank, shrouded in netting

and cables, slowly lifted from the dock. Men on the ship shouted instructions, and the troopers gazed at their charge, half in apprehension and half in relief.

It was odd, Bert thought, how one morning could so change a man's life. He had always admired Annaliese von Reger. He could remember when she had first come to live at Broad Acres, and how she would sometimes drive into the village with Lady Mackinder. He had only been fifteen then, but quite old enough to appreciate that tanned and almost boyishly slender body, so excitingly set off by the lustrous golden hair and the splendidly moulded features. He supposed he had had his first wet dream about Annaliese von Reger, had willingly cycled the three miles out to Broad Acres with the papers every day in the hopes of catching a glimpse of her. He hadn't, as a rule. She slept late. But had become more exciting in her absence, because one day during the summer holidays, when he had been helping out in the shop and Lady Mackinder had telephoned for something special, he had volunteered to run it up on his bicycle, as ever in the hopes of seeing the German girl. Again, he hadn't. But Mr Robbins, the butler, had sent his mind whirling through space by warning him not to go round the back of the house, because Miss Annaliese was out there, sunbathing. 'With nothing on,' Mr Robbins had added, with lordly disapproval.

Bert had wondered if Mr Robbins had ever seen her, and been quite jealous. But his dreams had grown even more demanding.

'Squad 'tention,' he snapped, and the men came to attention. 'By the left . . .'

Their boots clumped on the dock and then on the gangway as they entered the bowels of the ship where Sergeant Butler waited, in the midst of milling officers, ship's and regimental, and milling men, too. 'C Troop, Section sixteen, Sergeant.'

Butler consulted his pad. 'D Deck, starboard side, cabin seven. That means the right side, Corporal.'

Butler thought he was an ignorant ninny. 'Yes, Sergeant,' Bert said. 'Are we allowed on deck to wave Blighty goodbye?'

'When your gear is stowed,' Butler told him. 'And you'd better make it snappy.'

Bert led his three men forward, along various corridors, passing other men still hunting for their accommodation, others already in their cabins and arguing over who was to have which bunk. To reach D Deck it was necessary to descend another set of stairs. 'For Chrissake,' commented Trooper Mullings. 'We're going to be below water level.'

They were all recruits, and all in a state of high excitement and apprehension. That their corporal was younger than any of them was irrelevant; he was the only one who had seen action.

'You'll never know it,' he assured them, finding the right number and opening the door. 'That porthole stays shut the whole voyage.' He surveyed the four bunks. 'All right. Mullings and Payne, top bunks. Griffiths, you can have the other lower.' Griffiths was inclined to fart in his sleep, and Bert didn't want him on top. 'Now, get this gear stowed, on the double.'

They fell to work. Three large, sweaty, exuberant West Country boys. But then, he supposed he made a fourth. Only he was light years in front of them. He had been in battle, and seen men killed. He had stood on the beach at Dunkirk, behind the General, and watched his comrades die. Amongst them, the General's own son. Annaliese's husband. But there too he had been light years ahead of his men.

He hadn't been jealous when Annaliese had married Captain Mackinder, as Ian had then been. He had long recognized that she was to be ranked with the various film stars, such as Veronica Lake, whose pin-up photographs adorned the interior of his suitcase, but who would never be near enough to be touched. In many ways Annaliese reminded him of Veronica Lake, physically – except that she was taller. And having her married to a Mackinder meant that she would be remaining at Broad Acres, for him to see from time to time. He had been genuinely sorry to see Colonel Mackinder, as Ian had become so rapidly under the stress of war, dying from a Jerry bullet. He felt almost related to the Mackinders, in an outside way. But he had felt more sorry for poor pregnant Annaliese. He had not supposed he would after all see much of her in the future.

'Atten-tion.'

The voice roaring down the corridor could only belong to Regimental Sergeant-Major Brothers.

'Bit early for a kit inspection,' Griffiths muttered. But they promptly stood to attention in front of their bunks, shoulder to shoulder.

The Sergeant-Major loomed in the doorway, then stood to attention himself to allow Colonel Wilkinson to look inside. 'All well, Corporal?' the Colonel inquired.

'Yes, sir!'

'Very good. Carry on.'

'Yes, sir!'

The Colonel and Sergeant-Major disappeared, and the adjutant appeared instead, following them, accompanied by a sergeant with a clipboard and paper.

'Ah, Manly-Smith,' Major Mackinder said. 'Any complaints?'

'Not as yet, sir!'

'Well, let's keep it that way. At ease.' Fergus Mackinder followed his commanding officer.

'I suppose their cabins are on A Deck,' Mullings remarked.

'With private shower and toilet,' Payne added.

'They're the brass,' Bert reminded them. 'That's what being brass is all about. Privileges.'

But the brass didn't have all the privileges, he thought, as he continued with his unpacking. Perhaps because they were brass, and unable to see the good things in life which lay just beneath their noses. He would have bet a year's pay that Major Fergus Mackinder had never gone sunbathing with his beautiful sister-in-law. Or if he had, would have known what to do about it.

But *he* had. He had not expected it to happen the way it did, but now he looked back on it, he knew that it had all been inevitable. When that day last month Mr Robbins had told him that although the General and Lady Mackinder were out he could wait for them to return if he cared to do so, and had suggested he sit in the conservatory, he had added. 'And mind you stay indoors.'

'Don't tell me,' Bert had said. 'Mrs Mackinder is sunbathing.'

'That's right,' Mr Robbins had agreed. 'So you stay put, young Bert.' Mr Robbins had not been impressed even by the two stripes on his sleeve.

But Mr Robbins, in then leaving him to himself, had been guilty of a grave dereliction of duty – if it had been his duty to guard Mrs Mackinder's privacy. No sooner had he been sure that the butler had retired to his pantry, or wherever it was butlers spent their time, than Bert had slipped out of the conservatory door, and taking care to keep the various hedges which surrounded the garden between him and the kitchen wing, had walked, apparently aimlessly, hands in pockets and beret tilted on to the back of his head, down the slope. And he had found what he had been looking for.

He had meant to do nothing more than look, gasp an abject apology, and return to the conservatory. Just to look at her, once, had been his dream for so long it had to be realized. Her reaction, so different from the angry surprise he had expected, had taken his breath away. For a moment he had ceased acting, and been genuinely afraid of what he had done. But only for a moment. The sight of her lying there, smiling at him, of her breasts, so much fuller than he had expected them to be, and her buttocks, her pale silky pubic patch and her long legs, even the slight stretch marks that discoloured her pouting belly, had made him harder than ever before in his life. The idea that she actually wanted him to make love to her had caused him to droop again with apprehension, but he had soon been ready again, and by then she had been assisting him, sliding down his trousers and putting her hands inside. His entire life to that moment had never possessed a moment like that – but it had immediately been surpassed when she had allowed him to touch her in turn.

Then memory became fuzzy, as they had writhed against

40

each other in a huge spasm of damp warmth, and he had been aware mostly of touching and feeling, rather than seeing and knowing. Oddly, his principal recollection was of his tunic, which he had not had the time to take off, being stained with the milk oozing from her nipples as he had hugged her too tightly. She had been amused at that. 'My baby,' she had said. 'My baby. You must come to Mother again, some time.'

'Oh, yes,' he had promised.

He had not been able to. Even when the regiment had paused for that one night in the depot, there had been no time. But he had written her a letter, explaining. And when next he was home he would see her. He had no doubt about that. Because there was so much to do and to say to her. She had to love him, the way she had given herself to him. Of course she was a lot older than he, and as Ian Mackinder's widow, light years wealthier, he had no doubt. And he was a long way from twenty-one. What Grandpa would say were he to announce he wanted to marry Annaliese Mackinder did not bear thinking about. Or the General, for that matter. But he would be twenty-one, eventually; when that happened, he was prepared to face even the General. Because if she loved him, as she did, all things had to be possible.

'Visitors ashore,' rang through the ship's Tannoy. 'Visitors ashore.'

'Just like if we were taking a bloody pleasure cruise,' Payne commented.

'Personnel to the upper decks if desired,' came another voice, that of Sergeant Butler.

'Let's go,' Griffiths said, and led them into the corridor, which was suddenly jammed with men, all trying to gain the stairs leading up. Christ, if we were torpedoed, Bert thought. None of us would ever get up from down here in time. It was the first time he had ever been aware of being afraid. Not even when he had watched those fellows brewing up in that fierce tank battle in Flanders, during the retreat to the coast, had he been actually afraid. But the sea was an alien element to him. And he had so much to live for.

41

He was carried upwards in the flood of men, and reached the deck, to stare through the evening at the blacked-out houses of Plymouth, too many of them just gaunt shells as a result of German bombing raids. There were thousands of people out there, on the other side of the fence which protected the dock area, going about their business, making tea and reading the newspapers, listening to the wireless and perhaps even making love, apparently unaware that several hundred men were at that moment embarking to fight for their lives; on the dock beneath him Bert could see only a handful of stevedores and policemen.

'Bit different to the last time, eh, Bert?'

Bert came to attention. Fergus Mackinder had this habit of treating him as a friend. An inferior friend, of course. But still a friend. 'Yes, sir,' he agreed.

In October 1939 there had been the regimental band playing, and cheering crowds. Not a sneaking away into the dusk. Just a year ago, he thought. What a year!

'Well, we must be sure to finish the job and get home again in a hurry,' the adjutant said. 'Eh, Bert?'

'Yes, sir!'

'Because when we do, I'm going to be married, Bert.'

'Are you, sir? Congratulations. May I ask to whom, sir?'

'Why, to my brother's widow. We got engaged two days ago. Seemed sort of natural, don't you know? Good night, Bert.'

'Action stations! Action stations!'

The words pumped through the ship, and the troopers rolled out of their bunks, cursing and swearing, pulled on their clothing and grabbed their rifles, before gathering in a huddle in the corridor and making their way up the stairs to the deck.

This was becoming routine, now. There had been seven U-boat alarms since leaving Plymouth. There had been three in Biscay, and each had been terrifying. Then they had gained the security of Gibraltar, sheltering beneath both the rock and the warmest blue skies most of them had ever seen. For two days they had basked, the entire

42

regiment being allowed ashore to bathe in the sea, feeling like tourists – and very properly dressed in the costumes, which concealed them from shoulder to thigh, that had been issued with their tropical kit – while the population had stared.

Then they had been on their way again. Only four days to Malta, they had been told. But they had been a long four days: a submarine alarm every night.

They emerged into the darkness of the decks and fell in at their assembly points. Hopefully, if the ship was tor-pedoed, most of the men would be saved; they had been assured that there were sufficient lifeboat places for them all. But once again they would be without tanks, and as useful as a regiment of ants.

The utter darkness of the warm night was a place of sounds rather than sights. They could hear the whoop whoop of destroyers charging to and fro, and they could see the bright phosphorescent gleam of the wakes. As their eyes grew accustomed to the darkness they could make out the shapes of the other ships in the convoy, lumbering along, every man in the fleet with his fingers crossed. They saw no submarines, and no torpedo tracks. And there were no explosions.

'Just another false alarm, eh, Corporal?' asked the adjutant.

Bert was on the outside of his men, against the rail, and here was Mr Bloody Mackinder pushing his way through the throng. Doing his duty, of course. Mr Bloody Mackinder was always doing his duty.

No doubt he would do his duty when he had put his ring on Annaliese's finger and crawled on to her belly, Bert thought. But suppose he never did? Suppose this ship were to lurch suddenly, and someone fall against him, and pitch him over the side? It could happen.

But not in a calm sea. And not Bert Manly-Smith, he thought sadly. It was not his type of thing . . . perhaps in North Africa. But perhaps not even then. Because the poor chap wasn't at fault. The fault was at least partly his, for not making the effort to go up to Broad Acres when they had been at the depot. There had been no time. But he could have made time. The real fault was Annaliese's. German bitch, he thought, as he had thought a hundred times since the evening they had left Plymouth. She had taken what she had wanted from him, but she had never intended to give anything in return. She was a Mackinder, and he was a common soldier. So, she would marry her dead husband's brother. Good luck to her. But he would know more about her than Mr Bloody Fergus Mackinder ever would.

How he wished they were on their way to fight Germans, rather than Italians.

'Aboukir Bay,' remarked Johnny Wilkinson, peering at the coastline unfolding itself before them through his binoculars. 'My God, Fergus, what history lies over there.'

Wilkinson was given to flights of fancy, Fergus well knew. There was a difference of just six months in their commissions, which was the only reason Johnny was Colonel and he was adjutant. They had served together and fought together long enough to be friends. But it was still a grim thought that he might have to follow Johnny Wilkinson through his career, step by step, six months behind.

'It looks bloody hot,' he remarked.

'Feels hot, too,' the Colonel agreed. 'Makes a change from shivering in Flanders, eh?'

They had been wearing tropical kit for several days, the men seeming oddly weedy in their shorts as their bare knees glowed either too white or too sunburned; too many of them were knock-kneed, a strange failing for cavalry troopers, even if most of them had never sat a horse. Too many of them were calfless as well, and sadly lacking in shoulder. Perhaps the sun and the heat would fill them out, and broaden them out. The old regiment had been composed of professional soldiers, men who had been fighting fit and proud of it. Too many of these recruits had never been truly fit in their lives in depression-ridden England.

All things to be remedied, Fergus reflected – even if they did not seem to bother the CO. Wilkinson was one of those men who ambled through life with good-humoured

44

insouciance. There was much virtue in this attitude. Fergus had never seen Johnny Wilkinson either in a flap or in a hurry. He remembered him at Dunkirk lighting his pipe and saying 'Damnation!' when the blast from a bomb had knocked him over and blown out his match. That was the only time Fergus had ever heard him swear. Such a relaxed attitude undoubtedly communicated itself to his men.

But Johnny Wilkinson had not watched his brother killed and then posthumously awarded the Victoria Cross, and Johnny Wilkinson did not have a father named Murdoch Mackinder who possessed every decoration in the book save the Military Cross – he had never had the time for that – or a line of ancestors every one of whom had been a soldier of the utmost distinction. Johnny Wilkinson was not in a hurry, to avenge and to follow.

And Johnny Wilkinson was not engaged. There was another reason for haste. It was odd, that after their conversation back in August he had had no real doubts Annaliese would say yes when he asked her, yet he had still been as nervous as a kitten. Time had been so short, and he had been still feeling the effects of Mom's and Dad's obvious if carefully muted unease about the idea. He didn't know if they might have somehow forbidden the concept in his absence.

But she had said yes without hesitation, and he had held her in his arms for the first time. A moment to treasure. There might have been more. Almost he had felt that she would have welcomed him in her room that night. It would have been simply done, with the servants and Aunt Philippa all safely asleep. And he had certainly been tempted. But then he had reflected that he was Fergus Mackinder. When he took his wife to bed it would be on her wedding night. And if Annaliese had in her past been forced to yield to men's passions, she would be the more reassured to know that her future husband was both an officer and a gentleman.

He was sure she had been relieved at his decision.

So, all to fight for, and win for. He had every intention of doing that – so long as Johnny Wilkinson didn't slow him up too much.

'Alexandria,' Colonel Wilkinson said, sitting outside his tent and gazing at the rooftops and minarets, which were some four miles away. 'Do you realize that city is more than two thousand years old, Fergus? I can hardly wait to have a closer look at it.'

Fergus thought they had looked at it closely enough already. The transports had been piloted through the myriad shipping in the huge harbour, their decks crowded with eager men looking the height of absurdity in their sun helmets with the sky-blue flashes and with their stockings rolled down just above their boots. They had disembarked on to even more crowded quays, surrounded by *fellaheen*, who mixed with the British officials and sailors and soldiers, shouting questions, offering advice, calling for '*baksheesh*', and stinking to high heaven, while their women, surprisingly unveiled, had gazed at the troopers from doelike eyes concealed by long black lashes. The rest of them was entirely concealed as well, by their *haiks*, or long cloaks, but when they moved they revealed shapely brown feet, bare except for their sandals, and no one could doubt there was a lot of shapely brown body under each *haik*. The men had rustled with anticipation, which was something to concern any adjutant. But he was more concerned with the apparent lack of security: every one of the spectators might have been an Italian spy.

They, and everyone else, had watched the tanks being swung ashore, leaving no one in any doubt that this was an armoured regiment; some of the bastards had even attempted to climb up and look inside, and had had to be driven away almost physically. The crowds had cheered as the men had manned their machines and trucks, the engines had been started – with some anxiety after nearly two weeks at sea – and the regiment had moved off in a clank of exhaust fumes. Dad had told him of landing in places like Bombay and Berbera and Basra, and marching the regiment behind its band through the streets of those tropical towns with the maximum of pomp and ceremony . . . but where was the point in leaving England in such secrecy to arrive here in such publicity?

They had rolled through the town, the trucks with the staff and the medical section and the mechanics and the cooks and the rest of the support leading the tanks, expecting to move straight up to the line. According to the reports they had been given, the Italians were at a place called Sidi Barrani, fifty miles inside the Egyptian border, and only two hundred and fifty miles from Alexandria itself. But outside the city they had been met by a staff major, who had directed them to pitch the tents with which they had been issued on this benighted spot. The men had been delighted. There was food already cooking, they were on firm land again and utterly safe from any submarine, and they were situated on the edge of a vast beach.

'I'd mount a perimeter guard, if I were you, Colonel,' the Major had said. 'These people are absurdly light-fingered. But you chaps have been in India, haven't you?'

'Yes, and if we saw anyone not wearing uniform prowling around the camp we blew his head off,' Fergus said, already thoroughly bad tempered.

'My dear fellow, you can't do that here,' the Major protested. 'Our business is to keep the Gyppoes happy. And I'll tell you, it hasn't been easy since the Eyeties made their move.'

'So when do we go up to the front?' Fergus asked.

'Well, I suppose we can move you in a month.'

'A month?' he bawled.

'My dear fellow, nothing's likely to happen before then. The Eyeties advanced with five divisions against our two, last month. Well, we had to fall back, of course, although we made them pay for every step they took. So they got across the border, to Sidi Barrani, and there they dug in. Would you believe it? They haven't moved another step since then.'

'So they're waiting for reinforcements,' Fergus said. 'They could start advancing again at any moment.'

'Well, that's possible, I suppose. If they do, you'll get

47

sent up, of course. But before then, your chaps have to be acclimatized. Can't go rushing off into battle, don't you know, without acclimatization. Next thing, half your command will be down with sunstroke.'

'If we stay here too long, half our bloody command will be down with VD,' Fergus growled.

'Ah, that's something you have to watch,' the Major agreed. 'I have here a list of the best houses. I'd recommend you have that mimeographed and distributed amongst your NCOs. Oh, and by the way, old man, if I might make a suggestion, don't let your men loose except in parties of at least half a dozen, and tell them to stay off the wine. They won't, but they might drink a little less. Oh, and you'll have to learn how to manage in the desert, eh?'

'Manage in the desert?' Fergus demanded.

'I'll send along a man. Sergeant-Major Blair. Just the fellow. It's not as easy as it seems. Well, Colonel Wilkinson, I hope you'll be comfortable. Couldn't ask for much more, eh?' He had gestured at the sea, which lay virtually at their feet in deep blue profusion, the sky, which contained not a cloud to suggest that it ever rained, and the desert, which stretched in a brown miasma inland for as far as the eye could see. 'I'll bet it's raining at home. Oh, by the way, the boss will probably be up to inspect you in a day or two. I'll try to get you fair warning. Toodle-oo.'

He had boarded his staff car and bounced away, leaving Fergus furious and even Wilkinson slightly irritated.

'The fellow seems to think we're wet behind the ears,' the Colonel remarked, following which he had sunk into the camp chair provided by his batman and made his remark about Alexandria. To which he now added, 'The chaps look happy enough.'

The 'chaps' were having the time of their lives. They had pitched their tents, in orderly rows which reminded Fergus of bivouacking on the North West Frontier, save for the mass of parked tanks and trucks behind (instead of horses), had stripped off, and were splashing about in the sea like children – no costumes today: Fergus reflected that if he had thought their knees too white he hardly had a

48

description for the myriad naked backsides being presented to his gaze.

'I'll set sentries,' he decided, and rounded up his squadron commanders. 'Captain Bentley, A Squadron will be responsible for the western perimeter. That faces the enemy, incidentally. Captain Allack, B Squadron will take the southern perimeter, the desert flank. Captain Romerill, C Squadron will take the eastern perimeter, looking towards Alexandria. At the moment, that's the most dangerous flank, in my opinion. I want sentries patrolling, day and night. Understood?'

'Understood,' they agreed.

'As soon as we can get them out of the water,' Allack suggested.

They had all been lieutenants only six months ago. Promotion was clearly going to be rapid in this war – but it was also going to sort out the men from the boys.

'I suggest you do that now, Mr Allack,' Fergus told him.

'What is the situation as regards leave, sir?' inquired Romerill. 'The lads have been asking.'

'I'll organize a system of passes. Tomorrow.'

'And for officers?' Bentley murmured. He had at least been at Dunkirk. 'I'd like to have a look at Cairo, while we're here.'

'I'll see what the Colonel has to say,' Fergus told them. 'But get those sentries posted by nightfall.'

Wilkinson was naturally very amenable to granting leave; he wanted to have a look at Cairo himself. 'I mean to say, Fergus, it would be stupid to go home from service in Egypt and have to admit we'd never seen the pyramids.'

'With respect, sir,' Fergus pointed out, 'the record indicates that the pyramids are going to be there for a while yet no matter what happens in this war. But home might just not be if we don't win it.'

'Fergus, you take life too seriously,' Wilkinson remarked. 'All work and no play makes Jack a dull boy. Even Wellington spent his time fox hunting in the Peninsula when not actually fighting the French.'

Next day a rota was set up, and sixty men were allowed into Alexandria, while Allack and two lieutenants drew the first pass down to Cairo, driving away in one of the command cars with a great deal of glee.

'My turn tomorrow,' Romerill said with satisfaction.

'But today we'll work,' Fergus told him.

He had the entire regiment doing callisthenics on the beach for an hour after breakfast. Then he held a rigorous kit inspection, and tank inspection too; even after twenty-four hours sand was starting to appear everywhere. 'That rifle will never fire,' he pointed out to one of Corporal Manly-Smith's men, Trooper Griffiths. 'You get that sand out, and you keep that sand out, understood?'

At lunch time Sergeant-Major Blair arrived in a truck, accompanied by a sergeant and two privates. His uniform was faded to a sort of whitish yellow and his boots had seen better days, but he wore medal ribbons and his red face suggested the wearying experience of war. 'Driving practice, sir!' he informed Wilkinson.

'Well, have a bite of lunch first,' the Colonel suggested, 'and then I suppose we'd better wait until it cools off a little, eh?'

'The Eyeties don't always take a siesta, sir!'

Wilkinson looked at Fergus, eyebrows raised.

'I think the Sergeant-Major has a point, sir,' Fergus said.

'Oh, very well. Driving practice! Whatever will they think of next? Carry on, Major.'

Fergus assembled all the officers left in the camp, and all the NCOs as well, to listen to what Blair had to say.

'Over there is a large lake, you may have noticed,' the Sergeant-Major announced, pointing behind the city. 'That's the last water any of you are going to see, except the sea, for the next few months. And even that is brackish, not fresh. Out there' – thumbing over his right shoulder – 'is the desert. It is miles and miles of damn all, and then more miles and miles of damn all. There ain't no water out there, and there ain't no food. So a regiment, a brigade, a division, an army, travels with everything it needs. That means

50

where you go with your tanks, your trucks go with you. There ain't no signposts neither, and don't bother to make a note of physical features for future identification; you get a breeze, next time you come by it'll all have changed. So you travel with your compasses, everywhere, and you note your mileage, all the time. Now, sir,' he turned to Fergus. 'If you'd like to come with me?'

He indicated his own truck, and Fergus and most of the officers got in with him. Sergeant-Major Brothers and Sergeant Butler divided the NCOs between them in two of the regimental trucks.

'Do come back for dinner,' Wilkinson suggested with a grin as they set off.

The three trucks left the road within two miles of the camp and bounced over uneven ground, which rose and fell in gentle undulations, until all sign of life had disappeared. Then the Sergeant-Major braked, and summoned his class. Fergus had already made a note that movement in the desert was impossible to conceal; the plumes of dust which had arisen from their wheels hung on the still air. Now he made another note, that the mid-afternoon heat was lethal; it seemed able to burn right through his tropical jacket, and as this was in any event short-sleeved, he could feel his forearms scorching. His beret seemed glued to his head and he hastily changed it for his pith helmet – but the relief was only marginal. Another must, he was realizing, was some kind of tinted glasses to repel the glare.

That would make them look even more like bloody tourists, he thought.

'Now, gentlemen,' Blair announced. 'This is the terrain over which you gentlemen will be doing most of your fighting. Down there is a *wadi*. That's a dry riverbed. Up there is a *gebel*. That's a hill. There ain't nothing else. And what we're standing on is the desert. The stony desert. You won't have no difficulty in driving across this. But the desert ain't always stony. Some places it has sand. Over there' – he pointed to the south-west – 'is what they call the Quattara Depression. That's soft sand, miles and miles of it. Not even a tank can get through that without bogging down. Further west, in Libya, there's the Great Sand Sea. Even the Touaregs don't attempt to cross that, on camels. But mostly the desert is a mixture of sand and stone. The trick is being able to tell which is which. Now, then, who's going to volunteer?'

Sergeant Butler stepped forward, accompanied by Corporals Clarke, Manly-Smith and Roberts.

'Right-ho. What I would like you to do, Sergeant, is take that truck and drive to that *gebel* over there and back. It's not more than a mile.'

Butler himself got behind the wheel.

'I'll come with you,' Fergus said, and sat next to the sergeant.

'You follow us,' Blair told the sergeant who was driving his own truck, and got in beside Fergus; the corporals climbed into the back.

'Off you go,' Blair said.

Butler engaged gear, and the huge truck began to move. Butler drove with due caution for the first minute, then changed into top and began to bounce at about thirty miles an hour, steering straight at the hillock.

Blair pulled his nose. 'I should slow down if I were you, Sergeant,' he remarked.

Butler turned his head to look at him, fortunately taking his foot off the accelerator as he did so, for before he could speak the truck suddenly slewed sideways so violently Fergus thought it was going over. However, Butler was a very good driver, and turned into the skid, bringing them to a halt facing back the way they had come. 'I see what you mean, Sergeant-Major,' he acknowledged.

'Sand,' Blair commented. 'Didn't spot it, did you?'

'No, I didn't.'

'Neither did I,' Fergus admitted. 'But your people did.'

The truck which had been following them had turned away, and was some fifty yards to their right, also stopped.

'Well, sir, they've been trained to it. By me,' Blair added modestly.

'Yes. Well, Sergeant, I think we had better get over there and join them,' Fergus said

52

'Yes, sir.' Butler engaged gear, and released the clutch. The engine roared and the wheels churned. Butler increased speed, and the roaring grew louder.

'Sand,' Blair commented again.

Perspiring, Butler put the truck into reverse. The roaring grew louder yet, and sand flew in every direction. But the truck didn't move.

'If you keep that up, you'll bury her,' Blair told him.

'Then what the bloody hell do I do?' Butler shouted, red in the face. 'Begging your pardon, Mr Mackinder.'

'What does he do, Sergeant-Major?' Fergus asked.

'He digs it out, sir.'

Fergus looked at Butler, who looked back. 'We don't have any spades.'

'Pays to be equipped, in the desert, sir.' Blair jerked his thumb, and Fergus saw the sergeant and the two privates leaving their truck to walk towards them. They carried spades and strips of reinforced canvas. 'Sand channels,' Blair explained.

They all disembarked, and two of the corporals were given a spade each. They were certainly going to need it; the truck had sunk to its axles, and Fergus discovered the ground was so soft he very rapidly sank to the uppers of his boots.

Sweating and muttering, Manly-Smith and Clarke began to dig the sand away from the rear wheels, watched by their instructors and their comrades.

'You have to catch it right,' Blair explained, 'or it all slides back in. Now! Haste, Sergeant. Get those channels in.'

Butler and Roberts dropped to their hands and knees, forcing the canvas down against and in front of the tyres.

'Other side, quickly,' Blair commanded.

They hurried over and did the other side.

'Right,' Blair said. 'Now you three fellows push, and you drive, Sergeant. Once you get on to the channels you'll be all right.'

Fergus stood to one side with the instructors, while the corporals, red in the face and dripping perspiration, put their shoulders to the back of the truck. Butler got behind the wheel and revved the engine, sand flew into the faces and uniforms of the unfortunate corporals, but at last the wheels were got on to the canvas, gripped, and the truck moved forward – twelve feet, or the length of the channels, before promptly bogging down again.

Butler glared at Blair, who had been walking beside him. 'What now?'

'You do it all over again. You're lucky, Sergeant. There's firm ground only twenty feet away. Two more digs, and you're there.'

'Jesus Christ,' Bert Manly-Smith muttered.

'Some sand patches can be several hundred feet across,' Blair remarked. 'Drive into one of them at speed and you're there for the night.'

Fergus thought they might very well be there for the night anyway; it was now an hour since they had left the rest of the class, who were watching them through binoculars. It took them another hour to get out of the sand, and then Butler drove very cautiously up to the foot of the hill, while Blair, having made his point, told him what to look for to avoid entering another sand patch. Then they drove back to the rest of the class.

'Time for a cuppa, I would say, sir,' Blair suggested to Fergus.

'Unfortunately, we didn't bring any tea with us,' Fergus pointed out.

Blair winked. 'Always be prepared in the desert, sir.' His sergeant produced various bags from the back of his truck, while his two troopers took an empty four-gallon petrol can, made of thin sheet metal, and cut it in half. One half they punched full of holes with their bayonets, and filled it with sand and gravel. Then, from another petrol can, this one half full, they poured a liberal splash into the primitive stove. A match was struck, and the can flared into flame.

Watched in fascination by the class, the sergeant's water bottle was emptied into the other half of the can, and this was placed upon the flames. It boiled in seconds, and then from the various bags tea, sugar and powdered milk were

54

added, and stirred vigorously, again with a bayonet. Blair tested it, and then, using a rag to stop himself from being scalded, lifted the can and held it out to Fergus. 'You first, sir.'

Tentatively Fergus took both rag and tin, and raised it to his lips. It was boiling hot, but amazingly tasty, and refreshing. He swallowed, and handed it to Bentley. It then made the rounds, each man taking a swig, before the last of it came back to Blair, who finished it. He grinned at Fergus. 'It ain't a bad life, sir, if you don't let it get you down.'

'We have one hell of a lot to learn,' Fergus told the Colonel. 'And not all that much time.'

He put his drivers to work every day, cursing and sweating, but learning. And he put his officers through their paces as well. 'You normally won't have more than three men with you,' he told them when they complained. 'So you'll have to give a hand if you get stuck. You may as well know what it's like.'

The men grumbled even more, but he could watch them becoming more fit with every day, as their white bodies tanned and in the heat their chests and shoulders expanded, and their legs grew more muscular as they jogged round and round the camp and in and out of sand traps. When their friendly staff Major arrived to warn them that General Wavell was going to pay them a visit the next day, accompanied by the commander of the army in the field, Major General O'Connor, Fergus felt the regiment might just be up to scratch.

General Sir Archibald Wavell turned out to be a tall man with a little moustache and a somewhat abrupt manner. He wore breeches and old-fashioned boots and leggings. Major General Richard O'Connor was altogether shorter and more compact, and more casually dressed, in trousers. Both wore mufflers and heavy coats, for the weather had suddenly turned decidedly chilly; it was now mid-November.

They were met by Wilkinson and Fergus, and then driven on an inspection of the regiment, which stood to attention in front of its tanks and trucks.

'Fine-looking men,' Wavell commented when they returned to the command tent for lunch. 'How many were at Dunkirk?'

'Only about fifty per cent,' Wilkinson told him. 'But the rest are coming on well.'

'How soon can you move up?' O'Connor asked.

'One more week should do it,' Wilkinson said.

'We can move up sooner if necessary, sir,' Fergus said.

Wavell looked from one to the other. 'One more week will be fine,' he agreed. 'But I want you in position with the armoured brigade by the end of this month.' He looked at O'Connor.

'The Italians have been reinforced to a total of ten divisions, so far as we are aware,' O'Connor said. 'They had five when they advanced in September. They've made no move since crossing the frontier, but with such an accretion of strength it seems likely that they will do so now. We propose to pre-empt them and counter-attack at the beginning of next month.'

'In what strength, sir?' Wilkinson asked.

O'Connor gave a brief smile. 'We muster two divisions, Colonel. But with your chaps we have an armoured brigade, which is better than anything on the other side. I think we have every chance of success, if only because they won't expect us to start anything with such inferior forces. What I am telling you is in the strictest confidence, of course. Not even your squadron commanders are to know. You are merely moving up to take your places in the defensive line. Understood?'

'Yes, sir,' Wilkinson and Fergus said together.

'Action at last,' Fergus said, when the generals had left.

'Yes. I think the lads are just about ready for it,' Wilkinson conceded.

'Then why wait another week?'

'Because I haven't got down to Cairo yet. And I mean to do that, tomorrow. We'll go together, Fergus.'

'Really, John, I'd rather . . .'

'I insist upon it. You have been working far too hard. You simply have to take a break before we go into action. It could be weeks before we get back here. So we will take two nights off. Bentley can command here for two nights. Don't argue, Fergus. This is an order.'

'Brass,' Bert Manly-Smith remarked, as he fitted himself into the crowded truck and watched the command car disappearing down the road to Cairo. 'They get to visit the pyramids while we get to visit Alexandria.'

'Alexandria is older than Cairo,' Trooper Payne protested. He was a well-read fellow. 'Much older.'

'So Bath is older than Bristol,' Bert retorted. 'I know which one I'd rather visit on a pass.'

His men merely exchanged glances and raised their eyebrows. The corporal had changed over the past couple of months. Since leaving England, in fact. When they had first joined the regiment, and been stationed at the depot and then in East Anglia, he had been full of good humour and advice. But on the voyage out to Alexandria he had become more and more morose, and since landing had been very difficult to share a tent with. Much less an afternoon on the town.

But it was the last afternoon on the town, any town, they were going to get for some time. For some of them, perhaps, for ever. The troopers hadn't been deceived by the information they had been given, that they were to move up and take over a section of the defensive perimeter facing Sidi Barrani. They had no doubt at all that the brass knew the Eyeties were about to launch another offensive, and they were required to try to stop them. The recruits were about to fight their first battle. They reached Alexandria in a strange mixture of apprehension and euphoria.

'Christ, you wouldn't think there was a war on,' Bert growled as they marched through the crowded streets. The *souk* was in full swing, they were surrounded by eager vendors anxious to sell them anything from carpets to paintings, and they soon accumulated a gaggle of little boys, some of whom had a smattering of English. 'You want house, *effendi*?' one asked Bert.

'That's exactly it,' Bert said. He wanted to fuck the pants

of the plumpest Gyppo bint he could find, and stop himself thinking about Annaliese.

'I show,' the boy offered.

'You think he knows a good place?' Griffiths asked.

'What the hell?' Bert replied. 'They're all alike.'

'The sergeant gave you a list,' Payne complained.

'What the hell does he know about it? Lead on, son.'

The boy held Bert's hand, led him through the crowd. The other three exchanged glances, shrugged, and then followed. Everyone seemed to know where they were going, and grinned at them and offered advice, in Egyptian. So they had no idea what it was.

Then the boy led them out of the crowds and down a narrow and dark side alley, which smelt of drains. 'You think we're going to be sandbagged?' Mullings asked nervously.

'They'd never take on four troopers,' Griffiths protested. 'Oops! Three troopers and a corporal.'

The boy had stopped before a door set in the wall, and knocked once.

'You're sure this is a good house?' Bert demanded.

'The best,' the boy asserted.

The door was opened by a woman shrouded in a *haik*; it was difficult to ascertain her age. The boy spoke in Egyptian, and she stepped aside to allow the four troopers inside. The darkened hall into which they had been admitted smelt very little better than the street outside. But there were giggles from somewhere beyond the inner door, which sounded promising.

'You come,' the boy said, going to the staircase.

'Don't we get to choose?' Griffiths asked.

'All is good,' the boy said, his foot on the first step. 'You come.'

Bert followed, and the men followed Bert. They climbed the stairs and found themselves in a corridor which stretched away from the street and seemed to indicate that the house was far larger than it had appeared from the outside. There was a barred window at the far end which admitted some light, and they could see a succession of doors leading off.

The boy opened the first door. 'You come in,' he told Bert.

'See you later,' Bert said, and went inside. The room contained an iron bedstead with an uncovered horsehair mattress, and nothing else. Not even a washbasin. But what the hell, he thought; I'll wash her off in the sea when I get back to camp.

'You strip, eh?' the boy asked, and closed the door on him.

Bert took off his uniform and underclothes, sat on the mattress. He hadn't had a woman since Annaliese. He hadn't wanted one. After hearing about how she had betrayed him, he had wanted one even less, and had not applied for a pass throughout the regiment's stay in the camp by the beach – much to the disgust of his crew, because no men had been allowed into Alexandria save under the command of an NCO. But suddenly he wanted one very badly. He was as hard as a rock at the very thought of it. He should have had one long ago, and got rid of the woman from his mind. But he was going to do that now.

The door opened and he stood up in anticipation. But it was the boy again, who looked him up and down in appreciation, and said, 'You pay first, eh?'

'You're the head ponce, right? At your age? How much?'

'One pound.'

'You have got to be joking.'

'One pound,' the boy said. 'This is a very good house.'

Well, he was there, and he wanted. Bert picked up his trousers, found the money, held it out. The boy took it, folded it into his pocket, and then removed his shirt and fez. Bert watched him with only mild interest. Then the boy dropped his pants as well, to reveal himself just as aroused as Bert was. 'You want me first, or you?' he asked.

Still Bert didn't understand what he meant. The boy grinned at him, went to the cupboard in a corner of the room, and took out a jar of grease. 'I make it easy, eh?' he suggested.

The penny dropped in Bert's brain. 'You silly bastard!' he snapped. 'I came here for a woman, not a boy.'

'A woman? There are no women here, *effendi*. Save my mother.'

'Who ought to be ashamed of herself. I'll have my pound back.'

'You have paid, *effendi*,' the boy said, his face set in stubborn lines. 'Now come into me.'

Bert was suddenly very angry. He swung his hand. The boy ducked but not far enough. Bert's fist caught him on the side of his head and he tumbled across the bed. Bert picked up the boy's pants and retrieved his money, then pulled on his battledress and stepped outside, where his men were already waiting.

'Jesus, Corporal,' Payne said. 'This place . . .'

'Forget it,' Bert said.

'Mama, Mama,' the boy was screaming, and was now joined by a chorus from his compatriots in the other rooms. There was a good deal of noise from downstairs, and when the troopers reached the steps they found themselves looking at half a dozen young men, most considerably older than their recent companions, and bigger and stronger, too.

One of them said, 'You give us back the money, *effendi*.'

'You be damned,' Bert told him.

The young man looked at his fellows, and spoke in Egyptian.

'Corporal,' Griffiths asked, his voice trembling. 'What are we going to do?'

'We,' Bert announced, feeling happy for the first time in two months, 'are going to break this fucking place up.'

'Now there is a sight I had never expected to see,' Colonel Wilkinson said. 'Stop the car a moment, will you, Peters.'

'Yes, sir!' The car stopped at the side of the road.

'The wonder of the world,' Wilkinson said reverently.

Even Fergus was impressed. It was something over a hundred miles from Alexandria to Cairo, and the road had been dusty and not in the best of repair. It had also been crowded, with military as well as civilian traffic, which might vary from huge trucks making for the coast road and presumably the army entrenched before Sidi Barrani, to

60

donkey carts laden with dates or household goods. It had been a tiring journey.

The road had also followed the river, and that had been of endless interest. If Wilkinson was absorbed by man's previous puny efforts on earth, Fergus found the sight of the river, which had been flowing through this desert ever since time had begun, far more evocative. Because Egypt was a desert to either side of the river, at a distance of not more than ten miles. And yet, within that so narrow strip, all was cultivation and profusion.

But now nature's artistry and man's had come together, and he had to admit it presented an unforgettable sight. To their left was the railway line, which they had accompanied all the way from Alexandria, first on their right, but crossing it a few miles farther back. Beyond the line was the river, and beyond the river rose the rooftops and minarets of Cairo, glowing in the late afternoon sun. While in the strongest contrast, on their western side of the river, on a low plateau there rose the perfectly triangular shapes of the pyramids, guarded, at a lower level, by the massive body of the Sphinx.

'Four thousand years,' Wilkinson said. 'Give or take a century or two. Napoleon once fought a battle on this very spot. The Battle of the Pyramids. That must have been a marvellous occasion.'

'Let's hope we don't have to do the same,' Fergus commented.

'He formed squares, and repelled Mahomet Ali's cavalry,' Wilkinson said. 'I can just see it. Ah, well, drive on, Peters.'

'Yes, sir,' agreed the patient driver.

Wilkinson had booked them rooms at Shepheard's, and after a bath and a change of uniform, they went to the Gezira Club, where they gathered in the bar with a large number of other officers. 'Royal Western Dragoons,' remarked one colonel. 'Had no idea you were in Egypt, old boy.'

'Well, sir, you must be the only person in Egypt who doesn't know we're here,' Fergus said. 'Or in Libya, either.'

'I know, dashed difficult to keep things quiet here. I've been down in the Soudan, actually, making sure all is well there. Just got back in time for Jacki's party. You fellows are going, I suppose?'

'I'm afraid not,' Wilkinson confessed. 'We don't know anybody named Jacki. We're certainly not invited.'

'My dear fellow, that doesn't matter. You must come. When are you off for the front?'

Fergus coughed, but Wilkinson was already speaking. 'Two days' time.'

'Then you simply must come. Oh, indeed, I insist. You'll be my guests. Harrison is the name. Jacki is an old friend. Yes . . .' he frowned at their pale-blue undress uniforms. 'I'm sure we can fit you out with something to wear. As soon as we've had another whisky. Party doesn't start until eight.'

Mess jackets and trews were provided, albeit taken from a Scottish regiment. 'I feel like a spy,' Wilkinson remarked.

'And I think perhaps we should behave like spies,' Fergus suggested, retying his bow tie in an effort to get it straight. 'We don't know who'll be at this beastly party. I really don't think we should tell anyone that we're moving up to the front in the next couple of days.'

'Don't you think they know already?' Wilkinson asked. 'But we'll be mum if it makes you happy.'

The party was in a flat in a building overlooking the Nile, and even the pyramids, although they were now lost in darkness. Presumably there were blackout regulations for Cairo, but nobody seemed to pay them the slightest notice, and indeed the whole city was a blaze of light.

The flat itself was large and ostentatiously furnished. It belonged to a titled lady who was apparently either widowed or divorced – Fergus never did discover which – but liked to be called Jacki and was obviously very rich. Her hobby was, as she admitted, entertaining British officers. 'Well, you are all doing such a frightfully good job, don't you know, keeping Musso out of the Gezira Club. We poor females must do our bit.'

She was about forty, thin and angular, with an apparently bottomless ability to drink gin and enough jewels to pay for the war effort on her own. 'Rumour has it she's looking for a husband,' confided Colonel Harrison. 'But I don't think she's looking very hard. I say, fellows, let's circulate.'

The room was crowded, with a mass of officers, as well as a smattering of civilians, and even one or two Egyptians, obviously very upper crust. There was also a matching number of women, all wearing evening gowns and seeming to be competing for the prize for displaying the deepest décolletage, either front or back; their ages ranged from what seemed to be teenagers to elderly matrons, and they also included several Egyptian ladies. Fergus decided to approach one of these, as it was their country, however occupied by the British, and try to discover something about what they were like. He found it heavy going, however, between trying to balance smoked salmon sandwiches – the food was provided by a finger buffet – and champagne in one hand, and talk with the other: the lady he had chosen spoke poor English.

'You would do better in French,' a voice sparkled at his elbow, and he turned to look at a tall, dark young woman, with green eyes which matched the quality of her contralto. She smiled at him. 'I'm Monique Deschards,' she explained. 'And you are Major . . .?'

'Fergus Mackinder.' The décolletage of her midnight-blue gown was as deep as anyone's, and she had a wealth of heavy brown hair. He could hardly remember ever having been so instantly attracted to anyone.

'I knew you were Scottish, from your uniform. Gordon Highlanders, is it?'

'Ah . . . yes.' Fergus had never actually told a lie in his life, and to lie to this magnificent creature seemed doubly disgraceful.

'Fatima has lived a sheltered life,' Monique Deschards said, continuing to smile at him.

Fergus had lost all interest in Fatima. 'Your glass is empty,' he protested.

'Why, so it is.' She gave an artificially helpless glance to left and right.

'I'll find you a refill,' he volunteered.

'I will come with you,' she said. 'If I lose my glass, I may never see it again. Or you,' she added.

He reminded himself that he was engaged to be married, to the most beautiful girl in the world. But he was off to battle in two days' time, and Monique was just a ship, passing in the night. But what a delightful ship.

They found themselves on the balcony, looking down at the river. 'Do you think I should wear my ring?' she asked.

He didn't know what to reply to that.

'My trouble is,' she confessed, 'that I don't know whether my husband is alive or dead.'

'Good heavens,' Fergus remarked: he was on his fourth glass of champagne.

'He was in the Maginot Line when it was overrun, and was posted missing. He could be a prisoner.' She glanced at him. 'But if he was a prisoner, would I not have been informed?'

'Well . . .' of course you would have, he wanted to say. But that might depress her. 'It would be likely.'

'But not certain. It is a very difficult position for a woman to be in. So . . . I came out here to join my father. He is in business in Cairo. That was lucky for me, eh?'

'Oh, indeed. And for Cairo.' He had spoken without thinking, and instantly regretted it, especially as she did not reply. 'I was in France,' he ventured, hoping to mend bridges.

'I did not doubt it. You were at Dunkirk.'

'Ah . . . yes.'

She smiled, in the darkness. 'You think I am a spy.'

'Well . . . it's a good rule to keep one's movements to oneself. In wartime.'

'But you are in Cairo. You cannot keep this secret. From me, at the least.'

'Well . . . I suppose I can't,' he agreed.

'And in the next few days you will move up to the front to fight the Italians.'

'I'm not at liberty to say.'

'But why else would you be here? And everyone knows there is going to be a battle in a few days.'

'Do they?' he asked in alarm.

'Of course. The Italians are about to attack.'

'Ah.' He gave a faint sigh of relief. 'Yes, I suppose they could be.'

She gazed into the night. 'You will drive off into the desert, to kill, or be killed. The desert is very beautiful, but not when one is dying.'

'I suppose not,' he agreed.

She glanced at him. 'When do you return to your camp?'

'Ah . . .' But surely there could be no harm in telling her that. 'The day after tomorrow.'

'You are spending tomorrow in Cairo? Doing what?'

'Well . . . my colonel wants to have a look at all the antiquities, I imagine.'

'Then let him. Why do you not let me show you the desert. At peace, and beautiful? Before you begin to destroy it?'

'Do you know,' Fergus said, 'I think that would be an absolutely splendid idea.'

3

The Desert, 1940–41

'Well, well,' remarked Johnny Wilkinson. 'Off to the desert with a femme fatale, eh?'

'I am certain she is not a femme fatale,' Fergus objected. 'She is a war widow. Like . . . well, Annaliese. I suppose.'

'Something you want to remember,' Wilkinson said severely. 'I'll leave you to it.'

He departed with several other officers for a closer look at the pyramids.

'Do you wish to look at the pyramids?' Monique asked, when, a few minutes later, she arrived at Shepheard's in her father's touring car.

'Not right this minute,' he said. 'Everybody else is doing that.'

She smiled. 'I promised you the desert.'

They drove across the bridge and took a road leading to the south-west. They passed the pyramids, huge and much less perfect at close quarters, on their right, but Fergus found a lot more to look at nearer at hand; Monique wore a white linen dress with a blue cardigan – it was still fairly early in the morning and decidedly cool – and sandals, and her hair was kept from blowing all over the place by a bandeau: the canvas roof was down. He found her a quite beautiful picture.

She glanced at him. 'The desert is an evocative place.'

'I'm sure it is.'

'But you do not find it so.'

'When you're in an armoured regiment, sand becomes merely a damned nuisance. Oh, my God, I shouldn't have said that.'

'Then I will forget you did. But today I can tell you do not really belong to the Gordon Highlanders.'

Because without thinking he had put on his usual uniform. Another stupid mistake. My God, he thought, if she really is a spy . . .

'So I will forget both what you wear and what you said,' she volunteered. 'I find the desert beautiful.'

She gazed in front of her at the road, while for the second time in her company he mentally kicked himself. But she was the sort of woman one instinctively made these remarks to. 'This road,' she said, 'leads to an oasis. It is about fifty miles. And not all of it is as good as this. But we could make it for lunch. And, surprisingly, there is quite a good restaurant there. Would you like that?'

'I think that would be a splendid idea. If you can spare the petrol.'

She laughed. 'There is always petrol, if you know where to look. Today the tank is full.'

The road did indeed deteriorate, quite quickly, but it was absolutely free of traffic, and Monique was a superb driver. Fergus found himself wondering how well she would do under the eagle eye of Sergeant-Major Blair. But Monique Deschards would do very well under anyone's eye, however eagle. And however often she had to twist the wheel she remained cool and unhurried, although, as it warmed up and she removed the cardigan, he noticed little traces of damp at her armpits. These he found entrancing.

While she talked throughout the journey, about France, which she obviously loved dearly, about the guilt she felt at having fled, her anxiety to get back. 'When we return,' she said. 'Your army and mine, eh, Fergus?'

'Oh, indeed,' he agreed enthusiastically.

They reached the oasis, and she took him for a walk around the village, a kaleidoscope of closely packed houses painted in a variety of pastel shades, pinks and blues and yellows, all huddled beneath the tall tower of the minaret, and clustered around the bubbling pool of water which irrigated the green fields that surrounded the houses for a distance of about half a mile before ending abruptly in stony desert. 'There is so much water under the desert,' Monique said. 'If one only knew where to look.'

67

Lunch was somewhat crude, goatsmeat and soggy beans, but it was heavily spiced and the wine was good if heady. After the meal, as the sun was now very hot, Fergus helped Monique put the canvas hood up, and then leaned back as she commenced the homeward journey. But after they had driven for an hour she pulled off the road. 'I have drunk too much wine to concentrate,' she announced. 'I think I need a siesta before we go on. Unless you would like to drive.'

They gazed at each other. He should say yes, I will drive, he knew. But he also had drunk too much wine. Not too much to be unable to drive. Just enough not to wish to, but rather to wish to prolong this marvellous day to its ultimate moment. 'I think a siesta would be rather a good idea,' he said.

Monique smiled, and kicked off her shoes. 'The back seat is more comfortable.'

He didn't know whether she was actually inviting him, or not. 'Supposing someone comes along.'

'And you have not brought your revolver? Never mind, there is a pistol in my handbag.'

'Oh.' That hadn't been what he had meant at all.

'One must always be prepared, in the desert.'

Sergeant-Major Blair had said that. He wondered if this girl had tea and milk and sugar, and an empty petrol can, in her boot.

'But it is unlikely anyone will come along,' Monique said. She opened her door and stepped out. The breeze whipped her skirt and her hair. 'It is a delightful feeling, to stand barefoot in the desert,' she said. 'It robs one of one's inhibitions.'

Fergus opened the door and got out as well. He was going to hate himself tomorrow. This evening, perhaps. But this was a here and now situation, which might never be repeated. With a woman who so obviously wanted. 'Yes,' he said, as he walked round the car.

Monique turned into his arms.

'Oh, I say, really!' remarked Johnny Wilkinson. Fergus didn't know what the Colonel had done with his last twenty-four hours in Cairo – they hadn't seen each other until they had got into the staff car for the drive back to camp – but he certainly had a hangover. Neither of them had exchanged more than a word on the bumpy journey, and they had returned to find Captain Bentley in an extremely unhappy mood.

As was the Colonel, now that he had read the report. 'Four of my men, breaking down half of Alexandria? These people are our friends. Our allies!'

'There appear to have been extenuating circumstances, sir,' Fergus murmured, having read the report in greater detail.

'What extenuating circumstances can there have been to causing a riot?'

'Well . . . perhaps you should read Corporal Manly-Smith's testimony, sir.'

Poor little bastard, he thought. Setting off for a last night on the town, and winding up with a totally unexpected situation, while he . . . in the desert, sand gets everywhere. But sometimes delightfully so. He had cleaned the sand from between Monique's toes, while she had lain, half asleep and exhausted, on the back seat of the car. Her feet had dangled over the edge, then. Before, they had been separated. One had certainly been out of the door. The other had been hooked over the front seat, to brace herself. He didn't know where his had been.

That had been quick, violent, urgent. They had both wanted, so desperately . . . and perhaps, he thought, for the same reasons: separation from their loved ones. Although he felt that Monique did not really love her husband. Did that mean he did not really love Annaliese? That was an unworthy thought. In any event, it was not one he was prepared to consider too deeply at that moment. Of course he loved Annaliese: he and Monique were merely ships that had passed in the night, both needing a port.

But it had been a very long night. They had driven back to Cairo in a kind of euphoric stupor, and when they had reached the hotel, she had said, 'I would like to come up.'

So she had. No one had even raised an eyebrow. He felt

that raising an eyebrow in Shepheard's simply wasn't done. They had shared his shower, bodies pressed against each other, and then they had dried each other, and shared his bed, pressed against each other. Room service had provided dinner; Monique had laughingly disappeared into the bathroom while it was being served, and then they had sat opposite each other, naked, while they had eaten and drunk.

Surprisingly, that was his most clear-cut memory of their time together. Making love to Monique had been too all consuming for one sense, like sight, to stand apart; it had involved all the senses rolled up together. And looking at Monique, without having that jumbled sensation, had only been possible while they had been at once sated and eating.

He had never imagined that he would ever have dinner opposite a naked woman. Just being in the company of one had always appeared an unnerving prospect. How often had he dreamed of joining Annaliese in her secret hideaway, and lacked the courage? But no courage had been necessary, with Monique; it had seemed the most natural thing in the world. So, what would he carry into battle with him the day after tomorrow? A dream of golden hair, and suntanned limbs which he had never seen? Or a memory, of equally long legs, equally suntanned, but delightfully, startlingly, white at buttocks, groin and breasts: Monique was not a nature worshipper in that sense. She was much more voluptuous than Annaliese. Her breasts could hardly be cupped in a hand, her buttocks overflowed from extended fingers. But they were tight buttocks, and there were powerful muscles in her thighs and belly, and she had never been a mother. And the hair on her mound was like purest silk.

She had smiled, then laughed, at the moment of orgasm. And a great many other moments besides. She was a widow. Like Annaliese, but she had not forgotten how to live. Annaliese should smile more often. But would she smile at the moment of orgasm?

'Hm,' Wilkinson commented, having glanced at Bert's statement. 'I suppose they were pretty upset.'

'And we are going to need every fit man when we move out,' Fergus pressed. 'We have too many on the sick list as it is.'

'I take your point. But it is still reprehensible, the habit of this army of heading for the nearest town looking for women the moment they have a pass. I mean, suppose we had started looking for women the moment we got to Cairo, eh?'

'Very reprehensible, sir,' Fergus agreed.

'Very good, Major. They will have to be punished. A fortnight's loss of pay and privileges. And Manly-Smith to be reduced to the ranks.'

'With respect, sir, Corporal Manly-Smith is a very able tank commander.'

'He can command a tank as a private for the next few weeks. Let him earn those stripes back.'

'Yes, sir,' Fergus said sadly.

'Bloody hell,' Payne grumbled.

'You should grumble,' Bert told him. 'I've lost my stripes.'

Mr Bloody Adjutant Mackinder, he thought. My friend! One day, he thought. One day . . .

But for now it was necessary to concentrate as the regiment roared and rattled along the coast road that led from Alexandria to the wire, as the border was called. They made a long column, sixty tanks and some thirty trucks, and the dust settled on them and over them and behind them. They were at last going back to war.

'Christ, what a country,' Griffiths remarked.

There certainly was not a lot of feature to it. To the right there was the sea, and to the left there was the desert, flat and monotonous. They rumbled through various villages, all of which had unpronounceable names: Dikheila, Bahiq, Hammann, Alamein, Diraziya. They passed Roman ruins at a place called Taposiris.

Beyond Alamein the road, which had been following the coast in a roughly south-westerly direction, turned north-west, still following the coast – they were rounding the sides of a huge shallow bay. When they stopped for lunch their guides informed them that the enormous, impassable Quattara Depression lay to their south, leaving this coast road the only possible way for a military column to reach Libya – or for the Italians to reach Alexandria.

But that afternoon the country became more dramatic, with high ground rising away to their left – the Libyan Plateau, they were told – and well before dusk they came upon the army. A very small army, less than thirty thousand men, British, Australians and Indians, making up roughly two divisions. There was also a small park of tanks, to which the regiment was directed.

'Now that you are here, gentlemen,' Brigadier Jock Campbell said to Wilkinson and Fergus, 'we have an armoured brigade. Welcome to Mersa Matruh.'

'All well?' Fergus paused for the twentieth time in his inspection of the tanks.

Bert and his crew came to attention. 'All well, sir!'

'We will move out at midnight. Get some sleep while you can.'

'Yes, sir!'

'It'll be good to be back in action, eh, Private Manly-Smith?'

'Yes, sir!' And maybe you'll get your head shot off, you lousy bastard.

'A chance for you to get your stripes back,' Fergus told him. 'You will, you know.'

'Yes, sir!' No thanks to you, you ass-licking shit.

Fergus passed on. He felt a sense of pleasant excitement. On several counts. In just over two weeks it would be Christmas. It would be very odd to spend Christmas in this dust and sand, while even if it was cold enough for a sweater once the sun set, and a blanket at night, there was no possibility of snow. Even on the North West Frontier Christmas had been a time for snow and fires; here they would be bathing in the sea.

If they were bathing at all. In front of them were odds of at least five to one. Yet the army was quietly confident. And

72

behind them was all Egypt, waiting for their victory. Monique Deschards, waiting more than most. But he should not be taking the thought of Monique Deschards into battle. If he thought about anyone other than the enemy, it should be Annaliese.

'There they go,' Wilkinson commented. The senior officers waited by the command truck, which contained such things as a desk and a wireless operator, as well as their batmen and endless cups of tea. Now they all raised their heads to look up at the darkness above them, which had suddenly been filled with the drone of aircraft as the RAF prepared to deliver the first blows of the battle. A few moments later they listened to the crump-crump of bombs – the Italian lines were only a few miles away. Then the whole night exploded, as the army's own artillery opened fire, and were joined by the squadron of warships off the coast. These had moved up as soon as it was dark, and now the flashes of their big guns could clearly be seen. The Italian position became an inferno of flame and noise.

'Rather good to be on this end of it,' Bentley commented.

Wilkinson was checking his watch. 'Time, gentlemen. Now remember, markers have been laid down. And when we move forward, follow the guides through the minefield. There is a passage through; some Italian tanks were seen using it yesterday. That's our way. No straying. Good hunting.'

The captains returned to their squadrons, Wilkinson and Fergus boarded the command truck. This would be the first time he had gone into battle in a truck, Fergus thought; he would far rather have been in a tank. But he would never sit in a tank, in combat, again, except if, as colonel, he might lead his men into the fray: he would not be actually commanding the tank. And that presumed he would indeed be colonel, one day. It was an odd feeling that so important a part of his life was behind him.

'The regiment will move out,' Wilkinson told the telegrapher, who immediately relayed the command. The tank engines had already been started, and now they clanked ponderously forward. All around them was noise and creaks and bangs, but the sound of the army moving into position was muffled by the explosions in front of them.

The flaps of the truck were up, and Fergus could look left and right, at the three squadrons, and at the truck loads of Indian infantry, the Eleventh Division, which were accompanying them. They were to take up their position before the village of Nibeiwa, which reconnaissance had suggested was the least heavily defended portion of the Italian line, and where that telltale gap in the minefield had been spotted. Theirs was the responsibility for the breakthrough. It really was an imposing sight, he thought. The three squadrons were spread out, Bentley's A Squadron in front, Allack's B Squadron to the right, and Romerill's C Squadron to the left. Inside this vast moving, armoured laager were the trucks, those of the regiment – command vehicles, supply vehicles, vehicles containing the mechanics whose job it would be to repair any damaged tanks or trucks, medical vehicles, cookhouse vehicles – as well as the infantry transport. As they moved away from the road, sand clouded into the air and began to settle everywhere, making visibility very poor. As it grew lighter, the Italians would certainly know they were coming.

Fergus realized that it was indeed growing lighter; the self-inflicted sand storm had temporarily ceased as the regiment came to a halt at its appointed position. In front of them the barrage continued, but now it was a matter of checking watches again.

'Regiment will advance at oh seven hundred,' Wilkinson transmitted. Fergus wondered if he should not have uttered the regimental prayer at this moment, but Johnny Wilkinson was not a man for dramatic gestures. Now that there was no possibility of a change in orders, the Colonel jumped from the command truck and ran forward to join A Squadron, leaving Fergus in charge of the support echelons. It was galling, but it went with the job of adjutant.

He continued to look at his watch, and to left and right as well. The brigade lay in a shallow depression, surrounded by hills. The hills themselves were occupied by advance parties of the Indians, who no doubt could see the Italian position. Beyond the hills, on their right, the rest of the army was already in action; the barrage had been lifted to fire at the Italian south and rear, and the rattle of rifle and machine-gun fire, as well as, occasionally, the shouts of the troops, could be heard. That was the holding attack, designed to pin down the main Italian force. While they cleaned up. Oh six fifty. Oh six fifty five. Oh six fifty eight. Oh six fifty nine. The adrenalin was flowing now, as well as the sweat.

'Oh seven hundred,' Wilkinson said, over the wireless.

Fergus leaned out of the command truck and fired his verey pistol into the air. The light glowed even in the morning sun, as the shell curved over the regiment and dropped back to earth. Several others were let off at the same time, and at that moment the barrage ceased.

The tanks roared forward, following the markers which had been laid down during the barrage. Dust and sand rose into the air, and the morning was filled with screaming noise. Bentley's squadron was into the gap and their two-pounder cannon were barking to left and right, followed by the other two squadrons; the trucks were now halted, their crews preparing rifles and machine guns just in case of a setback. But there was not going to be a setback. Presumably the enemy were firing too, somewhere. Fergus saw a tank burning in the distance and, levelling his binoculars in an effort to see whose it was in the swirling gloom, realized it was Italian. Then he saw another.

'Regiment will turn north,' Wilkinson said.

Now they were out of sight in the haze, and the battle could only be followed by the voices on the wireless, but clearly the flanking attack had been a success; the Indian infantry brigade was now moving through the minefield, looking for their Italian counterparts.

'Bring support forward, Major Mackinder,' Wilkinson commanded.

Fergus gave the order and the trucks advanced, in single column, through the gap in the minefield. Now some of the dust had settled, and he gazed at a scene of utter destruction, with some twenty tanks burning or already burnt out. Those of their crews who had managed to get out in time stared at him with their hands held high. He ignored them.

But not far beyond there were many more Italians, a vast crowd which he estimated as at least five hundred. They were walking towards the minefield, unarmed, with their hands either in the air or clasped on the backs of their necks. And guarding them was a single steel-helmeted British soldier, stockings slipped down to his ankles, cigarette hanging out of one corner of his mouth, fixed bayonet gleaming on the end of his rifle.

'Supply to Command,' Fergus said into the wireless. 'Would I be right in assuming we have won a victory?'

'You would be correct,' Wilkinson replied. 'The Italians are in full retreat; those who have not surrendered. But we have been ordered to pursue. Let's have your trucks up here, Fergus.'

Incredibly, the regiment had lost not a single tank, had suffered not a single casualty.

'First battle I have ever been in and had no work to do,' remarked Surgeon Captain Lewis.

'They just didn't seem to want to fight,' Captain Allack said, joining the senior officers for a cup of tea.

'Well, let's head west,' Wilkinson said. Even he was looking elated. 'Next stop, Tobruk.'

It was indeed, virtually. The troops called the operation the Desert Gallop. The attack had commenced on Monday, 9 December, Sidi Barrani itself was occupied on Wednesday. The following Tuesday, the 17th, Sollum and Fort Capuzzo were captured, with another twenty thousand prisoners. After a brief break for Christmas, the advance was resumed, and Bardia surrendered on Sunday, 3 January 1941. This time forty-five thousand Italians laid down their arms, and a hundred and thirty tanks were taken. And on 27 January General O'Connor's army entered Tobruk.

By then it had long been apparent that the only enemy

worth worrying about was the desert. But the desert was a formidable foe. The armour was required to lead the gallop to keep harassing the Italians and never give them time to create a new defensive position – presuming they had any idea of doing that. But this approach meant that the regiment advanced as a single tactical unit, often out of touch with other elements of the army for days at a time. Thus they moved with what they could carry in their trucks. Food consisted of bully beef, marmalade, biscuits and tea; there was no variety. Water consisted of a gallon per head a day; from this had to be found every drop one required to drink, to shave, and to wash. The approaches to this problem were varied, and occasionally remarkable; there was, of course, no possibility of requiring any man to look like a soldier on parade. Thus while shaving was universally demanded, washing was not. At the same time, washing was necessary, because the sand got everywhere. Some men endeavoured to ignore it. Some contented themselves with merely rinsing face and hands and between the legs. Others carefully washed a small portion of their body every day, because if the sand was most unbearable in the crotch or the anus or armpits or around the face – anywhere related to hair or an orifice – it was intensely irritating even on the arms and legs, especially when those arms and legs were heavily sunburnt. But the water was never sufficient. The inside of each tank stank like a lair.

And the sand did not only attack human beings. That was incidental. It also found its way into every moving part of every vehicle. Breakdowns were frequent, and the mechanics were kept busy often twenty-four hours a day. Several of the trucks had to be abandoned simply because they ran out of spare parts, but the tanks were kept going by sheer dermination.

There was also the hazard of not knowing exactly where they were. The country was, as Sergeant-Major Blair had described it outside Alexandria, just miles and miles of damn all, and the compass was indeed as vital as a gun. While when the wind began to blow, and the sand became stirred into vast clouds, the entire world disappeared into a swirling yellow mist. Then it was a matter of merely keeping the vehicle in front of you in sight, and praying you would not become bogged down. Handkerchiefs were tied across noses and mouths because even with the windows tight shut the sand got inside the vehicles. After one such storm one of the trucks had vanished. Wilkinson halted the advance and sent out a tank patrol, but it returned empty-handed. 'Poor devils,' the Colonel commented.

In all of this they were inclined to forget the enemy. He turned up every so often, but usually to surrender. Told to stay where they were until the infantry arrived to take them into custody, the Italians sat by the roadside in contented obedience. There were brief flurries of fighting, when some enemy tanks would attempt to bar their advance, but the Italian armour was too light, and soon, on each occasion, half of them were blazing and the others either fleeing for their lives or waving white flags from their cupolas. 'Some God damned war,' Bentley commented.

It was important for the army to capture Tobruk, because it was the first really good harbour west of Alexandria, and therefore it could be used by the Royal Navy to supply the troops, a very necessary factor, as they had just about come to the end of their reserves of everything. But Tobruk rapidly became even more important to the rank and file, because in the captured town there were already reserves of everything.

The regiment had been engaged with the last of the retreating Italian armour, west of the town, while the infantry cleaned up the garrison and forced their way into the port itself. Once the white flag was hoisted General O'Connor declared Tobruk out of bounds to any troops not on duty, but it was too late. Fergus discovered, when he came to check up, that although all the tanks were neatly parked, half of their crews were missing.

'I don't suppose you can blame the poor devils, but you'd better go and see if you can get them back,' Wilkinson said.

Fergus took a command car and Sergeant Butler and drove through clouds of smoke from burning oil dumps to the perimeter. They were briefly stopped by military police, but allowed to drive on when Fergus explained his purpose, and soon after came upon a quite fantastic scene. The principal street into the town was named Via Mussolini, but the sign had already been defaced and replaced with 'Pitt Street'. They passed a hotel, once apparently known as the Albergo Tobruch, which was now named 'Young and Jackson's'. Then they saw a party of Australians, the most remarkable soldiers Fergus had ever beheld, for they marched beneath Italian national and regimental pennants, using their bayonets as flagpoles, while they carried an enormous collection of miscellaneous booty – swords, revolvers, Italian badges, monogrammed ashtrays, sashes and whistles, which last they blew as they saw the officer.

They weren't his responsibility. He drove on to the centre of the town, where the scene was even more chaotic. For troops limited to bully beef and tea for the past six months, Tobruk was a treasure house. Here were soldiers helping themselves to tinned fruit and fresh vegetables, to two-gallon tins of pulped tomatoes and huge boxes of spaghetti.

There were also, needless to say, women, squealing happily as they ran in and out of doorways, willing the Tommies to follow. Few were slow to do so, but Fergus didn't suppose there were going to be many cases of rape. And at last he saw some of his own men.

'Stop the car, Sergeant,' he told Butler. 'Let's round them up.'

'Why, Major, darling,' Bert Manly-Smith said. 'You nearly missed all the fun.'

Discipline was restored, and the advance resumed. On Thursday, 30 January Derna fell, but then it was reported that the Italians had dug in outside Benghazi, and that here at last they could expect to fight a proper battle.

'This is the decisive moment,' O'Connor told his senior officers. 'The enemy are aware that we are at the limit of our communications. We will improve on this once the navy gets Tobruk working again, but right now he will hope to counter-attack whenever he judges the moment is right. This we must prevent. We must, indeed, deal him a knockout blow now, while he is still reeling. Now gentlemen, he is retreating along the coast road, to Benghazi, where he is well fortified. He will assume that we will follow in the same way, thus stretching our lines of communication even further. He assumes we have no choice. Well, he is right, as regards our infantry and supply column; the mountains of the Gebel Akhdar guard his inward flank, the sea his outward, and trucks cannot cross the desert. But tanks can. The enemy conceives this to be impossible, because tanks need supplies of petrol, water and food as much as anyone. This is where we are going to surprise him. It is approximately two hundred miles, as the crow flies, from Gazala to Beda Fomm, behind Benghazi. Two hundred miles of desert, but it is south of the Gebel Akhdar. My intention is that the armoured brigade, living on its own, as it were, will cross to Beda Fomm and take the retreating Italians in the rear. Pressed as they will be by our infantry on the coast road, it is my opinion that we may be able to conclude this campaign within the next week.' He looked over the faces of the tank officers. 'You understand that there can be no thought of breaking off any action in which you may be engaged, and retreating. You will not have sufficient fuel to regain the main body.'

The Brigadier nodded. 'We understand that, sir.'

'Then good hunting.'

'A good, old-fashioned cavalry raid,' Fergus said. 'My old man told me about those, in the Boer War.'

'In the Boer War, a trooper could always eat his horse if he got bogged down,' Wilkinson pointed out. 'So we don't want to make any mistakes.'

The tanks were loaded with every can of petrol for which room could be devised. Each man carried four days' iron rations in his haversack, and two water bottles; there would be no washing or shaving until the battle was over. The guns were cleaned and greased time and again, as were the

80

engines – because there would be no mechanics, either. But so far the tanks had performed marvellously well.

Then the armoured brigade moved out.

They had suffered so few casualties, and managed to avoid so many breakdowns, that there were still some two hundred tanks available. They drove across the desert at a steady fifteen miles per hour, stopping only to fill up. Obviously they could not go into battle with cans of petrol strapped to the outer bodies of the tanks, and so the calculations involved had to be very exact.

They drove into a yellow and brown wilderness, upon which a flawless blue sky glared down. That they could be seen for miles was obvious from the huge sand plumes which rose up from the tracks . . . but they were relying on the fact that there was no one, for miles, to see them. They stopped again at dusk to refill and eat, and then pressed on into the night, following the glow of the light on the rear of each squadron commander's tank. Fergus, who had no intention of missing this show, drove with Romerill at the head of C Squadron. They brought up the rear; Wilkinson was in his usual post with Bentley and A Squadron, in front.

After the heat of the day, the chill of the night was a great relief. At two they stopped again, to refill, eat, allow the drivers to stretch their legs and have an hour's sleep. 'We're on schedule,' said Brigadier Campbell.

Their final stop was made at dawn. The last of the spare petrol was poured into the tanks, before they moved on, dead slow now, both to conserve fuel and to conceal their approach as much as possible.

They rolled up gentle slopes and down others. As the sun came up they saw the bulk of the Gebel Akhdar rising some thirty miles to their north, but they could also see where the hills tailed off to the sea in the west; they had passed round the mountains. And a few minutes later, topping another rise, they looked down on a sizeable village, from the guarding fortress of which there floated the red, white and green Italian tricolour.

'Beda Fomm,' the Brigadier announced over his wireless.

In accordance with previous orders, the brigade now split into regiments; they were not interested in Beda Fomm itself, only in the Italian armour. The dragoons turned more directly north and passed east of the town, which was now certainly awake to the fact that a large armoured force had mysteriously emerged out of the desert. They could hear Italian being chattered over their radios, and the garrison artillery began to open fire, without any effect.

Holding their course just to the west of north, the regiment lost sight of the rest of the brigade, which was making more directly for the coast road to their west, but they were kept informed by radio relays, several tanks being detached to make sure contact between the two wings of the force was maintained. The road was reached by the larger force with the sea now on the left hand for the first time since leaving Egypt.

'Enemy tanks reported approaching from Benghazi,' came the word along the relay. 'Section Three will maintain course and speed.'

'That's us,' Wilkinson told his men.

They were still motoring over the desert at something under ten miles an hour, conserving fuel and their own position as much as possible. If the garrison at Beda Fomm had observed that part of the British force had passed to the east, heading north, the town was now out of sight, and no one could be sure where they were.

Soon they heard the sound of gunfire from the west, and excited chatter came over the radio. 'There's one hell of a lot of the bastards,' was one of the more intelligible remarks. 'And this time they seem to want to fight.'

'This time they don't have anywhere to go, unless they can break through us,' Wilkinson commented.

Still the regiment held its course and speed, until the order came from Brigade to complete the encirclement: 'Section Three will swing due west and engage the enemy in its front.'

'Hooray!' Romerill shouted.

'Amen,' Fergus agreed.

In squadrons, three rows of twenty tanks each, the

regiment moved up the next slope and looked down on the coast road. To their left a fierce battle was going on, with British and Italian tanks engaged in a confused mêlée. To their right were masses of men and trucks, but these were some miles away. Directly in front of them was at least a regiment of fresh Italian tanks, hurrying towards the scene of battle.

'Regiment will engage,' Wilkinson said. 'Our objective is to destroy those fellows.'

The tanks rumbled down the hill. For a few moments the Italians seemed unaware that they were being approached from their flank. Then excited comment and orders flowed across the air, and the tanks swung to meet this new threat.

'Fire as you bear,' Wilkinson commanded.

The two-pounders barked, the tanks bucked and roared, and their interiors became over hot, and filled with nostril-blocking odours, from cordite to humanity. 'Christ, he's at it again,' Bert growled as Griffiths started to fart. He knew the fellow wasn't afraid; it was just his stomach's reaction to the excitement of action. 'There's a bugger,' he snapped. 'Line her up, Phil. Line her up. Traverse right, for Christ's sake. Range three five oh yards. Fire!'

Payne wrestled with the cannon sight, and pressed the button. The tank shuddered, and Bert, peering out through the slats, gave a whoop. 'Brewed the bastard. Here's another. Christ, they do mean to fight. Round, Bill. Round for God's sake.'

Mullings swung the wheel and the tank slewed round, almost in its own length, throwing the men inside about like toys.

'For Christ's sake,' Griffiths complained, nearly dropping the shell he was passing to Payne.

'Near one,' Bert said. 'Hit the bastard, Phil! Hit him.'

The gun roared again, and then there was a funny noise. Bert was not quite sure what it was, because for a few seconds he was unconscious. But he woke up rapidly enough to find his clothes on fire. In fact, he was sitting in the middle of a huge gush of flame. Instinctively he knew that to breathe was to die, and that he was going to die in any

83

event, in a matter of seconds, if he didn't get out. He looked to his left, at Mullings, and to his right, at Payne. They were already dead. So was Griffiths. But above his head the hatch had been blown away, and there was precious air up there.

Bert released his belt and clawed upwards. His hands touched burning metal and he screamed. But he would not stop, drove himself onwards, and fell down the outside of the tank, using the last of his consciousness to roll over and over in the sand in an attempt to smother the flames consuming his battledress.

'Brew-up!' Romerill snapped. 'Got the blighter. Good shooting, Corporal. There's another . . . shit, that's one of ours.'

Fergus peered through the slit, saw the tank in flames, and the number. 'Five two,' he said. 'Christ, that's Manly-Smith.' He watched in horror as a body emerged from the cupola and half rolled, half fell on to the sand, where it kept on rolling. Bert Manly-Smith!

'Poor beggar,' Romerill commented. 'Hard a-starboard. Here's another.'

The tank turned so abruptly it came to a screaming halt, and stalled. Desperately the driver tried to re-start, but although the engine turned over it wouldn't tick.

'Flooded,' the Corporal said tersely.

'And we're sitting ducks,' Romerill growled. 'Hit that fellow, Corporal.'

The gun roared, and Fergus released his seat belt. 'I'll be right back,' he said, and threw up the hatch.

'Sir?' Romerill inquired, looking up. 'Major, for God's sake . . .'

But Fergus was already out of the cupola and sliding down the outside of the tank. As he did so the engine re-started, and the vehicle began to move.

'Major!' Romerill bellowed, but Fergus stepped aside. Now he could look left and right. He had never been in the middle of a tank battle before – except inside a tank. The scene reminded him of something from a science fiction novel gone mad, a contest between monsters on the moon, perhaps. So much sand, overlaid by smoke, was swirling to and fro that visibility was down to less than fifty yards. In and out of this almost solid fog huge shapes emerged, belching flame, and then disappeared again, while all around him the enormous combined roar of their guns and their engines seemed to seal off this part of the world from any other.

But within sight was the burning Crusader. And a few feet beyond it the also glowing body of the one man to emerge. Fergus flung himself forward as he heard the roar of a gun, reminding himself that if he could hear it he was still alive, rolled across the sand, and came up to Bert. He hurled himself on top of the boy, careless of the flames, and rolled them both to and fro in the sand. Dimly he heard a roaring very close, and looked up to see an Italian tank passing only a few feet to his left. He wondered what it would be like to be squashed by a tank? Presumably one wouldn't have time to feel much. But identifying the body would be a problem.

The flames were out, and Bert was alternately groaning and screaming. Fergus rose to his feet, carrying the injured man in his arms, looked left and right. Some time while he had been on the ground the Crusader had exploded as the flames had reached its petrol tank, and now it burned merrily, giving off a tremendous heat but providing some shelter from the holocaust surrounding him. He decided his best plan was to stay close to it until he recognized someone, although that had to be pretty soon, or Bert would die. Then he saw No. 41 reappearing through the murk.

'Thank God!' he shouted, and waved one arm.

The tank slewed to a halt beside him; the hatch was still open. 'Take him in,' Fergus gasped. 'But easy. His clothes are burned to his body.'

Romerill and one of the crew came out to take Bert in. 'That was an incredibly brave thing to have done, sir,' Romerill said. 'You could've been killed.'

'I hadn't expected you to get going again so quickly,' Fergus confessed. 'What's happening?'

Because the noise had slightly diminished, and the sand and smoke haze was starting to clear.

'I think they're pulling out,' Romerill told him. 'But Major . . . the Colonel has brewed up.'

General O'Connor surveyed the officers gathered in what had been the Italian Officers' Club in Benghazi. 'I am sure you would all like to know the final tally,' he said. 'Well, gentlemen, to speak in round figures, we have taken one hundred and thirty three thousand Italian prisoners, four hundred tanks, and eight hundred and fifty guns. I think we may claim that the Italian Army has effectively been destroyed as a fighting force. This has been achieved as at loss to ourselves of five hundred and fifty men dead and missing, just over twice that number wounded, and ten tanks.'

He paused to allow his words to sink in, and someone shouted, 'Three cheers for General O'Connor!'

They roared their approval, and the General smiled; he knew that it had been his leadership, and especially his decision to send his armour across the desert to enclose the enemy in the jaws of a pincer, that had truly made the difference. 'Thank you, gentlemen. I would only like to say that I am proud to have led you. And even prouder to say that, now that our advance units have taken El Agheila, all Cyrenaica is ours.'

'When do we invade Tripolitania, sir?' someone asked.

'Give us time, Major. Give us time. We need to replenish in a big way. We need to get Tobruk in full working order as a port. We will invade Tripolitania, no doubt about that. But when we are ready. Thank you, gentlemen. Major Mackinder, a word if you will.'

Fergus moved forward through the other officers, brain spinning; he still had not come to terms with the fact that Johnny Wilkinson was dead. Bentley had survived, wounded, and had told him that the Colonel had died as he had lived: his last words after the tank was hit had been, 'My word, those fellows can shoot, after all.'

O'Connor gestured Fergus into a small inner room. 'Sit down, Mackinder.' The General also sat down, as did his ADC. 'Cigarette?'

'I don't, sir.'

O'Connor nodded. 'I'm recommending that you are confirmed as CO of the Westerns, Mackinder.'

Fergus raised his head. 'Thank you, sir.'

'You are the obvious man for the job, in more than one way. Or you should be. Tell me, how is the trooper you picked up?'

Fergus gulped. He'd had no idea the General knew anything about that. 'He is badly burned, sir. But I believe he is going to be all right.'

'Good. It'd be a pity if he were to die, after your effort. A splendid effort, Mackinder. But hardly one expected of a commanding officer.'

Fergus opened his mouth and closed it

O'Connor smiled. 'Your action was observed by an Italian colonel, who apparently nearly ran you down while you were rescuing Manly-Smith, and who insisted upon bringing it to my attention. I therefore required Captain Romerill to give me a full report on the incident, and he confirms in every way what the Italian colonel said. I intend to forward these reports together with my recommendation.'

Fergus swallowed. 'Yes, sir,' he said.

'I would estimate they will give you a medal. You certainly deserve one for so gallant an action. As to whether they will consider that your behaviour in abandoning your tank to save the life of a single trooper was consistent with the responsibilities of a commanding officer, I cannot say.'

'With respect, sir,' Fergus said. 'I was not in command of the tank, and at that moment I had no idea that Colonel Wilkinson was dead.'

'Oh, quite. I shall put that in my report as well.' The General held out his hand. 'It's a privilege to know you, Fergus.'

Fergus stood outside the door of the command tent and watched the truck bouncing over the uneven ground towards him, grinned as he saw the officer getting down from beside the driver. 'Tommy!' he shouted. 'Welcome back.'

Bentley saluted. 'They were kind to me, Colonel.'

Fergus shook hands. 'Thank God they were, Major; I've been doing two men's work.'

'And you're to get the VC.'

'Yes.' Fergus was embarrassed.

'That'll make three in the family. That has got to be unique. What does your old man think about it?'

'Well, I haven't actually heard from him yet. I only got the news yesterday. How the hell did you find out?'

'It's all over Benghazi. So, what's been happening?'

The two officers gazed over the sand at the horizon, shimmering in the distance. The command tent was pitched on a slight rise, allowing Fergus to overlook both the regiment, encamped in the hollow behind him, and the desert to the west, but the only things visible out there were the three outposts, situated on other hillocks looking west. 'Not a lot. The Eyeties are too afraid to move, and Sir Richard isn't ready yet.'

For O'Connor had also been promoted, to lieutenant-general, and given a knighthood, for his brilliant Desert Gallop.

'So I'm back in time,' Bentley said with considerable satisfaction. 'I'm looking forward to seeing Tripoli.'

'Yes,' Fergus agreed. 'I have a notion it's not going to be quite such a romp, this time. There are Germans over there.'

'Germans?' Bentley was incredulous.

'Yes. Armoured units. Some of our fellows had a skirmish with them just beyond El Agheila a couple of weeks ago. There don't appear to be very many of them, but they're obviously intended to stiffen up the Italian resistance. So . . .'

'I'd like to have a whack at the Germans,' Bentley said.

'Oh, so would I. And we're going to get it. Glad to have you back, Tommy. Now get yourself settled in.'

The truck had also brought mail. There were letters from home, full of congratulations for the brilliance of the campaign in which Fergus had shared. It seemed all

England was basking in the sunlight of a victory at last. But no one up there yet knew any details, although Wilikinson's death had been reported. 'I expect you'll get the regiment,' Dad had written. But he hadn't known. Or about the Victoria Cross. That hadn't sunk in yet. It had been his dream, always. But it hadn't crossed his mind when he had leapt out of the tank to rescue Bert.

There was a complex character. Because included in the mail was a letter from the hospital in Cairo: 'It is difficult for me to express my thanks to you, sir, as I understand that you saved my life,' Bert had written, his hand as stilted as his choice of words. 'I would appreciate your knowing, sir, that I am and must remain grateful to you for the rest of my days on earth, and this I shall do. I therefore, sir, tender my most humble apologies and look forward to the day when I can rejoin the regiment.'

Fergus wondered if the pain and shock had affected the poor young idiot's mind. What did Bert Manly-Smith have to apologize to Fergus Mackinder for? What *could* he have to apologize for? At any rate, he intended to see that the lad got his stripes back. He deserved them.

He sat in the canvas chair outside his tent and looked down at his command. His command! It already bore the mark of Mackinder. But then, it had, even when poor Johnny Wilkinson had been alive; it was, after all, not yet a year since it had last been commanded by a Mackinder. Now the men, even the padre and the medical staff, fell in for their keep-fit classes every morning without being summoned, just as they oiled and greased their weapons and their machines with loving care. They were veteran soldiers now. They had fought, and they had won. Long gone were the white skins. Those had accompanied the spic and span tropical kit into memory. Now their uniforms were that whitish yellow he had first seen on Sergeant-Major Blair outside Alexandria.

Alexandria! he thought. And Cairo! And Monique! Since the campaign had ground to a halt he had had too much time to think, and it had been mostly about Monique. Which distressed him. He was engaged to be married to

Annaliese – and he had let her down with a bump. No soldier on active service could be expected to remain chaste, but when he took a woman it should be some nameless and virtually faceless whore, who provided a function yet could never interfere with the course of his life; it should never be with a lovely, vital woman who was impossible to get out of his mind. Because he knew that the next time he got leave, which could not be long delayed, he would wish to return to Cairo and find Monique again.

But why was he guilty? Monique had demanded nothing of him save his body. Which was all he had demanded of her in return. Not a word of endearment had passed between them. She was a sensible, sophisticated woman, who had wanted sex and had chosen a partner. It was up to him to be no less sophisticated, and forget such crazy ideas as loving her. He could not possibly love her; he loved Annaliese.

How he wished this war would get moving again, so that he could occupy his mind in combat. In leading his men into battle. His men, for the first time.

But O'Connor's plans were being frustrated by events beyond his control. Towards the end of the previous year the Italians had invaded Greece, with no more success than they had obtained in Egypt. The Greeks had defeated them and hurled them back. So Hitler had gone to the aid of his ally there as well. Only on a much larger scale than in Africa. It was obvious that the Greeks could not take on both the Italians and the Germans, so Wavell had been required to send an army from Egypt to fight in the Balkans. Those men had been the reserves for which O'Connor had been waiting to resume his westward advance.

Even worse, a large proportion of the logistical support he had been awaiting had been diverted to Greece as well. It looked as if the long-heralded invasion of Tripolitania was going to be delayed still further, and all the while the Italians, now that they had been reinforced by some German elements, would be preparing a stiff resistance, no one could doubt. Thus the Eighth Army sprawled, comfortably, dispersed on what was essentially garrison duty. El Agheila was held by an infantry regiment. The dragoons were in reserve, some ten miles back, encamped just off the road to Benghazi, but close enough to the sea to enjoy it; Fergus could see the blue from his tent. The rest of the army was also in cantonments, in and around Benghazi itself. Once again, it was difficult to remember that they were at war, it was so peaceful, sitting here in the desert, waiting. A restful time.

Had been a restful time. Fergus frowned as the telegrapher hurried towards him. 'Message from Major Lawton to all units, sir,' he gasped. 'He is being attacked.'

Fergus sat up. 'By what?'

Lawton commanded a flank guard situated a further ten miles into the desert.

'Armour, sir. German armour.'

'Holy hell!' Fergus was on his feet. 'Sound stand to. Fall the men in. And find me Major Bentley.'

The trooper hurried off, and Fergus buckled on his revolver. 'Break camp,' he told Waterman, his batman. 'Hurry.' German armour? Now indeed he could hear the distant sound of gunfire. He went to the wireless truck. 'Does HQ know about this?'

'Yes, sir.' The telegrapher was listening again, while the notes of the bugle summoned the regiment to assemble. 'El Agheila is under heavy attack.'

'Christ!' Bentley had arrived. 'I thought they were done.'

'Apparently they don't know it,' Fergus snapped. 'Get me Brigade. Ask them for orders.' His instincts were to go to the aid of Lawton. But if Agheila was also in difficulties . . .

The radio was a jumble of voices, asking, commanding, imploring . . . the telegrapher raised his head. 'El Agheila has been ordered to evacuate and fall back, sir.'

'On us. Right. Major Bentley, have the crew fall in and the engines started. We must be prepared to counter-attack the enemy the moment the garrison at Agheila reaches us.'

'Yes, sir.' Bentley hurried off.

'Sergeant-Major, move the trucks to the rear,' Fergus said.

'Yes, sir.' Brothers followed Bentley. The engines started, and the trucks rumbled along the road towards Benghazi.

'Enemy tanks reported north-east, sir,' the telegrapher said.

Behind them! Fergus snapped his fingers. The Germans must have sent their tanks across the desert, just as O'Connor had done.

'We're to fall back on Brigade, sir,' the telegrapher said.

'Fall back?' Fergus was incredulous. 'What about the people from Agheila?'

'Brigade is to concentrate, sir. Before Benghazi.'

'The Germans are commanded by a chap called Rommel,' Brigadier Campbell told them. 'He's an experienced tank officer. He was one of the fellows who led the panzers through France.'

I wonder if he's the chap we fought that day? Fergus thought, with Dad in so remarkable command.

'As far as we have been able to discover, he has perhaps a panzer division with him here. That would mean we could be outnumbered, but we beat the Italians when we were outnumbered, so there is no reason to suppose we can't beat these fellows. Rommel is trying the same flanking movement as we carried out successfully last month. Well, we are going to go out there and hit him before he completes it.'

'Yes, sir,' they chorused happily. Germans, Fergus thought. Those were the fellows he really wanted to fight. Annaliese's people. But Annaliese wanted them beaten as badly as anyone.

The brigade moved out, a screen of tanks scouting. They advanced into the desert for some miles, then they heard cannon fire, and the scouts returned. 'Enemy armour beyond the next hill,' they reported. 'Supported by artillery. One of our tanks has brewed.'

'Artillery?' the Brigadier queried. 'Out here in the desert?'

That didn't make sense, and the brigade prepared to attack. They topped the next rise, the three regiments alongside each other in column of squadrons, and there paused to take stock of the situation. In front of them, some five miles away across a shallow valley, there was at least a brigade of tanks; it was impossible to say whether they were German or Italian. But they were presently parked, behind a screen of rather small and obviously highly mobile guns, supported by infantry – and the infantry were definitely German.

'Those are anti-aircraft guns,' the Brigadier commented over the wireless. 'Not artillery.'

No one replied; they could all see the British scout, which was still burning in the valley.

'Brigade will attack,' came the order.

'Follow me,' Fergus told his men, and the dragoons rolled down the hillside. They reached the bottom without mishap, within about three miles of the enemy, and then the anti-aircraft guns, brought down to aim horizontally, opened fire. Fergus could see the flashes, but had no idea where the shells were going until there came a sharp expletive over the wireless followed by silence from that source.

'Brewed,' Martell, the new commander of A Squadron, observed.

'There is another, sir,' remarked the corporal driver.

Fergus twisted his head left and right. It was difficult to see clearly, especially as they were now enveloped in sand and the British tanks had started to return fire. But what he could see he didn't like. At least five of the attacking tanks were out of action. In ten minutes they had lost half as many machines as in the entire earlier campaign, and they had not yet closed the enemy.

'Fall back,' the Brigadier commanded.

'Fall back?' Martell looked at Fergus in dismay.

'Obey orders,' Fergus told him.

Obviously they were risking unacceptable casualties – from anti-aircraft guns? The tanks turned and fled for the hills, followed now by the German armour. The shooting was fierce and several more British tanks were knocked out, for the loss of only one of the Germans.

'We'll give the bastards a taste of their own medicine,' the Brigadier said. 'Prepare to receive enemy tanks,' he told the support group.

'What might be called a tactical withdrawal,' Martell observed.

The brigade raced over the undulating desert, and came in sight of their assembly point, and, reassuringly, a row of anti-tank guns waiting for the enemy to appear in pursuit.

'Spread out, make your way behind the artillery, and regroup for counter-attack,' the Brigadier said.

'A Squadron will steer two four five,' Fergus said. 'B Squadron will steer two six oh. C Squadron will steer two seven five.'

The squadrons opened up as they altered course, allowing the anti-tank guns a clear field of fire. 'There they go,' Martell shouted happily as the British guns exploded.

Fergus unbuckled his belt and threw up the hatch to stand in the cupola and look back. The Germans – he had no doubt now that they were Germans – were coming over the last rise in line abreast, and the British anti-tank shells were bursting amongst them. But none of them seemed knocked out, and certainly they didn't stop their advance as they belched flame and smoke. Fergus turned back in dismay and watched two of the support lorries exploding, while one of the guns had also been hit. 'Holy hell!' he said. 'Our guns can't stop them.'

'Pull out,' the Brigadier commanded. 'Fall back on Benghazi. Pull out.'

They fled for their lives, confronted with a situation they had never envisaged. The effect on morale was disastrous. In France the British troops had felt they had been let down by their allies; when British armour had had the opportunity to fight the German panzers, they had generally given as good as they had received. But here they had been routed, by tanks which were more heavily armoured and armed than themselves – and by anti-aircraft guns being used as anti-tank weapons, and possessed of singular penetrative power.

But more than even the sheer physical effects of their defeat, it was the unexpectedness of it, after the glorious euphoria of the Gallop. Now they could only gallop back again, because there was no time to think. The Germans, supported by the rejuvenated Italians, kept striking as hard as the British had done the previous two months. Flanking forces kept being sent through the desert to cut the British lines of communication. Benghazi had to be abandoned, and the intention apparently was to make a halt at Derna. But the Germans outflanked the British yet again, and the Eighth Army barely got out of Derna in time. Some of them. Because here catastrophe struck. Lieutenant-General O'Connor, the man the army expected to stem the tide of defeat, together with General Neame, VC, were supervising the withdrawal of the last troops when the Germans arrived.

The news of General O'Connor's capture was the final blow to the British morale; now their sole objective was to regain the comparative safety of Egypt. Fergus had never experienced anything like it. In France at least it had been a fighting withdrawal. Now, whenever he wanted to stop and fight, the orders were the same: pull out, as quickly as you can – the enemy are behind you. More often than not they weren't yet, and the constant retreat was crushing – but not so crushing as the thought of exposing their tanks to those deadly AA guns.

Nor did they escape unscathed in any event. Trucks were destroyed or bogged down or simply broke down; and so did tanks as their support groups dwindled. The army fell apart. General Wavell, preoccupied with the equal disasters taking place in Greece and Crete, had to take violent steps to stabilize the situation. He threw an Australian division into Tobruk with orders to hold the port at all costs, and commanded the rest of the battered army to re-form inside Egypt, behind the narrow Halfaya Pass, which the troops had already renamed Hellfire Pass. Here they attempted to make a stand, but the German armour came storming through. The regiment was in the thick of the fight, and lost heavily. Even Fergus had to accept the orders for another withdrawal.

They fell back to Sidi Barrani, where it had all begun, so gloriously and optimistically, the previous December. Here they were again told to make a stand. But they knew there was no way they were going to halt the German armour. Fortunately, this time there was no attack. Fergus and his men gazed wearily and despondently to the west, only slowly realizing that they were at last being given a reprieve. The Germans had reached the end of their supplies and their line of communication. But one hundred and thirty-two British tanks – two thirds of the total with which they had commenced the battle – had been lost, and a large number of men. It had been a shattering defeat.

4

England, 1941

'I have the most tremendous news,' Murdoch said, letting the front door of the flat bang shut behind him.

'Hitler's dead,' Lee suggested.

'No. Or at least, if he is no one's admitting it. But even if he were, this news is better. Fergus is to get the VC.'

Lee stared at him, mouth open.

'It's true,' Murdoch assured her. 'Seems he saved Bert Manly-Smith's life at the Battle of Beda Fomm. Isn't that marvellous?'

'Oh, Murdoch, I'm so glad.' She hugged him. 'Three VCs in one family. Oh, I'm so proud of you all.'

'What is more,' Murdoch said. 'The battle was a howling success and the Italians have been knocked right out of Cyrenaica. That's half of Libya, you know. The only sad thing is that Johnny Wilkinson has been killed. You remember Johnny?'

'Vaguely,' Lee said. They had not met since before the war, when Johnny had been a lieutenant.

'But even that . . . well, it means Fergus has been confirmed as colonel.'

'What a celebration we are going to have. Oh, Murdoch . . .' she raised her head to listen to the siren.

He kissed her on the nose. 'Later, perhaps.'

Since the previous October the Luftwaffe had carried out raid after raid, mainly on London; there had indeed been only two twenty-four-hour periods in which not a bomb had fallen on the capital, and sometimes the raids had lasted all night. Most devastating were the fire storms caused by the dropping of vast numbers of incendiaries; there had been occasions when the entire city had appeared to be in flames, and the press had talked, in grim jest, of the Second Fire of London.

Yet people had become almost accustomed even to living in such a hell. Houses might be knocked down, water and gas mains shattered, all the ordinary comforts of life disrupted, but life itself went on in as nearly normal a fashion as possible.

And Lee insisted on remaining in London. Murdoch felt she was needlessly exposing herself to danger, but he understood that she wanted to share his; equally, being in London meant that she could be near Helen, and see her and the grandchild at least once a week. This was a great blessing for her. 'I'd go mad out in the country with just Annaliese and Philippa,' she would say.

'And little Ian,' Murdoch would suggest.

'Yes,' Lee said, without enthusiasm. Although she had telephoned Annaliese to congratulate her on her engagement, and they had both got down for a brief Christmas celebration, Murdoch also knew that Lee had felt uneasy with Annaliese these past few months. Annaliese, after the shock of nearly being taken away from Broad Acres and interned in the early days of the war, had married Ian somewhat hesitantly and anxiously. If his death had left her temporarily distraught, becoming engaged to Fergus had given her the confidence she had left behind when she had fled Germany, and in the absence of Lee she had virtually assumed the direction of life at Broad Acres. Lee had been uncertain what to do about it. As Fergus's wife, Annaliese would certainly inherit the estate, but that was still hopefully some years in the future. Yet if Lee's immediate reaction had been to slap the girl down, she could not help but remember how when she had married Murdoch, old Florence Mackinder had voluntarily withdrawn into the granny wing and encouraged the young wife to get on with managing the house. Of course, Florence Mackinder had already been a widow for some years, and had perhaps been happy to get rid of the responsibilities. This was far from Lee's position.

The situation had been embarrassing, and Lee had been happy to return to the noise and disruption, and danger, of

London. 'We'll sort things out when this is over,' she told Murdoch.

But that didn't look like being in the very near future, even if Wavell's troops were routing the Italians in Africa.

Murdoch was also concerned that his own life had become so very separated from Lee, mentally. That had only happened once before, just prior to the outbreak of the Great War, when secret orders and counter-orders had been flying to and fro, and he had been unable to tell her where he was, what he was doing, and why he was doing it. Once the war had actually started, although they had been physically separated, sometimes by thousands of miles as when the regiment had been sent to the Middle East, he had yet been able, whether by letter or leave, to share his thoughts and emotions with her. And after 1918 they had become far closer. Lee had accompanied him to India and shared all the physical dangers of the Mahsud uprising. And when this war had started she had again accompanied him when he had gone to Holland as head of the military mission. Again they had shared their thoughts and his responsibilities.

But this new command Churchill had given him precluded sharing, with anyone. He had a staff, with whom he could discuss points of view as an aid to making decisions. But the decision, as to who was to be used, and where he or she were to be sent, was his alone. And it was the loneliest business he had ever known. He was used to making decisions; he had been in command of something, ever since 1907 in Somaliland, when as a captain he and his squadron had been detached to operate against the Mad Mullah. But, as he had told the Prime Minister, the decisions had always involved himself, as well as the men he had ordered into danger. This was a wholly different situation. He met men, and women, sized them up, and then sent them out into the blue. He never knew whether or not he would ever see them again, whether or not they were actually betraying him – or at least their colleagues – whether or not they died with his name cursed on their lips in Gestapo torture chambers or against bullet-scarred walls.

Because too many of them had already suffered that fate.

Yet they, and therefore he, had achieved some notable triumphs. It had been his agents who had unearthed the German decision to send an armoured division to North Africa; that hadn't done the Italians too much good, as yet. Even more important, his agents had discerned vast German troop movements into Eastern Europe. They, and Murdoch, had no doubt this meant that Hitler was going to make war on Russia; the unnatural friendship between the Nazi and Communist regimes had shown visible signs of creaking during the past few months. He had given that information to Churchill, and presumably Churchill had seen that it reached Stalin. But the Russians had not made any positive response.

And the German Army had become diverted into the attack on Greece, which was turning out to be another victory for them. It was going to be a long war, all right.

He had gained other insights into what was going on across the Channel and in Berlin, which he found even more interesting, and pregnant with hope for the future. He had learned, for instance, of the existence of a considerable underground movement against Hitler – in the Wehrmacht. He did not suppose many of the generals involved were against the bestiality of the regime; they were merely concerned that Hitler, having failed to invade and conquer England last autumn, might after all be going to lose the war, and that, were he no longer there, they might, at this moment when their arms had been blessed with unbroken success, be able to negotiate a peace which would leave Germany the hegemony of Europe. Murdoch could not help but wonder if Paul was one of them. God, he thought, if the newspapers were ever to discover that snippet of gossip: that the eldest son of Sir Murdoch Mackinder was actually a colonel in the German Army! But how he hoped that Paul was one of the anti-Hitler conspirators. And if he was, what vistas that might open up.

Unfortunately, Churchill was not interested in pursuing that possibility. He had said that he would never deal with Nazi Germany, and in that embracing phrase he included the army which had carried out Hitler's orders. When

Murdoch had pointed out that he entirely agreed that Germany had to be at least reduced to its pre-1937 borders, and, this time, adequately and permanently disarmed, but that surely a first step in the direction of reaching that goal had to be the elimination of Hitler, the Prime Minister had growled, 'Bring me proof that they will do it.'

That proof he had been unable to obtain, as yet. But he was making every effort to get in touch with the conspiring generals, through his agents. The thought that he could soon be corresponding with Paul was all but unbearable.

'They're early tonight,' remarked the woman in the cot next to the Mackinders, as the booms of the bombs started to reverberate through the cellars.

'Yes,' Lee agreed. 'Hardly worthwhile undressing. We'll be back up for dinner.'

Because it was only seven o'clock on a warm late April evening.

'There was a letter from Harry today,' she said, sitting on her cot beside Murdoch. 'I forgot to mention it when you began telling me about Fergus. His battalion is being shipped out.'

'Where?'

'The Philippines. What does that mean, Murdoch?'

'Well . . . the Philippines have always been used as a training ground for the Marines. So it could be just routine. On the other hand . . . it could equally be a warning to Japan not to get too ambitious now that we have our hands full over here.'

'Would they?'

'They've always been ambitious.'

'And you think the Americans might come in with us if the Japanese were to attack us?'

'I would hope so.'

'Oh, boy,' she said. 'That would be just great. Like the last time. Oh, boy, we'd be certain to win, then.'

'We are certain to win, now,' Murdoch reminded her.

She glanced at him. 'I wish I had your confidence.'

He kissed her nose. 'I wish you did too. But you do

realize, my dearest girl, that if America were to come in, then Harry would be in as well, whether he likes it or not.'

'Yes,' she said. 'I do understand that. But we're all in this already, Murdoch. We have to be. It isn't right for Harry to be sitting on the sidelines.'

'I'll say amen to that.' He raised his head as the entire cellar shook. The lights promptly went out.

'That was closer than usual,' someone remarked out of the darkness.

'Well, we've been lucky for so long . . .' There was a tremendous crash.

Murdoch was aware of a great deal of weight, which seemed to be pinning the lower half of his body. He was also aware of pain, but this was nothing more than an irritation; his brain was working quite clearly.

But it was for the moment uncertain of its whereabouts, and his nostrils were blocked with dust. He sneezed and blew, and that cleared his ears as well. Before, the only sound had been a faint singing in his head. Now he heard creaks and thuds, and groans, and wails of pain from close at hand. And suddenly realized what had happened.

'Lee,' he gasped. 'Lee!'

'Murdoch? Where are you?'

He swept his hand to and fro, and found her. The bed on which they had been sitting had collapsed, and they were both on the cellar floor, still beside each other. 'Are you all right?'

'I think so. What happened?'

'I would say the building took a direct hit.'

'Oh, my God! I had chops waiting on the kitchen table for dinner.'

'Well, I would say "had" is the operative word. Tell you what, we'll go to a restaurant.'

'When?' she asked.

'When we get out of here.'

'General Mackinder, sir,' a man said urgently. 'General Mackinder!'

'Here,' Murdoch answered.

'My wife, General Mackinder. She's not moving. She's not speaking.'

'Damnation,' Murdoch said. 'Lee, can you find the torch?'

'I'm looking,' she said.

A match flared further off in the cellar, and then died again. Now the conversation, and the appeals for help, became widespread.

'She's dead,' the man said despondently. 'I know she's dead. Will you look at her, General Mackinder?'

'I'm afraid I can't, right this minute,' Murdoch confessed. 'I seem to be pinned by something. As soon as I can see . . .'

'Got it,' Lee said. 'Oh, blow. It's broken.'

'Well, can you move?'

'I think so.' He listened to her scrabbling about, and felt her dress against his arm. 'Are you really stuck?'

'Yes.'

'I have a torch,' someone called from the distance, and a light beam crossed the darkness. They might have been better off without it, as there was an immediate chorus of screams and exclamations. For the light revealed a tangled mess of joints and timbers, collapsed around the beds in spidery profusion, above which the ceiling of the cellar appeared as either gaping holes or precariously balanced timbers. And on top of the timbers would be all the piled rubble of the building.

'Oh, my God!' Lee gasped. 'If that stuff comes down . . .'

'Yes,' Murdoch agreed.

'Aaagh!' someone screamed from the far side of the cellar. 'Water! It's pouring in.'

'We're going to drown,' someone yelled.

There was a general rustle, and some ominous creaks from above them.

'Murdoch!' Lee begged him to take control.

'Please, ladies and gentlemen,' Murdoch shouted. 'Keep still unless you can move with total freedom. Please do not touch or put any weight on these fallen timbers. That water can only be from a broken main. It cannot possibly rise high enough to be dangerous.' Some of the panic subsided, and Murdoch called again. 'Mr Jameson, is that you?' He had recognized the voice of the man with the torch.

'That's right, General.'

'Will you shine the torch at the stairs and see if they are clear. Mr Wainwright, we will get to your wife in a moment.'

The chorus of noise gradually ceased as Jameson's torch beam searched the darkness. 'Can you move?' Murdoch asked Lee again, in a low voice.

'Yes.' She was kneeling beside his head. 'Oh Murdoch, there's a beam fallen right across your legs.'

'Yes.'

'Are you sure you're all right?' Her voice dropped to a whisper. 'There is water, seeping across the floor.'

'I'm sitting in it. But don't worry about it,' he assured her.

'I can see the stairs, General,' Jameson said. 'There are some timbers across them, but I think it should be possible to get up.'

'Very good.' The stairs were round a buttress of the wall from where he and Lee were, and Murdoch couldn't see them himself. 'I would like a volunteer to make his, or her, way to the stairs, and see if it is possible to reach the street and summon aid.'

'I'll do it,' Jameson volunteered.

'Only if you can find someone to replace you holding the torch.'

'I'll go,' said a woman.

'Well, be absolutely patient and careful, Mrs Jordan,' Murdoch told her. 'If you shift one timber, the whole lot may come down. If you can't get through, come back and we'll wait for daybreak.'

'Daybreak,' Lee muttered. 'That's hours away.'

'So you be patient,' Murdoch told her.

'She's dead,' Wainwright sobbed. 'I know she's dead.'

Mrs Jordan, a middle-aged mother of four – fortunately her children had been evacuated to South Wales – briefly came into the light of Jameson's torch as she crawled towards the staircase. Then she vanished from Murdoch's vision again. 'Can you get through?' he asked.

'I think so. Pays to be small, don't it?' she asked with a nervous giggle.

'Good girl,' Murdoch said. 'Now, anyone else who can get out, without touching or moving any timbers, do so. Mrs Jordan, will you find the nearest help? Mr Jameson, will you keep shining your torch on the stairs?'

The rustling began again, but now it was a controlled movement; Murdoch had taken effective command.

'I loved her,' Mr Wainwright said. 'Oh, God, I loved her.'

Lee crawled over the remains of the beds to sit beside him. 'Help will soon be here, Mr Wainwright.'

'I should think you could get out, Lee,' Murdoch said.

'I think when we go, we'll go together,' she told him.

She was being as courageous as ever. But when, several hours later, the firemen started moving the fallen timbers and masonry to free him, she collapsed into Murdoch's arms exhausted from the tension of waiting. He was the last to be dug from the rubble, the timber pinning his legs being carefully lifted as soon as there was room. 'It's hospital for a check-up for you, Sir Murdoch,' the fire officer said.

'I feel perfectly all right,' Murdoch protested.

'You could've broken some bones in there,' the man pointed out. 'At your age that could be serious.'

'My age,' Murdoch snorted.

Lee was taken up with him, and before the ambulance drove them away, together with the sobbing Wainwright and his dead wife – one of the falling beams had crushed her skull – they were able to see the ruins of the block of flats; theirs had been the penthouse. There was simply nothing left, save rubble.

'Now there is absolutely no reason for you to remain in London,' Murdoch said.

'Agreed,' she said. 'But you'll come with me.'

'You know I can't, my love.'

'But what will you do?'

'I'll take a room at the Cavalry Club. They'll look after me.'

'Until it's bombed too,' she said, and shuddered, looking at Mrs Wainwright's silent body. 'We are going to win, Murdoch? Say we are going to win.'

'We are going to win,' he promised her.

Murdoch's legs were badly bruised, although no bones had been broken, and he was kept in hospital for a month, much to his annoyance. The day he was released he was commanded to call at Number Ten.

'I hope you're all right?' Churchill demanded.

'It seems so.'

'It never occurred to me that you'd do such a damn silly thing as continue to live in that flat of yours. Suppose you'd been killed?'

'That thought did cross my mind as I lay in that cellar. Several people were killed.'

'I know, and I grieve for them. But it is the indispensable ones who must survive. Is Lee all right?'

'Yes. Shaken. She's gone back down to Somerset.'

'Well, that's a relief. Murdoch, there is misfortune everywhere. This *Bismarck* business . . . God knows we got the wretched thing, but it took everything we have available, and to lose *Hood* to a single salvo . . . I lost some sleep over that one. Now we are being thrown out of Greece. The Greek Army has surrendered, and we are being forced to leave, or surrender ourselves.'

'Good God!' Murdoch said. 'That gives Hitler all Europe.'

'Quite. Belgrade has been bombed flat, and the Yugoslavs have also surrendered. They were our last hope of a European ally.'

'Well,' Murdoch said, 'it was always likely to happen. But if we can take over North Africa . . .'

Churchill gave a brief, humourless laugh. 'We have been walloped, in Cyrenaica. Or rather, right out of Cyrenaica.'

Murdoch could only stare at him in disbelief.

'It's a fact. The same Italians we had running like a pack

of sheep, strengthened by a single German panzer division, have beaten us out of sight. O'Connor is gone.'

'Killed?'

'Taken prisoner. I believe Fergus is all right. But we've lost most of our tanks.'

'How in the name of God did it happen?'

Churchill shrugged. 'Complacency, perhaps. The troops were very dispersed, and were unable to concentrate in time to meet the surprise attack. Then there is talk about some new weapon the Germans have, which just eats up our tanks.'

Murdoch frowned. 'I can't accept that. I am sure we, I, would have heard about that.'

'I am sure you would have, too. But I want you to work on it. I hate to say it, but there was also some superior generalship. This fellow Rommel seems to be quite brilliant. There's to be a debate in the House. They're very unhappy.'

'There's no chance they'll turn against you?'

'I doubt that. We still hold Tobruk. That's a sally port on the German flank. A thorn in his side. And I'm sending out additional troops and replacement tanks just as quickly as they can be found. But . . . Wavell will have to go.'

'Wavell?' Murdoch asked in consternation. Archie Wavell and himself were contemporaries.

'He's a fine soldier, and we owe him a great deal. But there has to be a restoration of morale. And the quickest way to do that is to find a new commanding officer.'

Murdoch's heart was beginning to pound. He was only two years the older. And he knew as much about handling tanks as any man; he had virtually founded the British Armoured Corps. But he had to protest. 'That seems damnably hard. Would he have been beaten if he hadn't had to send so many men to Greece?'

'Perhaps not.'

'Well, then . . .'

'War, as you know as well as I, Murdoch, is a choice between horror and catastrophe, at every step. None of us can escape that, or the consequences. For God's sake, I'm not sacking him. He's too good not to employ. He just needs a change of scene, a change of objective. He'll go to India as Commander-in-Chief there. That'll frighten the Japanese.'

'And who'll go to North Africa?'

Churchill grinned at him. 'Auchinleck.'

'Auchinleck? He's already in India.'

'So they'll swap. I know what you'd like me to say, Murdoch, and I wish I could say it. But it can't be you. The House wouldn't go for it. Not right now. We need a younger man, who will put pep into the men out there. One of the reasons I'm relieving Wavell is that he's simply too old for the job. For all his talent, his brilliance, if you like, he has allowed himself to be worn down by the responsibility of running half a dozen fronts at the same time. Libya, Somaliland, Greece, Iran, Palestine . . . it's too much. I simply can't replace him with an older man. For God's sake, Murdoch, you're almost sixty.'

'How old are you, Winston?'

'Well . . '

'You are sixty-seven, all but. And how many fronts are you running?'

'I feel it, I can tell you. I'm sorry, Murdoch. I've made my decision.'

'Winston, you know, and I know, that I am the man to beat Rommel. Why not tell me the truth?'

Churchill sighed. 'Try to understand my position. If the facts about Paul ever became known . . .' Churchill was the only person other than Lee and Murdoch himself who knew of the relationship. '. . . and I had given you a fighting command, the Government would fall.' He brooded for a few seconds. 'It might anyway, even if you are officially retired. Anyway . . .' his grin was softer. 'I need you here. Find out about that German gun. And get me something concrete on where Hitler means to go next.'

'Russia,' Murdoch said. How that moment of madness forty years ago kept returning to haunt him. But there was no use being disappointed – and he did have a vital job of work to do.

'So you said before. But he sent his troops into the Balkans.'

'He was forced to, by that Greek business. He couldn't let Musso take another black eye. That in turn caused the Yugoslav business, which involved another change of plan. But if you're right, and Greece means to pull out . . . what's going to happen to our troops there?'

Churchill's shoulders were hunched. 'I told you. We're evacuating.'

'Back to Egypt?'

'No. Not unless we have to. We can't just go into a place and then run like hell whenever a German army appears. There'd be the devil to pay, especially in America. Lindbergh is already accusing us of prolonging the war unnecessarily, dragging in neutral after neutral when we don't have a hope of winning. Oh, Roosevelt has repudiated him, but there's no doubt a lot of Americans feel like that. We don't have enough men to hold Greece on our own. But we can hold Crete, and that I mean to do. They'll have to come across water to get at us. That should give us a splendid opportunity to kill them.'

'We'll need all the air cover we have.'

'All the air cover we can spare. I can't guarantee it'll be sufficient. We have to defend this island as well.'

'Winston,' Murdoch said, 'why not pull out altogether, no matter what the Americans may say? If I'm right, and Hitler does mean to attack Russia, why not give him every encouragement to do so? That would be the most effective way of killing a lot of Germans. And a lot of Communist Russians as well.'

'We don't know you're right, Murdoch. But we do know that he can't let us sit in Crete and develop it into an unsinkable aircraft carrier moored on his flank. We'll fight that battle first. And you get back to work. Now that the Germans have spread all over the Baltic, your field is doubled. Use it.'

Of course the Prime Minister was right, Murdoch knew: war was indeed a choice between horror and catastrophe.

But both needed to be inflicted upon the enemy as effectively as possible. And Russia and Germany were both, under their present regimes, enemies of everything Great Britain stood for; their mutual destruction could only be to Britain's advantage.

And his own? Russia was the home of that vicious young woman Yasmin Bogoljubova, who had attempted to assassinate him before the war. No doubt she had had a very good reason: Murdoch had executed her mother, who had been a Mahsud princess, for the mutilation and murder of captured English soldiers on the North West Frontier. He still could not help but feel that Yasmin would be far better employed in resisting the German panzers than in planning his destruction.

Instead, from his desk he watched the destruction of the British force in Crete, the gallant and costly attempt of the Royal Navy to bring off another Dunkirk. At the end of the day only one thing mattered: Britain had suffered another heavy defeat.

As in France, it could perhaps be attributed to the collapse of an ally. It was the situation in North Africa which worried him most. A letter from Fergus did nothing to reassure him. The British had been in full flight before General O'Connor had been captured; the general's disappearance had merely turned the flight into a rout. Fergus was perfectly frank about it. But unable properly to explain it – save that fear of the unexpected, and of superior enemy weaponry, was contagious.

This at least was his department, Murdoch thought. But what he turned up was even more disturbing. The Germans had no new secret weapon. They had merely used an eighty-eight millimetre anti-aircraft gun as an anti-tank gun, with devastating effect. And the British apparently had no comparable counter. He submitted his report both to Churchill and the War Office, and urged them to get on with developing one as rapidly as possible.

Meanwhile, as Churchill had pointed out, the whole of Europe, save only for the Iberian Peninsula, Switzerland and Sweden, was his field. And of course, Soviet Russia.

But he had never used Soviet Russia as a jumping off base or as a route: it was too dangerous. On the other hand, he had used Yugoslavia and Greece, and there he had some catastrophes of his own, as the Gestapo moved in behind the Wehrmacht and began rounding up suspects, who had perhaps been taking it too easy in their neutral hide-aways.

'Seven have just disappeared,' said Commander Methuen, his Chief of Staff. 'And four more have informed control that they no longer wish to be considered. I wonder we don't turn them in as well. Bloody swine.'

'We can't blame them,' Murdoch said. 'What we have to do is replace them.'

'Eleven agents, just like that?' Methuen snapped his fingers.

'We must have some available.'

'We have. But they're still training.'

'Recruits?'

'A little thin on the ground at the moment. There is one who is quite promising, but she's French. Mind you, the more people we have in France the better. Would you like to see her?'

'Of course.' Murdoch insisted on meeting all of his potential agents personally, not only because that enabled him to sum them up more accurately, but also because he could not contemplate them being sent to their deaths by a man they had never seen.

He was seated at his desk next morning when Methuen opened his door. 'I have Madame Monique Deschards with me, General Mackinder.'

Murdoch gazed at an intensely attractive young woman. She was not beautiful, in the way Annaliese was beautiful. Perhaps she was not even pretty; her features were too large and too strong. But her eyes, huge and intelligent, sparkled, and her wide mouth was used to smiling, while there could be no denying the probable splendour of the very full body beneath the blue serge suit and the blue and white vertically striped linen blouse.

111

'General Mackinder,' she said, in almost perfect English. 'I think I have met your brother.'

'Indeed?' He gestured her to a chair. 'Where would that have been?'

She sat down and crossed her knees. Her legs matched the rest of her. 'In Cairo. Oh, before last Christmas.'

Murdoch smiled at her. 'You are practising flattery, Mrs Deschards. I don't have a brother. The man you met was my son.'

She also smiled. 'I did not know that, truly.'

'Fergus suggested you come to me?'

'He never mentioned you to me at all, General. Is that not strange?'

'Not really,' Murdoch said. 'He probably assumed I would be known to everyone.'

'Then I must apologize for my ignorance.'

'If my son did not send you to me,' Murdoch said, 'why did you come?'

'I went to Cairo after my husband was posted missing in action,' Monique said. 'Now I know that he is dead, and I would like to do something for France. I secured a passage to England, and went to General de Gaulle, and his Free French organization. But they are recruiting soldiers, and I am not a soldier. Nor am I a clerk. They suggested I come to see you.'

'I am also recruiting soldiers, Mrs Deschards.'

She gazed at him. 'But obviously women as well as men.'

'My soldiers fight unsung and unhonoured. They seldom die in battle with the shouts of their comrades in their ears. Rather do they die in filth and squalor, in loneliness, and after suffering great pain and humiliation. Do you really suppose such a fate is worth risking?'

'War is a risk for everyone, General. It is also filthy and squalid, for everyone. And I can tell you, it is also lonely for everyone.'

Murdoch studied her. Her personality was quite compelling. He could not blame Fergus for chatting her up in Cairo. Lucky devil. 'There would be a period of considerable, and very arduous, training before I could use you,' he said.

'I understand that, General.'

'And then you would embark upon an even more lonely life than you endure now. You will be able to have no friends, only contacts. And you will have to do many terrible things.'

Monique smiled for the second time. 'I would have one friend, surely, General: you.'

The thought of her haunted him. He had not been so instantly drawn to someone since he had met the Princess Chand Bibi – and she had turned out to be a disaster. It was not a case of loving Lee any the less for being attracted to another woman; his love for Lee was constant, and strong enough to withstand any distraction. But he was a man to whom the occasional woman provided an immense impetus to his own life. There had only actually been three to do so: Margriet Voorlandt von Reger, Chand Bibi, and Jennifer Manly-Smith. He didn't know if Monique Deschards would be a fourth, but he did know that he was impatient for another five days to pass so that he could make his weekly visit to his training establishment . . .

He was met as usual by Colonel Lowndes, and Mrs Bryant. Mrs Bryant looked after the female section of the 'academy', as they called the country house which had been given to him for his work; Murdoch believed that the sexes should be kept in strict segregation throughout training. She was a small, homely looking woman with grey hair and soft eyes – and she was the toughest human being Murdoch had ever encountered.

'Monique Deschards,' she said, without curiosity. 'Oh, yes, General. She is quite a find. She is so eager. Would you like to see what I mean?'

'Yes,' Murdoch said, 'I would.'

Mrs Bryant led him into the wing reserved for the women, and along various corridors, then down a flight of steps. He was surrounded by noises, and was reminded of his only ever visit to a girls' boarding school, when, after his return from India, he had attended one of Helen's speech days. But on that occasion Lee had been at his elbow. Now he felt strangely isolated.

The stairs took them below ground, which even in summer was centrally heated. Now he listened to more martial noises, including, his experienced ear told him, the sounds of revolver shots. Mrs Bryant led him along another corridor, and then carefully opened a door for him to step through.

Now he inhaled cordite, and human sweat – oddly overlaid with feminine perfume. He blinked in the half gloom, found himself in a large cellar, some twenty yards across. Immediately in front of him there was a table on which rested the revolver he had heard. On the near side of the table there were four people, a male instructor and three women; all wore singlets, shorts and tennis shoes. A fourth woman was engaged in trotting round the room, but she stopped when the door opened, and she and everyone else in the room came to attention. The girls at the table had their backs to the door, but Murdoch recognized Monique immediately, from the wealth of dark brown hair which was gathered in a ribbon on the nape of her neck. Like them all, however, she remained at attention, looking into the room and not at the door.

'Carry on, Mr Hunt,' Mrs Bryant said.

'Yes, ma'am. Carry on, Betty,' Mr Hunt said.

The girl named Betty, on the far side of the room, resumed jogging. She made a fascinating sight, as, short and somewhat plump, and wearing no brassiere, she jogged past the table and continued on her way, sweat dribbling out of her hair. She did this five more times, and then Mr Hunt said, 'Now, Betty!'

Betty stopped at the table, breath coming in great gasps, picked up the gun, and turned to face the far wall, which was suddenly illuminated as Hunt pressed a switch. Over there stood the cardboard cut-out of a man, half turned towards them, hand thrust forward as if he too was armed; behind him the wall was padded with piled mattresses to prevent the risk of ricochets. Holding the revolver in both hands, Betty fired six times. The bullets thudded into the mattresses; two of them seemed to brush the target.

Betty lowered the gun in dismay, and made a remark in some foreign language; she was fair, and Murdoch recalled that she was Norwegian.

'Yes,' Hunt agreed. 'I want you to be fast, but not so fast that you miss the target altogether. You are quite dead.' He half turned his head, awaiting instruction from behind him.

'Monique,' Mrs Bryant said.

'Monique,' Hunt repeated. He took the revolver from Betty's hand, and began to reload it with cartridges taken from a box on the table. While Monique began to jog round and round the room. And if Murdoch had found Betty fascinating, he found Monique breathtaking. Heavy breasts sliding up and down beneath her singlet, muscles trembling in her calves and thighs, dark hair swaying to and fro as she ran, sweat starting to trickle down her temples, she was an entrancing spectacle. And she was very fit; she did not pant as Betty had done.

'Shooting accurately when one has just engaged in violent physical activity is difficult,' Mrs Bryant commented, softly. 'But it is what these girls will have to do, if they ever have to shoot at all.'

'Yes,' Murdoch said, watching Monique.

Round and round the room she ran, eight times in all, and then Hunt said, 'Now, Monique!'

The reloaded gun lay on the table. Monique stopped running, picked it up, turned, her left hand coming up to join her right as she levelled the weapon at the illuminated target. The six shots rippled away almost as one. The first missed, but the next three cut into the thick cardboard, as did the sixth.

'Good shooting, Monique,' Hunt said. 'This time I would say that *he* is dead.'

Mrs Bryant stepped back into the corridor, and Murdoch followed her, closing the door. 'She is excellent material,' Mrs Bryant remarked. 'In every way. It would be a great shame were she to be expended too soon.'

'Sit down, Mrs Deschards,' Murdoch invited. 'Mrs Bryant has given you a very good report.'

'Thank you, General.' Monique sat in front of his desk and crossed her knees. He thought she might have lost a little weight; that would hardly be surprising. But she was more attractive than ever.

'How did you find the training?'

'Very thorough. I did not know you English were so thorough.'

'Our faults are mainly those of over-confidence, rather than carelessness,' Murdoch said. 'Now, Mrs Deschards, I want you to think very carefully. This is your very last opportunity to change your mind.'

'How can I?' she asked. 'Now that I know so many of the secrets of your organization?'

'Oh, you cannot quit my organization now,' Murdoch agreed. 'But I could employ you here in England. Perhaps as an instructress at the academy.'

'Do you make this offer to everyone?' Monique asked.

'Almost,' Murdoch lied.

Monique smiled. 'I wish to fight the Germans. Tell me what you wish to do with me.'

I, Murdoch thought, wish to invite you out to lunch, and then take you to a hotel, and go to bed with you, and stay with you there all night. No doubt Lee had been away too long. But this was more than an idle fancy, he knew. Had the circumstances been at all different, the situation less serious . . . and had he not had to send her to her death at the end of it. Perhaps, when she returned, he thought.

'There is a plane leaving England tonight,' he said. 'I wish you to be on it. Commander Methuen will give you all the information and gear you need. There will be people waiting for you at your destination, and they will give you further instructions.'

'Thank you, General,' she said.

'I wouldn't, Monique. You can thank me when you get back.'

'When will that be?' she asked.

As soon as I can decently arrange it, he thought. 'When you have completed your tour of duty,' he said. 'In about six months.'

116

She nodded. 'I will look forward to it.'

So will I, he thought. He stood up, and she did also. He held out his hand, and she shook it. 'I would like you to come back, Monique,' he said. 'So be careful.'

She gazed at him. 'I would like to come back too, General,' she said. 'I will be careful.'

The door closed, and he sat down again. For several minutes he was unable to concentrate. But a week later he was distracted in another direction: the Germans invaded Russia.

5

The Desert, 1941–42

'I am sorry, Colonel Mackinder, but my daughter Monique is no longer here,' said M. Soubret.

Fergus gazed at him in dismay.

'She became bored with Cairo,' Soubret explained. 'She wanted to be doing something to avenge her Robert, eh? So I managed to get her a passage back to England, to join General de Gaulle and the Free French.'

'Good Lord,' Fergus muttered.

'So . . . but perhaps you would come in and have a coffee,' Soubret invited.

'Ah . . . no, thanks very much. I'm only in Cairo for twenty-four hours. I just dropped by to pay my respects. If you are in touch with your daughter, would you give her my regards?'

'Of course I will do that, Colonel. She will be honoured to know that so distinguished a soldier has called upon her.'

Because of course, all Cairo knew that he was to get the VC. All Cairo knew everything. But all Cairo had suddenly turned into a drab, dreary, disappointing dump.

How his heart had leapt when he had been informed that replacements were arriving, and in Cairo rather than Alexandria: the Mediterranean had become just too dangerous for British shipping, and so it was being routed round the Cape of Good Hope, which of course entailed even longer delays in the always awaited appearance of men and munitions.

It was unusual, to say the least, for the colonel of a regiment to travel two hundred miles to meet a bunch of recruits. But it had been the only way he could legitimately give himself leave to visit Cairo – there had been no time for holidays during the previous three months, as the Afrika

Korps and the battered Eighth Army had glared at each other across the sand, each trying desperately to build up sufficient strength for an offensive.

There had been limited attacks and counter-attacks. General Wavell had been duly reinforced after the collapse of March and April and a special convoy laden with the new 'I' tanks – which hopefully would be able to stand up to the German armour – had been rushed, at whatever risk, through the Mediterranean to replace the Eighth Army's losses. The operation had been code-named Tiger, and thus the tanks had been christened Tiger Cubs. They were splendid pieces of machinery but – perhaps due to the haste with which they had been dispatched – subject to more than the usual number of defects and breakdowns. The General had made an abortive attempt to relieve Tobruk, which had failed, mainly due to those weaknesses in his armour – especially galling to those who had to drive and fight the tanks. Yet in fact Tobruk was doing very well, supplied by sea. The Royal Navy had actually been able to take off half the garrison – as demanded by the Australian Government, which apparently felt their soldiers were being abandoned to do all the fighting in Tobruk while the rest of the army basked in the sun and bathed in the sea – and replace them with fresh troops. On the other hand, as the Germans and the Italians built up their submarine fleet in the Mediterranean, and German long-range Condor bombers were stationed in Italy itself, the casualty lists grew amongst the ships, and it was obvious that a land offensive was going to be very necessary if Tobruk was to be retained. As it had to be, as much for propaganda value as anything else. It was Britain's sole trophy in North Africa.

But a large-scale attack had been delayed, partly because of the decision to route the supply convoys round the Cape, and partly because General Wavell was being replaced. The troops on the ground viewed this with mixed feelings. Wavell had directed O'Connor to that great victory over the Italians, and had then been forced to weaken his army by sending so many men to Greece. He had also, while all of this was going on, masterminded a brilliant campaign in

119

East Africa which had destroyed the Italian armies in Ethiopia and Somaliland and Eritrea, and restored the Emperor Haile Selassie to his throne in Addis Ababa. To be sacked after all that was unjust, almost everyone felt. Yet most of the troops also felt that they would have been defeated in the desert even had they remained at full strength. The suddenness and vigour of the German attack, the deadly power of those eighty-eights, the complacency with which their own forces had been spread out, were facts nobody could gainsay.

Morale had certainly not fully been re-established. The men would obey orders to go into action, but they expected to be beaten . . . and that was no recipe for victory. So perhaps a new commander-in-chief was the answer. Fergus personally was happy with the new man. General Sir Claude Auchinleck had a brilliant record. Only three years younger than Dad, Fergus knew, Auchinleck had been a junior contemporary of Murdoch Mackinder at Wellington College, before following him to Sandhurst. The two men were good friends, and indeed their careers had in many ways been similar, for Auchinleck had also served in both France and the Middle East during the Great War, and on the North West Frontier of India, although his tour of duty had been in the middle thirties. He had been involved in the abortive expedition to Norway in 1940, before being sent to India to organize the defences there against a possible Japanese attack. He was due to arrive any day now, and then surely things would take a turn for the better.

With him, as Chief of Staff, was coming General Neil Ritchie. A relatively young man, only forty-four years old, Ritchie had been on Auchinleck's staff for the past year, and so the two men obviously worked well together. While Auchinleck's choice as the new commander of the Eighth Army was General Sir Alan Cunningham, who had actually led the victorious forces in East Africa. There was all to look forward to.

In the desert. But not in Cairo. Because, Fergus knew in his heart, he had come here to take Monique to bed and know once again the utter joy of that night last November.

His whole being was directed to that, to clear his sexual decks, as it were, before taking on the Germans again. Of course he was being terribly lucky. Had she been there, had they slept together again, he might well have fallen in love with her. He wasn't sure he hadn't half done so anyway. And that would have been the most caddish thing in the world to do, when Annaliese was waiting for him at home. But if he could so easily fall for another woman, how deep was his love for Liese? This bothered him. He was not by nature promiscuous. He wanted to direct his love and maintain it in a steady stream at a particular woman. Annaliese. So he had been terribly lucky, that temptation had been withdrawn.

So what you do, Fergus my boy, he told himself as he stood on the pavement and inhaled the sights and sounds of Cairo, is get hold of the porter at Shepheard's, and tell him you want a good bint, and let him organize it, and screw her until she can't move, and then put all women out of your mind until the coming battle is over. That was a sensible approach to the problem, the sort of approach, he felt, that Dad would adopt.

He turned briskly.

'Colonel Mackinder, sir!'

Fergus checked and turned back, saw Bert Manly-Smith striding towards him, wearing a new, smart uniform – complete with a corporal's stripes on his arm – and beret, brightly polished boots gleaming in the sunlight, and now drawing himself to attention and snapping a salute, regardless of the passers-by who had suddenly to avoid walking into this rock erected without warning in their midst.

'Bert!' Fergus saluted in turn, then said, 'At ease,' and shook hands. 'It's good to see you. I see they've given you your stripes back.'

'Yes, sir. I'm told it was on your recommendation, sir.'

'Well, I think you were treated a little harshly last year, in all the circumstances. And now you're fit again?'

'As a fiddle, sir. Just completed three days' leave.'

Fergus frowned at him. 'You could have gone home, you

know, Bert. After a bad burn like that, it would have been the right thing to do.'

'I wanted to stay here, sir. I wanted to rejoin the regiment.'

'And the regiment will be pleased to have you back, Bert. Well, tomorrow you can help me meet some replacements, and get them out to Mersa Matruh in one piece.'

'Yes, sir. I shall look forward to that, sir. Joey will be with them.'

'Your brother?'

'Wrote me, sir. He's joined up. Well, the regiment, of course. He said he'd be here some time this summer.'

'Well, that's splendid. I'll look forward to meeting him again.'

'Thank you, sir.'

'Very good, Corporal. Carry on. Meet me at Shepheard's Hotel at eight thirty tomorrow morning.'

'Yes, sir. Sir . . .' Bert suddenly turned crimson, and resumed standing to attention.

Fergus frowned at him. 'What's on your mind?'

'It's just that . . . I never thanked you for saving my life.'

'Yes, you did, Corporal. In your letter.'

'Yes, sir. But . . .'

'You also apologized. I assume for rather disliking our decision to demote you. We had no option. The Egyptians have to be kept at least prepared to accept our troops here. We can't go around beating them up, no matter what the provocation. But the matter is now closed.' Fergus smiled. 'And between you and me, Corporal, you did a damned good job.'

'Thank you, sir.' Bert looked as if he wanted to say more, then saluted again. 'Oh eight thirty tomorrow, sir, at Shepheard's Hotel.' He marched off.

He was an extremely odd fellow, Fergus thought. But he had a lot to offer as a soldier. If he could just keep out of trouble he might do quite well.

At the same time, he was a bloody nuisance. Seeing him, especially at that moment, had reminded Fergus too much of home, and Annaliese. There was no way he was going to

122

enjoy an Egyptian whore now. He sat in the bar at Shepheard's and got quietly drunk, instead.

General Auchinleck was a large man with craggy, determined features. He looked out across the faces of the officers seated in front of him, and gave them an encouraging smile. 'At ease, gentlemen,' he said. 'You may smoke if you wish.' He waited while various cigarettes and pipes were lit before resuming. 'It is a pleasure to be here. But I must tell you that I am here to carry out a specific purpose. That purpose is, firstly, to relieve Tobruk, and secondly to recapture Cyrenaica. I may regret as much as you that General Wavell has not been permitted to complete the task he so ably began, but that decision was not mine. Mine, ours, is the burden of completing that task.

'Now, let us consider the situation. The enemy still occupies Halfaya Pass, and in some strength. Our reconnaissance estimates that he musters something like four hundred tanks. I'm afraid these are in the main heavier and more heavily armed than the best of ours; our tank battles will therefore have to be fought at close quarters and with superior numbers. We also know that he has fortified his position, with minefields, to a considerable depth. He relies upon the fact that the Quattara Depression prohibits any wide turning movement. We are therefore faced with a situation that our attack must be delivered approximately where he expects it – we may feint with one hand and punch with the other, but it will still have to be over a limited area. It will still have to penetrate those minefields. And it will still have to face heavy losses in tanks, and men, from those eighty-eights. These are facts we have to look in the face. I know there is not a man here will shirk the business of advancing, regardless of the risks involved, but I am determined not to fight a battle until we are certain to win it, and I am equally determined that this time, when we arrive on the borders of Tripolitania, we are going to stay there until we are ready to advance to Tripoli itself.

'This means that I am not going to launch any attack until I have the materiel to do so successfully, and to sustain our advance. I wish you all to be clear about this, and to make sure your men understand it too. We are here to win, not to indulge in vain heroics to satisfy the politicians at home.' He paused. 'And I can tell you there are quite a few of those who expect us to advance tomorrow, simply because I *am* now here. However, I have informed those who matter of my intentions, and I look to their full support. My estimate is that we require at least a two-to-one superiority in tanks, or say, three armoured divisions, to carry out our purpose on the scale and with the results I am determined to achieve. It is my task to see that I obtain that margin of superiority over the enemy. It is your task, at brigade and regimental levels, to see that your men, and your machines, are maintained in the highest possible state of readiness and fitness for the coming offensive. There will be an offensive, gentlemen, and it will be a victorious one. You have my assurance on that. Thank you.'

'What's so big about a German?' demanded Corporal Manly-Smith. 'We fought them in Flanders, didn't we?'

'And got licked there too,' Sergeant Butler pointed out.

The group of NCOs sat on the beach, basking in the sunshine, and watching the troopers bathing. As he had felt so often before, Bert found it difficult to appreciate that they were actually at war, and virtually in the front line. 'Like hell we did,' he argued.

'Well, they certainly licked us back in March,' Butler insisted. 'While you were in hospital, Bert. You weren't there. You didn't see.'

'You trying to tell me we can't beat them now?'

'I didn't say that. I'm just saying they are one hell of a lot tougher than the Eyeties. And that fellow Rommel is pretty smart.'

'In Flanders we were fighting under the General,' remarked Corporal Hennessey.

'The Colonel is all right,' growled Sergeant-Major Brothers. 'If they'd give him a chance. It's the brass bothers me.'

124

'I think they're doing the right thing,' Butler argued. 'Wait till we're ready, I say.'

'And suppose Rommel attacks first?'

'Then we stop him first. That might make our job easier.'

'Only if everybody stands and fights,' Brothers said.

Oh, we'll stand and fight, Bert thought, and watched the naked body of his younger brother emerging from the sea. They were in different squadrons, and therefore did not see as much of each other as he had feared; for all his pretended pleasure to Fergus Mackinder, he had been appalled to hear that Joey was coming out to serve in the regiment. The fact was that he and Joey had never been close. He supposed Mum's feelings had had something to do with that. Because if he wasn't actually a bastard, Mum had been pregnant when she had married. She hadn't confessed that to him until he had been a teenager. Then she had wanted to share things.

He had been resentful. Not, oddly, of the fact that he had been so nearly a bastard. He thought he would actually have preferred that. What he resented had been the condescension of that fellow Ralph Manly-Smith – he could never truly consider him as Father – in marrying the sergeant-major's daughter he had put in the family way. Everyone, even Grandpa Yeald, seemed to think he had acted like a proper gentleman. But he hadn't, in Bert's opinion: he had acted like a proper squire, and he had, by doing so, made all of their lives into a mishmash of attitudes and uncertainties.

And then to go off and get himself shot through the head following the General in the last of those wild cavalry charges in which that old madman had sought fame by leading whenever possible! Ralph Manly-Smith had earned the Victoria Cross on that campaign, for commanding a forlorn hope into the heart of the Mahsud stronghold. That had set the seal on his gallantry, in the opinion of everyone – except his eldest son. That VC had been Mum's proudest possession; she had carried it everywhere with her. Thus when she had died in Holland it had disappeared. Bert wasn't worried about that: she would probably have willed it to him had she had the time.

Poor Mum. He didn't even know *how* she had died. She had been engaged on some kind of hush-hush work, with the General, of course, and bingo. He wondered if he hated the General.

But then, he had hated Fergus. Sometimes, he still wanted to hate Fergus. But how could you hate a man who has saved your life? And whose future wife you have seduced? Or had she seduced him? He didn't suppose that mattered, save that he so wanted to explain that to Fergus, and perhaps to warn him, that a woman who was the daughter of a general – because old von Reger had been a general in the Wehrmacht – and could carelessly offer herself to a common soldier, was maybe not going to make an ideal wife for an officer. But he just couldn't. For one thing, he couldn't imagine Fergus's reaction to that information. For another, it was difficult to feel, in his heart, that he owed Fergus all that much. Fergus had not rescued him, Bert Manly-Smith. Fergus had done what was expected of a Mackinder, and played the bloody hero. And been more than adequately rewarded for it.

All he knew was, that if Ralph Manly-Smith hadn't also acted the bloody hero, and got killed for it, Bert himself might have been an officer too, and able to make his own play for Annaliese von Reger. Except . . . would he really want to do that, knowing what she was like? He had been tempted, to go home, and see her again, and discover if she was still as randy as ever. But he hadn't. He couldn't do that to Fergus.

If he had been an officer, then he too would have been expected to act the bloody hero at the drop of a hat, and he might have got his head shot off.

He wondered if the person he really hated was himself?

'The balloon has really gone up. The latest reports are that the Russians have been taken completely by surprise, and are retreating, or surrendering, everywhere.' General Auchinleck poured the wine himself. He was fond of tête-à-tête supper parties with his senior officers, and Fergus was a regular guest, because of the general's

126

friendship for Sir Murdoch: Auchinleck had often dined at Broad Acres and had known the Mackinder boys since their schooldays.

'Damned good thing,' remarked Brigadier Campbell. 'If they get to slaughtering each other it'll be better for the rest of us.'

'Ah, but we are going to fight with them,' Auchinleck said. 'The PM is making the defeat of Germany his prime objective, and worrying about what happens after that, after that.'

'Does this affect our plans, sir?' Fergus asked.

Auchinleck gave a grim smile. 'Not if I can help it. But of course, everyone is now clamouring for us to launch our attack here earlier than planned. To help the poor Russians. Quite makes you sick. When did the poor Russians ever help us, when we desperately needed it?'

He was unusually bitter, and Fergus understood some of the pressure which was being brought to bear on him. And respected his determination to do things his way or not at all. But he was taken aback when, after the meal and while they were enjoying their brandies and cigars, Auchinleck suddenly turned to him and asked, 'What do you suppose your father would do, Fergus?'

'Oh . . . ah . . . I'm sure he'd act exactly as you are doing, sir.'

'Don't you believe it. He'd have waved his sword and led the armour straight down Halfaya Pass, guns blazing. And do you know something? He'd have got away with it. He always did.'

'Yes, sir. But don't you think that the fear he might not always get away with it is the reason he hasn't been given a fighting command in this war?'

'Point taken. But I have no doubt he's doing a great job in that hush-hush establishment of his. Although, you know, I wish he *had* been given a fighting command. Things might have been different. Give him my regards when next you write, Fergus. Tell him we are going to do our best.'

General Auchinleck had laid his plans for an offensive in the middle of November, and to this he adhered, despite increasing unrest in the Government in London at this lengthy delay, and despite increasing fears that Rommel might strike first or that, if not preoccupied in North Africa, the Axis might attack Malta in overwhelming strength. However, Rommel too was clearly awaiting reinforcements which were at that moment committed to the invasion of Russia, as Murdoch was able to confirm through his network of agents. Thus the 'Auk' was able to adhere to his dates even if he had failed in his efforts to bring the Eighth Army up to the strength he desired, of three full armoured divisions. By mid-November, under the overall command of General Cunningham, it consisted of two corps, the Thirteenth, commanded by General Godwin-Austen, and comprising the Fourth Indian Division, the New Zealand Division, and the First Army Tank Brigade, and the Thirtieth, commanded by General Norrie, comprising the Seventh Armoured Division (made up of the Seventh Armoured Brigade and the Twenty-Second Armoured Brigade), the Fourth Army Brigade Group, the First South African Division, and the Twenty-Second Guards Brigade Group.

The plan, naturally, was the same as that used by O'Connor nearly a year before; there was no other available. The Thirteenth Corps was therefore required to make a frontal assault on the German position, while the Thirtieth Corps, which was mainly armour, would swing as widely as possible into the desert, slash into the enemy's flank, and drive for Tobruk, only seventy miles away. But this was to be a battle on an altogether larger scale than O'Connor's; the tank strength alone had been raised from around two hundred to no less than seven hundred and twenty-four machines. This was about double the estimated German strength, which in fact provided almost the margin of superiority Auchinleck sought, and half of the tanks were the new fast-moving cruisers, the Tiger Cubs, with which the regiment had been re-armed, and which had hopefully had all their wrinkles ironed out. There were another two hundred in reserve.

It was impossible to suppose that the accumulation of this large force, which of course included the emplacement of vast supply dumps, or the obvious manner in which it would have to be used, could provide any possibility of surprise. Yet tactically this did seem to happen. The attack was aided by a break in the weather, for no sooner had the preliminary bombardment commenced than the skies opened and a torrential downpour followed. The order to advance was given, and the tanks rolled forward, very slowly at first, as they were following the sappers who were going to clear a path through the minefield – no fortuitous movement of enemy armour had been observed this time.

With the rain clanging on the tanks like pebbles, and limiting visibility to only a few yards, it was even more eerie than advancing in a sand storm. Fergus rode with Captain Allack and B Squadron, in the centre of the regiment; from here he felt he could exercise a greater tactical control of the situation. But for two days there were few tactics to be employed. On 18 November, a Tuesday, the armour felt its way cautiously from behind the frontier wire to the El Abd Track, the nearest thing to a road in the desert. This day they encountered no enemy at all. On the following day they crossed the track, and moved on. By now they had ascertained that there was a German Mobile Corps stationed about the oasis of Bir Hacheim, roughly due west of the El Abd Track. A small holding force was detached to mask this possible threat, while the rest of the armour made north for the Capuzzo Track, some fifteen miles further on. This was the key to the whole manoeuvre, as because the British and Australians were still holding Tobruk, the Capuzzo Track was Rommel's main line of communication.

Dominating the Capuzzo Track was the village of Sidi Rezegh, which was situated on the top of a ridge some hundred feet above the vital road. On the south the rise to this ridge was quite gradual, but on the north, above the track, it made a very steep escarpment, so obviously its seizure would enable the British to dominate the road and it would be very difficult to retake. Equally important, close to it was a large enemy airfield, which would also be dominated from the village.

The drive north from the El Abd Track was exhilarating, for only enemy patrols were encountered, and these were quickly dispersed. Orders therefore came for the Corps to split up and seek the enemy armour, which had to be around somewhere. Fergus could not help but feel that this principle, dispersal rather than concentration, was what had got them into trouble earlier in the year. But at least the Seventh Armoured Brigade, with its Support Group, was detached to seize and hold Sidi Rezegh.

'Let's go,' Brigadier Campbell told his men, and the tanks surged forward across the desert, racing into the town to the discomfort of the surprisingly small garrison. 'Well done,' the Brigadier said. 'We are here, and we now wait for the rest of the army to come up. This is the decisive point.'

Fergus stood his men down for a meal, watched by the curious Arabs, who did not seem the least concerned to have exchanged their German and Italian masters for British. 'I suppose because you've all been here before,' Joey Manly-Smith suggested.

'We didn't have time to stop in places like this,' Bert told him. He had come across to make sure his little brother was all right, but in fact the regiment had suffered no casualties at all. 'We were in a hurry, the last time.'

'We're going to be in a hurry again, pretty soon,' Butler told them. 'Jerry can't leave us here.'

And indeed, before they had finished their meal, the alarm was given: 'Enemy armour in sight.'

Fergus hurried forward, while the villagers hastily got inside their houses; they knew there was going to be trouble.

'There seem a hell of a lot of them,' the Brigadier growled, studying the dust storm to the north-east through his binoculars. 'For an army which only has four hundred tanks. I would say there are damn near that number heading this way.'

'That means we're outnumbered two to one,' remarked his Brigade Major, somewhat unnecessarily.

'Make to General Norrie,' Campbell said. 'Enemy attack on Sidi Rezegh imminent, with approximately three hundred tanks.' He grinned at his officers. 'One should never exaggerate, gentlemen. Add to that: Request support.'

'Urgent?' inquired the Brigade Major.

Campbell considered. 'I think you could mark that urgent, yes. Now, gentlemen, our business is to hold this village until the army comes to us. Fergus, I want you to withdraw your regiment, as quickly as possible, down the rear of the hill. Move to the west, and when I say so, launch a flank attack on the enemy. You understand you will be outnumbered.'

'Yes, sir,' Fergus said. About six to one, he thought.

'However,' Campbell went on, 'if he has already committed himself to attacking the village, and it is my intention to wait until he has, your counter-stroke may just throw him into confusion, and force him to retreat. That should gain time for the entire division to concentrate.'

'Yes, sir,' Fergus repeated, and hurried off. 'Let's go,' he shouted over the loudhailer, and the tank crews hastily abandoned their meals and climbed into their vehicles.

'Are you returning here, sir?' Bentley asked.

'In a little while,' Fergus assured him, and, sitting next to Captain Allack, he rolled out of the village and down the slope behind. 'Regiment will assume squadron line ahead,' he ordered, and stood in the cupola to watch the sixty tanks form up.

'Another half mile,' the Brigadier said over the wireless; he was watching them from above. 'Then halt and await orders.'

The regiment proceeded to the west, round the edge of the escarpment. In another half mile the Capuzzo Track came into view, but the enemy armour was still out of sight. Here they waited, for about half an hour, while to the north of them firing began, and looking up the hill they could see shells bursting in the village, and hear the rumble of the rest of the brigade returning fire.

'Stand by, Westerns,' came the voice over the wireless.

Fergus picked up the mike: this was the first time he would lead the dragoons into battle as their colonel.

'Move,' came the command. 'And good hunting.'

'Advance,' Fergus said to Allack, and the tank went forward. Heart pounding, Fergus thumbed the mike. 'Gentlemen,' he said, 'the regimental prayer.' He drew a long breath. 'May the great God of battle, who has guided the fate of this famous regiment on many a hard-fought field, and never failed to lead it to distinction, grant that on this day, faced as we are with a host of enemies of our King and our Country, every man will do his duty, so that should we fail in our ordained task, it will yet be said of us, they were the Royal Western Dragoon Guards, who fought and died according to the ancient valour of their regiment and their blood.' He waited for the rumble of repeating voices over the wireless to cease, and for Allack's tank to turn the corner of the ridge and sight the German armour. Then he added, 'Gentlemen, there is your enemy!'

'Hurrah!' shouted Corporal Manly-Smith, and his cry was echoed by fifty-odd other tank commanders.

The entire regiment rounded the ridge. The German tanks were already surging up the steep slope behind the belching guns, and for the moment they were taken unawares. 'Where?' Allack inquired quietly.

'Hit them amidships,' Fergus said, closing the hatch and sitting beside him.

'Left hand down,' Allack told his driver, and the tank swung to the north. 'Traverse right fifteen degrees. Range one thousand yards. Fire!'

The two-pounder roared, and then again. The tank filled with cordite and other odours as well, as they drove straight at the Germans. 'Bloody thing bounced off,' the gunner complained.

'Same fucking story as the last time,' Allack said in despair.

'Aim at the tracks,' Fergus told him, and grabbed the mike. 'Aim at the tracks,' he repeated. 'They can't have reinforced the tracks.'

The gun was depressed and fired again.

'Sand,' Allack commented. 'Up a shade, Ada.'

'Christ!' exclaimed the loader. 'Talk about brewing.'

Fergus looked to either side, and gulped. He counted five of his lead tanks already knocked out as the Germans detached several squadrons and these turned their heavier guns on the approaching British regiment. 'Keep advancing,' he said into the wireless. 'Close the bastards.'

'Got one,' the gunner crowed as he neatly shot the tracks off a panzer, causing it to slew round and stop. But its gun could still fire, and did so, time and again.

Now Allack's squadron was in the midst of the enemy, blazing away left and right with their two-pounders. At this close range they were doing more damage, but not half so much as they were suffering. Fergus felt physically sick as he saw some more of his men being fried alive in blazing tanks, others throwing themselves from the cupolas to be cut down by the machine guns which were the Germans' secondary armaments.

'Brigade to Westerns,' came the voice over the wireless. 'Withdraw your tanks behind Sidi Rezegh. Repeat, withdraw your tanks behind Sidi Rezegh.'

'Oh, shit,' Allack complained.

'Obey orders,' Fergus told him, and thumbed the mike. 'Dragoons will withdraw to the west. One-hundred-and-eighty-degree turn, driver.'

The tank slewed round, still firing. All who could followed. The battle still raged for the next few minutes, then the Westerns were racing for the shelter of the escarpment. Fergus threw up the hatch to count, and his sickness grew: there were only thirty-six tanks left out of the sixty he had led into battle.

'Well done, Dragoons,' the Brigadier said. 'That did the trick.'

Fergus couldn't believe his ears, looked back in surprise to see that the German armour was also pulling back, disconcerted by the fury of the flank attack they had just suffered. Nor had they gone entirely unscathed: if their casualties were considerably less than those suffered by the regiment, there were still a dozen panzers immobilized or burning at the foot of the escarpment.

'Well done, Westerns,' he said in turn. 'Well done.'

They regained the village, and Fergus was able to report to the Brigadier. In fact, Campbell had seen for himself that tank for tank the British cruisers were no match for the German panzers, and this sombre fact now dominated the battle. The rest of Thirtieth Corps soon came up, and the Afrika Korps soon renewed their assault. The regiment, having suffered such heavy casualties, was kept in reserve in Sidi Rezegh, but the other regiments and brigades launched counter-attack after counter-attack against the enemy, always with the same result: the Germans were invariably checked for a few hours, but the British casualties were heartrending. This constant pounding went on for two days, at the end of which Thirtieth Corps had lost more than four hundred tanks, or a staggering two-thirds of its strength. The Germans had lost about half that number, so that the odds still seemed to favour the British, but from the way more and more panzers were appearing from the north, it was evident that the original intelligence estimates of the total German tank strength had been grossly under-estimated. At this juncture, the support of his infantry having failed to materialize – the South Africans, under-trained for desert warfare, were virtually cut to pieces – General Norrie sadly determined that he must abandon Sidi Rezegh and fall back on El Abd Track to reorganize his shattered command.

This was a bitter blow to the tank crews, who had fought so hard and so well, and apparently unavailingly. But in fact they had not sacrificed themselves entirely in vain. Rommel had felt called upon to use every tank at his command – which actually numbered five hundred and eighty-eight instead of the approximately four hundred reported by Intelligence – and with the panzers thus thoroughly distracted, General Cunningham had turned Thirteenth Corps' holding attack on the coast into a fully fledged onslaught, thus executing the most perfect of all military manoeuvres: the punch becomes the feint, and the feint becomes the punch.

The Axis front fell back, and curled to its left, that is, against the coast, where it was pinned down by the weight of British forces. The infantry reserves were thus able to move forward and resume the battle for Sidi Rezegh while the panzers themselves were endeavouring to recuperate, and now at last, the weather having cleared, the RAF was able to assist and blast anything hostile that moved; they had complete command of the air. The village was taken and re-taken several times, but the battle was now starting to sway the British way, for the main Axis infantry remained pinned against Bardia and Sollum on the coast; the RAF was also effectively preventing supply columns from using the Capuzzo Track, and the garrison in Tobruk was mounting a sortie to link up with the approaching Allied forces. Thus, amazingly despite the defeat of his armour, Cunningham was poised for victory, when there came a dramatic intervention.

The brigade had been arranged in a 'leaguer', a square with the tanks and artillery on the outside and the trucks inside, and Fergus had just finished inspecting his battered command, after snatching a few hours' sleep – no one had had any for forty-eight hours. Several more tanks had been lost even in the defensive positions about Sidi Rezegh, and only twenty-seven were fit for action – but this was more than in most of the other armoured regiments. The human casualties were no less depressing. Some hundred and thirty men, a quarter of the ration strength of the entire regiment, were missing or known dead; another seventy-odd were wounded – a horrifying reversal of the normal casualty ratio, but when a tank brewed in the middle of a battle there was virtually no hope for those inside. Among the dead were Captain Romerill, Lieutenants Edison and Smith, and Sergeant-Major Brothers, while the recently-arrived Captain Petheridge was wounded. Fergus promoted Butler to sergeant-major, but made no other field changes, as he only commanded little more than one squadron in any event. He was relieved, however, to learn that both the Manly-Smiths had survived; Bert had, as usual, been in the thick of the fight, but this time his tank had emerged unscathed.

Again as usual, he had an opinion to offer. 'We have to get better machines, Colonel, sir,' he said. 'Otherwise they are going to keep us hanging by the short and curlies.'

'He's right, of course,' Fergus confessed to Bentley as they had a frugal supper. 'It's asking too much of men to send them into battle with inferior weapons.'

He had just turned in for some more precious sleep when the alarm went. 'There's a breakout, sir,' gasped the telegrapher.

The Brigadier summoned his regimental commanders. 'That fellow Rommel has gathered what remains of his armour and punched east,' he said. 'As all our reserves are commited to the battle, there is nothing between him and Cairo. He must be caught and brought to battle, regardless of the cost. All units must be ready to pull out in fifteen minutes.'

Desperately men finished their dinners and clambered into their machines; the tanks had happily been refuelled and re-armed that morning. Fergus took his place in the cupola of Allack's tank and fired the verey pistol to bring the pitifully small force he now commanded into column behind him. The other armoured units of Thirtieth Corps were also under way, and they raced over the bumpy ground, seeking the enemy.

'You have to hand it to that bastard for nerve,' Allack commented.

'He's stuck his neck out too far this time,' Fergus growled. 'And by God we're going to cut it off.'

They roared through the night, while the RAF swept above them looking for the enemy. The panzers were spotted just before dawn. Rommel of course lacked the fuel to make a plunge for Alexandria or Cairo; his aim had been to relieve the pressure on his infantry by swinging up behind the Allied forces in turn. But lacking air superiority it was a forlorn hope. The British armour this time held a watching brief, content to leave the work to the RAF, who tore into the panzers with their machine guns, cannon and bombs. Soon Rommel realized that he was in danger of losing his precious Afrika Korps, and was in full retreat, harried by the Seventh Armoured Division, and as usual, giving as good as he got.

The regiment regained Sidi Rezegh to find the enemy gone. But the surprises of this remarkable battle were not yet over, for now they learned that they had a new army commander. It appeared that General Cunningham had wanted to call off the struggle for Sidi Rezegh, in view of the exorbitant casualties his men were suffering. General Auchinleck had himself flown into the battle area to see what was happening, had determined that the battle would be continued to victory, regardless of casualties, and had replaced·Cunningham with his own Chief of Staff, Ritchie.

The rights and wrongs of so exceptional an occurrence – the replacement of a commanding general in the very middle of a battle – could not be gauged at regimental level. There was still a lot of hard fighting to be done, as Rommel tried desperately to extricate his infantry. The entire Seventh Armoured Division now numbered only a hundred and twenty tanks, but they were again thrown into the battle, and again found themselves outgunned by the panzers. But Rommel was now thinking only of escape, and on 8 December General Ritchie was able to announce that Tobruk had been relieved.

That Auchinleck had made the right decision became obvious when the casualties were tallied. Including the garrisons that had been cut off in Bardia and Sollum and forced to surrender, the enemy had lost thirty-three thousand men, whereas the Allies had lost only just over ten thousand in killed and missing – of these, less than three thousand were positively identified as dead – and some seven thousand wounded. Even more revealing were the tank figures: three hundred Axis tanks had been destroyed in the battle, against only two hundred and seventy-eight British. Many more had been put out of action, temporarily, but because the Allies had held the ground these were now available to be repaired and put back into service. Had the assault been called off on account of unacceptable casualties, it would have been a catastrophe.

Of the British tank losses, the vast majority had been suffered by the Seventh Armoured Division, and Fergus would dearly have loved to take his men out of the line to recuperate, but this was impossible, as the orders were to mount the maximum possible pursuit of the enemy. The days of the Desert Gallop seemed to have come again, as the armoured columns roared to the west, accompanied by the RAF. The Axis retreat became headlong, but as had happened the year before, when the Allies reached El Agheila and the borders of Tripolitania, they had to call a halt to let their supply columns catch up with them. By then it was January 1942, and what was happening in the desert had suddenly become of small importance in the larger view. Even as, on 8 December, the siege of Tobruk had been raised, the news of the Japanese attack on Pearl Harbor had been received. Now it was indeed a world war.

Fergus had no time even to consider the implications of the entry of the only two remaining great powers into the conflict until February, when at last the Seventh Armoured Division was allowed to return to Egypt, its place being taken by the First Armoured Division, just sent out from England, and reputedly the finest in the British Army. With their new uniforms, and their unscarred tanks, they made a proud show as, pennons flying, they rolled past the battle-weary veterans of the desert campaigns.

'Green as grass,' Bentley commented, watching through his binoculars some of the supply trucks making heavy weather of the sand. 'Let's hope Rommel doesn't come again until they've had a chance to get sunburned.'

Fergus made no reply to that. He agreed with his adjutant, and he was dismayed to see that the replacements were armed with the same vehicles which he had watched shot to pieces around him before Sidi Rezegh. Of course, with the RAF controlling the skies, and reinforcements pouring into Egypt – the total ration strength of the Allied armed forces in North Africa was now over half a million men – things were different this time. Or were they? Without warning, and with hardly more than a hundred tanks, of which nearly half were Italian, Rommel launched a sudden and savage counter-attack, now at last supported by the Luftwaffe. The First Armoured Division mustered a hundred and fifty tanks, but were torn apart by the panzers, and again as had happened a year before, the entire Allied front crumpled into headlong retreat. Benghazi fell, and Derna, and the so recently victorious army was almost back to Tobruk before Auchinleck, again interfering personally in the battle, checked the German advance, and left the two exhausted armies glaring at each other across the desert.

Fergus was too busy to worry about what was happening to the west; there was still a great deal to be done even in the Delta. There were his men to restore to full health as rapidly as possible – the mental strain of a long modern battle could produce results very akin to a prolonged nervous break-down. Then there was the complete reorganization of the regiment to be undertaken; he was told that there would be replacements soon enough, and his surviving tanks, and men, had to be the cadres on which these replacements would grow. Thus he was required to make his recom-mendations immediately. Petheridge was sufficiently badly wounded to be returned to England, so Fergus gave B Squadron to Lieutenant Mather, and C Squadron to Lieutenant Brown, both of whom were promoted to captain. As they each had only eight tanks under their command, the absence of any lieutenants to assist them was not immediately important. Fergus also had to re-establish his NCOs. Butler was a tower of strength here, and happily agreed when Fergus promoted Bert to sergeant. 'Always in the thickest fighting, that boy,' the Sergeant-Major said. 'He's a born soldier.'

Then there was the dismal business of sitting down with the padre and writing to the next of kin of those who had been killed; there were so many, this occupied him for some time.

139

On a happier note, there were letters to and from the family. The biggest news from home was that Harry was now fighting as hard as anyone, as the Japanese surged through the Philippine Islands. Fergus gathered that Dad and Mom were worried for their youngest son, naturally, but at the same time content that their entire family should be taking part in the struggle. They wrote too about the destruction of the London flat, but assured him that they were both well, and that Broad Acres had not been damaged in any way, so far.

They also said conventionally nice things about Annaliese, but Fergus decided that they had not yet become fully reconciled to the fact that she was again going to become a daughter-in-law. On the other hand, Liese's letters were full of love, and desire, too. Reading them made him feel more than ever guilty over that brief beauty with Monique Deschards. He wondered where she was now, and what she was doing? But he would never see her again.

He replied in kind, and then took himself off to Cairo. This was at least partly because he was commanded to do so, in order that he could be invested with the precious crimson ribbon by the British Resident. It was also an occasion for meeting the Lord Privy Seal, Sir Stafford Cripps, who was on his way to India to attempt to persuade people like Nehru and Gandhi to cease their agitation for independence until the Japanese had been dealt with. Cairo was, however, not merely a stopover for Cripps, as Fergus discovered when the following evening he was invited to the Commander-in-Chief's flat, where he discovered, to his surprise, that it was to be more of a supper tête-à-tête than usual: he was the only guest.

'I get precious few quiet evenings,' Auchinleck told him. 'And I haven't had a chance to talk to you since before Sidi Rezegh. What did you think of it?'

'I think thank God you made us go through with it, sir,' Fergus said.

'I didn't ask you here to be flattered, Fergus. I want some criticisms.'

'Well,' Fergus said cautiously, not at all sure what the

General was looking for, from him, when he must have received reams of reports from the various brigadiers. 'Tactically, we need better tanks. I don't think our armour is inferior to the panzers', but our two-pounder gun is too light except at very close quarters. I think this has been proved by the fact that when we get into a mêlée we do as well as they. It is when we are moving up to the attack that we suffer the most casualties.'

'Go on.'

'Then we don't have an adequate anti-tank weapon, nothing to compare with their dual-purpose eighty-eights. And most important of all, sir, having regard to the differences I have already mentioned, our strategy of dispersion is a poor one. If it takes two of our tanks to kill one German panzer, then we must always have two of ours available. Our armour was thrown into the Battle of Sidi Rezegh piecemeal. Surely, as Sidi was the whole object of our attack, all the armour should have been concentrated on it, and not dispersed to look for the enemy. Once we held Sidi, he would have had to come to us. As he did. Only he would have met our entire force at once.'

Auchinleck nodded. 'There were tactical mistakes. But it is this sense of inferiority that our armoured personnel have which is most worrying. Have you mentioned any of this to your father?'

'Well . . . no, sir.'

'Why not? Not a misguided sense of loyalty to the Eighth Army, I hope. The best thing you can do for the Eighth Army, for us all, is to bring these facts to the attention of those who can correct them. I am trying. But I need all the help I can find. Your father has Churchill's ear. That may be most important.' Auchinleck had dismissed his servant, and now he poured them each a goblet of brandy. 'I wouldn't like our conversation to go any further, Fergus, but the Government don't really understand what is happening out here, and if they are not careful, they are going to land us in one hell of a mess. They complained when I took so long to mount our offensive in November, but they were delighted with my apparent success. Yet I was never in any doubts as to how it would go, and continue to go. In fact, as regards tank losses we came out better than I had hoped. But since then things have gone badly. I don't want to take any credit away from Rommel. He is a brilliant tactician, and he came back far quicker than I had thought he possibly could. The fact is that he was reinforced more quickly than I could be, because the Axis have been getting their convoys through the Mediterranean whereas ours are being diverted round the Cape of Good Hope. But it is also a fact that he counter-attacked before he was reinforced, and that the First Armoured Division simply fell apart. I am convinced that he began his attack just as a probe, which he took advantage of when he saw how well it was going. Churchill is furious. He cannot understand how a hundred and fifty virtually new tanks, manned by fresh troops, could have been routed by a hundred and twenty old bangers manned by men who had so recently been defeated. The fault of course lies partly in the tanks themselves, of course, and partly in the fact that ours were fresh troops, unused to the desert, whereas Rommel's men were all veterans.'

'With respect, sir,' Fergus ventured. 'Isn't the truth of the matter that Rommel always leads his attacks in person, whereas you are tied to Cairo so much of the time?'

Auchinleck grinned. 'You're back to the compliments, Fergus. You could even be right. But then, the biggest fact of all is that Rommel has Libya to worry about, and nowhere else. I have to fight him, and administer Egypt, and keep an eye on Palestine, and deal with Rashid Ali in Iraq, and butter up the Turks, all at the same time. I simply have to spend most of my time here. Anyway, they're not interested in excuses at home. With things going so badly elsewhere – Singapore, Hong Kong, Malaya, the Germans getting set to resume their Russian advance – the powers that be badly need a victory, and they reckon that here in the desert is where they are most likely to get it. They are also once again concerned that if we don't keep the enemy fully occupied here in North Africa he may launch an all-out assault on Malta. Well, we are going to keep him occupied, and they are going to get their victory, but only if we attack on our terms, not Rommel's.' He paused. 'Do you mind me talking like this?'

'I appreciate it, sir,' Fergus said.

'They are clamouring for me to launch another offensive. They keep reminding me that my ration strength is enormously greater than Rommel's, that I have more tanks . . . and they grumble like hell when I ask for still more. That's the real reason why Cripps stopped by, you know. To tell me personally that the Government wants an offensive, now! I just cannot convince them that merely having more men and more machines is a waste of time unless those men and machines are as good as the enemy's. That means as well trained and acclimatized. I am determined not to throw my people into battle merely to be cut up. That would be criminal. When our preparations and the training of our replacements are completed, then we shall attack. I should be most grateful if you would explain all of that to Murdoch. He will understand it, and it's just possible he may be able to get it across to the PM.'

'I will certainly try to do so, sir,' Fergus said. 'But supposing Malta were to fall. Wouldn't that have a disastrous effect on our situation here?'

'As we can no longer use the Mediterranean as a supply route, I cannot see that the fall of Malta could be in any way as disastrous for us as to lose the Eighth Army. Warfare is a matter of choosing the lesser evil. Our strength will continue to grow here, regardless of the Mediterranean situation. If Malta falls, perhaps Rommel's strength will grow more quickly than it is now doing, but I still think we will grow faster. That is something else that needs to be explained.'

'Yes, sir,' Fergus agreed.

He returned to the Delta in a pensive frame of mind, understanding, perhaps for the first time, the many problems that went with the independent command of a large body of men. Dad had always made it seem so simple. But Dad must have had the same doubts, been subjected to the same pressures. He did as Auchinleck had asked, and wrote home as fully as he could, explaining the difficulties and asking Murdoch to convey them to the Prime Minister.

Then it was back to work. The build-up of forces continued, replacements arrived, men and machines, and it was a matter of training them in desert techniques and survival. The men were very eager, but also very green. They also, unfortunately, had a very healthy respect for the name Rommel, and Fergus began to realize that it was a matter of crucial importance that the Auk gain a victory as dramatic as that of the previous year – and that this time he should hold on to it.

But the General was still not ready, in his opinion, when peremptory orders arrived from London that he must attack no later than the dark moon period of June. This political direction of a commanding general in the field was unheard of since the days of the Peninsular War, and caused a stir. Many expected the General to resign. But like a good soldier he accepted the decision and made his preparations for an offensive. Unfortunately, Rommel struck first.

Fergus had just taken the regiment back up to the front, and had indeed been greatly impressed by the huge defensive system which had been created, almost reminiscent of what his father had told him of Flanders during the Great War. Here were what were known as 'boxes', foursquare fortresses designed to resist enemy armour. They didn't look like fortresses, and to the recruits, seeing nothing but empty desert, they seemed a joke. But they were surrounded by minefields and carefully embedded concrete pillboxes, as well as buried dumps of food and fuel and ammunition. The General had clearly given much thought to resisting marauding columns of enemy armour, and this certainly seemed one answer. In theory, the panzers were to be allowed the freedom of the empty desert, but be unable to crack any of the strong-points, around which they might flow like an incoming tide around various concrete moles, but from which they could be counter-attacked at the right moment.

Even the British armour was concentrated in boxes, and

if this was ultra-defensive thinking to Fergus's mind, he assumed it was because the army was not yet ready to take the offensive.

The sudden appearance of the German tanks, careering out of the desert behind blazing guns and supported by their mobile artillery as well as the Luftwaffe, did not therefore frighten anyone, as it had done further west on two previous occasions. If it was a probe, such as had started the last Rommel offensive, it would hopefully soon discover that this time there was going to be no headlong Allied retreat. If it was the commencement of a battle, the army felt total confidence in its new defensive position, and if Rommel blunted his panzers immediately before the British were ready to launch their own attack, so much the better. The brigade thus contented itself with firing at any enemy vehicles which came too close, and awaiting the orders for a counter-thrust.

Within a couple of days, however, it became obvious that this was indeed the opening of a battle, and that the German target was Tobruk. The panzers hurled themselves at the various boxes which had been set up to block their advance, and disconcertingly, some of these supposedly impregnable positions began to crumble. The Seventh Armoured Division was also subjected to heavy attacks, in its position east of Bir Hacheim, which was being defended with the utmost skill and gallantry by the Free French. These onslaughts were repelled, and the regiment knew they were giving as good as they were getting, but to their dismay no orders came to counter-punch and relieve the French. Day after day passed, with the panzers apparently being allowed to run free in the belief that they would simply wear themselves out.

'When are they going to let us go?' Bentley grumbled. 'For God's sake, we're not fortress troops.'

It was not until 4 June that the division was 'let go', and then it was too late. The panzers, having recoiled from their initial onslaught, had been reinforced, and yet again in the open desert the German machines and gunfire were overwhelming. Soon the British armour was as usual being ordered to pull out. This time the troops were angry. 'When are we going to beat the buggers?' Sergeant Manly-Smith moaned, banging his fist into the side of his tank.

Losses had been heavy, but when the casualty figures were estimated, they still seemed on the right side of the ledger. The panzers had lost some four hundred tanks, as against three hundred and fifty British; on both sides a number of these would be repairable, depending on which side eventually held the field; there were in any event still over three hundred British vehicles ready for immediate use, two hundred and fifty of these being cruisers. More disturbing was the loss of men, over the army as a whole; the total was estimated at about ten thousand, and the Germans and Italians could hardly have suffered less, as their infantry had been battering against the South African division holding the coastal road – but of the Allied total some eight thousand were thought to be prisoners of war. This suggested that despite the boxes, there had been a crumbling of morale in some places as the panzers had advanced.

Once again it was a case of everything to the rear. The general orders were clear enough, and confident enough. The Eighth Army would fall back on Egypt, and the vast amount of men and materiel which was now pouring up the Red Sea; these included some three hundred and fifty new tanks, which would entirely make up any losses. This would mean that Rommel, if he continued his attack, would be stretching his lines of communication to the limit, and be ripe for a counter-stroke. The strategy also involved letting Tobruk be invested once more, but only temporarily – and it had survived investment before. This time the garrison was to consist in the main of South Africans, and was to be commanded by General Klopper, of the South African Division.

This decided, the Eighth Army, resentfully and sullenly, pulled back to their old position between Sidi Barrani and Mersa Matruh. Their officers did their best to raise morale, assuring them that it was indeed nothing more than a tactical ploy which would bring them a decisive victory in the near future. Unfortunately, the old hands had heard it all before, twice. While the recruits were merely bewildered. Real warfare in the desert, with the heat and the sand and the thirst, the screaming panzers and the equally screaming aircraft overhead, bore not the remotest resemblance to mock warfare on Salisbury Plain.

Fergus had never known the morale of the regiment to be so low. Men sat around in groups when off duty, muttering at each other. When required to entrench the muttering grew more intense. They saluted their officers while they looked at the ground, and the effect they had on the replacements who hastened up, fresh-cheeked, from Cairo, was disastrous.

Fergus called an officers' conference. 'This is a very serious matter,' he told them. 'And it must be checked, and reversed, at once. Now, this is what we are going to do. We are . . .' he checked to look at the telegrapher, who had entered the room without knocking. 'What the devil . . . ?'

The corporal's face was quite white. 'Colonel, sir,' he stammered. 'News has just been received . . . Tobruk has surrendered.'

PART TWO

VICTORY

6

England, 1942

'This is quite catastrophic,' Churchill declared. 'What in the name of God more can we do? We appoint a fine fighting soldier to overall command; we give him damn near everything we have; we allow him as much freedom of action as we dare, having regard to the whole world situation . . . and he gets beat.'

'He's saved the Eighth Army,' Murdoch protested mildly.

'Saved the Eighth Army? I didn't give him the Eighth Army to save it. I gave it to him to drive Rommel out of North Africa. And I don't know that he has saved it. Do you realize there is the most tremendous flap going on down there? They are talking of evacuating Cairo. They are burning their code-books. Some blithering idiot of a naval officer has commanded that the entire stock of binoculars in Alexandria be thrown into the harbour to prevent them from falling into the hands of the enemy. This is after we have allowed Tobruk, with enough supplies to keep an army going for three months, to be handed over to the Afrika Korps. It is quite unbelievable.'

He paused, and Murdoch waited. The PM clearly had considerable problems at that moment, too many for his own to be mentioned.

'Well, we are not going to evacuate Egypt,' Churchill growled at last. 'Auchinleck will have to go.'

Murdoch sighed, but he had known that decision was inevitable, even if no suggestion of evacuation had come from the Commander-in-Chief himself.

Churchill had heard the sigh. 'More than the last time, it's a matter of restoring morale. It is a matter of restoring morale here in London as well, I can tell you.'

'So who is going this time?'

'Alexander. Perhaps I should have sent him in the first place.'

Murdoch thought he might just about be right. He did not know Harold Alexander well: there was a considerable difference in their ages, Alexander being ten years the younger. Yet for that very reason he would probably be a sound choice: he was, equally, seven years younger than Auchinleck. He was also a soldier of the most undeniable courage and tenacity of purpose; the last time Murdoch had seen him had been on the beach at Dunkirk, when as general officer commanding the evacuation, he had been the last to leave, and had inspired everyone with his quiet confidence.

But there was a problem. 'I thought Alexander was already earmarked to be Eisenhower's deputy, when we launch Torch,' he said. The Anglo-American decision to undertake an amphibious attack on the western Mediterranean coast of North Africa, so as to catch the Axis forces between two fires, had been recently concluded and was still known only to a very few people.

'That's true. But we will have to have him back. I'm giving the Americans Bernard Montgomery instead.'

'Hallelujah!' Murdoch murmured.

Churchill shot him a glance. 'What have you got against Montgomery? I know he hasn't had a very brilliant war, but he simply hasn't had the chance since we were thrown out of France. Now's his opportunity to do what he can.'

'Oh, quite. I was just thinking that he's not everyone's cup of tea. He can be . . . abrasive?'

'You mean damned cocky,' Churchill suggested. 'Eisenhower will have to grin and bear it. But in addition to replacing Auchinleck in Cairo, I also intend to make some changes in the whole command structure of the Middle East. Holding a command which covers everything we have to defend from Iran west is too much for one man. I see that now. It is a change I should have made before. Alexander will have overall command of North Africa and responsibility for defending the Suez Canal; Auchinleck will take the rest of the Middle East.'

'That's a little rough on Auchinleck,' Murdoch pointed out. 'If he had only had to worry about Libya he might have pulled it off.'

'I accept that,' Churchill said. 'That is a stroke of ill fortune. But in the present circumstances there has to be a change.'

'And who will get the Eighth Army? Or are you retaining Ritchie?'

'No, I am not. He has clearly lost the confidence of his troops. As to who is to replace him, I wish to God I knew. It will have to be Strafer Gott, I suppose.'

'You'll hardly do better. But Strafer took over Thirteenth Corps from Godwin-Austin before Rommel's attack. He's been as much involved in the disaster as anyone.'

'From what I have been able to gather, Thirteenth Corps has come out of this débâcle better than anyone else. Which is to Gott's credit. Anyway, I haven't made a firm decision yet. I intend to fly out to Cairo myself, and see the situation on the ground personally. I also intend to inform Auchinleck of my decision regarding him in person as well; I can hardly do less.'

Murdoch nodded. He knew that Churchill, like himself, never shirked his duty. 'When are you leaving?'

'Tomorrow. Now then, have you got the man for Yugoslavia?'

Murdoch grinned. 'Yes. Myself.'

Churchill frowned at him. 'I am really not in the mood for jokes, Murdoch. Not today.'

'Sorry. It really would be just up my street. I have parachuted before, you know.'

'Crawling about a lot of cold mountains with a bunch of bandits is up your street?'

'Well, I rather gather that a good number of the guerillas are soldiers who refused to accept the surrender of the Yugoslav Army. They could become a useful fighting force. But the main reason is that my reports have told me that Paul is now in Yugoslavia. A general, would you believe it.'

Churchill's frown deepened. 'You wish to go and fight your own son?'

'If necessary. But you know I have always had a feeling that Paul was never whole-heartedly behind Hitler. I won't deny he's a Nazi. But it's Hitler we want to get out. And if there is an underground movement, and Paul is interested in it, and I could contact him . . .'

'We'll get Hitler by smashing him from the front,' Churchill growled. 'Who are you sending?'

Murdoch sighed. 'Brigadier Durden. He knows the area.'

'What orders have you given him?'

'As we discussed. We have contacts there already, and they are expecting a high-ranking British officer. He will be dropped by parachute at an agreed place, with his staff, which I am limiting to three people. As I say, these Chetniks, as they call themselves, will be waiting for him. He will make contact with their leader, this fellow Mikhailovitch, and set up a liaison with him. He will observe the Chetnik operations against the Germans, and relay back to us their requirements.'

'Within reason,' Churchill reminded him. 'You say these people are expecting him. You realize we know nothing about this Mikhailovitch save that he was an officer in the Yugoslav Army who wishes to continue fighting. We know nothing about these so-called Chetniks, either, save that they have taken to the hills. Are you certain Durden won't be jumping straight into a trap?'

'No,' Murdoch said. 'But if we are sending a mission to these people, we must accept this risk; it could happen at the jump or weeks later. I don't like doing it, Winston. You know that. But if it must be done . . .'

'It must be done. We need the support of people who refuse to surrender their country. That is the kind of underground I can work with. Keep me informed.'

Murdoch nodded and stood up.

Churchill grinned at him. 'And if Durden can open useful contacts with General von Reger, without jeopardizing his mission, then you may give him my permission to do so.'

154

Murdoch sat at his desk and considered writing Fergus. But he really wasn't in the mood. Fergus had survived this latest setback, and Murdoch had no doubt he would be up to his ears in it, reorganizing the regiment and restoring its morale. But in any event, he would not appreciate having unhappy domestic news foisted on him.

Not even the news that his only surviving brother might well be dead? As a United States Marine, Harry had taken part in the gallant defence of the Bataan Peninsula against the Japanese armies which had come flooding down Luzon and overrun Manila. With his comrades he had retreated to the island of Corregidor, dominating Manila Bay, and there had fought to the last bullet, while so many other garrisons in other parts of the world had surrendered. It was impossible not to feel bitter about Singapore and Tobruk. Of course Percival had reported that the Japanese had captured Singapore's freshwater reservoirs and that to continue further resistance would have made life intolerable for the large civilian population trapped in the island city, but the fact remained that eighty thousand British troops had surrendered with arms in their hands and ammunition in their belts to a hardly greater number of the enemy. Equally, Klopper had reported that Tobruk was a 'shambles' from German artillery fire, yet there again over thirty thousand soldiers had laid down their arms to an attacking force of hardly *half* that number, while still in possession of all the sinews of war. However grim it might be to think it, had every two men in Tobruk taken one German with them as they died, the war in North Africa would now be over, with an Allied victory.

The defenders of Corregidor had not considered surrender. They had fought, encumbered with civilians and with an ever growing number of seriously wounded or seriously ill, against the Japanese Army, Navy and Air Force, until an unlucky bomb burst had set off their magazine and all their ammunition. Then, disarmed, they had raised their arms and passed into the horrors of Japanese captivity. But Harry Mackinder was not on the list

155

of those gallant men. He had apparently not lived until that final catastrophic moment.

Murdoch supposed he would never forget breaking that news to Lee. Harry had been their youngest child, and therefore Lee's baby. That he had opted for American citizenship, her own citizenship, had had to be a source of pride to her, however she had shared Murdoch's disappointment that he would not be an army Mackinder. And true to the tradition that she had married, she had been honestly angry that Harry had not come back to fight for king and country as his brothers were doing. It was not possible to be angry any more. Lee had wept, as she had not done over Ian.

But Ian had not been less on her mind, because of Ian's widow. Another cause for anger. Annaliese was apparently feeling the strain of being cooped up down in Somerset, with nothing but female company, and her baby to care for. Lee had been greeted, on her return there, with a tale of woe from Philippa of how her niece-in-law often went out in the evenings, into Bath or even Bristol, apparently to the pictures. But, as Philippa had taken to waiting up for her to return, she had observed that it had too often been with bright eyes and gin-laden breath.

'Which I have seen and smelt for myself since returning here,' Lee had written him. 'Can you imagine, a well-bred young woman going to a pub by herself? Can you imagine who she might meet there?'

Murdoch could imagine very well, nor did he suppose Annaliese had ever been to a cinema at all, at least by herself. It lay heavy on his mind. He had never told Lee of that remarkable conversation in the porch at Broad Acres. It was not something he ever proposed to do. Certainly if the girl was marrying Fergus. But could he allow her to marry Fergus? Annaliese was a young woman with ants in her pants in a way that her mother had never had. Should Fergus not know that? But how could he write a man who has just suffered defeat in battle and tell him that his fiancée was close to being a whore? He had tried to tell Ian that, once, and it hadn't worked.

156

The alternative was to go down to Broad Acres himself . . . and do what? *He* had taken the girl in and given her a home. No one else. Lee had been aghast from the moment he had told her what he felt he must do, but with her unvarying loyalty she had accepted his decision. He had virtually adopted the girl, and he had personally killed her father, after watching her mother die. To throw her out, send her to an internment camp, would be a betrayal of every chivalrous instinct in his body.

So, go down to Broad Acres and put her across his knee, and wallop her? He had a suspicion she might enjoy that. Far more to the point, he had a suspicion that he might enjoy that as well – far too much.

How he wished he could go out to Egypt and join the troops there. He wouldn't care if he wasn't in command. Just to get into a tank and see the enemy through the slit. He was a fighting soldier. He had always been a fighting soldier. Always in the past the uncertainties of personal problems had been resolved in the glorious certainty of physical action, win or lose, kill or be killed. Riding into battle with an utterly fearless unconcern for personal safety, he had always won. Now he sent other men and women into battle, and watched them from afar, and could share neither their triumph nor their tragedies.

'The mountains are called Maglio and Durmitor,' Murdoch explained, pointing to the map. 'They're each about seven thousand feet high, but there is a valley between. Still high, but fertile country, well wooded, with plenty of conceal-ment. Where that long, narrow lake is.' He grinned. 'We'll endeavour not to drop you in the water.'

'Rather close to Sarajevo, isn't it?' Brigadier Durden asked.

'Fifty-odd miles,' Murdoch told him. 'But the Germans only control the towns and the main roads. Fifty miles is a long way in that situation. For a German.'

'Yes,' Durden agreed. 'And General von Reger is in Sarajevo.'

'That is his command headquarters, according to our

157

latest reports. You understand that he should be approached with the utmost caution. We don't know if he will be receptive.'

Durden nodded. 'But you feel it will be worthwhile, sir.'

'Yes,' Murdoch said. 'I met the General, when I was in Germany before the war. He struck me as being a very sensible fellow.' He had not of course told Durden that Paul was his son.

'Right-ho,' the Brigadier said. 'Well, I think that about ties it up. When do I go?'

'On Thursday, you fly out to Cairo via Gibraltar. Thence to Cyprus. The actual flight is from Cyprus.'

'Will do.' Durden grinned. 'Four days.'

'Stay sober,' Murdoch recommended. 'Now, I'd like to meet your team.'

Durden raised his eyebrows.

'A weakness of mine,' Murdoch said.

'Quite, sir. I haven't told them what the op is, of course.'

'I wouldn't have expected you to. What *have* you told them?'

'That we are undertaking a mission into enemy-held territory, and that we may be away some time. Nothing more than that.'

'And they are all volunteers?'

'Oh, indeed, sir.'

'Good. Then I would like to meet them. Bring them along tomorrow.'

Brigadier Durden appeared rather like a ringmaster, as he stood in the doorway to Murdoch's office. He was, in fact, showing unwelcome signs of strain this last week. Well, Murdoch thought, he was being almost literally launched into the blue. He was the ideal man for the job, on paper: he was a logistics expert, he had known Yugoslavia before the war, he spoke Croat, and his hobby was mountaineering. He had fought in Norway and received the Military Cross; no one could question his courage. Murdoch had picked him from several volunteers for this mission, and he had no

158

doubt at all that when the mission actually began Durden would be as cool as necessary.

He was more concerned with the possible reactions of the three men accompanying the Brigadier, who as yet did not know their fate. Three men? Murdoch's jaw dropped as he surveyed the two men and the woman standing before his desk. All wore battledress, but . . . he looked at Durden.

'Captain Percy Markham, sir.'

Murdoch shook hands.

'Sergeant Ronald Evans, sir.'

Another firm handclasp.

'Private Mary Edmunds, sir.'

'Private.' Murdoch gazed at her. She was a tall, somewhat raw-boned young woman, pleasant-faced and with curly fair hair peeping out from beneath her forage cap. She looked tough and fit enough, but . . . 'I'm pleased to make your acquaintance,' Murdoch said. 'I am sure you will all be a credit to the service. Good luck, and thank you.'

They saluted and filed out.

'A word, if you will, Brigadier,' Murdoch said.

Durden closed the door.

'What the hell is going on?' Murdoch inquired.

'Sir?'

'My dear fellow, you can't take a woman parachuting into the Serbian mountains.'

'Why not, sir? She volunteered.'

'For a mission. Not a mission like this. And with three men . . .'

'Private Edmunds speaks Croatian and German, sir. Amongst other languages. She is a highly skilled linguist. I picked her for her qualifications over several men.'

Murdoch gazed at him.

'And *you* use women, sir,' Durden reminded him.

'Only after I have personally supervised their training. And I don't like doing it. I don't like this one at all.'

'She won't let us down, sir.'

'I was considering the other side of the coin, Brigadier.'

'I can assure you, sir . . .'

'Simmer down,' Murdoch told him. 'I wasn't thinking of

you or your men. But she is going to have to live rough with a lot of Serbs.'

'With whom we shall be fighting, shoulder to shoulder. I will make Edmunds's well-being my personal concern, sir.'

Murdoch knew he wasn't trying to be funny; a sense of humour was something the Brigadier entirely lacked. 'Very good, Durden,' he said. 'I was just taken aback. Carry on.'

The Brigadier saluted.

'I'm not sure it isn't indecent,' Murdoch grumbled to Methuen.

'Yes, sir,' the Commander agreed. 'But she did volunteer, and she knows she's going to be with a lot of men. It's the thought of if she were to be captured by the Gestapo that worries me.'

'Yes,' Murdoch said. 'It worries me, too. I worry about all of them.'

'I know that, sir,' Methuen said. 'That's why . . .' he gave a kind of gulp.

Murdoch raised his head. 'Say it.'

'I think Deschards has gone.'

'What? What makes you say that?'

'There has been no report this week. So I contacted Pleinhomme, and asked him to check. He has just come back to me. Her rooming house was raided, nine days ago. Gestapo. The neighbours heard shots, and then they saw people being removed.'

'Dead people?'

'Live people. But not in very good shape. One of them was certainly a woman.' Methuen watched his superior's fingers curling into fists. 'I'm sure she will never betray us, sir, or her contacts.'

'Yes,' Murdoch said. 'Deschards will never betray us.' But she will die cursing us, he thought. Me, at the least. He got up. 'I'm going to the Cavalry Club.'

'Yes, sir,' Methuen said unhappily.

Murdoch didn't even feel like getting drunk. He lay on his bed and stared at the ceiling, remembered Monique jogging round and round the cellar, so confidently, so

160

powerfully. And then blowing that target to bits. Shooting accurately after extreme exertion is difficult, Mrs Bryant had said. Had Monique undergone extreme exertion before having to shoot for her life? Either way, she hadn't succeeded.

And now Durden, setting off into the blue, with his three volunteers . . . while he lay on his bed and sweated. God damn, he thought, to have a command . . . the telephone jangled.

Murdoch lifted the receiver. 'Yes?'

'I have a call for you, General,' said the hall porter. 'It's Commander Methuen.'

'Put him through.' Murdoch's heart began to pound. It had to be news of Monique. Perhaps she had evaded the Gestapo after all, in which case he'd bring her back out, right away. 'Commander?'

'Sorry to disturb you, General,' Methuen said. 'But we have just received a top-secret communication for you from the PM.'

'I'll be right down,' Murdoch said, and dragged on his uniform.

Churchill had wired, in code, to General Sir Alan Brooke, Chief of the Imperial General Staff, copied to Lieutenant General Sir Murdoch Mackinder, on special assignment to his Majesty's Government: GOTT KILLED IN AIR CRASH THIS MORNING HOURS AFTER ACCEPTING COMMAND EIGHTH ARMY STOP FATE HANGS HEAVY AT TIMES STOP SUGGEST VERY SERIOUSLY MONTGOMERY FOR VACANT POSITION STOP ALEXANDER CONCURS STOP IF YOU AGREE AMERICANS WILL HAVE TO BE SQUARED STOP SUGGEST CIGS CONTACT EISENHOWER AND MACKINDER PUT POSITION TO MONTGOMERY STOP MOST URGENT DECISION TAKEN AND IMPLEMENTED IMMEDIATELY STOP HOT STOP CHURCHILL.

Murdoch picked up the phone and called the War Office. He had known Alan Brooke for many years, as he had known his predecessor, Sir John Dill, whom Brooke had only replaced as CIGS the previous December, owing to Dill's ill health. 'Yes,' Brooke said. 'It's an odd world. Poor old Strafer. Anyway, we don't have any choice but to go along with Winston's idea. I wouldn't wish Montgomery on anyone, much less an army suffering from low morale, but there is no one else. You go along and see him, Murdoch. And the best of luck.'

Murdoch left next morning, driving down to the south of England where Montgomery was presently in command. He had of course known Montgomery as long as he had known most of the other generals in the British Army, without ever coming into close working contact with him; Montgomery was six years the younger man. Murdoch knew him for a painstaking soldier who had a reputation for holding, and expressing often enough, the opinion that few of his contemporaries really understood the art of modern warfare. Which probably accounted for the fact that he had had the least opportunity of all the senior British commanders to distinguish himself, although he had commanded an army corps in France before Dunkirk; no one really wanted either to command him or work with him, and that Alexander had agreed with Churchill over giving him the Eighth Army spoke volumes for the new GOC Middle East's confidence.

Murdoch therefore approached the meeting with some caution. But his fighting record as well as his seniority was an asset. He was greeted most courteously and entertained to a decidedly simple lunch, at which no wine was offered. 'I assume you've come to see how my troops are getting on?' Montgomery asked when the meal was finished and they retired to the General's office to drink coffee in private.

'As a matter of fact, no,' Murdoch told him. 'I was asked to come and see you by the PM. With the agreement of Brooke, of course.'

Montgomery, a sharp-featured little man with a small military moustache, raised his eyebrows. 'An emissary from the corridors of power,' he remarked. 'Have the Yanks objected to me?'

'Not so far as I am aware,' Murdoch said. 'But it has been decided that they can't have you.'

'Is that so? Why not?'

'We want you to take the Eighth Army.'

Montgomery turned his head to frown at him.

'As you probably know,' Murdoch said, 'it's in pretty bad shape. Not only did it take a shellacking from Rommel, but it has the idea that the man cannot be beat, that his tanks and guns are superior to ours.'

'The reports I've read indicate that they are,' Montgomery observed.

'That may be, although steps are being taken to remedy this. The point is, the army has to be restored to its full fighting capacity, and Rommel has got to be beaten. Otherwise Malta is going to fall, and then probably Egypt.' He didn't add that in such an eventuality Torch would probably have to be abandoned, and perhaps the whole of North Africa, and ultimate victory would have receded by another year at least, even with American aid.

'Oh, I can see that,' Montgomery agreed.

'Well, will you take the command?'

Montgomery stared in front of himself for several seconds. Then he said, 'Has it ever struck you, Murdoch, just how whimsical Fate can be when she decides to play tricks? She takes a professional soldier, who has devoted his life to his country and his career, who has fought in the Great War and obtained some little distinction, who has progressed through the various grades of seniority until he arrives at the rank of lieutenant general, and is given command of an army. It could be said that he has arrived at the pinnacle of his ambition, of his career. And then, with a snap of her fingers, the fickle jade takes it all away.'

'My dear fellow,' Murdoch protested. 'I am sure it isn't going to be anything like as bad as that. The Eighth Army is restorable. My own regiment is with them, and my son. They are just looking to be led. As for that supposed inferiority in weapons, I can tell you in confidence that President Roosevelt has authorized the immediate transfer of three hundred Sherman tanks to Egypt. They are the very latest American machines, and are superior to anything possessed by the Afrika Korps. I really see no reason for you to be that despondent.'

Montgomery had turned his head, and was frowning again. 'Despondent? I am not in the least despondent.'

'But what you just said . . .'

'Good Lord!' Montgomery gave a sudden grin. 'I wasn't speaking of myself, Murdoch. I was speaking of poor old Rommel.'

It occurred to Murdoch, as he drove back to London that afternoon, that Montgomery might indeed be the one man who could beat Rommel. More than ever he wished he could be there, to see and hear for himself, rather than have to wait for Fergus's letters.

But when he regained his office, he forgot all about the Eighth Army. 'I'm afraid it just isn't our day, sir,' Methuen said. His voice was tense.

'What's happened now?'

'Brigadier Durden has had a heart attack.'

Murdoch sat up straight. 'A what?'

'A heart attack, sir.'

'But he was passed as absolutely fit.'

'I know, sir. I suppose he must have been under a greater strain than we realized.'

'Yes,' Murdoch said. 'Where is he?'

'The Middlesex Hospital.'

'I suppose I'd better get down there. Let them know I'm coming, will you. Is he conscious?'

'Ah . . .' Methuen hesitated. 'When I meant the hospital, I actually meant the morgue, sir.'

'Good God! Just like that?'

'I'm afraid so, sir. The mission is due to depart on Thursday. Shall I cancel it? I'm afraid there isn't time to brief a replacement in time. Even if we can find one.'

Murdoch stared at him.

'Sir?'

'Leave it with me for a few hours,' Murdoch said. 'It doesn't have to be cancelled yet.'

He called for his car and drove into Buckinghamshire, found Mrs Bryant in her office. 'Deschards,' Mrs Bryant said. 'Now that is a shame, General. But she was careless, letting herself be taken alive. I gave her a full supply of cyanide tablets.'

'We don't know she was taken alive,' Murdoch said. 'But supposing she was, what will they do to her?'

'Do you really want to know?'

'Yes,' Murdoch said. 'I do.'

Mrs Bryant's shoulders rose and fell. 'A body search. Very unpleasant. A flogging. The Gestapo are fond of flogging women. Electric shocks. This is their latest toy. They attach them to various sensitive parts of the body.' She gazed at Murdoch. 'There are a lot of those. Then a cell. And then a firing squad. Or just a bullet through the inspection hatch. It's all very unpleasant. Far better to bite the cyanide capsule.'

'Yes,' Murdoch said. 'Take me downstairs, will you, Mrs Bryant.'

She got up without comment, led him down the stairs. Mr Hunt had his usual four girls in the cellar. 'Give the young ladies a ten-minute break,' Murdoch requested.

'Dismissed for ten minutes,' Mrs Bryant said.

The girls gave Murdoch anxious glances – he had of course met them before sending them here – and filed out. Murdoch removed his uniform, stripping to his underwear. 'Test me, Mr Hunt,' he said.

Hunt looked at Mrs Bryant, and received a quick nod.

'Very good, General. You'll find a pair of plimsolls over there. Will you put them on and start running?'

Murdoch obeyed. He quickly began to sweat. But he kept himself fit by playing squash at least three times a week and did not find the jogging unduly hard. Indeed he soon began to enjoy it, lost count of the number of times he circled the room, was surprised when Hunt said, 'Now, General.'

He stopped at the table, picked up the revolver, used his left hand as it slipped on his sweat-wet palm, turned to face the target as it came into light, and squeezed the trigger six times. Cardboard flew in every direction.

'Nice shooting!' Hunt exclaimed.

165

'Indeed,' Mrs Bryant said. 'I wish some of my girls could have seen that. I mean, at sixty . . .'

'Don't say it,' Murdoch suggested. 'But you think I'd pass your tests?'

'That one,' Mrs Bryant told him. 'There are others.'

'I really feel we should do something about that aircraft, sir,' Methuen said. 'And the three staffers. They don't know about Durden's death yet. But it's hardly fair to cancel at the very last minute, and they're due out tomorrow.'

'We are not going to cancel,' Murdoch said, sealing the third envelope on his desk.

'You've found a replacement, sir?'

'Yes,' Murdoch said. He held out the three envelopes. 'The two to be mailed are to be sent in four days' time. Yours can be opened then.'

Methuen glanced at them. One was addressed to the Right Honourable Winston Churchill, PC, the second to Lady Mackinder, and the third to Commander Methuen. 'My God, sir,' the Commander protested. 'You're not . . .'

'I am taking a few days off to go into the country, Commander. Understood?'

Methuen swallowed. 'There is going to be the most utter hell to pay, sir.'

'Which is why you know nothing about it. The moment you do know something about it, which will be when in four days' time you obey orders and open your sealed envelope, you can call for all the help you can get to fetch me back.'

Methuen gazed at him. 'May I beg you to reconsider, General? I mean, at your age . . .'

'You mention my age and I'll cashier you,' Murdoch growled.

'But really, sir. Yugoslavia . . .'

'Is apparently the only place I am going to be allowed to fight the enemy, Methuen. Beggars can't be choosers. You just carry out my orders.'

'I'm sorry to bring you up to London, Lee,' Churchill said.

'It's simply that I cannot come down to Somerset.' He tapped the letter on his desk. 'I assume you've had one of these?'

'Yes.' Lee's face was tight. But not as tight as the Prime Minister had feared.

'He's a cunning rogue,' Churchill said. 'He was actually on his way out while I was on my way back. He landed in Gibraltar going east hours before I landed there coming west; our aircraft must have passed within a few thousand feet of each other at one stage. But he managed to keep his identity secret, travelling as this poor fellow Durden. He even got away with it in Cairo and Cyprus. His staff must have been sworn to secrecy too. And of course Methuen must have known his intention, even if Murdoch says he didn't.'

'Did he get to Yugoslavia?' Lee asked.

'Oh, indeed he did. The required code signal was transmitted by wireless. Murdoch usually gets where he wants to, by hook or by crook. He really ought to be locked up for his own protection. Sixty-one years old, and jumping out of aeroplanes. How ridiculous can you get?'

'So what happens now?'

'Now? Well, I have already issued the most peremptory order for him to return as soon as is practicable.'

'Which he will ignore.'

'I'm afraid that would be in character. Lee, it is essential that Murdoch's presence in Yugoslavia be kept an absolute secret. Our mission was going to be top secret anyway, but to let it be known that we have sent a lieutenant-general, and probably our most famous lieutenant-general, to contact the Serbian guerillas would invest that theatre of war with an importance out of proportion to the rest of our war effort. I shall, of course, inform the President, in the strictest confidence, but no one else outside of us three and Murdoch's personal staff must know; to the world he has been taken ill and is in a secret hospital somewhere in this country. Will you promise to adhere to that?'

'Of course,' she said. 'It might be a good idea to book that hospital bed right away; he's going to need it when I get through with him, after he comes back.'

Churchill grinned. 'After he's been cashiered, you mean.' He stroked his chin. 'Although there's no precedent for cashiering an officially retired general. Lee . . . are you really very angry with him?'

Lee sighed. 'Of course I'm angry with him, Winston. But I'm also very proud of him. He's acting entirely in character, and it was that character I first fell in love with, after the Mad Mullah's men had stopped shooting holes in him. Winston . . . he is going to come back?'

Churchill rested his hand on top of hers as it lay on the desk, fingers clenched. 'Murdoch always comes back, my dear. It is his most enduring characteristic.'

7

El Alamein, 1942

'Gentlemen,' Sir Claude Auchinleck had said at the end of July, standing before a huge map of north-western Africa. 'We have been outgunned and outdriven by Rommel once again. But he has reached the end of his resources, for the time being, and we are being replenished every day. So, here we are, and here we are going to stand until we are ready once more to attack. The plans for this are well laid, and if we have lost Tobruk, the RAF intends to do as much damage as possible to the enemy lines of communication by raiding as far back as Benghazi.

'But we can expect Rommel to come again, because he must, before we are ready. If he cannot beat us, decisively, before our reinforcements arrive, he cannot beat us at all. So this time his attack must fail. I wish to leave no one in any doubt about this. Our position is a strong one, if defended with determination. It is only thirty-five miles from the sea, here at Alamein, to the Quattara Depression. This doesn't give even Rommel too much room for manoeuvre, and those entire thirty-five miles have been sown with mine-fields. I have no doubt that he will find his way through the mines; our objective must be to cut him to pieces when he does.

'Now the key to the position, apart from the presence of the Depression on one flank and the sea on the other, is these three ridges.' He began to touch the map with his wand. 'Way down in the south, overlooking the Depress-ion, is Hunter's Ridge. Approximately twelve miles north-east of Hunter's Ridge, and thus actually behind our position, is the Alam al Halfa Ridge. Both of these are natural defensive positions. But the best position of all is this one, the Ruweisat Ridge.' Again he touched the map.

'You'll see it lies in the very centre of our position, ten miles due south of Alamein Village. It is two hundred feet high, and steep sided.

'Now then, gentlemen, in addition to the front before Alamein, where we are organized in great depths, we are going to hold Ruweisat in strength: I am allotting the First Indian and the Second New Zealand divisions, together with the Seventh Armoured Division. As I propose to hold nothing south of that, not even Hunter's Plateau, you will observe that I am deliberately giving Rommel a good deal of desert to play with. I hope, and believe, that he will do just that. He will never chance his precious panzers on a frontal assault on the Alamein position. He will undoubtedly do as he has done before, and seek to utilize the desert flank. He will find his way through the minefields between Ruweisat and Hunter's, because his probes will tell him that the front there is lightly held. When he is through he will discover that it is not held at all, and he will make one of his great swings to the north. He will not attack Ruweisat, because he will be able to see as well as anyone how strong it is, and how well defended. He will seek to go further east, but because Alam al Halfa is another natural obstacle, he will seek to swing up to the north between Ruweisat and Alam. That is the moment when the Seventh Armoured Division, debouching from Ruweisat in the south, will catch the Afrika Korps in the flank and hopefully bite it off.' He had paused for a last time to look over their faces. 'I have to tell you, gentlemen, that I intend to command this battle personally, and that there will be no retreating from the positions I have outlined. Good day to you.'

That had been in July, and when Rommel had attacked, only a few days later, things had turned out very much as Auchinleck had predicted. Fergus had entered the battle with some misgivings. The fall of Tobruk had had a stunning effect on the already low morale of the army. The fact that Auchinleck himself was to command, and that he had chosen probably the strongest natural position in North Africa to do so, had been encouraging, but against that had been the news that kept seeping up the railway from Alexandria, of wholesale preparations for evacuation, of wholesale panic as well.

And above everything lurked the suspicion in the minds of the armoured units that their tanks and their guns were inferior to those of the Germans. A battle, and a victory, were very badly needed.

There was no victory, but after a week of hard fighting the Afrika Korps had been checked and hurled back. The battle, known as the Battle of El Alamein (and later renamed the First Battle of El Alamein), was fought according to the General's plan, and at the appropriate moment Fergus and the dragoons roared down the slope of Ruweisat, with the rest of the division, indeed catching the panzers in the flanks. There had been another glorious mêlée, with brew-ups in every direction, and as usual, at close quarters the cruisers had done very well. But they had not routed the enemy, who withdrew in good order behind their mobile anti-tank screen, and when the British sought to press home their advantage, the eighty-eights once again took a frightful toll. However, Rommel had realized that this time the Allies intended to hold their positions no matter what it cost, and he was not going to break through without prohibitive losses; he had pulled his troops back out.

The Eighth Army was more relieved than jubilant. If they were at last beginning to feel that they had a position which could be defended, and a commander who was determined to defend it, they also knew there was no way they could take the offensive and beat the enemy while he could destroy their tanks at a ratio of two to one.

Yet Auchinleck had every reason to be satisfied, and to look forward to that accretion of strength, mainly those three hundred Sherman tanks promised by the Americans, which, with their seventy-five millimetre guns and their heavier armour, would be superior to anything possessed by the panzers, and would hopefully neutralize the eighty-eights. Fergus was therefore utterly surprised when, only a week after the battle had been concluded, and while the

171

regiment were still seeing which of their tanks could be restored to working order – and he was still composing letters of condolence – the General appeared in his leaguer, which was still on Ruweisat Ridge.

'At ease, gentlemen,' he told Fergus and Bentley and the padre, Captain Long. 'I just dropped in to say goodbye.'

They stared at him in consternation.

'I am being replaced as GOC Middle East by General Alexander,' Auchinleck explained.

'But why, sir?' Fergus asked.

'I would say because I have not yet beaten Rommel conclusively, which is what the armchair politicians in England consider I should have done.'

'Where are you going?' Bentley asked.

Auchinleck's smile was bitter. 'Oh, I am to command what might be called the Middle East East, as opposed to the Middle East West. That is to say, Iran and Iraq. It is felt that for one man to be responsible for the whole area is too much.'

'But . . . both you and General Wavell were in command of the whole area,' Fergus protested.

'Our masters have changed their minds. One could almost say they have come to their senses. Well, gentlemen, I will repeat the words I used when I took up this command. As I regretted that General Wavell had not been allowed to finish the job he had begun with so much distinction, I regret not being allowed that opportunity myself. But I would like you to know how much pleasure it has given me to command you, and I know that you will give General Alexander the same loyal service as you gave me.'

He shook hands with each of them, and Fergus felt a lump in his throat. 'May we ask who is going to command the Eighth Army, sir?'

Auchinleck smiled. 'Now, that is good news. General Gott is moving up from Thirteenth Corps to the army command. If any man can beat Rommel it will be Strafer Gott.'

That was the first week in August. Within two days General Gott had been killed in an air crash while surveying his extended new command. General Ramsden assumed temporary command, and then the army waited, once again with dwindling morale, uncertain as to what was going to happen next. But at last news was received that their new commanding officer was arriving.

The regiment had been given a few days' rest and relaxation behind Alamein – they could easily regain Ruweisat at the first sign of any new move from Rommel – and although it was early in the morning the troopers were already bathing with a crowd of Australians and South Africans, who were responsible for the line in front of Alamein itself. Their officers were breakfasting, and enjoying mail from England, such of it as was enjoyable.

Harry was missing, believed killed! Fergus had never known his younger brother all that well. He had been close to leaving Wellington when Harry, five years his junior, had first gone there. Then their paths had separated, and if he had looked forward to having his baby brother in the regiment, eventually, that prospect had disappeared with Harry's determination not to become involved in military matters. Fergus remembered being angry about that mainly because he had observed how upset Dad and Mom were. After that there had been no contact between them at all. Harry had even been in Paris, scribbling away at his interminable novels, when the war had started and the BEF, including the regiment, had gone to France – but he had never come up to see his brothers, and when the going had got rough he had escaped to the States. Fergus remembered thinking, jolly good riddance.

Now the poor little blighter, having belatedly tried to make amends by joining the American Marines as that country had been drawn ever closer to war with Japan, had got himself killed. His life, in Fergus's opinion, had been a disaster.

But what was he to say about his own? Annaliese was definitely unhappy. She felt that Lee and Philippa didn't like her. Apparently they were always criticizing her clothes and her habits. It really was an impossible situation for a girl like Liese to be in, he felt. As a German she could hardly go out and get a job, although as the widow of a British officer she could hardly be called an enemy alien. She was having the worst of all worlds, with no prospect of marriage while the war dragged on, and especially while this stalemate continued in Africa. Yet Mom appeared to be behaving as kindly to her as ever, and had even bought her a second-hand motor car so that she could be more mobile – within the range of her petrol coupons. He didn't know who to believe.

On top of all that was a letter from some brigadier in Cairo, informing him that a group of his men had been observed on the streets of the city improperly identified; they had not been wearing their regimental flashes. Would he kindly see that this did not happen again. Ye gods, he thought, what a way to fight a war.

He folded the letters into his breast pocket, looked up, and watched a staff car bouncing along the road to divisional headquarters. Fifteen minutes later a bugle played assembly. Men raced from the sea, hastily dragging on at least their shorts, while their officers looked for orders or the enemy.

A tank – one of his tanks, Fergus realized – had been parked in the centre of an uncluttered area, and towards this the men were being directed. They formed a vast, muttering, uncertain group, totally confused. Their officers felt their way through them and stood in front, to watch the staff car return from Corps Headquarters and draw up beside the tank. In it were several high-ranking officers, including the Acting Army Commander, General Ramsden, his Chief of Staff, General Sir Francis de Guingand, and Thirtieth Corps Commander, General Sir Oliver Leese. But all eyes were upon the somewhat slight figure who was first from the car, and who then climbed up the side of the tank and leaned against the cupola. He looked over his amazed audience, and they looked back; he was very casually dressed – but for the gold braid on his cap it would have been difficult to tell he held any rank higher than captain.

He waited, and slowly the shuffling and muttering ceased. Then he spoke, in a high, clear voice. He tapped the tank on which he stood. 'I have been told that the Germans have better machines than this. I am here to tell you that is utter rubbish. A tank is only as good as the man who commands it. Just as a rifle is only as good as the man who is firing it. No better, and no worse. You . . .' he pointed at them. 'Every man of you, is worth two Germans. Don't forget that.'

He paused to let that sink in, and Fergus suddenly felt the adrenalin begin to flow. Why hadn't he thought of telling his men that? So what if it wasn't true? If they believed it, they would make it come true.

'My name,' the General announced, 'is Montgomery, and I am your new Commander-in-Chief.'

He paused to let that sink in too. 'Let me tell you now,' he went on, 'that standing here today, I am the proudest man in the British Army. The fame of the Eighth Army is renowned wherever fighting men gather together. You are the best soldiers this nation of ours possesses – and that means you are the best soldiers in the world. Your deeds testify to that. You have fought, and won, time and again. Where you have been driven back, you have always recovered to fight, and win, again. Well, you are never going to be driven back again.'

Another pause, and Fergus glanced to left and right. Not a man was moving, but every face seemed to glow; for too long they had received criticism instead of praise.

'My mission,' Montgomery said, 'and yours, is to hit that man Rommel for six, clear out of Africa.'

This time there was a rustle; it was very nearly one of applause.

'It will be difficult,' Montgomery told them. 'He is a capable soldier. All Germans are capable soldiers. It is in their blood. But we are fighting for a cause, and we have a mighty ally on our side: the great Lord above. He will not fail us, and we will not fail him, any more than we will fail each other. As of this moment, the Axis forces in North Africa are doomed. I want every man to be certain of that. Dismissed!'

The men stared at him for a moment longer, then someone – Fergus recognized the voice as belonging to Bert Manly-Smith – shouted, 'Three cheers for the General! Hip-hip . . .'

The hurrahs raced skywards, and Montgomery smiled, and saluted.

'Some speech,' commented the padre.

'Words are cheap,' Bentley pointed out. 'What did you think of him, Fergus?'

'I'd rather see, and hear, him at close quarters before I make a judgement,' Fergus said. 'But he has certainly made the men happy. If he does nothing else, he's worked a bloody miracle there.'

He had his opportunity within twelve hours, as the new General summoned a meeting of all his senior officers, from colonel up, for that same evening. They were assembled from all over the command, in the army headquarters; chairs were provided, but no ashtrays. 'The General cannot abide smoking,' they were told by Guingand, who was organizing things.

This caused a grumble, but a few minutes later they were on their feet and standing to attention as Montgomery entered. He walked through their midst, and was introduced to each man in turn. 'Mackinder,' he remarked, as he shook Fergus's hand. 'I know your father. Good man.' Then he passed on, and took his place on a hastily constructed platform at the far end of the room, where a large blackboard had a huge map of the area pinned to it. Montgomery gave the map only the briefest of glances, before turning to face them, and inviting them to sit.

'I do not propose to start this meeting for two minutes,' he announced. 'In that time, will everyone who has a throat to clear, a nose to blow, a chair to scrape or a shoe to shuffle, kindly do so. There will be no movement and noise, once I commence speaking.'

He paused, and the officers looked at each other in consternation. Then an outbreak of coughing swept the room, while they tried to conceal their grins. The man certainly had a novel approach, Fergus reflected. But there was something irresistible about it.

'Now,' Montgomery said, when he was satisfied that the room was, and would remain, quiet. 'I intend to enlarge upon what I told the men this morning. I have been given a mandate by the Prime Minister: it is to destroy the Axis forces in North Africa. This I intend to do just as quickly as possible. If there is anyone in this room who doubts my intention, or has the slightest reservations that it will be accomplished, he has my permission to withdraw. Now.'

He looked over their faces; no one moved. 'It follows from what I have just said,' he went on, 'that I have given instructions that any and all plans concerning the possibility of a withdrawal to the Delta are to be burned. There will be no withdrawal. I did not come here to defend Alexandria, or Cairo. I came here to defeat Rommel. Nor did I come here to enjoy myself.' He looked around with obvious distaste at the solidly constructed wooden building. 'Officers will as of this moment live in their Armoured Command Vehicles. This is not a seaside holiday camp; it is an army. A British army!

'Now, I have no intention of assuming the offensive until I have got this army up to the strength and morale I require . . .'

There was a faint stirring. They had heard such words before.

Montgomery waited for the noise to subside. 'I have therefore requested two more armoured divisions to be attached to this command, and these, the Forty Fourth and the Tenth, will soon be here. We will also await the arrival of the Sherman tanks, and it will be necessary to train the crews in their use. How will they be used? It is my purpose to create an elite armoured striking force, rather on the lines of the Afrika Korps itself.' He gave a brief smile. 'It does no harm to learn from the enemy, from time to time. But we also have a lot to do. It is my impression that a good part of this army is only half trained. I know there are a considerable number of you who have been in North Africa for some time, and who have fought the enemy more than once. I envy you your experience. But there are even more of you, and of your men, who are replacements and who need to be brought up to the high standards that this army now requires. This training will commence immediately. Incidentally, there is nothing like severe training for restoring morale.

'Now, it will be said that if we delay too long we risk Rommel attacking first. Gentlemen, it is my earnest wish that he will do so, if he will allow me a fortnight to settle in. When he attacks, we will not merely check him, we will defeat him. For this purpose I propose in the main to continue the arrangements made by General Auchinleck, which are admirable. There will be this difference, however: instead of merely luring him on to the Alam al Halfa Ridge, in order to attack him in the flank, I will station the two new armoured divisions there, so he will be met with armour from the front. Now there is a point here I wish to make perfectly clear. I have studied the reports of every battle we have fought against Rommel over the past eighteen months, particularly with regard to his so-called superiority in tanks. It is apparent to me that this superiority has been nothing more than superior tactics, not weapons. He has got a very good anti-tank gun, I will agree. But we have been committing suicide upon it. What have our tactics always been? To launch our tanks against his. What have his been? To demonstrate in order to bring our tanks on to the attack, and then to retire behind a screen of those highly mobile eighty-eights and blow our machines to pieces. Where our armour has been refused, he has simply proceeded to the rear of our positions and blown our administrative units to pieces, thus forcing our retreat.'

He paused to let his analysis sink in, and Fergus scratched his head. Montgomery had never fought a desert battle – yet he had put his finger on a glaring, and repeated, mistake.

'There will therefore be no counter-attacks, and no armoured battles in the future . . . except on our terms. When the panzers attack us, whether they turn for Ruweisat, held by the Seventh Armoured Division, or for

Alam al Halfa, which will be held by the Tenth and Forty-Fourth, they will certainly be met by our armour – but by our armour entrenched and acting as concentrated artillery: we will be able to hit him and he will not be able to hit us. Our armour will not be launched until I am satisfied that he is in full and genuine retreat.

'Now as to his strategy. Will he attack the desert flank? I believe that he will, because that is the only course open to him. As to whether that is the only course open to us, when we launch our own assault, remains to be seen. Thank you, gentlemen. I will inspect each of your brigades and regiments individually, over the next few days. Good evening.'

'I think he means business,' Fergus told his officers. 'He simply can't shoot a line as arrogant as that unless he means to fight.'

He felt more confident than for many a long month. Much as he liked Auchinleck personally – and could tell that it would be very easy to dislike Montgomery in equal proportion – and admired his immense qualities as a fighting soldier, the Auk had never had the gift of projecting quite such a massive personality, or such massive confidence. And Fergus's confidence grew when the regiment was visited by the GOC a few days later, and after the inspection, in which Montgomery as usual found the time to give the troopers every possible encouragement, he was informed that the dragoons were to form part of the elite striking force. 'It cannot be formed until the Shermans arrive, of course,' the General said. 'And before then we shall have some fighting to do. But that's what we're here for.' Then he studied Fergus for a moment. 'I am an infantryman, not a cavalryman,' he said. 'But I know that the coming battle will be won by our armour. I would like one of those berets, Colonel. Would that be possible?'

'Of course, sir.' Fergus signalled Bentley, and a brand-new beret was quickly produced.

'Hm,' the General said, trying it on. 'Very comfortable. Thank you, gentlemen. I will wear this into battle.'

Rommel launched the onslaught they had been expecting on the night of 30–31 August. This was, however, just on the fortnight Montgomery had wanted, and in that time he had made the necessary preparations to receive the enemy. Although he continued to hold the area south of Ruweisat lightly, he had doubled the number of mines sown there, with the result that when the German and Italian infantry moved forward to clear a path, they found the going very much tougher than they had expected. Thus the entire attack was delayed.

It continued, nevertheless, but so heavily were the panzers and the Italian armour strafed by the RAF that the planned encircling movement soon became merely an assault upon the Alam al Halfa Ridge – which indeed gave the battle its name.

This raged for three days, while the rest of the armour stood on the defensive and the Seventh Armoured Division chafed at their inactivity – despite the General's homily on their future tactics – sitting behind the Raqil Depression, within a few miles of the German line of communication. And being ordered to remain there. Montgomery did not deliver his counter-attack until the morning of 3 September, when he reckoned the enemy were withdrawing and had dispatched their anti-tank artillery to the rear; then the Tenth Armoured Division and the Second New Zealand Division were sent south-west against the enemy, and the Seventh Armoured Division was hurled against his communications. For another three days a fierce battle raged, with hardly time to eat and no time to wash or sleep. There were tanks all over the place, guns cracking, caterpillar tracks flying off, men dying, but now the Germans were dying in at least equal numbers: it slowly began to dawn on Fergus that the enemy were short of petrol, as he observed several panzers simply stopped, and able to be hit until they exploded.

The regiment suffered heavy casualties too. To maintain themselves over this hectic period they needed the support group in close attendance, and a marauding German panzer got in amongst the trucks at one stage. The result was chaos, and a good deal of destruction. Fergus's ACV was blown to smithereens, and Major Bentley with it. RSM Butler died as well. But B Squadron, hastily summoned by radio, got back in time to dispose of the intruder, and by 7 September the battle was over, and the Axis forces had withdrawn beyond the minefield.

It had been fierce while it lasted. Axis losses were put at three thousand human casualties, fifty tanks, thirty-five anti-tank guns, and four hundred lorries: the lorries were the most vital. The British had lost less than two thousand men, but sixty-eight tanks. However, even the fact that yet again the German armour had proved its superiority could not dampen the feeling of victory that spread through the Eighth Army. Twice in succession now Rommel had hurled his famous Afrika Korps against them, and twice in succession he had failed to dislodge them; this time he had been driven back in disorder.

In fact, as they learned later, the German Field Marshal – he had been given his baton for taking Tobruk – had actually been too ill to fight the battle, and this may have influenced the result; soon he returned to Germany for treatment. That did not dispel the feeling on the part of the British that they were at last turning the corner. And this feeling was increased with the arrival, at the end of the month, of the Shermans. Huge armoured monsters, yet capable of great speed and endurance, and armed with a seventy-five millimetre gun – the same bore and hitting power as the famous French field artillery in the Great War – it was difficult to see how they could be stopped.

There had, of course, been the usual casualty lists to deal with. By now Fergus had secured the promotion of Allack to Major as his second in command. He also had to replace Butler as RSM, and he had great pleasure in promoting Bert Manly-Smith to that august rank. Bert was not yet twenty-one, but he had seen more service than any other member of the regiment except Fergus himself. 'I reckon I could make general, sir, at this rate,' he said proudly. 'If only my old mum could see me now.'

181

Or my old dad, he thought; the bastard.

The regiment was given a month in which to familiarize themselves with the new machines, for not only were Montgomery's preparations nearly ready, but he did not have as much time to prepare as he might have liked. Only he and Alexander and their closest staff associates were aware that Torch, the Anglo-American invasion of the other end of North Africa, was scheduled for 8 November. These landings would of course take place in French-held territory, nominally at least under the control of the Vichy Government. Thus a great deal would depend upon the attitudes of the French commanders in Algiers and Morocco: would they welcome the Americans as old allies with whom they could work to defeat the common foe? Or would they, out of loyalty to Pétain and, more likely, fear of German reprisals, join hands with the Axis forces in Africa and make the invaders fight for every inch of ground? Clearly the difference in estimated casualties between the first and second eventualities would be enormous.

It was felt that the best way to encourage the French not to oppose the Allied armies would be for the Afrika Korps to have been resoundingly defeated before the landings took place. This meant that the battle for which everyone was waiting had to be fought very shortly. It was, in fact, scheduled for the night of 23–24 October, on which there was a full moon.

Montgomery's plan was essentially simple, as are all good plans. 'Hitherto,' he told his assembled officers, 'every desert battle has been fought the same way, on either side. As the enemy's seaward flank cannot be turned, his desert flank has been attacked. Thus, for example, in both of Rommel's last thrusts, we knew exactly where he would begin, and could make our dispositions accordingly. Our previous successful operations have also begun with a turning of the desert flank. But these have led essentially to a disorganized series of encounters, in which the enemy has been able to use his armour as he chose, and in which our tanks have been drawn on to those massed eighty-eights. What is more, not one of these battles has been decisive, however much territory has been gained as a result of the action. Indeed, as you know to your cost, that extra territory has always turned out to be a liability. The newspapers at home may have loved to scream that we rushed through Tobruk and Benghazi. But we are not here to please the newspapers or to gain showy, but irrelevant, and temporary, successes. We are here to destroy the Afrika Korps and its Italian subsidiaries. That is our only duty. That is the duty we are going to carry out.

'I therefore intend to fight a battle in the oldest of tactical fashions, to destroy the enemy. The main thrust will be here in the north. It will be a crumbling attack of infantry, preceded by bombardment from the air and from our heavy artillery. This attack will be carried out by Thirtieth Corps, General Sir Oliver Leese.' He looked at that officer as he spoke. 'Once the infantry have forced their way through the minefields, and "fixed" the enemy, then Tenth Corps, Lieutenant-General Sir Herbert Lumsden, comprising our two new armoured divisions, will pass through the gap opened by the infantry, and engage and destroy the enemy armour.' Once again he looked at the General involved.

'Operations in the south will be in the care of Thirteenth Corps, Lieutenant-General Sir Brian Horrocks.' He nodded at that officer. 'He will have with him the Forty-Fourth Division, the Thirtieth Division, the Free French, and the Greek brigade. As well,' he added with great deliberation, 'as the Seventh Armoured Division. Now this is the flank on which Rommel will expect our main attack, and he will be even more certain of it because his old enemies the Seventh Armoured Division, the Desert Rats, will be stationed there. So Thirteenth Corps will certainly attack. But this will be our feint.' He watched the disappointment in the faces of the officers of the Seventh Armoured Division. 'Never fear, gentlemen. You will get your chance – when the enemy is in full retreat. Now I want everyone to be clear about one thing. As I say, this is going to be an old-fashioned battle, a slogging match. It may last a week, perhaps ten days. We are going to suffer considerable casualties. Our aim must be to inflict even more casualties on the enemy. We are here to kill Germans. I want every man in this room, and I want every man in this room to make sure that every man in his command, has only one idea when we advance – to kill Germans.' He grinned at them. 'I want even the padres to be keen on killing Germans. They can kill one every day of the week, and two every Sunday.'

There was a roar of delighted applause. Suddenly Fergus knew that they were going to win, that, as Montgomery had said on his first day, Rommel was doomed.

'First time we've ever been in reserve,' Brigadier Campbell grumbled. 'Still . . . we really will be the cavalry this time, out to harry the defeated enemy.'

No one doubted that Montgomery would do as he had said he would, and destroy the Afrika Korps. The preparations for the attack were on a scale Fergus had never seen before, although his father had told him about similar operations in the First War, before, for example, the decisive Battle of Amiens in 1918. All movement of troops and supplies was made at night, and the dumps of petrol and ammunition were carefully concealed by morning, while to convince the enemy that the main attack, as usual, would be coming on the desert flank, elaborate dummy dumps and army headquarters, as well as assemblies of wooden tanks and guns, were established behind the southern front. This was largely the work of Lieutenant Colonel Geoffrey Barkas, who revealed a genius for camouflage.

The actual forces being used in the battle were also on a scale Fergus had not known before. Montgomery commanded an army of very nearly two hundred thousand men, compared with O'Connor's thirty thousand of two years before. He had at his disposal over a thousand tanks, of which two hundred and fifty were the new Shermans, and well over two thousand pieces of artillery, of which more than half were anti-tank weapons. As near as could be determined by reconnaissance, the Axis forces amounted to approximately half of these totals, in all three areas. Only in the air was there anything like equality: seven hundred and fifty RAF planes, of which a third were bombers, were opposed to just under seven hundred of the Luftwaffe.

The Seventh Armoured Division was returned to its old stamping ground just north of the Raqil Depression, behind the mass of the Forty-Fourth Division, and there they waited. For the next fortnight after the General had issued his briefing, the RAF flew nightly sorties, blasting at the enemy's lines of communication: everyone knew that the Afrika Korps was desperately short of petrol, and that of the remaining five-hundred-odd Axis tanks, half were inferior Italian machines. It had also been learned that Rommel had returned to Germany on sick leave.

'Everything comes to he who waits,' Allack commented. 'This time it's all going our way.'

The battle commenced at 2140 on 23 October, under a brilliant moon, when the entire British artillery opened fire on the enemy position. The noise was tremendous, even twenty miles away to the south, and the northern sky was repeatedly cut by the flashes of light, while every so often there would be a bright glow from behind the enemy lines, showing that something had been hit. Waiting by his new ACV with Allack and the three squadron commanders, all wearing greatcoats as the desert chill began to spread, Fergus looked out at the stillness around him with a feeling of awe.

Twenty minutes after the barrage had begun, at 2200, the infantry started their advance in the north, and at the same time Thirteenth Corps infantry moved forward as well. Stand by, came the order to the Armoured Division, and the dragoons manned their tanks. But after that nothing happened. The noise in the north continued to be tremendous, and from snatches of reports and commands over the wireless Fergus gathered that the Australian and New Zealand infantry were advancing steadily, but that in the centre, the Fifty-First Division was meeting un-expected resistance, and taking longer than anticipated to clear a way through the minefield.

The same thing was happening in the south. Although this was only supposed to be a feint, Montgomery was well aware that the Axis right flank was held mainly by Italians, and he clearly had it in mind that should a dramatic breakthrough be effected, the Desert Rats could be loosed in a conventional swing to the right through the enemy minefields. But the night dragged on, and although there was fierce fighting in front of them, no orders came to the armour to advance; the Italians were defending their ground with enormous resolution. Indeed, soon after daybreak orders arrived from GHQ instructing General Horrocks to break off his attack, but to keep the enemy engaged.

'That's that,' Allack said glumly.

'The battle isn't over yet,' Fergus reminded him.

In fact it had hardly begun. Short of fuel and ammunition, outnumbered by two to one, the Germans and Italians continued to fight with enormous courage and determination, and after three days the Allied attack had ground to a halt, with the only positive gains the penetration by the Anzacs of the area just to the north-west of the Miteiriya Ridge, dominated by a hill named Kidney by the Allied soldiers. Montgomery now called a halt to reorganize his forces and prepare for a further advance, and Rommel, hastily recalled from Germany after his replacement, General Stumme, had died of a heart attack, took advantage of this breathing space to launch a counter-attack on Kidney Ridge. The battle flared up again around this position for several days, and to their great relief the Seventh Armoured Division were at last ordered north to reinforce the troops there – operations in the south being at a standstill.

Fergus found preparations being made for a fresh breakthrough just north of the Anzac position, and this time heading for the coast. For this Montgomery intended to use all three of his armoured divisions. The panzers had suffered so heavily in the battle for Kidney Ridge that they had been withdrawn, and the way seemed clear, but Rommel had also weakened his southern front and pulled some Italians up to the northern sector, and once again the fighting was far more severe than expected. Certainly the Italians had never resisted so stoutly in the past; it was not until after the battle that the Allies learned that there was insufficient petrol left for the Axis forces to use their trucks, so that if a withdrawal became necessary, the Italian infantry knew they were going to be left behind.

This renewed attack was code-named Operation Supercharge, and commenced on 2 November. The Second New Zealand Division advanced and cleared a path through the minefield, allowing the armour hopefully to debouch. The Ninth Armoured Brigade led the way, while the First and Seventh Divisions waited anxiously for their chance. Suddenly all hell broke loose in front of them, and the most stricken messages returned from the Brigade: it had run into a battery of the deadly eighty-eights and in little more than fifteen minutes eighty-seven of its hundred tanks had been knocked out.

The heavier machines were then ordered forward. 'Action at last,' Fergus told Captain Brown of A Squadron, with whom he was riding.

Both the First and Seventh Armoured Divisions raced through the gap. The enemy anti-tank battery was quickly overrun – even the eight-eights couldn't make much impression on the Shermans, and the orders were given to swing up to the north.

The remainder of the panzers were waiting for them. 'Tally-ho,' Fergus bawled. There was no time to say the regimental prayer, as the armour surged at each other. As with so many previous tank battles, once it became a mêlée it was impossible to decide what was happening beyond a range of a hundred yards or so, because of the immense dust clouds whipped up by the tracks. Comment flowed across the air, and Fergus gave what orders he could, endeavouring to keep his regiment together and under his control, while the gun traversed left and right, and exploded again and again: range-finding was irrelevant as the enemy were so close.

It was the first time Fergus had used the huge seventy-five millimetre in battle, and the results were stupendous; the panzers were armed only with fifty-millimetre cannon. Yet they fought with all the courage and skill they had always revealed in the past, and although they were finally forced to withdraw, more for lack of petrol, it was later discovered, than by being outgunned, the British armour was itself too short of fuel and ammunition immediately to follow.

But the battle was won. News came in that the Italian infantry were streaming to the rear, and that even the panzers were racing west – what was left of them.

'Now's our chance to finish the job,' Fergus said, drinking tea hastily brewed for him – in half a petrol can – by Sergeant-Major Manly Smith and Trooper Waterman. 'Where the devil are those fuel trucks?'

It was nightfall before the replenishments of fuel and ammunition arrived. The dragoons were glad of the rest after the heat and exhaustion of the battle; they and their machines were all covered in sand and dust and oil. But they were nonetheless desperate to get on after the fleeing enemy, and were distressed when no orders came to advance. They buried their dead, sent their wounded to the rear, and Fergus inspected the tanks – he still commanded over forty – while they listened to the RAF droning overhead.

Montgomery himself arrived the next day. 'Good shooting,' he commented, as he gazed at the burned-out panzers. 'Good shooting.'

'When can we go after them, sir?' Fergus asked.

'When we've regrouped, and got some fuel supplies up. When we advance this time, Mackinder, we aren't coming back.'

That made a good deal of sense, but it was galling to be told to sit tight for another eighteen hours while the infantry moved through the remaining minefields and mopped up such Axis forces as remained. It had been a stupendous victory. Some twenty-five thousand of the enemy were dead, and another thirty thousand prisoners of war – more than half of Rommel's entire army. He had lost three hundred and twenty tanks, and a thousand guns. Once again it was instructive to discover that the British armour had actually lost five hundred tanks, or five to three of the enemy; the losses in Shermans was far less in proportion, but the fact remained that the Germans had again revealed themselves as masters of armoured warfare. The real difference was that the British losses could be replaced, the German couldn't. The same went for aircraft, where again the British had suffered more heavily, ninety-seven to eighty-four. The big catastrophe for the Germans was the losses in men and guns occasioned by their having to retreat; the British lost only a hundred guns and they suffered thirteen thousand personnel casualties.

The pursuit was finally launched on 5 November, headed by the three armoured divisions. The orders were to cut across the desert and try to reach Mersa Matruh before the enemy, and complete his destruction, as the RAF weren't meeting with the success expected. But too much time had been lost, and to make matters more difficult, the following day the skies opened and a torrential downpour limited visibility to a few yards and turned the desert into a lake. The supply trucks couldn't keep up in these circumstances, and the armour soon ran out of petrol, to find themselves stranded in long lines south of the coastal road. Their own inability to move did not stop the Italians from seeking them out, to surrender. It was back to 1940 again, but the infantry had no choice, as they were totally without either food or ammunition. They were sent to the rear.

Fergus took Bert and went up to the road itself to have a look, at a scene of utter destruction. Presumably the Germans had looked at something like this in and around Dunkirk in 1940. But here, in the brilliant sunshine which followed the rain, it appeared more poignant, the abandoned trucks and tanks, the discarded equipment, which included everything from oil drums to radio sets and binoculars, and the exhausted, crushed groups of men, Italian and German, waiting to be taken prisoner.

'Hell, they're only men after all,' Bert commented.

189

'Aren't we all, Sergeant-Major,' Fergus agreed. 'I imagine we looked like that on the beach at Dunkirk.'

Fuel finally arrived, and the armour moved forward again. By now they knew they were not going to catch the remainder of the Afrika Korps; it was a matter of driving them back until Rommel was forced to stand and fight. And that that was going to happen sooner than later was made evident when on the second day of the pursuit news arrived of the landing of more than a hundred thousand British and American troops at Casablanca, Oran and Algiers. Despite fierce resistance from French naval units, the invaders established themselves ashore, and it was evident that the end of the Axis empire in North Africa was in sight. Indeed, a ceasefire between French and Allied forces was agreed as early as 9 November, whereupon Rommel, who had been showing signs of standing at Sidi Barrani on the Egyptian frontier, hastily pulled out and began another headlong retreat, to El Agheila at the other end of Cyrenaica.

The pursuit now began to resemble a road race. The weather having improved, the trucks were able to keep up with the tanks, and the armour careered along the roads, cutting corners wherever possible. Benghazi was recaptured on 20 November, and after a pause to regroup, the advance was resumed, with the result that on 13 December Rommel abandoned El Agheila and withdrew into Tripolitania.

'Well, hallelujah,' Allack commented as they saw the minarets of El Agheila and realized there was no resistance awaiting them. 'How many times have we been here, sir?'

'This is the last,' Fergus promised him. He had no doubt of that now.

Orders arrived to attempt another flanking movement to see if the Afrika Korps could finally be eliminated, but once again Rommel skilfully evaded the pincers. Yet he had to keep withdrawing to the west, and on Christmas Day the Eighth Army entered Sirte. 'Just names on the map, for so long,' Fergus mused.

By now they were learning of the huge battles being

waged on the borders of Tunisia, as the Germans there put up a desperate resistance, and they were anxious to get there to assist their comrades. Early in January they found themselves before Tripoli, where the Afrika Korps were supposed to have dug in. Montgomery now sent a personal message to his weary but still exhilarated troops, calling for a final supreme effort to capture this last Libyan stronghold.

That the Germans were intending to fight for Tripoli, reconnaissance made clear. But nothing now was going to stop the Eighth Army, and they had been reinforced by the Free French striking north across the Sahara from Chad.

'For Christ's sake, sir, this is what it's been all about from the beginning,' Bert told Fergus.

Tripoli was stormed on Saturday 23 January. As far as the Royal Western Dragoon Guards were concerned, that finished the job they had been sent to do more than two savage years before.

8
Yugoslavia, 1943

A twig snapped, and the entire forest seemed to freeze. Certainly the men and the woman perched on the hillside held their breaths, peering into the darkness below them, while the very wind that constantly soughed through the pines seemed to drop.

Murdoch felt a hand on his arm; Kostitch was pointing with his other hand. Kostitch had eyes like a cat.

'How many?' Murdoch whispered. Taught by Private Edmunds, he had picked up sufficient Croat to enable him to carry on a simple conversation.

'One man,' Kostitch replied. 'As instructed.'

'A brave man,' Murdoch observed. 'To come to us, alone.'

'No braver than ourselves,' Kostitch said. 'To wait for him.' He stood up, his tommy gun thrust forward. He was a small man, and looked heavier than he was in his winter gear and with his spare cartridges draped round his neck.

Murdoch followed his example. He too was huddled against the cold, for this early May of 1943 was colder even than February had been. Or Christmas.

It had been an odd Christmas. Yet he had felt, by then, that he was amongst friends. Certainly he had been welcomed in the heat of the previous August, when he and his three staffers had parachuted into these mountains. They had been spotted and seized immediately by the partisans who held this Montenegran-Serbian border. But the suspicion had quickly changed to welcome when they had identified themselves as British. The guerillas had supposed they were the advance guard of an invasion force. They had been disappointed there, but had yet been happy to know that they were recognized in London.

For Murdoch, that had been a bad beginning. His information had been that the Chetniks would be expecting them – but the people amongst whom they had landed knew nothing of that. It had not taken him long to discover that there were several groups operating in the mountains, all ostensibly against the Germans, but also revealing remarkable rivalry, and even hostility, amongst themselves.

It had taken him several weeks to persuade his new friends – or were they really his captors? – to permit him to make contact with General Mikhailovitch, as the guerilla leader styled himself. It was Mikhailovitch who had previously been in touch with London; the group led by Colonel Kostitch – another self-created rank, for Kostitch admitted that he had been only a sergeant in the Yugoslav Army before its destruction by the Germans – were afraid that the General would appropriate Murdoch.

Mikhailovitch had certainly wanted to do that, had insisted on 'entertaining' the General for several weeks. It was Murdoch who had refused to abandon his first friends. If, before he left London, he had assumed that he would operate from Mikhailovitch's headquarters – and certainly would have expected Durden to do so – he had not, as it turned out, liked the General, who had an abstract air about him as though he was continually wrestling with vast problems. No doubt he was, but Murdoch had a job to do, and he wanted it done. He was also disturbed by the absence of any great urgency about operations, or indeed any operations at all, against the Germans.

Mikhailovitch had willingly supplied him with a list of his requirements. It had been as long as his arm, and quite a few of the items had been absurd. He had wanted tanks and aircraft and artillery, with which he claimed he could drive the enemy out of Yugoslavia. But the Yugoslav Army had possessed tanks and aircraft and guns, and still been shattered in a couple of days. Anyway, such items could not possibly be dropped from an aircraft. When Murdoch made these points, Mikhailovitch had noticeably cooled towards him.

He had cooled even further when Murdoch had told him

that part of his mission was to contact the commanding officer of the German garrison in Sarejevo, General Paul von Reger. Mikhailovitch had clearly never heard of General Sir Murdoch Mackinder, and he could hardly suspect a British general of treachery, but he wanted no part of negotiations with the Germans – he said. When Murdoch had insisted that he was going to carry out his orders, no matter what hindrances were put in his way, Mikhailovitch had been happy to let him go back to Colonel Kostitch's group.

Kostitch had himself been doubtful, but by then he had realized that Murdoch was a fighting soldier par excellence, and he was willing to be led. He and his following, which numbered some seventy-five men, women and children, had been subjected to one of the periodical German sweeps into the mountains soon after Murdoch's return from the north, in late October. Armoured cars had rattled along the road through the valleys, men had leapt out armed with machine guns as well as rifles, and bullets had scythed into the trees as the grey-clad figures had moved up the slopes.

They had, disturbingly, known exactly where to make their attack. The guerillas had watched them coming, and had been aghast when the Germans had deployed immediately beneath their current headquarters. If the men would have had little difficulty in melting away into the upper slopes, their wives and families and livestock could not be moved so quickly. It was then that Murdoch had proved himself, taking command of twenty men, and checking the German rush with a series of brilliant little delaying actions, while the rest of the partisans had rounded up their campfollowers and seen them to safety. Even so it had been a disaster. Most of the goats had been lost, and several men. Sergeant Evans had died in that brief battle. Yet the group had been saved, and would grow again. And Murdoch had become a hero in their eyes. After that, they would do whatever he wished.

Not less had Murdoch grown to respect them. He had come to Yugoslavia with at least an equal amount of suspicion,

194

and it had been heightened by their first contact. Here were indeed bearded, badly dressed bandits. But their weapons were new and clean; taken from the Germans, Kostitch proudly explained.

Murdoch had been more than ever concerned for Private Edmunds's safety, in the midst of such an uncouth, and desperate, fighting force. But there had been nothing to fear. The partisans expected a man to have a mate for his sleeping bag or blanket, if only to keep warm: but no woman was made to sleep with anyone she wouldn't accept. If the Englishwoman was a constant source of interest – there was no privacy in the guerilla encampment and Private Edmunds had different habits to the Serbian women, who were as interested in her ablutions as their menfolk – no one questioned her right to sleep alone, any more than they questioned Murdoch's decision to do likewise. Once Kostitch had realized that Edmunds was not Murdoch's own bedmate, he had introduced him to a buxom young woman and indicated that she had recently been widowed and needed a man. Murdoch had declined with thanks, and she had been accepted by Sergeant Evans, with some apologies. Now she was a widow again.

Murdoch had also been impressed by the guerillas' fighting qualities, at least when resolutely led. They undoubtedly had an inferiority complex as regards the Germans, but this was hardly surprising: the British Army in Africa had apparently had an inferiority complex regarding the Germans until the Battle of El Alamein, news of which arrived just before Christmas and greatly enhanced his reputation. He knew it was going to take a good while to overcome this in Yugoslavia, because the Germans had the more men, the better weapons, the better training and discipline, and they had uniforms, which are always a great help to morale. They also had adequate medical supplies. He discerned that, as far as the guerillas were concerned, these had to be his first objectives.

He could contact Cyprus by the wireless equipment he had brought with him. Evans had been the telegrapher, and thus his loss had been more than merely a tragic one. But

Captain Markham had also had some training with radio, and was able to take over. Thus Murdoch could send out his request for more and better weapons and ammunition, clothing and medicine. Sending and receiving were two different things, however. For one thing, as the Germans undoubtedly monitored his calls – even if he did not think they had broken his code – the wireless had to be sparingly used; he allowed himself only one call a month, and as soon as it had been made, the entire group had to move, fairly rapidly, to a new location. This did not make the wireless very popular with the guerillas. For another, the dropping of goods into the mountains was no easy matter, at least, where the parcels could be found and not simply disintegrate. However, a trickle of supplies had started to reach them.

With the first batch had come a command from the Prime Minister for Murdoch himself to return home. Churchill was even prepared to land an aircraft wherever flat ground could be found, in order to pick up his errant hero. Murdoch replied that he would obey as soon as he could, but that at the moment it was impossible for him to leave.

This was only partly untrue. He still had not made contact with Paul, and he knew he was the only person who could do so with any hope of success. But equally, he was enjoying himself too much.

It was some fourteen years since he had campaigned, in mountainous country, against a brutal and ruthless foe. And indeed, to compare the Mahsuds with the Germans was like comparing a pussycat to a tiger. The Germans did not mutilate their prisoners – at least visibly – but they did just about everything else; and they were far tougher fighting men. The odd thing was that the partisans did wish to mutilate *their* enemies, in revenge for what had happened to their country, their families and friends. How odd is life, Murdoch mused; the wheel had certainly turned full circle, and now he was the desperate guerilla, fighting against the forces of an occupying country. How Chand Bibi must be laughing in hell. Where he had sent her.

He had, in fact, been somewhat appalled the first time he

had seen action with the partisans. It had been just before Christmas, and just after the first drop had replenished their store of arms and ammunition, which had suffered a heavy depletion during the escape from the German raid. The arms had, of course, been intended for the entire guerilla army but Kostitch had insisted upon keeping this first load. He had been delighted with the new weapons, and had been anxious to use them. Murdoch had, through one of the guerillas' cousins, who lived in Sarajevo and claimed to be in contact with the Germans – had he been the one to give away the location of their headquarters? This uncertainty as to whom to trust had been something else new to Murdoch, brought up in the traditions of comradeship that obtained in the British Army – begun a tentative negotiation with Paul. He had not, of course, dared reveal his true identity. But he had allowed it to be known that a British agent sought a meeting with the German general providing adequate safe conducts could be exchanged. He had thus been a little hesitant about starting anything which might imperil his plans. On the other hand, no reply had been received to his overture, and it might just be useful to stir Paul up. Thus he had agreed, especially when the colonel informed him that he had learned that a truck convoy was going to pass along the road through a valley a few miles to their west, making for one of the German hill fortresses.

'Christmas puddings for the Germans,' Kostitch had grinned. 'Why should we not eat them ourselves?'

Murdoch had still been learning this game; it had never been taught at Staff College or Sandhurst, at least in his day. Thus he was content to play a subordinate role; but he had no intention of missing the opportunity to see the partisans in action.

The guerillas had left their encampment the night prior to the expected convoy, and made their way over the mountains, forty-seven heavily armed men; Private Edmunds had wanted to accompany them, but Murdoch had refused to allow it.

They had reached the road well before dawn, and chosen their position carefully, where there were already patches in the rutted surface. Two of these patches, some two hundred yards apart, had been dug up, and explosives planted, their leads taken away into the trees; the surface had been covered again. Then the guerillas had lain beside their weapons, and waited. It was the most primitive plan Murdoch had ever seen, and for that reason he presumed it might work. Everything depended on how heavily the convoy was guarded.

Daylight came, and found them huddled and frozen; the temperature had dipped below zero during the night. The sun warmed them a little, but they had no breakfast, not even a cup of coffee. 'We will breakfast off the Germans,' Kostitch growled.

Murdoch and Markham rubbed their hands together and jogged on the spot to restore their circulation. Minutes later they saw a column of smoke rising from the next mountain. It might have been a farmer burning rubbish. But there was no farm up there.

'Stand by,' Kostitch told his men. He himself took his place by the plunger to explode the charges; his two machine-gun teams lay down, one on either side of the road. His tommy gunners crawled behind the nearest trees. Murdoch and Markham were also armed with tommy guns, in addition to their service revolvers, and joined them. It was the first time in more years than he could remember that Murdoch had gone into a limited action such as this under the command of someone else; he felt somewhat breathless.

Despite the morning cold they kept absolutely still as the noise of the trucks seeped through the valley towards them. Then the lead vehicle appeared; an armoured car. Behind it was an open truckload of soldiers, and behind them again four trucks with flaps down. It could be a trap, Murdoch thought, and each of those trucks be filled with machine guns. But Kostitch was a cautious man, and no one had been allowed to leave the encampment since the plan had been devised. Besides, the convoy was certainly heavily enough protected in any event: behind the supply trucks were another troop carrier and another armoured car. That last would be the problem.

Murdoch glanced at Kostitch to see if he would think better of the idea; there had to be at least sixty Germans in the convoy, as well as the two armoured cars. But Kostitch merely gave him a thumbs-up sign and a quick grin.

The first armoured car reached the first repair in the road and drove over it. Now Murdoch was definitely holding his breath. He could see the faces of the German soldiers, laughing and talking; he could see the cabs of the trucks, and felt his heart constrict: in one at least there was a woman.

Again he glanced at Kostitch, but now the Colonel was concentrating. The leading armoured car was just reaching the second road repair. Murdoch looked down the column; the first repair was between the last supply truck and the second troop carrier. He looked back at Kostitch, saw his arms go down.

Columns of mud and earth shot upwards as the explosions echoed through the valleys, taking with them pieces of metal, and of men. The first armoured car had been blown on to its side, although its stout sides and bottom had resisted the dynamite very well; its machine guns were however uselessly pointing at the sky. Further back, the rear had been blown off of the last supply truck, which stood at a crazy angle, while the engine had equally been blown off the troop carrier, which had burst into flames. Men hastily leapt from it, straight into a hail of tommy-gun fire, which scattered them like toys. The first machine gun was directed at the front troop carrier, and here too the execution was catastrophic.

The second machine gun was aimed at the armoured car. This was a distracting operation, as the bullets merely clanged off the armour, while the German machine guns turned and sent a stream of lead back into the trees. But it served its purpose as one of the guerillas, specially detailed, was enabled to leave the trees behind the car, run up to it, climb up, and drop a grenade through the hatch. The explosion was shattering, and flames belched from the windows.

All of this Murdoch noted almost subconsciously, for he was leaning against his tree, his tommy gun against his shoulder, and firing at the cabs of the supply trucks. He desperately wanted to kill that woman, for her own good, but at the same time he could not risk hitting the petrol tank of the lorry, and losing what was inside. But the brief battle was already over. The Germans had been too surprised and the partisans' shooting too accurate and sustained. Now grey-clad men either writhed on the ground in agony where they did not already lie still, or raised their hands into the air in surrender. Others climbed from the cabs of the supply truck. The first armoured car continued to lie helplessly on its side, and now someone opened the hatch and shouted 'Kamerad!' But one of the guerillas ran forward, thrust a grenade into the opening, and slammed the hatch shut again. A moment later the men inside were dead.

Those on the road now realized their mistake. But it was too late. They were already surrounded by the excited partisans, who stripped them of their weapons and their clothing under the watchful guns of their companions. Others raided the trucks, and began exploring the cases of food.

Others dragged the woman from where she had been crouching on the floor of the truck. She wore a grey-green uniform tunic and skirt, and a forage cap. She was no longer laughing. She did not strike Murdoch as being terribly attractive, being mousily blonde and somewhat over-weight; besides, her terror made her ugly, as she begged her captors in German.

'What are you going to do with these people?' Murdoch asked Kostitch.

The Colonel grinned. 'We cannot take prisoners, General. Besides, they do not take us prisoner.'

'Sir,' Markham said urgently.

The men were stripping the woman; she had fallen to a kneeling position, but they were still tearing her clothing away, as small boys might have torn the wrapping paper from a toffee. She shrieked and wept, and her pale flesh was turning blue with cold.

'Is that necessary?' Murdoch asked Kostitch.

'It is how they treat our women. You can have her first, if you wish, General.'

'Thank you, no,' Murdoch said, and reminded himself that this was what would have happened to Monique Deschards, before she too was executed. Only Monique would also have been tortured. He turned away, watched the German men being herded into a group. One protested, and was jabbed in the belly with his own bayonet. Blood spurted, and he fell to his knees, while the machine guns opened fire again. The Germans, stripped to their underwear, turned to run, and met more bullets, hailing at them. White flowed into red, and they fell in heaps. The last man had not ceased breathing when they were being dragged off the road.

By that time there was a regular queue at the woman. She had stopped screaming and begging, and only moaned and gasped as each man took his turn.

'It is a great victory,' Kostitch said. 'And we have lost only two men. You have brought us much good fortune, General. As you brought us the arms we need to win. Now we have German arms as well. Come along,' he shouted at his men. 'Enough of that. We must get these trucks closer to home.' He climbed behind the wheel of the first truck himself, grinning out through the bullet-shattered windscreen. 'You ride with me, eh, General? We shall have a good Christmas.'

Murdoch looked at the woman. As the men had finished with her, someone had thrust a bayonet through her throat, pinning her naked body to the ground. She choked, and bled, and cut her fingers on the blade. And died.

'By God, General,' Markham had muttered. 'Thank God you didn't let Edmunds come. We seem to have fallen amongst wolves here.'

'It takes wolves to beat wolves,' Murdoch reminded him, and climbed up to sit beside Kostitch.

★

Thus, as the Colonel had promised, they had had a good Christmas. It had been slightly delayed, as the hills to the west had been swarming with German soldiers out to avenge their comrades, and for that time they had literally to hibernate, in a cavern high in the mountain, huddled together for warmth as it was snowing outside and they dared not light a fire. But eventually the Germans had gone home and the partisans had been able to celebrate their victory.

'It sounds tremendous, sir,' Edmunds said. 'I wish I had been there.'

'Well, don't,' Murdoch told her. 'It was pretty grim. These people don't take prisoners.'

'Oh,' she said.

'And there was . . .' Markham began.

'Forget it,' Murdoch told him, as he ate his Christmas pudding.

And thought of home. Of Lee. He thought of her regularly; she alone was on his conscience. But they would have been separated had he been given the fighting command he wanted, and she would understand.

And perhaps at last he might be close to achieving something. There had been little activity during January and February; it had simply been too cold, and movement in the snow left too easily discernible tracks for the aircraft which often swooped low over the mountains in an effort to spot the guerillas' location. Yet the RAF transports had continued their monthly drops.

Mikailovitch had himself come for the second of these, the news of Kostitch's successful foray having spread through the mountains. 'One convoy,' he remarked contemptuously. 'Were we to be given enough weapons we would do better than that.'

'Just be thankful for what you have,' Murdoch said, and to Kostitch's disgust allowed the Chetnik General to take all the new gear.

The following month another group of men had appeared. 'Do not deal with these, General,' Kostitch warned. 'They are Communists. They are hiding further to the south, in Montenegro. They are not of our kind.'

'If they are fighting the Germans, they are of our kind,' Murdoch pointed out.

'They are destroyers of all that is good in life,' Kostitch argued. 'Worse than the Germans. Do you not know that people say, the Nazis will take your bodies, but the Communists will take your souls? I know the leader of these men. His name is Broz. He has been a Communist all his life. He fought with the Communists in Spain, and he has been trained in Russia. Now he calls himself Marshal Tito. Not general, mind you. Marshal! Ha! That is because he dreams of ruling Yugoslavia after the war.'

'Well, that is something we must keep an eye on,' Murdoch agreed. 'But Colonel, my mission is to arm and equip every man in this country who is willing to fight the Germans. Communist Russia is our ally in this struggle. Therefore Communist Yugoslavs are also our allies.' He gave the men the guns and ammunition, and they disappeared into the trees.

In between drops, the partisans had spent most of their time in their caves, trying desperately to avoid frostbite. Before long Edmunds had moved into Markham's sleeping bag, and indeed Murdoch was the only one of them who slept alone. He would then have welcomed a companion, but his apparent uninterest in sex had been noted, and he felt it was important to preserve some distance between himself and the guerillas. So he thought of Lee instead. Or of Monique Deschards. He felt he had at last done something to avenge her.

He had heard little of Mikailovitch since Christmas; the Chetnik leader had apparently decided that the British mission was not up to much. Nor had the Communists contacted them again. But Murdoch was content with this also: he wished to keep a low profile until he had contacted Paul.

For which purpose he had continued to put out feelers, and at last he was being rewarded. The cousin in Sarajevo had met with a positive response, thus he and Kostitch, and their men, and Private Edmunds – for her fluent German – were waiting on this snow-covered hillside. And a German was approaching.

A wolf, into a den of wolves. Kostitch had given safe conduct, but would he be able to hold his men?

The German had come by car, which was parked on the road in the valley; the partisans had sighed as they had watched it, alone, in their mountains. Now the man climbed the hill as he had been instructed to do, and stopped, as he realized he was surrounded. He spoke in German, and Edmunds translated. 'He wishes to speak with the English officer,' she said.

Murdoch stepped out into the pale moonlight. The German wore the uniform of an officer beneath his greatcoat, and now he saluted. Murdoch did likewise.

'General von Reger is willing to meet with you,' Edmunds interpreted. 'He is waiting for you now. He has promised you safe conduct to and from the meeting.'

'He is in the car?'

Edmunds spoke with the officer. 'No, at a place some miles from here. It is a private place. You are to accompany this man, sir.'

Murdoch nodded.

'I will come with you, sir,' Edmunds said. 'You will need a translator.'

'General von Reger speaks perfect English,' Murdoch told her.

'You have to get to the General, sir,' Edmunds said patiently. 'I am here because I speak German.'

She had a point. And she was desperate to work with the famous man with whom she had so oddly been thrown together.

'What is happening?' Kostitch asked.

Murdoch told him.

'I do not like it,' Kostitch said. 'It is impossible to trust these people.'

'They have trusted us,' Murdoch pointed out. 'And I am sure I can trust General von Reger. I have met him before the war.'

'I do not like it,' Kostitch said again.

'I will be back by dawn,' Murdoch promised him. 'If anything happens to me, Captain Markham will continue to act as your liaison with our people. Understood, Markham?'

'Yes, sir.' Markham shook hands with Edmunds and looked as if he wanted to do more.

'For heaven's sake,' Murdoch told them. 'Fall out for five minutes.'

Markham and Edmunds withdrew into the trees, while the German waited patiently, eyeing the partisans, who stared at him.

Edmunds returned, and she and Murdoch went down the hill. There was a driver in the car, but no one else. Murdoch and Edmunds got into the back of the Mercedes, and the officer sat in the front. The car began to move, slowly along the slippery road. 'Ask him how far,' Murdoch told Edmunds.

'A few miles,' she interpreted.

'Scared?' he asked.

'Not with you, sir.'

He squeezed her hand. 'If we're captured, we just take off our coats. We're both in uniform. The worst they can do to us is send us off to a prison camp in Germany. But I am sure it is going to be all right.'

He felt pleasantly excited, at the thought of seeing Paul again. Having lost two of his sons, he was suddenly realizing how much he valued the remaining two – even the illegitimate one. Who was also an enemy! But that was a whim of Fate. Paul would be forty-two, now. And clearly a man destined for high command – except that there would be no command left at all, when Germany had lost the war. But if Paul was one of those who cooperated in the elimination of Hitler before the final defeat, it might be possible to make something of his life, after all.

They drove into a village, where there were a great number of German soldiers, heavily armed, and prepared for action; machine guns were emplaced and even some mortars. The swastika flag drooped from the pole above the main building – once an inn, Murdoch estimated – and there were several cars as well as trucks parked in the little square before it. Of any previous inhabitants there was no trace.

The car came to a halt before the shallow steps, and the officer opened the door for Murdoch and Edmunds. They got out, and the two soldiers beside the door presented arms. 'The natives appear to be friendly,' Murdoch said.

The officer opened the door for them, and they went inside. 'He says the General is waiting for you upstairs,' Edmunds translated. 'But I am to stay here.'

Murdoch nodded. 'The General speaks perfect English,' he reminded her. And the meeting would necessarily have to be a very private one, for a variety of reasons. 'I'll try not to be too long.'

He went up the stairs behind the officer, who opened a door for him, clicked his heels, and saluted. And was dismissed by the man standing behind the desk. The officer waited for Murdoch to enter, then closed the door on him.

Murdoch stared at Paul von Reger. They had not seen each other for nearly three years, but he did not think either of them had changed, except that Paul now wore the uniform of a general instead of a colonel, and possibly there were a few more streaks of grey in his own black hair. As had happened the last time, Paul did not look pleased to see his father.

'I saw you get out of the car,' he said in English. 'Are you mad?'

'I hope not.'

'You, here in Yugoslavia, fighting with those thugs in the mountains, who rape and murder helpless women?'

'Those thugs seem to think there are more raping, murdering, thugs in the towns than in the mountains, Paul,' Murdoch said. 'Will you not shake my hand?'

'No,' Paul said, and sat down behind the desk. 'You are seriously compromising us both.'

'I don't see how. No one knows our relationship. And it is important that I speak with you.'

'Then speak,' Paul said. 'And quickly. Then leave, while you still can.'

Murdoch sat down. 'You must realize that Germany has lost the war, Paul.'

'Indeed?'

'You have been crushed at Stalingrad, defeated in North Africa. Soon there will be an invasion of Europe itself. You cannot hope to resist the combined armies of Britain, the United States and Russia. You can hope for nothing from Japan, which is also on the road to defeat, and even less from Italy. What have you got to go on fighting for?'

'So you would have us surrender. I believe you have been in Yugoslavia several months. You are out of touch with the news, Father. Perhaps you have not heard that Churchill and Roosevelt have announced that they will accept only unconditional surrender.'

'I did hear that. But I am sure they mean unconditional surrender from a Germany ruled by the Nazi Party. Were that party to be replaced by a more acceptable government, I am sure the Allies would be willing to call a halt.'

'Replaced? You seem to forget that I am a member of the Nazi Party myself.'

'I suspect you found yourself in it before you had time to think. Now I am asking you to do that, Paul.'

'To be a traitor.'

'To be a patriot. Surely it is more treacherous to watch your country sliding into an abyss, and do nothing about it? When you *could* do something about it.'

'Into the abyss,' Paul repeated. 'The abyss is already there, Father. It is called Soviet Russia. It is an abyss which is attempting to swallow all of Europe. And it will do so, unless we continue to fight it. Why do you not go home, and tell Roosevelt and Churchill that instead of fighting us, they should be fighting with us against the Communists?'

How odd, Murdoch thought, that this self-confessed Nazi and Colonel Kostitch really have exactly the same point of view. 'Perhaps that too could be achieved,' he said. 'Were you and your associates to replace Hitler.'

'I swore an oath to the Fuehrer, as supreme commander

of the German Army, Father. I will not break that oath. I am disappointed that you should think I might.'

They gazed at each other, Murdoch searching for some sign of weakness in his son's face, but Paul remained utterly cold. 'Then God have mercy on your soul,' Murdoch said. 'And the soul of everyone in Germany.'

Paul stood up. 'We shall look after our own souls, Father. Now, I will have my driver return you to your bandit friends. But if you will take my advice, you will leave Yugoslavia, as clandestinely as you came, and as quickly as possible. I am under orders to extirpate those vermin in the hills. And I shall do so. If you are with them, I will not be able to save your life.'

'I'll bear that in mind,' Murdoch said.

Paul saluted him. 'Heil Hitler! And goodbye, Father. We shall not meet again.'

Murdoch saluted in turn, and Paul went in front of him to the door. He opened it, and frowned at the two men standing there. They wore civilian clothes beneath belted topcoats, and slouch hats. 'Have you finished your private conversation, Herr General?' asked one, in English, and looked at Murdoch. 'That is your language, is it not?'

Murdoch looked at Paul.

'It is his language, yes,' Paul said.

'And I assume he is under arrest?'

'He is not under arrest. He came here under a safe conduct to discuss certain matters.'

'What matters?'

'Military matters, Herr Roebel. Nothing to do with the Gestapo. Our discussion is now terminated, and General Mackinder is now leaving.'

'General Mackinder,' the man called Roebel remarked. 'A famous name. You are fighting with the partisans, General Mackinder?'

'I am the head of a British military mission to Yugoslavia,' Murdoch said carefully.

'You are a spy, and a guerilla. On both counts you will be shot.'

208

'I am a British officer, in uniform,' Murdoch told him. 'I cannot be a spy.'

'But you are fighting with guerillas. They are not soldiers.'

'They consider themselves as soldiers.'

'They may consider themselves what they like. We know differently. If you wish to save your neck, General, you will agree to lead us to where we can find these scum. Then it might be possible to treat you as a prisoner of war.'

Murdoch looked at Paul; he was not conscious of any fear, only tension.

'I cannot permit this,' Paul said. 'I gave General Mackinder my personal safe conduct.'

'The matter is out of your hands, Herr General,' Roebel told him. 'The moment I discovered that you were entertaining a British officer, I telephoned Berlin. I spoke to Reichsfuehrer Himmler himself. He has authorized me to take charge of the prisoner, and deal with him as I think fit.'

'I do not believe you,' Paul snapped.

Roebel walked across the office and picked up the phone. 'The Reichsfuehrer is expecting a call from you.'

Paul stared at him, and some of the colour left his face; it was obvious that the Gestapo officer was not bluffing. Then he looked at Murdoch. He had saved his father from imprisonment once before, in Holland. It was too much to hope that he would take the risk again. 'He is not to be harmed,' he said.

Roebel grinned. 'I would not harm such a distinguished officer; what eventually happens to him is up to the Reichsfuehrer. I am sure I can discover what I wish to know from his secretary.'

'Where is Private Edmunds?' Murdoch snapped.

'Under arrest. As are you.' He spoke in German to his aide, who immediately produced a pair of handcuffs.

'I am sure that will not be necessary,' Paul protested. 'General Mackinder will give you his word that he will not try to escape.'

'I don't think I will do that, General,' Murdoch said.

'I would not accept it in any event,' Roebel said.

Murdoch's arms were pulled behind his back, and the handcuffs snapped on his wrists.

'I am sorry about this, General,' Paul said. 'And I wish to apologize. I will telephone my superiors immediately and endeavour to have my safe conduct honoured.'

'Thank you,' Murdoch said. But he didn't have too much hope of that. His venture had turned out badly, as Kostitch had feared it would. Now his business must be to ensure that Edmunds was not harmed in any way; he didn't like Roebel's threat.

She was waiting downstairs, also handcuffed. Her coat had been taken away, and her uniform was somewhat dishevelled, but she managed a smile, although her face was pale.

'Have they harmed you?' Murdoch asked.

'I think they were searching me, sir,' she said.

'The bastards.' He turned to Roebel. 'This lady is a British soldier, just as I am. If you harm her in any way, you will answer for it.'

'Oh, indeed I shall,' Roebel agreed. 'To my superiors.' He gave an order, and Murdoch and Edmunds were taken outside. Without their coats it was very cold, and the girl shuddered. There was a van standing in the yard, with its engine running. The door at the back was opened, and their guard, who had been joined by two other plain-clothes men, indicated that they were to get in. Murdoch went first, without difficulty, but Edmunds tripped, and was given a push which hurled her to the floor, gasping, her lip cut where her face had banged. His wrists secured, Murdoch could do nothing to help her. Nor was cursing and swearing going to help, he knew. It was necessary to keep as cool as he had always been, whether in the hands of a Boer Commando or the Mahsuds, and wait, and watch, and be patient – but deadly when the time came.

Two of the Gestapo men got into the van with them, and then they waited for the arrival of Roebel. They made no effort to help Edmunds get up, and when, panting and with a trickle of tears rolling from her eyes, she struggled to her knees, one of them put his foot on her shoulder and pushed her over again. She fell down and now did begin to weep.

'Hold on,' Murdoch told her. 'Just hold on.'

They waited for nearly half an hour, then the door opened again and Roebel got in. Immediately the van began to move.

'Your men have been ill treating Private Edmunds,' Murdoch told him. 'I am going to hold you responsible for that.'

Roebel grinned at him. 'I have been speaking with the Reichsfuehrer, telling him who I have captured. He is delighted. Do you know that you are the most senior Allied officer to be taken thus far? He is going to have you filmed when we get to Berlin.'

'I was talking about my interpreter,' Murdoch said coldly. Winston is going to flip his lid, he thought.

'It is she who is going to have to do the talking,' Roebel said, and gave an order. The two detectives each seized one of Edmunds's arms and dragged her to her knees, in front of Roebel. '*You* are not going to Berlin, Fraülein,' he told her. 'You are going to stay here, with us. And show us how to reach your friends, eh?'

Edmunds looked at Murdoch.

'You will be committing a crime, which will be remembered,' Murdoch told Roebel.

He grinned. 'Then let me give you something to remember,' he said. 'You, Fraülein, if you wish to save your skin . . .' he paused, to slide his hand round the line of Edmunds's jaw and into her hair. 'You will tell us exactly where your friends are. And you will tell us how to find this man who calls himself Marshal Tito. He is the one we want. You will tell us these things.'

Edmunds gasped.

'Speak,' Roebel ordered.

'I . . . I do not know where Marshal Tito is,' the girl said.

'You are lying. But it is no matter. I know how to make little girls tell the truth.' He slapped her face, four times, to and fro. Blood flew from her already split lip, and tears rushed from her eyes. Her body was racked by a huge sob.

Keeping still required an enormous effort. But Murdoch knew that movement would be futile and self-defeating. He could only kick, once. Then he too would be beaten up, without having accomplished anything. If he felt, in himself, as fit as ever, he was well aware that he was no longer a young man, that his bones were more brittle than they had once been, and thus that if he were to be injured, he would become a complete liability, and for a very long time.

The rest of the journey was a nightmare, as Roebel tormented the girl, sexually, and encouraged his men to do the same. They tore open her battledress blouse to put their hands inside and squeeze and pull her breasts, and they put their hands between her legs, again to squeeze and poke. Edmunds sobbed, her shoulders shaking, while Murdoch's hands and wrists became numb and he wished his brain could also go to sleep.

But at last they stopped for the night at another German-controlled village. Here they were separated, Murdoch being taken to the officers' quarters, while Edmunds was dragged off to the cells. Murdoch's wrists were released to enable him to shave and to eat, but all the time an armed guard was at his shoulder. In fact, he did not wish to eat, but knew he had to force something down to keep up his strength. 'What are you doing to Private Edmunds now?' he asked Roebel.

'Amusing ourselves,' the detective said blandly. 'She will remain here. With me. I will get what I want out of her before she dies. But you will continue your journey tomorrow. There is a plane waiting at Belgrade. You will be in Germany in two days' time.'

'And one day I will come back, and seek you out, and kill you,' Murdoch told him.

'One day may be too long for you, General. You are becoming an old man. I do not fear your one day.'

Murdoch could not help but wonder if he was right. Because suddenly he was feeling very old. It was fourteen years since he had campaigned amongst the Mahsuds, and seen men, and women, so horribly mistreated. Only fourteen years. But fourteen years in which he had lived in an atmosphere of civilization, and good feeling. Perhaps he had never supposed there could be anything else, in Europe. But this war was breaking civilization down, reducing men, and women, to the beasts they essentially were. It was a depressing thought.

And even more depressing was the thought that he might *not* be here to see it finished. He could not imagine life in a prisoner of war camp. But he knew it was going to be hard. Too hard for an old gentleman of sixty-two? He squared his shoulders on the narrow bed to which he was again handcuffed. He would survive, because he had a lot to do. A lot to avenge. The list began with Jennie Manly-Smith and stretched through two of his sons and Monique Deschards to that poor, frightened girl who was about to be tortured to death.

He had not expected to sleep, but was far more exhausted – emotionally even more than physically – than he had realized. He was surprised to be awakened by the cuffs being released from the bed, told to dress, and given some coffee and black bread for breakfast. Three cars, two of them filled with soldiers, were waiting for him, as was Roebel.

'I shall say goodbye, Herr General,' he said. 'I have a lot to do, eh, with your private?'

Murdoch merely looked at him, then got into the car, and the motorcade moved off. It was a crisp, cold morning, and if there was no snow on the road, it lay on the hills to either side. His guards apparently spoke no English. Neither did they seem the least brutal or even hostile; indeed, when they stopped for coffee about ten, the Lieutenant in charge took away the handcuffs. 'Gestapo,' he remarked contemptuously. 'Nein.'

Murdoch slapped his hands together and restored some circulation. But he kept thinking of what might be happening back in that command post.

They drove on, and came upon a stream of bullock carts, proceeding slowly along the side of the road. Horns blared, and the carts edged more to the side to give the cars room to pass. But they had to slow down, and were moving abreast of the carts, and the men sitting above the bulls, when the leading cart suddenly slewed across the road. The first car braked, but still hit it. The second, in which Murdoch was sitting, ran into the first. The third stopped short, and went into reverse, but the last bullock cart had also slewed sideways, completely blocking the road.

'Lie down, General!' someone bellowed in English.

Murdoch threw himself on the floor of the car as the shooting began. The men around him attempted to return fire, and one of them grasped Murdoch's shoulders to pull him back up, perhaps to use as protection. Murdoch struck him a swinging blow with the edge of his hand, so happy to be able to relieve his feelings in action at last. The German grunted and fell back against the cushion, and was shot before he could move again. The friendly Lieutenant who had freed his hands was already dead. For the partisans were now right round the car, shattering the windows to shoot in. Hands grasped Murdoch and pulled him out, while others fired into the petrol tanks of the cars.

It was all over in a matter of seconds, the three cars blazing, and the bullock carts being driven hastily away. Only two of the German soldiers had managed to get out, and both lay dead. Three of the partisans had been hit, one quite seriously, but they seemed very pleased with their success.

'General Mackinder,' said a lantern-jawed man, whose entire face was cast in the same granite mould. He was heavily armed and actually wore a khaki uniform, with a forage cap, and was speaking tolerable English. 'When we heard, from Himmler himself on the radio, who you were, we felt we had to regain you.'

'For which I am very grateful,' Murdoch said. 'Were you sent by Colonel Kostitch?'

The grim face relaxed into a grin. 'Kostitch? No, I was not sent by Colonel Kostitch. Now, we must get you out of here, eh?'

Murdoch was hurried up the hill and into another valley,

where there were more men waiting. There were, in fact, more men in these hills than he had seen since he had visited General Mikhailovitch. Had Mikhailovitch rescued him? In which case he would be prepared to like the man.

Certainly there were sufficient men here to carry out a major assault, and they were well armed.

'One of my people is still in the hands of the Gestapo,' he told his English-speaking rescuer. 'In the village where I spent the night. They wish her to lead them to Kostitch's hideout. And to tell them where this Marshal Tito is to be found.'

'How can she do that?' the man asked. 'You do not *know* where Tito can be found.'

'That is true. So they will torture her.'

'And she will lead them to Kostitch. He can take care of himself.'

'You don't understand,' Murdoch said. 'She is probably being tortured at this very minute. I would like to take some of your men down there to rescue her.'

The man studied him for a moment. Then he said, 'You are too used to playing the hero, General Mackinder. It is not possible to rescue the woman. That village is far too strongly defended; my men would be slaughtered to no purpose, and even if we got in, the Germans would certainly kill their captive before we could reach her. Had we artillery, mortars, perhaps . . . but we do not. Your army will not spare them for us. I am sorry, General. It is not heroic, eh, to abandon a damsel in distress? It is not British, perhaps. But this is not a heroic war, and you British will have to learn that before you can win it. We have had to sacrifice much, even our own homes and families, because we have had to balance what we would like to do against what is possible, and what is necessary so that the fight can continue. You must forget the woman. She will not be the only one to die. Now we must hurry. I have arranged for you to be taken to a deserted part of the coast, and I will arrange for a British submarine to come there and pick you up. Your Mr Churchill will be happy to do that, eh? To get his general back. And perhaps he will be grateful to us for rescuing you. He may even send us those mortars, eh.'

'I am sure he will. But you will have to cancel your arrangements,' Murdoch said. 'I am not leaving Yugoslavia. If, as you say, it is impossible to rescue Private Edmunds, then I mean to avenge her. You have very nearly an army here, my friend. If you lack the means to fight, I will provide those means. And only I can do it.'

The man studied him for several seconds. Then he grinned. 'I have heard, and read, much about you, General Mackinder. They have called you Britain's greatest fighting soldier. Now I can see why. It will be a great pleasure to have you stay here, and fight with us. And see to our supplies.' He held out his hand. 'I am Marshal Tito.'

9

England, 1943

Churchill said, 'Before Alamein, we never had a victory; after Alamein we never had a defeat.' This was an over-simplification, and was indeed a sad injustice to the brilliant, if temporary, triumphs of Wavell, O'Connor and Auchinleck. What the Prime Minister really meant was that before Alamein, however many tactical victories were gained, there had been no strategical successes: after Alamein, although there were to be tactical setbacks often enough, there were no more strategical checks. The Allies had the Axis on the run, and it was a matter of maintaining that advantage. This situation became yet more apparent when that same winter the Russians forced the surrender of the German forces investing Stalingrad.

But there was still a great deal of very hard fighting ahead, before the enemy could even be sealed inside Fortress Europe – much less the walls of that fortress breached. The capture of Tripoli might have seemed the end of their personal road to the Westerns, but Rommel continued to lie in front of them, now reinforced and refuelled, and there were enormous numbers of German and Italian troops in Tunis, determined to fight to the last. Thus it was necessary for the Eighth Army to continue their campaign, and on Thursday, 4 February 1943, they themselves crossed the border into Tunisia. From here they pressed on to the capture of Medenine, a fortnight later.

By then Rommel had assumed overall command of the opposing army, and letting the Eighth Army get on with it for the moment, he launched a shattering onslaught on the inexperienced American forces at Kasserine, in the west. Matters were put right by the Allied air forces, which harried the Germans into retreating, but true to his policy of conducting an active defence, Rommel returned to the attack again and again, and after a lone British brigade had covered itself with glory at Hunt's Gap by repelling a panzer onslaught equipped with the new Tiger tanks, he turned against the Eighth Army for the last time, attacking fiercely at the Medenine Pass.

The battle was reminiscent of the old tank mêlées further to the east, save that Montgomery kept his armour under strict control, and this time it was the British anti-tank screen that tore the panzers apart. This was actually Rommel's last battle in North Africa, as immediately after it he was recalled to Germany to command the troops holding the West Wall – the Channel. Yet the Germans remaining in Tunisia were as full of fight as ever, and when the Eighth Army came up against the strongly defended Mareth Line, they had one of their hardest battles of the war.

Here there was no possibility of waiting for the panzers to come to them: the line had to be forced. So, having sent the New Zealanders on a flanking movement, Montgomery launched the army in a frontal assault. The attack began on Saturday, 20 March, and lasted a week. The initial onslaught was brought to a halt on the Monday, and the following day the Germans counter-attacked so strongly that the Allies were forced to withdraw. But Montgomery was again equal to the situation, reorganized his battered troops, and sent them forward again. On Sunday 28 March the Eighth Army smashed their way into Mareth and once again the Axis forces were driven into retreat.

It had been as hectic an action as Fergus had ever known. The command tank of A Squadron in which he was riding was hit, and although the crew got out before it brewed, two of them were killed, including Captain Brown, while Fergus himself was hurt.

It was not a serious injury, and involved only a couple of broken ribs, but he had become so used to emerging from every battle unscathed that it came as a bit of a shock to find himself lying in a field dressing station. John Allack hurried forward to take command, but by then the victory had been won.

Of the British armour engaged, the Westerns had suffered the heaviest casualties, in both tanks and men. They were pulled back to rest and recuperate, while the campaign continued, to culminate six weeks later when the last German and Italian troops in Tunisia surrendered. By then Fergus was fit again, but astounded to read that the Germans were claiming to have captured, while on a secret mission to the Yugoslav partisans in the mountains of Serbia, General Sir Murdoch Mackinder. He just could not believe his eyes. What on earth was the old buzzard doing on a secret mission in Serbia? He could only have got there by parachute. At his age! It was at least reassuring to know that, according to the German report, he was in good health. But Father, a prisoner of war? Again, at his age? He wrote Lee asking just what on earth had been going on.

Whatever his concern about his father, he was delighted that his regiment's splendid behaviour, over the whole campaign, and indeed the whole two and a half years they had been in Africa, had been recognized by the award of two DSOs, one to himself and one to Allack, three MCs, to his squadron commanders, and eight Military Medals: one of these went to RSM Manly-Smith, who had also been wounded in the battle, shot through the fleshy part of the thigh.

The medals were presented by General Montgomery personally, and after the ceremony he drank tea with Fergus in his ACV.

'I suppose the big question is, where next?' Fergus ventured.

'That is of course up to our lords and masters,' Montgomery said. 'Although I would have supposed we will now assault Fortress Europe itself. And my bet would be here in the Mediterranean, which is certainly the weakest link. We are, however, to be allowed a breathing space of a couple of months. I suggest you take advantage of it. You, and quite a number of your men, have now been out here for two and a half years. Too long. I am issuing leave warrants, and I would like you to select those men who you feel are most in need of a short spell in England. I personally am selecting you.'

'But sir,' Fergus protested. 'My place is with the regiment.'

'Of course. But you will only remain an efficient regimental commander if you take a little rest. And I am sure you have this very odd business with your father very much on your mind. I think you should find out something about it. It is not a matter I propose to argue about, Mackinder. Your convoy leaves Gibraltar in three days' time, and there are aircraft seats available the day after tomorrow. Pick your men. You will, of course, give priority to those who have been wounded or may have domestic matters to be seen to. Major Allack will command until you return.' He held out his hand. 'Enjoy yourself.'

'Cripes, sir, but I shan't know what to say to anyone,' remarked Bert Manly-Smith, as the transport nosed into Plymouth Sound. It was a port all the troopers, and the three officers who had accompanied them, were glad to see. U-boat wolf packs had been very active off the Portuguese coast, and the men had to spend the entire voyage on deck and at their assembly points, and wearing their lifejackets, being allowed below only to perform the most necessary of human functions. Their ship had escaped unscathed, but they had watched three others in the convoy go down, their passengers and crews drowning in the oil-covered water. They had all decided they felt safer fighting the Afrika Korps.

But now they were safe. At home. Fergus rather agreed with Bert, and in addition, he had a good deal on his mind. During the continuous advance which had followed the victory at Alamein, the troops had obviously received mail very rarely and at irregular intervals. Even then, although he had received, from time to time, letters from Annaliese and Mom, there had been nothing from Dad. Yet Mom, in her more recent letters, had said more than once that Dad was fine, if very busy. It was unlike Dad ever to be too busy

220

to write, and it was equally unlike Mom to comment on his activities, even in a negative sense.

Now it was all explained. At least up to a point: Mom must have known what Dad was doing. The old rascal, he thought. But, Dad in a German prison camp? He could only remind himself that Dad was indestructible, and always successful. In any event he would soon find out the truth of the matter.

Just as he would soon hold Liese in his arms. After two and a half years! He wondered if she would recognize this gaunt, sunburned figure? If she would still want to marry him? Strange how his thoughts never included the word love. Because he had no proof that Liese did love him? Her letters were loving enough, but lacked passion, often as she repeated her anxiety to have him back home, safe and sound. But then, were his letters any better? And he was the guilty one, with Monique Deschards locked away in his secret mind, and dominating his secret heart, as well. He knew how that heart would leap were he to meet her again, just as he knew she was in England. Of course the possibility of their encountering each other was too remote to be imagined – but suppose he met someone who knew someone who knew this woman Deschards? That was not beyond the realms of possibility. Would he be able to stop himself from obtaining her address and rushing off to find her? He was a cad.

'Golly, what a shambles,' Bert commented, staring at the town as they disembarked. 'Do you reckon the village has been hit, sir?'

'There's been no report of it,' Fergus said. 'So what are you going to do with your leave, Sergeant-Major?'

'Sink a few dozen pints of beer, sir. While I tell Grandad all about it. He'll want a blow by blow description of every battle, from beginning to end.' He grinned. 'That'll be reason for another dozen pints of beer.'

'No girl on the horizon?'

'No, sir. I was a little young for that when I left Blighty.'

You're a little young for that still, Fergus thought. But

221

still, Bert was a sergeant-major. 'I should think you'll have no trouble in finding one now,' he suggested.

'Maybe I won't, sir,' Bert agreed. 'But a fortnight ain't much time to do a lot about it. Permanently, anyway. Time enough when we're home for good.'

'Well,' Fergus said, 'don't forget to spare the time to come up to the house for a drink. I know my mother would love to see you. You never met my fiancée, did you?'

'Gosh, yes, sir,' Bert said. 'When I was helping in Grandad's shop, before the war.'

'Of course you must have,' Fergus said. 'Well, I know she'd like to meet you again, too.'

'Yes, sir,' Bert said. 'I'm sorry about the General, sir. All the lads are.'

'So am I,' Fergus said. 'But I imagine he was doing what he wanted to. I'll expect you at the house, Bert.'

They separated, because although they were using the same train, of course the Colonel was travelling first class, and the NCOs and troopers were in third. That was just a fact of life, Bert thought, as he gazed out of the window at the countryside rolling by. Just as it was a fact of life that no matter what had happened to his father, Fergus Mackinder was going home to pat his retrievers on the head, and make sure the Daimler was still in working order, and stand on his porch and look out at his rolling acres of countryside, and hug his mother, making sure not to disturb her twinset or her pearls . . . while he was going home to squeeze himself into the tiny, smoke-filled and smoke-stained parlour where Grandad would be listening to the wireless, and play a game of draughts, and then go down to the pub and see if anyone there remembered him. He would probably get a bit of a welcome, he supposed. He was a man, now, in every way. As well as a war hero. Even that plump barmaid might give him a smile.

But Fergus Mackinder would also be going home to take his fiancée into his arms. Bert felt more than ever guilty about that – about every aspect of it. While they had been fighting together in North Africa, and especially after

Fergus had saved his life, he had been aware only of self-horror, that he could have allowed such a thing to happen. Equally had he felt guilty at being unable to warn his commanding officer of the character of the girl he was intending to marry.

Those feelings had persisted all the way home, although he had then known that he never would say anything to Fergus. But the sight of Plymouth had induced a subtle change in his feelings. The seaport might have been bombed to bits, but it was still recognizably the place he had looked at on that October night in 1940, when the regiment had embarked for Alexandria. Then his brain had been filled with the thought of what he was leaving behind – and only Annaliese mattered. But then his dreams had been so abruptly shattered by Fergus's telling him of his engagement.

The sight of Plymouth had brought those dreams back. Suddenly he wanted, all over again. And the woman had to be Annaliese. He wondered if he was in love? It was not something he had ever considered. But then, he had never before felt for any woman the way he felt for the German. Perhaps the very fact that she *was* a German, a member of the nation against which he was fighting, one of whom might very well one day blow his head off, made her the more attractive. If he went up to Broad Acres, and met her, and they looked at each other. and she had that look in her eyes again . . . therefore the only thing to do was to ignore Fergus's invitation. The Colonel would no doubt be offended, but Bert felt sure he could make up a suitable reason for not being able to find the time – even if he had to invent a woman. Even lying would be better than cuckolding the old man once again: the fellow had saved his life.

'Fergus?' Lee stared at her only surviving son, who was surrounded by leaping dogs. 'I heard the barking . . . oh, Fergus!' She ran down the front steps to throw herself into his arms, while Robbins the butler, who had actually opened the door, stepped back inside the house.

'If only you could have let me know you were coming!' Lee cried, her eyes filling with tears.

'Well, you know I couldn't do that, Mom. But I'm here.' He kissed her again, then held her away to look at her. Nearly four years of war had aged her in a fashion he hadn't noticed before he had left. The slight figure in the twinset and pearls was as neat and slender as ever, but the fair hair was more grey than yellow, and there were strain lines on her face. Yet she looked well enough. 'It is so good to see you.'

'And so good to see you.' Her finger traced the crimson ribbon on his breast, and then the red and blue one next to it. 'You are going to be as distinguished as your father.'

'That'll be the day. But, talking about Father . . .'

'Fergus, my dear, dear boy.' Philippa came hurrying up from the stables. 'I heard the noise . . . my, but you're looking well. You're burnt quite brown.'

Fergus embraced her and suppressed a wince. If his ribs were officially knitted, they were still susceptible to extreme pressure, and Aunt Philippa was a large, powerful woman.

'Fergus? Is it really you?'

Both the older Mackinder women stepped aside to let him look at Annaliese. Although it was still not the end of May, the weather was delightfully warm, and she had clearly been sunbathing. Now she was wrapped in a bathrobe, but it was obvious she had nothing on underneath, and her feet were bare as her hair was tousled. Fergus thought she looked delightful, as if she had just left her bed. He had almost forgotten how beautiful she was.

She had also taken the time to collect little Ian, or maybe he had been sunbathing with her; he wore only a bathing costume. He was nearly at his third birthday, and stood sturdily beside her, holding her hand.

'Fergus,' she said again, and came down the steps, Ian still attached. 'Darling, this is your Uncle Fergus.'

'Liese, one day you are going to catch your death of cold,' Philippa admonished. 'And give Baby chronic bronchitis.'

Liese ignored her, and was in Fergus's arms. He kissed

224

her mouth, and it opened for him. He held her close, forgetting the pain in his side, and she stood on tiptoe and pressed her pelvis against his. Oh, she loved him all right. And he loved her.

He released her, scooped Ian from the ground. The little boy had still been a feeding babe when he had left England. 'You don't remember me, do you?' he asked.

'You're going to be my new daddy,' Ian said.

Still holding him, Fergus kissed Annaliese again. 'It's so good to be home,' he whispered in her ear.

'Two broken ribs?' Lee asked. 'Oh, my God! How you must have suffered.'

'I was well looked after,' Fergus assured her.

'But . . . only two weeks?' Annaliese pouted. 'It hardly seems worthwhile.'

'We'll make every minute count,' Fergus promised, and sipped his whisky; he hadn't tasted Johnnie Walker Black since the last time he had been in Shepheard's Hotel in Cairo, and that seemed a very long time ago.

And that hadn't been his own drawing room. Now he sat, with the three women around him, and Robbins popping in and out every few minutes to make sure all was well; Fergus had already been down to the kitchen to say hello to Cook and the maids, and up to the nursery to introduce himself to Ian's new nanny.

He looked around him at the so familiar pictures, the ornaments and bric-a-brac, the chandelier and the other light fixtures. Then he looked at the women. Annaliese had dressed herself, slacks and a loose shirt and sandals. Again she looked absolutely delightful. He felt a great sense of wellbeing. And a great sense of humility, too, when he thought of all the fellows who would never come back to this: Wilkinson and Bentley, Brothers and Butler . . . and most of all, Ian and Harry.

'Now tell me about Dad,' he said.

'God knows what he was doing,' Philippa said. 'We don't.'

'We were all so surprised,' Annaliese said. 'We knew he

was in something very hush-hush, but not what it was.' She looked at Lee. As did Philippa.

Lee stood up. 'You'd better come into the study for a moment, Fergus.'

Fergus looked at Annaliese, who raised her eyebrows. Then he got up in turn and followed his mother into Murdoch's private room, where the reproduction of the charge in 1843 hung behind the desk.

Lee sat at the desk, unlocked one of the drawers, and took out a letter. 'What I am going to show you, and tell you, Fergus, is in the strictest confidence. The contents of this letter are known to very few people. One of them is the Prime Minister.'

'Sounds terribly important.' He grinned, trying to lighten her mood.

Lee gave him the letter and he scanned the contents. 'The old devil,' he commented. 'You mean he didn't even tell you what he was going to do?'

'He didn't even tell the Prime Minister,' Lee said. 'He apparently just acted on the spur of the moment when that man Durden died.'

Fergus raised his head. 'Now, Mom, you mustn't be mad at him.'

'Mustn't I?'

'So he couldn't let you know before he went. Of course he couldn't. But he did let you know. And . . . is he all right? I mean, Dad in a prison camp . . .'

'He isn't in a prison camp, Fergus.'

'Eh? But the newspaper report . . .'

'That is the confidential bit. The newspapers reported what the Germans put out on the wireless. But only a week later we received a code message, using Murdoch's private identification, from the partisans. Winston told me this himself, in the strictest confidence.'

'I don't understand,' Fergus confessed.

'Nobody understands. The Germans have not retracted their claim to have made him prisoner, but it seems almost certain that he isn't. And the whole world knows he went to Yugoslavia. Winston is hopping mad. But in the circumstance, he wants the fact that your father is actually free to be kept secret, at least until the Germans choose to confess that their claim was a hoax. Or a mistake. It's something to do with not having to admit himself that we have a lieutenant-general as our liaison officer with the guerillas.'

'Trust Dad to turn the world upside down. Gosh, he must be having the time of his life. I knew he wouldn't spend the entire war sitting at a desk. Not Dad.'

'Fergus, your father is nearly sixty-two years old. He *should* be sitting at a desk. Not crawling around a lot of mountains, living rough, being shot at . . . my God! If he isn't killed or really captured he'll probably die of pneumonia.'

'Now, Mom,' Fergus said. 'Admit that you're actually proud of him.'

Lee glared at him for a moment, then sighed and smiled. 'Of course I'm really proud of him. But I do worry so.'

'He'll survive. Dad always survives.'

'I know. That's what Winston says. But Fergus . . . no one must know the truth. No one.'

Fergus grinned at her. 'Mum's the word. But by God, I feel on top of the world.'

'So what's the great secret about Uncle Murdoch?' Annaliese asked.

They had had dinner, for which Fergus had worn mess kit and she had put on a blood-red skin-tight evening gown, and had worn her glowing golden hair brushed straight and slightly over one eye, which made her look like Veronica Lake, Fergus thought. Facially, indeed she rather reminded him of the famous actress, although she was much the taller woman. Either way, she was quite irresistibly beautiful.

And now they were alone, for the first time, sitting in the conservatory: Annaliese had added a stole, as once the sun had gone down the evenings were quite chilly.

'Oh, simply that he was engaged in something very hush-hush, and has been taken prisoner.'

'I told you that,' she pointed out. 'It was in the

newspapers. There has to be something more. Which Aunt Lee and now you will not tell me about.'

'Well, you wouldn't expect us to, would you? There's a war on. And I'd be awfully grateful if you wouldn't ask me anything more about it.'

'Because I am a German and you don't trust me.'

'As I have only two weeks, my darling, it seems rather stupid to quarrel. Of course I trust you. But I must respect the secrets which go with my job.'

She continued to stare at him for a few seconds, then she smiled. 'Of course. I am being stupid. It is just that I want to share with you. Everything.'

He squeezed her hands. 'And you will. As soon as this war is over, and I can tell you everything.'

'This stupid war,' she said. 'I cannot see why it drags on. It is no longer serving any purpose. Hitler cannot beat the Allies; the Allies cannot beat Hitler unless they can invade Europe, and there is no prospect of them doing that. It is time to call a halt.'

'We aren't going to do that either.'

'I know. I saw the news of the announcement by Churchill and Roosevelt. Unconditional surrender! Germany will never surrender unconditionally again. The war will last for ever.'

Were there tears in her eyes? In the semi-darkness of the conservatory he couldn't be sure.

'No it won't,' he promised her. 'I know it won't.'

'But you can't tell me about that, either. Fergus . . . kiss me.'

He was happy to do that, to slide his hands over her arms and round her shoulders and bring her against him, to kiss those moist lips and find that eager, questing tongue. It was an aggressive tongue, and it took him by surprise -- as it had done the night he had asked her to marry him, nearly three years ago, he remembered. It was, somehow, an unladylike tongue. What had Dad said about her nude sunbathing? Not exactly in keeping with a general's wife? Did generals' wives have aggressive tongues? Did Mom? That was an impossible thought.

Annaliese took her tongue away, but her cheek was pressed against his. 'Make love to me, Fergus,' she whispered. 'Oh, please make love to me.'

'Liese,' he said. 'We're going to be married.'

'I know. So what is to stop us? And Lee and Philippa have gone to bed. So have the servants. Oh, Fergus, I have waited so long.'

Thoughts tumbled through his mind. There was nothing to stop him. Nothing at all. She wanted. He wanted. My God, how he wanted. And they were going to be married.

But there *were* things to stop him. He wasn't sure whether he wanted to make love to her, or just a woman. As for making love to her before they were married . . . that thought hadn't troubled him for a moment with Monique Deschards. But he hadn't been going to marry Monique. They had been two people who had met under the stress of war, and had tumbled into each other's arms. They hadn't known each other for years and years, and they hadn't been going to spend the rest of their lives together. And Monique had not been going to become a general's wife. But Annaliese was. He had no doubt about that now.

Annaliese found his hand, and placed it on her breast; the flesh felt curiously hard beneath the fabric.

'Liese,' he said. 'We must wait.'

Her head went back. 'Why? Tell me why?'

'It's just that, on our wedding night . . .'

'For God's sake, Fergus,' she said. 'You know I am not a virgin, so what difference does it make?'

'Yes,' he said. 'I know that you are not a virgin.'

For a moment her face hardened. 'Your father has been speaking against me.'

'You were married to my brother,' he reminded her. 'And you are a mother.'

She gazed at him, with a slight frown, for a moment. 'Then you are not angry with me?'

'Of course I am not angry with you, my darling. I love you.' Perhaps if he repeated it often enough he would believe it. How could any man not love so magnificent a creature?

229

'But you will not take me to bed.'

'I will take you to bed when we are married.'

'But why? Why wait so long? Suppose you were to be killed?'

'That is exactly why I mustn't take you to bed.'

'Men!' She threw her hands in the air. 'I want you. I want you to make love to me. I want you, here!' She squeezed her groin.

He wished she wouldn't do things like that. Or say them.

'And I want you, Liese. As my wife. Nothing less than that.'

'Then let's get married. Now. Tomorrow. We can get a special licence. Oh, Fergus . . .'

'Liese.' He held her hands. 'I asked you to marry me when this war is over. I am not going to change my mind about that. As you say, I could be killed, at any time. I cannot ask you to bear the burden of having twice been widowed. Nor can I ask you to . . . well, feel under any obligation to me, because we have shared a bed. If I die, I want you to feel absolutely free to find yourself another husband, to find little Ian another father.'

He paused, uncertainly, because he wasn't at all sure those were the reasons for rejecting her. Could it possibly be that he didn't want to make love to Annaliese, even Annaliese, because of the memory of Monique? But that was absurd. He would never see Monique again. He couldn't carry her image, the recollection of that unforgettable lovemaking, through the rest of his life.

Annaliese gave him another of her long stares. 'Then I must be patient,' she said at last. 'Well . . . if you won't marry me and you won't fuck me, what are we going to do with your two weeks?'

Once again, her choice of words jarred. Where Monique had said 'fuck' more than once while they had been doing just that together, it had seemed entirely natural. With Annaliese it sounded forced. And Annaliese was going to be a general's wife. But he was determined not to be angry with her. Not after two and a half years, and not knowing when he would get home again.

'We have a lot to do,' he said. 'Principally just talk, and, well . . .'

'Neck,' she suggested. 'Like a couple of school kids. Even they at least feel each other up.'

'We have to get to know each other,' Fergus said.

'We have known each other for years.'

'And do we really know each other?'

Annaliese gave him another of her stares.

He hurried on. 'And then there's Bath to visit . . . I can hardly remember what the old place looks like.'

'And London,' she said eagerly. 'I should so like you to take me to London.'

'Why, we could do that. We'll take Mom along, and stay at Aunt Rosemary's, if she hasn't been bombed out.'

'Oh, yes,' Annaliese said sadly. 'Mom, and Aunt Rosemary. What fun that will be.' Clearly she had been thinking of a hotel, with perhaps only one room available.

'And then, we'll do some entertaining here.'

'Will we?'

'Of course. May as well let the county know I'm back. Oh, and that lad Bert Manly-Smith is coming up to see us. You remember Bert Manly-Smith, Liese? Rather gangling youth who used to help out at the village shop. Well, you'd hardly recognize him now. He's bigger than I am, and a sergeant-major.'

'Good heavens,' Annaliese commented. 'Yes, indeed, I remember Bert Manly-Smith. You mean he is in England, too?'

'He's in the village right this minute,' Fergus told her. 'Probably telling the lads how he won North Africa, single-handed.'

'There was this Jerry tank, see,' Bert told his audience. 'And there was another one here . . .' he arranged the glasses on the bar counter of the Marquis of Granby public house. 'And we were here.' He indicated his own pint mug. 'Now, then, you have to remember that the Jerries had bigger guns, then, and bigger machines, too. While we had our little two-pounder. But it's the man behind the gun that

231

matters, not the size of it. So we traversed to the right, lined the first one up, and bingo, shot the tracks right off him. Then we lined the second one up, and put a round right through his observation slit. Talk about brew. He went up like a firework.'

'That must have been some shooting,' observed Mr Bartlett.

'It was, if I say so myself,' Bert agreed modestly. 'Sighted that one myself, I did.'

'What do you really think about Montgomery?' asked Mr Linley.

These were all men who had given him Christmas tips when he had delivered their newspapers, and whom he had addressed as sir. Men who, only four years ago, wouldn't have dreamed of standing him drinks in a pub. Now they were bewitched by the badge on his arm, which showed a lion and a unicorn inside a laurel wreath and told everyone he held the highest non-commissioned rank in the British Army, and even more, by the blue, white and red vertical stripes on the ribbon above his breast pocket.

'Have another pint, Sergeant-Major,' invited Mr Cross.

'Well . . .' Bert looked at his watch. But it was only twelve fifteen, and there was nothing ahead but lunch with Grandad. He pushed his mug across the counter. 'Don't mind if I do.'

'Tell us about Tripoli,' Mr Bartlett suggested. 'I was there, once, back in 1926. I wonder if it's changed.'

'Well . . .'

The publican placed his tankard on the counter. 'There's someone asking for you, in the lounge bar,' he said.

'For me?'

The publican winked. 'I'd find out about it, if I were you, Bert.'

Bert hesitated. He had never been in a lounge bar in his life. But he was a sergeant-major, now. 'Can I take this through with me?'

'Of course. It's my beer.'

'Excuse me, gents, I'll be right back,' Bert said. He picked up his foaming tankard and stepped into the

232

corridor, then cautiously opened the end door into the smartly furnished lounge bar, and checked. The room was empty, save for Annaliese Mackinder.

She smiled at him. 'Why, Bert. I only discovered last night that you were home.'

She wore loose trousers, an even looser blouse, and sandals; her hair was tied up in a bandanna, and only a few yellow wisps were exposed. Her face was thus isolated, and more beautiful even than he remembered it. She was sipping a port and lemon.

'Aren't you going to say hello?' she asked.

'Hello, Mrs Mackinder,' he said, acutely aware that the publican could probably hear them through the hatchway to the public bar.

Annaliese was apparently aware of that too. She held out her hand, and Bert took her fingers. 'It is so good to see you looking so well,' she said. 'Colonel Mackinder told me you had been wounded again.'

'Nothing serious this time, Mrs Mackinder.'

Her fingers still held his, and now she drew him to a seat on the far side of the room. 'You must tell me all about it,' she said in a loud voice. 'About all the battles.' She sat down, still holding Bert's hand, and he sank on to the cushion beside her. 'I have the car outside,' she whispered. 'Come with me for a drive.'

'But Mrs Mackinder . . .' he couldn't do that. He couldn't let the Colonel down again. Besides, the risk . . .

'Listen,' she said, 'I have told everyone I'm driving into Bath to see the dentist, and that I won't be back until after lunch. Nobody can possibly know.' She stared at him. 'Don't let me down, Bert.'

He licked his lips. She wanted him. After nearly three years, she still wanted him. And she was the only woman he had ever wanted. His brain seemed to be spinning round and round. But another part of his body was more insistent.

Annaliese smiled at him, and finished her drink. 'Why, Sergeant-Major,' she said in a loud voice, 'I've my car outside. Let me drop you off.'

Bert gulped, and drained his beer.

'You away, Sergeant-Major?' asked the publican, looking through the hatch.

'Yes,' Bert said. 'Just remembered there's somewhere I have to go before lunch. And Mrs Mackinder has kindly offered me a lift.' He pushed his head through the hatch himself. 'Thanks for the drinks,' he shouted at his audience. 'See you tonight.'

He hurried through the door behind Annaliese. 'This is daft.'

'All love is daft,' she said, and got behind the wheel.

To his relief he saw that it wasn't the Daimler, but a small Austin; the front seats seemed very crowded. Annaliese turned the car and drove out of the village, towards Bath, but as soon as the houses were out of sight she swung down a lane.

'When did you learn to drive?' Bert asked, watching her. She made a fascinating sight, with her blouse drawing tight against her shoulders and underclothes, and then ballooning again, and her legs moving beneath the slacks.

'Ages ago. Driving gives one a sense of freedom.'

'Whose car is it?'

'Oh, mine. I asked Lee if I could have a car, and she said yes. Pays to have rich relatives.' She glanced at him. 'Can you drive?'

'Only a tank.'

'Doesn't make sense, does it, to drive a tank and not a car?' She had slowed, and now she turned down an even narrower lane. After a few seconds of bumping in the ruts, yet another turn brought them into the shelter of a high stile, which completely hid them from the road. There was a tree by the stile, which shaded the car, and in front of them the meadow disappeared over the brow of the hill.

'You've been here before,' Bert accused.

'Of course.'

'Who with?'

She glanced at him. 'By myself. When I don't have a friend, I'm just as happy by myself. Aren't you?'

'Women don't do that.'

Annaliese gave a low laugh. 'I bet they do it more than

men. There's no mess.' She opened her door and got out. 'I love this place. Here we can be really alone.'

'Suppose someone comes along?'

'No one ever does. There's no reason for anyone to.'

Bert got out too; he was as hard as a rock. But his bladder was full as well: all that beer.

'I'll just step behind the stile for a moment,' he said.

'Do it here,' Annaliese suggested.

'In front of you? Don't be daft.'

'Why? You must pee in front of other men, in the army.'

'Other men. I've never peed in front of a woman.'

'Why not?'

'Well . . . it ain't proper.'

'Everything is proper, if you both want it,' Annaliese told him. 'That's the secret, both wanting it. I want to see you do it.'

Bert hesitated, then unbuttoned his battledress trousers. He was so hard it was a struggle to get it out, and even harder to control it; he went crimson in the face.

'Oh, he's just splendid,' Annaliese said. 'Go on, do it.'

Bert obeyed. What a woman. But what a marvellous woman.

'Now,' Annaliese said when he had finished. 'Undress me, Bert.'

He licked his lips, in a mixture of uncertainty and desire. She wanted him, when Fergus was available. There was the incredible thing.

He stepped up to her, and she took him in her arms and kissed him, deeply and slowly. His flies were still unbuttoned and she put her hand down to hold him while she kissed him. He wanted to shout for joy: that was his principal memory of their last time together.

His hands were on her back; when she stepped away they scraped over her shoulders. 'Now undress me,' she repeated.

He didn't really know what to do, but he unfastened the buttons of her blouse, and it fell open, to reveal a white undergarment which seemed to be brassiere and petticoat and knickers all in one. It was made of satin and lace, and through it her body seemed to beckon him.

Annaliese kicked off her sandals and shrugged the blouse from her shoulders. It fell to the ground. 'Now the pants,' she said.

These had a waistband, and buttoned up the back. He released the catch, and she turned round so that he could undo the buttons. The pants slid gently down over her hips and gathered about her ankles. He stared at her bottom and legs. She wore no stockings; he was surprised at that.

Annaliese stepped out of the pants, and turned to face him. 'Now the cami.'

'I don't know how to do it,' Bert confessed.

'It's very simple,' she told him. 'You just take the straps from my shoulders, and slide the whole thing down.'

Heart pounding, Bert obeyed. This was far better than the last time, because the last time she had been already naked, and simply too much to take in at one go – so he had taken in hardly anything, only the feel of her hand on his penis, and the sight of the milk on his tunic. There would be no milk today. Today he could savour each piece of her, as he uncovered it.

He slid the straps from her shoulders, aware that she was staring at him, but with her eyes only half open. He slid the straps right down to her wrists, and only then looked at her breasts. They were smaller than the last time, because she wasn't feeding. They were, in fact, small breasts. But they were beautifully shaped, and had hard nipples.

'Kiss them,' Annaliese commanded. 'Suck them. Suck them hard.'

He obeyed. At that moment he would have done anything she told him to. He pressed the breasts together and managed to get both nipples into his mouth at once, had a tremendous urge to bite, but resisted the temptation.

The camiknickers had slipped further, and were waiting round her thighs. He stooped to slide them down and uncover her pubes. Annaliese gave a little shake of the hips and the garment joined the rest on the ground. She stepped

236

out of it, and remained with her legs spread. 'Kiss me there too,' she said.

Bert raised his head to look at her. He couldn't believe she would really want that.

'Have you never kissed a woman there before?' she asked.

'No,' he said. And wanted to ask in turn if she had ever been kissed there before. But he didn't dare.

'Then do it to me,' she said. 'And make me yours.'

He liked the sound of that, buried his face in the silky curls, held her buttocks to bring her harder against him.

'Oh,' Annaliese said. 'Ohhh!'

She tore at his clothes, but she was even more mystified by the intricacies of battledress than he had been by feminine undergarments. He released her to help her, and they rolled on the grass together. She wanted to take him into her mouth as well, and for a few glorious seconds they sucked each other, then she got him right side up and on top of her, but before he climaxed she wanted to change again.

'This way,' she panted. 'This way.'

She knelt, her legs spread. For the second time Bert was astounded. But if it was what she wanted . . . and it was the best he had ever had, with his groin thumping into her buttocks, while she took both their weights on her knees and elbows, gradually subsiding, so that when he came he was lying on her, and she was writhing and gasping beneath him.

'I can't breathe,' she said at last, and he rolled off her. She lay on her back, twigs and dirt clinging to her headscarf, arms and legs thrown wide; her right leg rested against his. 'That was so good,' she said. 'So good.'

'I never knew women felt like that,' Bert confessed.

'Women feel more than men,' she said. 'I had two. A small one when you were eating pussy, and then a big one when you were inside me. Bert . . .' She raised herself on her elbow. 'I'll have another dentist's appointment tomorrow.'

'But what will you tell him about missing today?'

'Silly! I don't really have any appointments at all.' She sat

237

up, and pulled the scarf from her head to shake out her hair. 'I just told everyone at Broad Acres that I did.'

'Oh, heck!' He sat up as well; their shoulders brushed. 'They're certain to find out.'

'Not that lot. Fergus was quite happy to spend the morning talking with his mother. About his crazy dad, I suppose.'

'Wasn't that something? The General, a prisoner. He'll escape. I swear he'll escape. But Fergus,' Bert said. 'I'm going to have to see him.'

'What about?'

'Well . . . us.'

'Are you out of your mind?'

'Well, heck, Annaliese . . .' it was the first time he had ever used her name. 'We love each other, and . . .'

'And we keep it just the way it is,' Annaliese told him.

'But . . . don't you want to marry me?'

'Marry you? Of course I don't want to marry you.'

'But you let me . . . you wanted me . . .'

'I want you to make love to me, whenever we can get together. I love making love with you, Bert. I've never had a man like you.'

'Then why won't you marry me?'

'Because it would be absurd. You haven't any money. Or a nice home . . . you couldn't even afford to give me a motor car.'

'Well, maybe not. But if we love each other . . .'

'Love is a matter of good sex,' she told him. 'It has nothing to do with life. Life is a matter of getting all you can and holding on to it.'

'And you have good sex with Colonel Mackinder,' Bert said sadly.

'No,' Annaliese said. 'I don't have any sex with Colonel Mackinder. He regards himself as a gentleman. I don't suppose I'll have good sex after we're married, either, if he's at all like his brother. That's why I need you.'

'But you still intend to marry him?'

'Well, of course. He's going to inherit Broad Acres when

238

the old people die. Think of that! I'll be mistress of Broad Acres.'

Bert got up and began to dress. 'And you expect me to come every time you call? To screw my Colonel's wife?'

'Don't be afraid, Bert. If anything ever did happen, I'd look after you. I promise.'

'I'm not afraid,' he said. 'I'm disgusted.'

'Bert!' She was on her knees.' You love me.'

'Yes. I love you. I want you. I want you as my wife. Not as Fergus Mackinder's wife.'

Annaliese's face changed, subtly, but nonetheless it had hardened. She also got up, and pulled on her camiknickers. 'I thought all those years fighting would have made you grow up.'

'I think they did,' Bert said. 'They taught me the meaning of words like comradeship. I don't suppose you understand that, Annaliese. But the Colonel and I have to lead our men into battle, together. We have to stand shoulder to shoulder when the bullets are flying, and to know that we can trust each other.'

'I am sure Fergus trusts you, Bert. And you know you can trust him.'

'But I know that he can't trust me. Can't you understand? For God's sake, he saved my life.'

She saw the shadow flitting across his face, and instantly understood the thought that had provoked it. 'He saved the life of one of his soldiers, didn't he, Bert? Because he was Fergus Mackinder, and he had to act the part. He didn't care if it was you. I bet he didn't even know it was you.'

'Does that mean I mustn't be grateful?' Bert muttered, picking up his beret and dusting it off.

'It means that you don't have to regard him as someone special.'

'He's also a friend,' Bert argued.

'Now really, Bert, can you honestly call Fergus Mackinder a friend? Have you ever been invited to dinner at Broad Acres? He's expecting you to call, you know. So that he can show you off to his mother.' She smiled. 'And me. "Do you remember that odd fellow Bert Manly-

Smith?" he asked. "He's a sergeant-major now. I've told him to come up and have a glass of beer. You'll enjoy meeting him again. Below stairs, of course." '

Bert got into the car, and she sat beside him. She started the engine and drove back towards the village. 'You've missed lunch,' she told him.

'So have you.'

'I'll get something in Bath. That way I can prove I was there.' She glanced at him. 'I'd like you to come along, but I think it'd be too risky.'

'Yes,' he agreed. 'It would. You can drop me at the corner.'

The car stopped, and he got out. Annaliese leaned out of her window and held his hand. 'You are the most exciting man I have ever known, Bert. The most exciting man I will ever know.'

He hesitated, then stooped to kiss her mouth.

Her fingers tightened on his, and she smiled at him. 'Walk out here tomorrow morning,' she said. 'And wait for me. I'll be here at eleven. That'll give us so much more time.'

She released him, engaged gear, and the car drove away. She had not waited for an answer. Because she already knew the answer. He was going to be there.

'It's been decided that tanks aren't going to be all that much good, in Sicily,' General Montgomery told the officers of the Desert Rats. 'Either on the beaches or on the terrain farther inland. The assault will be carried out by infantry and airborne troops. It is hoped that Italian resistance will not be prolonged; there are already encouraging signs of a crack in their determination to continue the war. But of course there are a considerable number of German troops on the island, and they, one assumes, will fight like the very devil. However, they will be overcome, and then we will proceed to the next logical step in our plan, the invasion of Italy itself. It is for this that you are being kept in hand, and it is for this that you must continue training at your very hardest. I look forward to having you under my command again then.'

The meeting was dismissed, but the General remained to speak privately with several of the officers. Amongst them was naturally Fergus.

'How was England?' Montgomery asked.

'Worth fighting for, sir. I wouldn't have hurried back if I'd known there was going to be this long delay in getting back into action.'

'You have work to do, licking all these recruits into shape,' Montgomery told him. 'And you'll have action again soon enough. Sicily is just going to be a sideshow. But not even the Royal Western Dragoon Guards can always be in the front of every action, you know. How is your father?'

'Ah . . . very well, I believe, sir.'

Which might not be a lie at all, he reflected.

'It's impossible to think of Murdoch Mackinder a POW. I imagine you can write to him. Give him my regards, and tell him we're on our way to get him out of that camp.'

'I will do that, sir,' Fergus agreed. He left the meeting and drove back to the regimental cantonment. They were once again in the Delta, where it had all begun so many months ago. But what a difference. Now indeed the sentries were required only for resisting pilfering; there was no armed and organized enemy anywhere on the continent of Africa. Thus the camp could sprawl in orderly lines, and the men could enjoy themselves, as much as possible . . . while their officers endeavoured to make them train as hard as ever. In Fergus's absence, the dragoons had been brought right back up to strength, in both men and vehicles. A good number of the former were very green, but proud to belong to a regiment which had added so many recent laurels to its already famous name, and proud to be taught by the veterans who had chased the Germans right across the desert.

Allack, and the three squadron commanders, Captains Mather, Hartley and Smithie, were waiting for him, together with the padre, Captain Long. The captains were themselves relatively new boys, eager for action, and desperately disappointed that they were not to take part in the invasion of Sicily. Fergus repeated Montgomery's admonishments as nearly as he could remember them, and sat down for a drink with John Allack. They were the only two remaining out of the officers who had landed at Alexandria in October 1940; there weren't all that many of the original men left, either – not more than a dozen.

Including Bert Manly-Smith. There was the devil of an odd chap, Fergus thought. During the closing stages of the African campaign, and even more on the voyage home to England, he had thought he was getting through to the boy. But following their arrival in the village, Bert had changed again. He had become withdrawn, sullen even, had refused to come up to the house for that offered drink.

Fergus had been offended by that, had reflected that what could have been a very successful career – there was no reason why Bert shouldn't wind up as an officer and even attain field rank, he was so young – would certainly be spoilt unless he could learn to keep his moods under control. He had then tried to rationalize. Bert was undoubtedly a somewhat mixed-up youth. Having an officer for a father, and a sergeant-major's daughter for a mother, must have been totally confusing. Of course, Ralph Manly-Smith had died before either of his sons had been old enough properly to remember him, and Jennie had been, as Fergus remembered her, a remarkably sophisticated and well-bred young woman, even if she had been RSM Yeald's daughter. He particularly remembered how fond Dad had been of her. But then she too had died, and Bert had been left with only his grandfather and brother. Enough to make anyone introspective. And presumably, Fergus thought, going home made it worse, whereas in the army he could concentrate on being the very good soldier he had turned out to be. Because, what did he have to go home for? Fergus had gathered he didn't have that much in common with his grandfather. But then, he didn't seem to have that much in common with his brother. There was not even a girl, apparently. What a lonely existence. Fergus wished he could help in some way. But when it came to women, it seemed he couldn't help himself.

It was so odd, really. There had been no hesitation over

242

Monique Deschards. They had seen each other, she had beckoned, and he had looked neither left nor right. Well, Liese had certainly beckoned.

Although she had not done so again after he had rejected her on that first night, had been apparently content with a good night kiss and holding hands while they walked in the garden.

There was no way of telling what she actually thought about his refusal to bed her. But he had become quite concerned about it, since leaving England again and being able to look at it objectively, as it were. Liese was a most lovely girl, and she was the girl he was going to marry. Yet he was afraid to touch her. Of course he had pretended that it was the proper thing to do to wait until they were married, but he knew that wasn't the truth. The truth was that however much he thought about her when he was away from her, the moment he got near her his sexual processes seemed to dry up. What he had to do, and before their marriage, was work out why.

Ian? It had seemed quite natural to replace him, and he adored little Ian, would not have wanted anyone different as his own son. But the replacement had been in the abstract, as a husband. Replacing him in bed had seemed a sufficiently remote contingency when he had proposed; he had never imagined that Liese would wish to jump the gun. Was he then afraid that she might wish to compare him unfavourably with his dead brother? He did not honestly think so.

Well, then, what of the other men, the men who had helped her escape from Germany, or even worse, the men she might have known before it had become necessary to escape? But surely those had been exorcized long ago. If they had not bothered Ian, why should they bother him? Again, he did not honestly think they did.

Thus it had to be Annaliese herself. And that, he knew, was the truth. He was afraid of the woman he intended to make his wife. There was a confession of weakness. But it couldn't be denied, at least to himself. He was afraid of being conquered. Because Liese was a conqueress. She had offered herself to him, but with the offer had come a challenge: match me if you can, but if you cannot, become my slave. To be Annaliese von Reger's slave might be a very pleasant existence . . . but it was not something he had in mind. He wondered if Ian had been her slave? Perhaps there hadn't been time. But perhaps once would settle the matter.

So why did he not settle the matter, once and for all, now that he had at last realized the reason? So it might mean acting the utter cad. But that would be preferable to a life of misery. Besides, he was Murdoch Mackinder's son. When Mackinders saw an enemy, or a problem, they charged it with their swords drawn. A fitting analogy. He should have done that long ago. Have at her, and were they not suited, call the engagement off. As she had reminded him often enough, he could hardly be accused of stealing her virginity.

That way, either way, lay happiness. And it would be done, the very next time he returned home.

As with all of his resolutions regarding Annaliese, that moment of truth seemed a comfortingly long way in the future. Nearly three years had elapsed between leaving England in October 1940 and returning there in May 1943; if the next break could hardly be that long delayed – it was inconceivable that the war could still be raging in 1946 – he did not suppose it was going to happen very soon.

But he was to be surprised. The invasion of Sicily went very much according to plan, for if the Germans put up as determined a resistance as had been expected, the Italians crumpled right away. The landings – Operation Husky – took place on 10 July; fifteen days later Mussolini was dismissed and arrested. No one immediately knew what would happen next, but that a change in Italian policy could be expected seemed obvious.

Meanwhile the invading armies surged onwards. An armada of six thousand ships had landed twelve British and American divisions on the south coast of the island, and although the Germans immediately hurled everything they had at the intruders, the Allies gained their lodgement and then forged steadily inland. Catania and Syracuse fell in the first week, and on 20 July Enna, the communications centre for the defence of the island, was captured.

The United States Seventh Army stormed Palermo on the north coast on 22 July, and spreading west at the same time, took Trapani two days later, the day before Mussolini's fall. The Germans might have hoped to hold their strong hilltop positions at Centuripe and Regalbuto, but the British and Canadians drove them out on 2 August, and on the 14th they were past Mount Etna. By then the Allied armies had been entertained by the behaviour of the American General Patton in slapping a soldier suffering from battle fatigue, but that did not stop the advance. Taormina was taken on 15 August, and two days later the Axis forces evacuated Messina for the Italian mainland.

Preparations were instantly made for the invasion of Calabria, and the armoured divisions were now moved from Egypt to Sicily. The men were jubilant at going into action again – for many of them it would be for the first time – but this was an odd campaign for veterans like Fergus or Bert or Allack. The crossing was made on 3 September, the British fourth anniversary of the beginning of the war, and accomplished without a great deal of difficulty, for Italy was still in a state of utter confusion; indeed, an armistice was secretly signed between the new Italian Government and representatives of General Eisenhower on the day of the invasion, although it was not made public, for various reasons, until five days later. But already the Allied troops were welcomed as friends and liberators by the Italian people, and by such soldiers as could escape the clutches of the retreating Germans.

Predictably, this caused even greater confusion, as the German forces attempted to disarm and imprison their erstwhile allies while fighting off the invaders, and to add to their troubles another assault was now made, at Salerno, just south of Naples, by the US Fifth Army assisted by the British Tenth Corps. In these circumstances the advance was rapid. The Eighth Army, given the eastern side of the peninsula as their field, were in Brindisi only eight days after landing at Reggio, and on 16 September the two armies, Fifth and Eighth, linked hands; the toe and heel of Italy were secure.

By now the fraternization between the troopers and the Italians, or at least, the Italian women, was becoming a serious problem. In the desert there had been no women, save for the occasional heavily veiled Bedouin. One had saved one's lust for civilization, wherever that might be found, and even then, it had to be strictly bought sex. Suddenly the men were surrounded by extremely attractive, visible, white and willing young women, who were prepared to make any soldier a very happy man for no more than a bar of chocolate. They were ignorant of most of the facts of life, and the incidence of VD suddenly became alarming. RSM Manly-Smith here proved a tower of strength – for all his youth he did not appear to be interested in Italian women any more than in British – but Fergus was heartily glad when after a brief pause for regrouping, the advance was resumed.

To continue at almost breathtaking pace. The important rail junction of Potenza fell on 21 September, and the even more important communications centre of Foggia on the 27th. On the left the US Fifth Army reached Pompeii two days later, and entered Naples on 1 October.

'At this rate we'll be at the Alps before Christmas,' Allack said jubilantly.

Fergus wasn't so sure. It was unlike the Germans to give up without fighting; it was a matter of how soon they could get their Italian affairs under control – but already their commandos had rescued Mussolini from his mountain-top prison and set him up in a new Italian Fascist state in the north.

At the beginning of November the Fifth Army fought their way across the Volturno, despite vicious German counter-attacks which showed that resistance was going to stiffen as the Allies approached Rome, and on the 19th, after even harder fighting, the Eighth Army crossed the Sangro, which was in flood. They continued to drive forward, but now the land was becoming mountainous, and by the beginning of December it was obvious that the tumultuous advance was grinding to a halt before the series of ridges dominated by the mountain of Cassino.

'I think even Rome by Christmas is to be optimistic,' Fergus told his men.

But they weren't going to see Rome at all. The next day orders came for the Royal Western Dragoon Guards to withdraw to Naples.

'Rest and recuperation, I imagine,' said the Brigadier. 'If it's going to become a slogging match, we will need to rotate all the units in turn.'

Yet it was odd that the choice of which regiment should be first withdrawn had not been left to him, and he was obviously put out.

Fergus led his somewhat bewildered men into the famous old city, a peculiar mixture of bomb-shattered buildings and bustling port. Staff officers showed them where to park their tanks and camp, just outside the town, and they were given time off to drive out to Pompeii and look at the ruins. Then they were visited by General Alexander himself. He inspected the regiment, before lunching with Fergus and Allack. 'You embark tomorrow,' he told them. 'But no one except yourselves is to know that until the order is given.'

'Embark, sir?' Fergus asked in a mixture of amazement and dismay.

'You're going back to England,' Alexander said.

'To England? All of us?'

'The entire Seventh Armoured Divison, yes. This regiment is simply the first to be pulled out. You'll leave your tanks here. They'll be moved back to the line by your replacements.'

'But . . .' Fergus and Allack looked at each other.

'I am not at liberty to tell you why this is happening,' Alexander said. 'Although you're obviously welcome to draw your own conclusions. I can tell you that General Montgomery has also been recalled to England, to take up an important new command. He has already left the Eighth Army. He has, however, been allowed to name one or two

247

units which he wishes to have with him in this new command, and the Desert Rats happen to be one of them. I think you should congratulate yourselves.'

'But . . . to leave the army, and in the middle of a campaign, sir . . .'

Alexander's smile was only a little bitter. 'I'm afraid this campaign is going to become something of a sideshow, Mackinder, which I am to have the honour of commanding. I will wish you good fortune in your new assignment.'

10
England, 1944

'Think we'll be home for Christmas?' Allack asked.

'With luck,' Fergus said.

'Shame we can't let them know we're on our way,' Long remarked. 'My dear old mum has a weak heart, and when I suddenly walk in . . .'

'We'll find some way of letting them know when we're in England,' Fergus promised him.

But in fact they didn't get home for Christmas, as they were held up in Gibraltar waiting for a convoy to assemble. Christmas was actually spent at the Rock, which was disappointing, especially as they were forbidden to fraternize with the locals and were confined on board their ships, sitting in the harbour, and staring at the Spanish mainland. Long led them in carol singing and the navy provided plum puddings, but it was a severe letdown.

'It really is most frightfully hush-hush, isn't it, sir?' Mather asked. 'What on earth can be going on?'

'Simple,' Fergus told him. 'It's the build-up for the invasion of France. That's obvious.'

'And we're elected, by Monty himself,' Allack pointed out. 'Rather a feather in our caps, what?'

To join all the others, Fergus thought. Of course he was excited about it. But he was even more excited to be returning home, however briefly, far sooner than he had anticipated. Because he had not forgotten his determination. So, was he also scared? Merely pleasantly apprehensive, he thought.

But he wasn't going to get home quite as quickly as he had anticipated. The convoy sailed just before the new year, and arrived, not in Plymouth, but in Southampton, the first week in January. It had been heavily escorted and there had been little U-boat activity, but on the way the regiment was ordered to deface all its badges and distinctive marks, so that when they disembarked they were totally nondescript; even so they were escorted from the docks in closed lorries and under heavy guard – their new tanks were apparently waiting for them somewhere in England.

'Anyone would think we were prisoners,' Sergeant-Major Manly-Smith commented.

A lengthy drive through Hampshire brought them to an army camp, where they were given quarters; it was certainly the home of an armoured brigade, for there were tanks everywhere, and security was even tighter – the camp was entirely surrounded with barbed wire. It was also, equally obviously, a temporary encampment. The officers might have huts, but the troopers and NCOs were provided with little tents, each to shelter two men, and each beautifully fitted out with two American Army cots . . . with sheets! 'By Christ,' remarked RSM Manly-Smith. 'It's sure as shit we're not going to be here long.'

But while they were there, they were going to be happy; there was an enormous NAAFI where everything except sex could be bought – and even that could be arranged on the QT – and a virtually round-the-clock film show to be watched when off duty.

Fergus and Allack were promptly summoned to Brigade HQ, where they met Brigadier Manton and Brigade Major Crawford. 'Welcome, gentlemen,' Manton said. 'It is an honour to have such a distinguished regiment under my command.' He glanced at the crimson ribbon on Fergus's breast. 'And such a distinguished soldier. I never served with your father, Colonel. Worse luck. And now he's a prisoner of war. What a shame.'

'Yes, sir,' Fergus said, hoping the Brigadier wasn't going to go on about it. He was also disturbed because Manton had never served in North Africa. They were really amongst strangers here.

'Well, sit down,' Manton invited. 'I am sure you have already worked out why you're here?'

250

'We've formed certain ideas,' Fergus agreed.

'You were brought back to England at the express desire of General Montgomery, who is now in England himself, taking up his new duties.'

'Will he be in supreme command, sir?' Allack asked.

'No, worse luck. Now that the Americans are in with us, it seems that they have to have the rank. Eisenhower will be Supreme Allied Commander. Have you met him?'

'Briefly, sir. He inspected the regiment while we were in Tunis, but after the fighting had stopped.'

'Yes, well . . . he remains the American choice.' Obviously he would not have been Manton's. 'Air Vice-Marshal Portal is Deputy Supreme Commander. But General Mongtomery is to lead the assault.'

'Do we know where, sir?' asked Allack.

Manton stroked his moustache. 'I am quite sure that the decision has already been made, but it has not yet been passed down the line. For obvious reasons. However, whether it is to be the Pas de Calais, the Bay of the Seine, or the Bay of Biscay, we do know that it is going to be France. Our training will therefore be organized on that under-standing. And we are going to train, gentlemen. I know that your men are battleworthy. But they must be kept that way.'

'Yes, sir,' Fergus agreed. 'Is there any possibility of leave? Quite a few of my people, including Major Allack and the padre, have been away from their families for more than a year.'

Allack gave a deprecatory cough, but Manton nodded. 'Yes. There will have to be arrangements for leave. I think you should make up a roster, Colonel Mackinder, begin-ning naturally with those people who have been longest away. They can go in batches of about twenty at a time. It is of course necessary to remind them that there is to be no careless talk, but actually, I don't suppose too much harm can be done. If the Germans don't know that we do intend to invade them, then they need their heads examined. And if they don't realize that we are probably shifting men back from Italy for that purpose, then they are not very bright.

What they do not know, and they cannot know, because we don't know it ourselves yet, is the time and the place. Thank you, gentlemen.'

Fergus and Allack made up their rota, which naturally meant that Fergus himself would be the last to get home. He was allowed to write, however, and although he had no doubt that, despite the Brigadier's sensible point of view, what he said would be mangled by the military censors, he was at least able to let Mom and Liese know that he was in England and hoped to see them before too long – presuming the invasion didn't actually start too soon.

He was, however, very quickly faced with a problem, when RSM Manly-Smith arrived in his office one day, together with his brother; Joey was by now a corporal. The two came in with tremendous clumping of boots, and sprang to attention before the desk, rather as if Joey was on a charge, Fergus thought.

'Family problems?' he inquired.

'Afraid so, sir!' Bert was naturally spokesman. 'The old man has had a heart attack.'

'Sergeant-Major Yeald? Oh, my God! Is he all right?'

'He's not too good, sir! Touch and go, the hospital says.'

'Well, you'll have to go and see him.'

'Corporal Manly-Smith will go, sir! With your permission.'

'You'll both go, Sergeant-Major. You're his only living relatives.'

'With respect, sir! I had home leave eight months ago.'

'This is an exceptional circumstance, Sergeant-Major. You will take your leave now.'

Bert gazed at him, face expressionless. 'Yes, sir!'

'And give Sergeant-Major Yeald my very best wishes for a speedy recovery.'

'Yes, sir!'

'And Bert . . . perhaps you'd be good enough to drop up to Broad Acres and put my mother and Mrs Mackinder in the picture.'

Bert hesitated for a moment. Then he said, 'Yes, sir!'

252

'Give them my love,' Fergus told him.

'Yes, sir!' Bert said, and marched his brother back out.

Poor old Bert Yeald, Fergus thought. An almost exact contemporary of Dad. Which made him brood a bit. Mom was right, of course: sixty-two – and Dad would soon be sixty-three – was an absurd age to be scurrying up and down mountains. He'd be the next for a heart attack, if he hadn't already had one.

The Manly-Smiths returned a week later. 'He didn't make it, sir!' Bert announced.

'Oh, hell!' Fergus said. 'I am sorry, Bert. He was a fine old gentleman.'

'We gave him a good send-off, sir!'

'I'm sure you did.'

'And Lady Mackinder sends you her best love, sir!'

'Thank you, Bert.'

'As does Mrs Mackinder, sir! And Miss Mackinder! And the boy, sir!'

'Oh, splendid. You saw them all, did you?'

'Yes sir! Most kind they were too, sir!'

'Thank you very much, Sergeant-Major. Carry on.'

'Thank you, sir! For the leave.' Bert marched out.

He really was a bit of a scream, Fergus thought.

A couple of weeks later the big brass arrived. General Montgomery was accompanied by General Eisenhower himself, as well as several other high-ranking American officers. The brigade put on a display for them, charging across the Hampshire countryside in their tanks, and then parading for an inspection. Eisenhower shook hands with every officer, and then addressed them in the mess hall.

'Some of you men,' the Supreme Commander said, in the measured tones he always employed when on duty, 'have fought against the Germans already, in North Africa and in Italy. You know the nature of the beast. For those who have not yet engaged the enemy, I say again, we are speaking of a beast. He is hardy, he is courageous, he is cunning, he is well armed, and he is well led. But he is still a beast. His deeds testify to that. I want every man here to remember that, and I want you all to instil that understanding in your men. Forget any preconceived ideas you may have about the glory of war, about exchanging a cigarette with a beaten foe, about shaking hands once the shooting stops. We are about to take our places in a crusade, a crusade to rid Europe of the most hideous disease with which it has ever been afflicted. It must be extirpated, so that not a vestige of it remains, so that it can never reappear to poison the lives of innocent men and women. That is our task. That is our business. And with God's will we shall carry it out.

'The way will not be easy. It will be hard. We are going to suffer grievous casualties. Make no mistake about that. But every man who falls will have died in a great and glorious cause, and in the performance of his duty. He will be remembered. Thank you, gentlemen.'

There was no laughter, as had so often accompanied a Montgomery briefing, and the officers felt depressed rather than exhilarated by what they had just been told.

'Makes one feel the SAC is living in a different century,' Allack commented. 'With respect, padre, I have never been able to feel there is anything religious about warfare, or that religion should have anything to do with something so primordial.'

'In many ways I agree with you,' Long said. 'One must of course believe one is fighting for the righteous cause . . .'

'But to talk of warfare as a crusade is going a bit far,' Fergus said. 'Back into medieval history, as John said. Of course, the Americans have always been supposed to live in a different century to us – but it's usually taken to mean the next one, not the last.'

Montgomery stayed on after the Americans had left, and dined with the Brigadier and the regimental commanders, giving them one of his famous pep talks, which considerably improved their mood. To the delight of the regiment, he was wearing the beret they had presented to him. He also found time for a quiet chat with Fergus, but of course was not prepared to discuss the weaknesses – or strengths – of

254

their commanding general. 'It's good to see your fellows looking so fit,' he said. 'I imagine they were glad to see the back of Italy?'

'Well, they rather felt they were running out, until they were told what happens next.'

'Have they been told that?'

Fergus grinned. 'In a manner of speaking, sir.'

Montgomery grinned back. 'Well, one thing is certain; France has got to be one hell of a more suitable tank country than Italy. But the SAC was right when he said it's going to be a tough one. You know our old friend Rommel is in command of the West Wall now?'

'I had heard that, sir.'

'I'm rather pleased about that,' Montgomery said. 'I feel we have some unfinished business. Any word on your father?'

'No, sir,' Fergus said, glad not to have to lie for a change.

'Hm. At least we can say we're now on our way to rescue him.'

'Yes, sir. Any idea when?'

Montgomery looked down his nose. 'I think I can safely say, it will be before Christmas, Colonel Mackinder.'

A weapons expert, Major Lewiston, came down to talk to them about what they were going to find across the Channel. The regiment was assembled together with its officers, who sat in front.

Major Lewiston stood on a dais, and was armed with a huge blackboard and several pieces of chalk, with which he dashed off various diagrams. 'It is true to say,' he told them, 'that a large proportion of the units manning the fortifications on the Channel are what might be called garrison troops; quite a few of them are from Landwehr regiments, that is, only slightly better trained than our Home Guard. They are either too young for sustained active service, or more usually, too old. However, it would be a grave mistake to assume that they will not fight to the death. They may no longer have the wind and the stamina to carry out prolonged assaults – but they will not be doing that: we will. They will be sitting in their fortified bunkers, and they are very well armed indeed. Remember this, gentlemen.

'Now, as I say, they are equipped with fortified bunkers. You may rest assured that the Royal Navy and the Americans, and the joint air forces, intend to saturate the entire landing area with high explosive before a single one of you steps ashore. However, experience in both the last war and this indicates that saturation bombing of fortified positions has no more than a very brief stunning effect. The physical damage and the casualties inflicted are always considerably less than projected, and the will of the bombarded troops to fight, once, as I say, they have recovered from that temporary numbing effect, is more often than not unimpaired.

'In this case, the German fortifications are very solid indeed: they have had nearly four years in which to perfect them. In the First War their dugouts were always marvels of ingenuity; some of them had galleries descending into the earth for two or three levels. Nowadays, these galleries are made of reinforced concrete, and some of them go down six floors. Let into a cliff face they can present a wall of fire some seventy feet high, and they will resist anything less than a direct hit from a high-explosive shell. Even one of those is unlikely to put the whole bunker out of action.

'These bunkers are armed with artillery, as well as machine guns, and they are emplaced to cover any possible landing areas. These are the areas you are going to have to use.

'However, before you reach the bunkers, you must reach, and cross, the beaches. Tides will play an important part here; the range can be considerable in some places on the French coast, and it is never less than several feet. The Germans have emplaced a very large number of underwater obstacles to hamper our landing craft, and they have also strewn wire in the shallow water. However, your main problem will be when you reach the beaches.

'These are sown with a great number, and variety, of mines. In the main these are anti-personnel devices; they will rely upon their artillery to destroy the tanks. But these anti-personnel devices are extremely unpleasant, and the utmost caution must be exercised in crossing any area not previously cleared by the sappers. They fall into two main categories. One is the old-fashioned dish, which carries a charge quite severe enough to blow off a man's leg. The other is our old friend the S, loaded with ball bearings, which can cause a pretty nasty mess. But this now has a variation, which makes it even more unpleasant, to my way of thinking. It consists of a charge which fires a steel rod upwards at great speed. Obviously this is a hit and miss affair. If you tread on it with your right foot, and it is aimed to the right, it will probably fly harmlessly past your shoulder. But if you tread on it with your left foot, and it is aimed to the right, you can abandon hope of ever becoming a father.'

That raised a laugh, but it was really very grim stuff. 'You wouldn't think any of us had a chance of even reaching those bunkers,' Allack commented.

'An old-fashioned storm,' Fergus said. 'Badajoz and all that. Enough always survived to get in.'

They gazed at each other.

'Well,' Allack said at last. 'We've both been damned lucky so far, Fergus.'

'Amen,' Fergus said.

Suddenly he was desperate to get home. This was disturbing. He had never been afraid before, of death or injury. Of course he had had the normal instinctive optimism of the fighting man: it'll always be the next bloke. He had watched that proved, time and again. He had been within six feet of his brother when that bullet had torn into him, and he had been sitting next to Brown when the tank had been struck. And his total misfortune was a couple of broken ribs and various bruises and scratches. Compare that with the old man, who had been wounded no less than thirteen times, several of them quite seriously.

When did a man's luck run out?

It was the beginning of April before the regiment had all had a brief holiday, and by then it was obvious that time was short. 'I'm afraid you can only have three days, Colonel,' Manton told him. 'And as from the fifteenth all leave is out. Understood?'

'Yes, sir?' Fergus agreed.

Three days. But that was time enough, and perhaps it would be a mistake for it to be any longer. Yet the train seemed to be taking an interminable time to thread its way through the West Country, and when it finally reached Bath he had the problem of finding his way out to Broad Acres, as of course he hadn't been able to let them know he was coming.

Fortunately he located a recruit on his way back to the depot, who was as thrilled as he was terrified when faced with the prospect of giving his own Colonel a lift on his pushbike's crossbar. 'Strictly illegal, of course,' Fergus told him. 'But it's my responsibility.'

'Yes, sir,' the boy gasped. 'I could take you the whole way, sir.'

'That's very kind of you,' Fergus said. But he insisted on stopping at the depot gate and squaring the matter with the sergeant of the guard, leaving that worthy also gasping at the apparition which appeared, and then disappeared again.

Even with the assistance of Private Witherspoon, however, it was ten o'clock at night when Fergus finally reached the gates of Broad Acres. He shook hands with his 'chauffeur', sent him off back to the barracks, and walked up the drive. Dogs barked, but they had already been locked up for the night.

Yet he was sure there were still lights on behind the blackout curtains, as he rang the bell.

Robbins opened the door a moment later. 'Mr Fergus? Good heavens, sir.' Hastily he took Fergus's haversack. 'Lady Mackinder is in the drawing room, sir.'

'Thank you, Robbins. Is my bed made up?'

'Oh, yes, sir. Your bed is always made up. I'll just make sure the heating is on in the room. Would you like a drink, sir?'

'Indeed I would, Robbins. A large Johnnie Walker Black.'

'Of course, sir.'

'And Robbins, I haven't had a square meal since breakfast.'

'Oh, quite, sir. Cold meats be sufficient? I'm afraid Cook has gone off.'

'Cold meat will be fine, Robbins; as long as there's enough of it.'

How good it was to be home. How the entire burden of the war dropped away from his shoulders as if it did not exist.

He opened the drawing room doors, gazed at his mother. She was listening to a music programme on the wireless, and knitting. 'Who was it, Robbins?' she asked, without raising her head.

'Trouble, as usual,' Fergus said.

Lee looked up, and laid down her work. 'Fergus!' She was on her feet. 'Oh, my darling boy. You do give me some surprises.'

He took her in his arms, kissed her. 'Always pleasant ones, I hope?'

'Always pleasant ones,' she said. 'But . . . Oh, Fergus, I'm so glad you're back.'

There were tears in her eyes. He kissed her again. 'I'm always coming back, Mom.'

'Yes.' She sniffed. 'I wanted to write, but. . .'

'I got your last letter.'

'Yes,' she said again. 'But I didn't . . .' she seemed to square her shoulders. 'You'll be wanting to see Liese.'

'Indeed I do. Is she in bed?'

'I should think so.'

Fergus sighed, mentally; there was no warmth in his mother's tone. 'Ah, Robbins.' He took the whisky, drank. 'Thanks, I needed that. I doubt she's asleep yet. Would you object very much if I went up?'

Lee licked her lips; it was almost a frightened gesture. 'No,' she said. 'No, I wouldn't object. But Fergus . . . don't be angry with her. She can't help what she is.'

Clearly they had been quarrelling again. He really would have to sort the pair of them out. But not until he had done what he had come here to do. He went up the stairs, heart pounding; he had never before actually set out to rape a woman. Only it wouldn't be rape, with Liese. He knocked, gently.

'Yes?' she asked.

'May I come in?'

'Fergus!' The door was pulled open, and she was in his arms. Naked. But of course Annaliese would sleep naked.

Her mouth was glued to his, and wherever he put his hands he found flesh, suntanned and firm and cool. 'Oh, Fergus,' she said.

He put the glass on the dressing table, lifted her from the floor, and carried her back to the bed, laid her on it. She gazed at him with wide eyes. 'I only have three days,' he said.

'And then?'

'All leave is out. We're going to invade Europe. Sometime soon.'

'Oh, Fergus.' She sat up to kiss him again. 'Three days.' Then she looked down at herself. 'You will be angry.'

'No,' he said. 'I could never be angry with you, Liese.'

'Fergus,' she said.

He was hungry. But hungrier for her. He held her breasts. For how long had he wanted to touch those breasts. She unfastened his buttons. For how long had he wanted her to do that. Now at last Monique Deschards was finally exorcized.

Naked, he held her in his arms. Her body writhed against his, and they rolled across the bed together, kissing and holding each other. Her hand was on his penis, and his was between her legs. They loved with a desperate passion born of a four years' wait. Then he was inside her, and spent only moments later. She continued to move beneath him for some seconds, before lying still.

'My God!' he said. 'I should have done that long ago.'

'Yes,' she agreed. 'I wish you had.'

He rolled off her to lie on his back, and she got up and went into her bathroom, returned with a warm wet cloth to wash him, kneeling beside him, while he took in her breasts and belly and legs and pubes and bottom, all the magnificent things that went to make up a woman. And realized that he had, at last, fallen in love with her.

260

'Have you seen Aunt Lee?' she asked, her face serious as she worked.

'Yes. She's downstairs. So's supper. I'm starving.'

'Then you must eat. I'll come down with you.' She got off the bed, pulled on a dressing gown, picked up the glass he had left on the dressing table and drank some of it. The simplest gesture in the world, yet the most intimate – somehow, more intimate than the act of love. He felt like bursting into song as he got dressed.

They went downstairs, hand in hand. The cold meat, bread, butter, lettuce and tomato were already set on the dining table, together with a bottle of Chablis.

Lee gazed at them in consternation. Poor dear Mom, Fergus thought: doesn't she yet know what a man and a woman do in a bedroom for half an hour together?

'Is everything all right?' she asked.

'Everything is just wonderful,' Fergus told her.

'But he has only three days,' Annaliese complained. 'Only three days.'

Lee gazed at her, hesitated, then kissed her on the cheek. 'Then you must make the most of them,' she advised.

Fergus kissed them both and sat down to eat, while the two women sat on either side of him. Robbins poured them each a glass of wine. Annaliese was perfectly relaxed, but Lee kept looking from one to the other, as if expecting them to tell her something. But for God's sake, Fergus thought: she couldn't possibly want it spelled out, chapter and verse.

He finished his meal, and Robbins gave him a large Hine. He lit a cigar and leaned back with a sigh.

'It must be hell, waiting,' Lee said.

'There are better ways to spend an evening,' he agreed. 'This way. Any news about Dad?'

'Only that he's alive and well. And apparently living with a lot of Communists. Can you believe it? Dad?'

'Well, we're all on the same side at the moment.' He finished his brandy and yawned. 'Would you mind very much if I went to bed?'

'You must be exhausted,' Lee agreed.

'We'll talk tomorrow,' he promised her.

'Oh, yes. There's so much to talk about.'

Presumably she would now wish to start planning the wedding. Because she assumed that once the Allies landed in Europe the war was all but over? He wished it could be as simple, and as brief, as that.

'You'll sleep in my room,' Annaliese told him as they climbed the stairs.

'I am exhausted.'

'Of course. But now that I have got you, my darling, I don't want to let you go again.'

They slept in each other's arms, and made love again when he awoke, just after dawn. He had never felt so rested, so relaxed, so at peace with all the world. He did not want to waste a moment of the day, and as Annaliese showed no inclination to get out of bed, he kissed her, went along to his room to shower and dress – in civilian flannels and sports shirt – and then downstairs for one of Robbins's enormous breakfasts. Aunt Philippa and Lee were already there, smiling at him.

'Fergus, you darling boy,' Philippa said. 'Every time I see you, you seem to have grown.'

'Well, it can't be army food,' he assured her, and tucked into the kedgeree and scrambled eggs – made from powder, but Cook could do even that successfully.

'Did you sleep well?' Lee asked.

'Like a top. Well, up to a point.'

She squeezed his hand. 'I am so happy it is going to be all right, Fergus. I can't imagine another man . . . but now, we really must decide what to do about it.'

He frowned at her. 'About what?'

'Well, obviously she can't have it,' Lee pointed out.

Fergus looked at Philippa, seeking information.

'You mean she actually told you, just like that?' Philippa asked. 'And you didn't blow your top?'

'Will one of you kindly tell me what the devil you are talking about?' Fergus requested.

Lee and Philippa looked at him, then at each other, and then at him again.

'Oh, my God!' Philippa remarked.

'I thought . . . last night . . .' Lee sighed. 'Then she didn't tell you she was pregnant?'

Fergus's jaw dropped.

'You can't be absolutely sure,' Philippa objected. 'And if she isn't . . .'

'She is, and she knows it,' Lee insisted. 'For God's sake, she's had a child already.'

'Will someone please tell me what is going on?' Fergus asked again. His brain was refusing to accept what it was being told.

'Your mother has this bee in her bonnet,' Philippa explained. 'Because Liese is two months late. It's not conclusive.'

'I am certain of it,' Lee said.

'How can she be?' Fergus asked. 'It is damn near a year since I was last at Broad Acres. And incidentally, last night is the first time we have ever slept together.'

'She has her car,' Lee said miserably. 'I gave it to her. She was so fed up, stuck out here in the country . . .'

'She used to be gone for hours,' Philippa remarked.

'I wanted to write,' Lee said. 'But I didn't know what to say. And as Philippa said, I could have been wrong. I was waiting for one more month, then I was going to tackle her. But then you appeared, and went to her room – you looked so happy when you came down. I thought she must have told you, and you'd accepted it. The situation, I mean. I suppose . . .' she gazed at her son. 'What are you going to do?'

'Find out the truth,' he said, and left the table.

'Fergus,' Lee called. 'Don't hurt her. Please.'

He climbed the stairs. His brain was spinning, but he didn't actually want any coherent thought to develop right at the moment. He was afraid of what it would be.

He opened the bedroom door. She was sitting up, and sipping the orange juice one of the maids had brought her. Last night he had supposed he had fallen in love with her.

263

What did he suppose now? But that also was too dangerous to put into thoughts.

'All fed?' she asked. 'I thought we could take a ride this morning. It is such a gorgeous day. Doesn't look cold at all.'

Fergus closed the door behind himself, and locked it. 'Can you risk riding?' he asked.

'Risk it?'

'In your condition.'

Annaliese's face seemed to tighten. 'What condition?' she asked.

'Mom seems to think you're pregnant.'

'Pregnant? How can I be pregnant?'

'That's what I asked her. But you must have missed a couple of periods.'

'A girl often misses periods. I'm run down. Through worrying about you.'

'Liese,' he said, speaking as gently as he could, trying desperately to suppress the raging anger which was threatening to take control of his brain. 'Tell me the truth.'

She gazed at him. 'You come back here,' she said, 'taking me by surprise. You throw me across a bed and virtually rape me. And then . . .'

'Liese,' he said again, his voice hardening. 'The truth.'

Annaliese drew up her knees. 'I was so happy,' she said, her eyes filling with tears. 'I thought . . .'

'That having got me into bed with you, it wouldn't matter. That if the baby was a couple of months premature no one would wonder why. Is that it?'

She gazed at him from beneath arched eyebrows. 'I'll have an abortion,' she said. 'I was going to, anyway, if you hadn't come back. I was just waiting to make sure.'

'You consider that murder and adultery go hand in hand, is that it?'

'I don't know what you are talking about. You come here, saying horrible things to me . . .'

'Liese,' he said. 'If you don't pull yourself together and start telling me the truth, I am going to *do* horrible things to you. If you have an abortion you will be murdering the child in your womb. Don't you realize that?'

'Oh, nonsense. I don't want the beastly thing.'

'And you don't feel that perhaps the father should have a say in it?'

'Him? I don't suppose he even knows how babies are made.'

'Who?'

Annaliese's face closed again. 'You're trying to trap me.'

'You have trapped yourself, Liese. I want the name of the man.'

'For God's sake,' she flared. 'You knew I wasn't a virgin when you proposed to me.'

'I didn't know you were also a whore,' he snapped. Perhaps that wasn't true, he thought. Perhaps he had known that all the time; Dad certainly had. But he had refused to believe it.

'You . . .' she swung her hand, but he caught the wrist, and then twisted it as the anger began to take control. She gave a little yelp and rolled on her face. 'You're hurting me,' she gasped.

Fergus swung his leg over her and sat on her thighs, still holding her wrist. He looked down on that beautiful back, those inviting buttocks, that seething pale yellow hair. She was absolutely the most beautiful woman he had ever seen. And equally the most filthily amoral.

'Tell me his name, or I'll break your arm,' he said.

'So that you can go and murder him?'

'So that I can decide what to do with you.'

'You . . .' she attempted to heave him off, and he bent her arm a little more. 'Ow!' she screamed. 'You're hurting me!'

'Fergus!' Lee called from outside the door. 'Fergus, let me in.'

'Not just now, Mom,' he said. 'Tell me.' Another twist.

Annaliese screamed, and began to cry.

'Tell me,' Fergus said, beginning to despair. He certainly wasn't going to break her arm. And did he really want to know? But he had to know.

'Bert,' Annaliese sobbed, soaking her pillow.

'Bert?'

265

'Bert Manly-Smith. That huge lout.'

Fergus released her arm, but remained sitting on her. His mind seemed to have gone blank. 'When he came back for his grandfather's funeral,' he muttered.

'That's when he gave me this,' Annaliese sobbed, pulling her arm up to hug it against herself.

'But he'd screwed you before?'

'Oh, yes,' she said, her tears beginning to dry as she prepared to defy him. 'He's been screwing me every time he came home. He's been screwing me for years!'

Fergus got off her, and she rolled on her back. 'Does it matter, Fergus?' she asked. 'I've screwed lots of men. And now I've screwed you. And I like screwing you. Does it matter?' She held up her arms. 'Come down on top of me, and I'll give you the best one you've ever had.'

'If I was to touch you, I would strangle you,' he said.

She sat up again. 'So what are you going to do?'

He hesitated. His brain seemed to have divided into two completely separate entities. One half kept telling him that this was the most beautiful woman in the world, for him, that she was the woman he had been going to marry, and that he had just spent a magnificent night with her: therefore that he must hate any man who attempted to get between them, and even more, hate her for allowing it to happen.

But the other half kept suggesting: Aren't you really relieved? So you had a great screw, but do you really want to be married to Liese von Reger? Did you ever? You never loved her. You fell in love with a woman who just drifted through your life and who you will never see again. So what are you so angry about? Didn't you cheat first, with Monique Deschards? Probably not, if Liese was to be believed. But he had believed he had done it first, and he had still done it.

Well, then, Bert Manly-Smith! Again the aggressive part of his brain was shouting, that bloody little swine, always polite, always trying to do his best while he was fucking the pants off his CO's fiancée. But the sensible part of him was recognizing that if Annaliese offered herself, there was

266

hardly a man in the world could refuse her, and more than that, to go back to the encampment now and have a set-to with Bert could only result in a catastrophe for the regiment, just as they were about to undertake the biggest action in their history. An action which was going to end the war and get Dad back, safe and sound. To do anything to jeopardize that would be far more criminal than anything either Bert or Annaliese might have done.

Besides, he could not prevent a ghastly little thought from sneaking into his mind. The regiment *was* about to go into the fiercest action in its history. Casualties would probably be very high. There was no saying that both he and Bert Manly-Smith would survive – or either of them.

Time enough to worry about what happened next when they were both back home. And if Bert did come home, well . . . no doubt he and Annaliese deserved each other.

Annaliese was gazing at him, trying to interpret the various expressions which flitted so rapidly across his face. 'Fergus?' she asked.

Fergus went to the door, unlocked it, allowed Lee into the room. She looked from one to the other. 'Fergus?'

'It seems you were right, Mom,' Fergus said. 'And Annaliese is pregnant.' Carefully he closed and locked the door again. 'The father is Bert Manly-Smith.'

'Bert? That boy?' Lee looked dumbfounded. 'He was always so polite.'

'One of the ways to a woman's heart,' Fergus agreed.

'But . . . what are you going to do?'

'She wants to have an abortion,' Fergus said. 'I am against that.'

'Oh,' Lee said. 'Of course, it isn't legal, but . . .'

'I am not interested in the legality of it, Mom. Annaliese is going to have that baby.'

'You mean you'll take him as your own, like Ian?' Annaliese asked, eyes shining.

'No, I will not take him as my own,' Fergus told her. 'His father is Bert Manly-Smith. But I am prepared to adopt little Ian. In fact, I insist upon doing so.'

'You mean we are still going to be married?'

'No,' Fergus said. 'You are going to marry Bert Manly-Smith, as soon as the war is over. Until then, you are going to live here, and behave yourself. Mom, I want that car taken away, and Annaliese is only to go out accompanied by either you or Aunt Philippa. She will have her baby, and she will sit tight until we come home from the war, at which time she and Bert will be married. And at that time we will arrange to look after Ian.'

'You . . .' Annaliese had gone quite pale beneath her suntan. 'You think you can just tell me how to live my life?' she demanded. 'Decide who I am going to marry? Who is going to have the care of my children?'

'Yes,' Fergus said. 'Because you don't have any choice. You attempt to leave Broad Acres, and I am going to have you locked up as an enemy alien. And you try any funny business, and you go out on your ear without a penny when they release you from an internment camp. I don't think even Dad will argue about that. You should try realizing that I am really being very good to you; many men would throw you out now. But you are my brother's widow, and the mother of my nephew. So you can continue to live here, in total luxury, until Bert comes home. But you had better goddamned well behave yourself.'

Annaliese stared at him, then looked at Lee. 'You are going to allow this to happen?'

'I entirely agree with Fergus,' Lee said.

'Well, you would,' Annaliese grumbled. 'He's your son. I'm just a helpless orphan.'

'Whom we took in,' Lee said severely. 'And made one of the family. I think you have behaved quite disgustingly. I don't see how Fergus could possibly be more generous.'

'Oh . . . I hate you. I hate you both. I hate you all!' she screamed, and threw herself across the bed on her face, to give the appearance of weeping.

Fergus jerked his head, and his mother accompanied him outside. 'I really am most sorry to stick you with this, Mom. But there is nothing else I can do.'

'Don't worry about me. It'll give me something to do. But Fergus . . . what about Bert Manly-Smith?'

268

'What about Bert Manly-Smith?'

'Well . . . aren't you . . . well . . .' her shoulders rose and fell.

'Aren't I going to confront him, and punch him on the nose? Or challenge him to a duel? This is 1944, Mom. Perhaps fortunately.'

'But you're going to have to tell him, something. Say something to him.'

Fergus shook his head. 'I don't propose to say anything to him, at this moment. And I don't want anyone else to say anything either. I want you to monitor Annaliese's mail, and make sure she doesn't write him.'

'But why?'

'Mom, Bert and I have to lead our men into action. The Regimental Sergeant-Major has at least as big a role to play as the Colonel in the life of the regiment. I expect him to be at my shoulder all the time. I don't really want him at my shoulder with all this on his mind.'

'Oh, my God! You don't think he'd kill you?'

'I'd prefer not to think that. But I know he wouldn't be very efficient. And neither would the regiment. Mom, we're in something that is bigger than Annaliese's squalid little lusts. You must understand that. And so must she.'

'Yes,' Lee said. 'Of course you're right. You are beginning to remind me of your father. You go and win your war, and I'll look after the home front. But Fergus . . . bring Murdoch home with you, please. I have a notion we are going to need him.'

Fergus returned to the encampment, a day early, and fortunately so, for the very next day they were visited by General Montgomery, who was apparently touring his entire command.

'As of this moment,' he told the assembled officers. 'All leave is cancelled, and all mail as well. Thus I am at last in a position to let you know what we are going to do.

'Now, as you know, while General Eisenhower is in supreme command of this operation, code-named Overlord, by the way, I have been placed in command of the actual assault. I must tell you firstly that the plans for this assault were drawn up before I was given my assignment, and that when I studied them I realized they were inadequate. I therefore insisted that the area of assault be increased, and naturally that the forces under my command also be increased. This will make our success the more certain. However, it has also meant a certain delay. The initial target date, a full moon and a high tide, was intended to be next month, May. This cannot now be achieved. But we will be ready on the appropriate dates at the beginning of June.

'My intention is to assault, simultaneously, beaches on the Normandy coast immediately north of the Carentan estuary and between that area and the River Orne. The object is to secure a lodgement, from which we will be able both to seize the vital Caen road centre on the left, and swing back to occupy Cherbourg on our right, with the use of its port and its airfield.

'Under my command will be two armies, our Second, commanded by Lieutenant-General Dempsey, in which this brigade will serve, as part of the Seventh Armoured Division, and the first American Army, under General Bradley. We have two additional armies in reserve, the First Canadian, under General Crerar, and the Third American, under General Patton.

'The assault itself will be an infantryman's affair. It will be their task to make the initial lodgement, destroy such of the enemy as have survived our preliminary bombardment, and create a bridgehead. With them will go the sappers to clear the minefields. Before the infantry assault, we shall have dropped two airborne divisions behind the enemy beach positions, and these will have caused as much disruption as possible, and will form interior beachheads, as it were, with which it will be our task to link up as quickly as possible.

'The armour will form the second wave. We have got to have reasonably unobstructed beaches to put your vehicles ashore, and we have got to have inland targets for you to move against; we don't want your tanks to become bogged down on the sand. However, landing the armour will take time, for obvious reasons. I am pleased to tell you that this brigade will be the first ashore, in advance of the rest of the Seventh Armoured Division. If all goes well, you will land on the morning of D-Day. I anticipate that the entire division will be ashore not later than two days after that.

'Now I will tell you about the strategy I intend to pursue. Our first objective is of course to gain that lodgement. Once that is done, my intention is to feint with my left, and strike with my right. That is, the British, supported by the Canadians, will move on Caen, which the Germans will have to defend, because of its road network, which includes direct access to Paris. We know that there are considerable armoured forces in France, and we further know that they are commanded by our old friend Rommel, who is not to be despised. It is my intention to force him to commit that armour, if it has not already been committed on the beaches, to the defence of Caen, and thus Paris from the west.

'As soon as he has done this, the two American armies will break out from their lodgements in a southerly direction. They will then pivot on the town of Falaise, to swing to the east, along the south bank of the Seine. As the Combined Air Forces have been instructed to destroy every bridge across the Seine, this movement will cut off, and trap, all the Axis forces south of the river. That is the initial plan.

'Now let us talk about the lodgement itself. Here we come back to Rommel. I have no doubt at all that he will in the first instance attempt to defeat us on the beaches. This is of course the only German plan which can have any hope of success. Now we know, from our experiences in North Africa, that Rommel is a commander who does not like set-piece battles. He is a man for the mêlée, for the sudden thrust which can be either exploratory or develop into a full attack should he find the opposition weak. He will therefore seek to prevent our armour from debouching out of the beachhead, and concentrating for a pitched battle, in which he must be overwhelmed by simple force of numbers.

'Now, I want to make it perfectly plain that no matter what happens there is not going to be another Dunkirk, another Greece, another Crete. One of those is enough for any war. Once we land in France this time, we are going to stay there. This means that no matter what Rommel throws at us, the Allied armour, and this means you, has got to blast its way ashore, and in such strength that it can defeat any force thrown against it by the Germans. I can assure you that it is going to be the most terrific party. I can also assure you that we are going to win. We are stronger in every department, and our air forces are going to give us constant tactical and strategical support, to limit the movements of German vehicles, and to prevent supplies from reaching their fighting men.' He grinned at them. 'I look forward to seeing you on the beaches.'

'So here we go,' Allack said.

'Hallelujah,' Fergus agreed, and gazed at the RSM. They had only saluted each other last night. Now he studied the boy, because Bert Manly-Smith was, still, only a boy. His large face with the curiously small features was composed and eager, as always when he was on duty. Did he look like that when screwing Annaliese? But he simply had to avoid such thoughts. Women, love, romance, babies, personal rivalries, had no place in what they were about to undertake. Only the enemy and the regiment mattered.

Besides, had he not now cuckolded Bert Manly-Smith, rather than the other way around?

'Everything ready, Sergeant-Major?'

'Every man ready to go, sir. I hope all was well at home?'

'Yes, Sergeant-Major. All was well at home.'

'Glad to hear it, sir.'

'Thank you, Sergeant-Major. Carry on.'

Presumably it would grow easier as time went on, and under the stress of action. But for an intolerably long time there was no action. April drifted into May, and tension slowly increased. Training was now completed; it was a matter of keeping fit, and keeping the mind off the immediate future. The regiment attended film show after film show, lost themselves in the swashbuckling of Errol Flynn and the villainy of Basil Rathbone, the comedy routines of Abbot and Costello, the manliness of Johnny Weismuller as he swung from tree to tree, the song and dance routines of Van Johnson and Betty Grable, and the sultry beauty of Veronica Lake. Only Miss Lake's pictures did the Colonel not attend. But the Sergeant-Major never missed one.

When the order came, on 1 June, it was almost anticlimactic. 'The brigade will move out at oh eight hundred tomorrow morning,' the Brigadier said over the Tannoy. The Brigade Major then gave details of the routes they were to follow. It seemed very complicated in view of the short distance that had to be covered, but Fergus discovered just how complicated it was going to be the next morning, when he led his men on to the most crowded roads he had ever encountered. Vehicles were converging from every direction, and soon progress slowed to a crawl. The results were chaotic. The tanks bore up very well, but it was the First of June, and true to tradition it was a glorious day, for all the wind streaks in the sky. The result was that as the sun got up the heat rose, and the truck radiators began to boil. Stopped trucks added to the general disruption, and all contact with the rest of the brigade was soon lost. Nor could it be regained, for the entire air was a kaleidoscope of voices asking directions, trying to contact the rest of their units, and swearing.

'Hell's bells, if it's like this on the other side of the Channel, Rommel is going to have a field day,' Allack commented.

'It'll be different over there, sir,' Bert said. 'Half of this lot will have been shot up before we make the beach.'

'Oh, cheer me up, Sergeant-Major.'

The day dragged by, but they were making progress, and at last the traffic thinned, and Fergus navigated them to the field outside Southampton which had been marked by the Brigadier and where they had been told to park and await embarkation. Here they discovered a small caravan, blocking the entrance through the hedge, a motorbike, and a single bored military policeman.

'Royal Western Dragoons?' he said, turning over the pages of a typewritten list. 'I ain't got no Royal Westerns down 'ere, sir.'

'Well, you have them down there,' Fergus said, and pointed back along the road at the tanks and trucks. 'So are you going to move that caravan, or am I going to crush it?'

'Well, sir,' the MP said, scratching the back of his neck.

Another motorcycle engine roared, and a Major arrived. 'Nineteenth Yeomanry?' he inquired.

'No,' Fergus said grimly. 'Royal Western Dragoon Guards.'

'Good Lord!' the Major commented, and consulted another typewritten list while the MP stood to attention. 'I don't think this is where you belong, sir. In fact, I can't find you anywhere. Are you *supposed* to be going to France, sir?'

'We are going to France,' Fergus told him. 'Have you tried looking under Seventh Armoured Division?'

'Desert Rats,' Allack suggested, having joined the mêlée.

'Seventh Armoured . . . oh, dear. Oh, dearie, dearie me.'

Fergus wondered if the idiot knew he was on the verge of becoming the first casualty of the invasion.

'You're not supposed to be here, sir,' the Major explained. 'You're supposed to be five miles away, over there. This field is reserved for the Nineteenth Yeomanry.'

'But they're not here,' Fergus said patiently.

'Well, no, sir.'

'And we are. And my men are dog tired; they have been driving, and inhaling dust and petrol fumes, all day. So we will use this field.'

'Well, sir, I don't know that I can permit that.'

'Major,' Fergus said. 'Look along this road. You will count sixty tanks and thirty trucks. I am now going to give them the order to enter this field. If you feel you cannot permit that, you have my permission to stand right here with your hand up saying "Halt!" And that goes for you too, Private. Now move it.'

The caravan was hastily removed, and the regiment entered the field.

Next morning they embarked.

PART THREE

TRIUMPH

11
Normandy, June 1944

It was three days after embarkation before the invasion armada sailed. For those three days the troops sat on board their transports in the Solent, and waited, while it blew better than a gale and teemed with rain.

'Ike will have to cancel,' Allack growled. 'He can never hope to put us ashore, and keep us supplied, in this weather.'

'On the other hand, the Germans will feel the same way,' Fergus argued. 'So it might be worth the risk.'

He worried for the morale of his men, after the build-up of actually boarding. But he needn't have. The Westerns had a sufficient nucleus of veterans to take three-day delays in their stride. The Landing Ships Tank which were to carry them were naturally moored alongside each other, and it was possible to get from one to the other without risk. Except that of stepping on someone's stomach. Every square inch of deck space was crowded, with men standing, men sleeping, men playing cards, and, most numerous, men eating. It was as if the fact that they might be supplied with difficulty once they got ashore had permeated down to trooper level, and every man was determined to stuff himself to the eyeballs. They queued up at the ship's galley, and as soon as they had finished eating they queued up again. The naval cooks took it all in good part; they regarded the dragoons with the air of surgeons aware that their patients were suffering from an incurable disease.

So did the sailors, as they went about their duties, saluting the officers and NCOs who patrolled ceaselessly. RSM Manly-Smith was as ever a tower of strength, constantly on the watch for anyone moping or gazing at the shore, jollying them out of it with a quip and a reminiscence

– he was now using the story of his Alexandrian experience as an in-joke, suitably embroidered, Fergus had no doubt . . . the only three who might have contradicted him were all dead.

He wondered how Annaliese would fare, as Bert's wife. Not very well, he supposed. But he was still determined to make her go through with it. Cutting off his nose to spite his face? He did not think so. He knew now that not only had he never loved her: he had never even really liked her. Which was why he had hesitated for so long before taking her to bed. He had fallen for an idea: Ian's widow; the mother of his nephew, whom he adored; and a beautiful woman, all wrapped up in one magnificent package. To complete the analogy, it was only when he had started peeling off the paper that he had realized the contents had been around just a little too long, and had gone sour.

So where did that leave him, when Johnny came marching home? He really did not know. Perhaps he could advertise for Monique. There was a laugh. A girl like Monique would long ago have got herself married.

'Cheer up, sir,' Bert said at his shoulder. 'Soon be on our way.'

Just as if I was some blasted recruit, Fergus thought. 'I hope so, Sergeant-Major,' he said. 'By God, I hope so.' Because if he didn't kill a German sometime soon, he'd kill Bert.

On the Sunday evening, 4 June, news was circulated through the fleet that the Allied Fifth Army had entered Rome. Nearly all the while that the regiment had been training in Hampshire, its erstwhile comrades had been banging their heads against that Gustav Line, dominated by Monte Cassino, which the Eighth Army had just reached in December. But it had at last been breached.

'If we don't get them from the West, we'll get them from the South,' Allack declared jubilantly. Then added, sadly, 'I always wanted to see Rome.'

'Let's hope there's enough left of it to be worth looking

280

at,' Fergus said. 'Tell you what, we'll go there together, when this is over.'

'You're on,' Allack agreed.

Next morning the Brigadier and Major Crawford came on board to inform them that they were sailing that afternoon. 'As you know,' Manton said, 'it is Monty's intention that we shall be the first of the armour ashore. I'm afraid, however, that there can be no question of our support group accompanying us; the trucks will have to wait for the construction of these artificial harbours the sappers have up their sleeves. It follows therefore, that our initial radius of operation will be limited to the fuel we can carry in our tanks. Tell your fellows not to waste it.'

'What happens when we run out, sir?' Allack wanted to know.

'We beg, borrow or steal some more, or we sit tight and wait for support to come to us. I'll be in touch as soon as we're ashore. But you may inform the men.'

There was no immediate reaction amongst the troopers; the eating and the card games went on as usual – but now there was an air of quiet desperation. This was it. Whatever dreams each man might have had in his secret mind, that, like a condemned prisoner, he could be reprieved by the news that Germany had suddenly surrendered, had now to be buried. The beaches were waiting, and would have to be stormed.

There was, however, considerable discussion amongst the officers when the other squadron commanders, Captains Smithie, Hartley and Mather, came on board Fergus's LST.

'One thing is certain,' John Allack declared, 'I'm not hanging back with the ACV waiting for some damned harbour to be built. For God's sake, that could take days. I'll ride with Sergeant Sullivan.'

Fergus had to agree; he couldn't be totally separated from his second in command. 'I'll leave you in charge of the support group, Padre,' he decided.

'Me?' Long demanded. 'What about divine service?'

'We'll wait for you to catch up with us. Tell you what, I'll

leave the Sergeant-Major with you. He'll see it all goes
according to the book.'

'Me, sir?' Bert asked when he was informed.

'That's an order, Sergeant-Major,' Fergus told him. For
Christ's sake, he wanted to say, I'm trying to save your life,
you silly twit.

Bert went off to board the landing craft carrying the
trucks and the ACV; that wasn't leaving until the next
morning.

The wind had dropped, but the skies remained grey and
leaden, and looking through his binoculars beyond the Spit
forts Fergus could see that the seas were still big.

Now the waiting was close to intolerable. The armada
started getting under way about noon, but as the initial
assaults were to be made by the infantry, it was late
afternoon before the LSTs finally began to move. Smithie
and Hartley returned to their own men while Fergus,
Allack, Mather and Long – who had insisted on coming
along with the first wave even if he understood he would
have to wait for the support group once they reached the
beach – moved amongst the troopers of A Squadron,
talking to them, laughing and joking with them, Fergus
being able to tell them stories of campaigning in France in
1940 – Allack had not joined the regiment until after
Dunkirk.

When the lead ship at last began to make its way down the
Solent, Fergus went up to the bridge. He looked back at the
support group, and received a wave from Bert, also
standing on the bridge; he wondered if they would ever see
each other again. 'Choppy outside the Solent, sir,' said
Lieutenant Moon, who was in command. 'Hope your chaps
are good sailors.'

Fergus wasn't all that worried about the men, but he
collected Sergeant Sullivan and went down to the lower
deck to make sure all the tanks were secured, and requested
the sailors to signal the other ships with their Aldiss lamps
in order that they too might have their precious cargoes
checked out. Then he returned to the bridge, to look with

some awe at the scene about him. The entire surface of the Solent – and this body of water, enclosed against the England shore by the Isle of Wight, was some twenty-two miles long and three wide – was covered with ships, of every size and description, and this after at least a third of the armada had already sailed.

'Just about seven thousand vessels in this op,' the Lieutenant said. 'Including little ones like us, of course. Biggest fleet ever to put to sea.'

While overhead, audible but not visible because of the low cloud – so much for the moon everyone wanted, Fergus thought – roared a continuous succession of aircraft. Most of these were bombers, off to continue their methodical destruction of every bridge and every road which could be of use to the Germans. But quite a few, Fergus knew, would also be carrying the various airborne detachments who would actually be the first in France, landing hopefully several miles behind the beaches further to disrupt enemy communications.

They drew abreast of the Needles, and soon turned south. Immediately the LST began to rise and fall, and to plunge as well; spray flew over the ramp and splattered across the tanks, even reaching the afterdeck where the men were. Within minutes the land behind them had disappeared, and, the sun long gone into the evening gloom, they were surrounded by the purple dusk.

But even the Channel seemed too small for all the ships which were at sea, crowding onwards, while destroyers, like anxious sheepdogs, scurried to and fro, the whoop-whoop of their sirens cutting through the evening.

Now men started to be seasick. Fergus felt all right – he had been on too many sea voyages, although never in a ship as small as this, and never with the prospect of action before he had even disembarked. He and Allack, Long and Mather, and the two lieutenants, Brereton and Openshaw, dined with Lieutenant Moon, and drank a lot of coffee.

'Might be an idea to have a kip,' Moon suggested. 'Nothing you can do for a couple of hours.'

He too was being as solicitous as a doctor about to see a

patient into the operating theatre. But it was sound advice, and Fergus passed it on to the men. He didn't know how many of them took it, but he dozed himself; Long, Allack, Mather and Brereton preferred to play bridge.

Fergus awoke with a start when the night exploded. He looked at his watch: it was just after midnight, and the sky in front of them, to the south, was suddenly a mass of fire and flame.

'There are seven battleships down there,' Moon told him when he went on to the bridge. 'Together with twenty-three cruisers. Softening Jerry up for you.'

The glare of the exploding big guns, and equally their booming reverberations, seemed to make the night darker than it actually was. Fergus peered out at the ships to either side, moving onwards in orderly lines. Every one was equipped with radar, and Moon had his face constantly buried in the eyepiece, but even so to Fergus's unnautical mind it was a miracle they did not all collide in one tremendous mid-channel smash.

The minutes, and the hours, ticked by, while the bombardment continued. Fergus was almost surprised when the darkness turned to grey, and then steadily lightened. Moon pointed. 'France.'

Visibility was actually quite good. Fergus rubbed his eyes and peered at the low green countryside in front of him, still some twenty miles away. They were in the Bay of the Seine, and there was land to their right as well, the Cotentin Peninsula, at the seaward end of which was the port of Cherbourg, so important to their plans. Closer at hand, also on their right, was the tiny, drying harbour of St Vaast La Hogue, where the British Navy had once won a famous victory.

But that was to be the American sector: the beaches were code-named Utah and Omaha, and already he could see, through his glasses, the landing craft surging at the shore, and the smoke rising from exploding bombs, mines and shells. Ahead of him were the British beaches, Gold, Juno and Sword. There too the Landing Craft Infantry were

284

surging through the surf, and there too there was a constant ripple of gunfire.

He looked over his shoulder. The battleships and cruisers were now behind them, huge grey monsters which continued to belch flame and smoke; somehow the LST had threaded its way past them in the dawn.

'Half an hour,' Moon remarked, and from the drawer of his chart table took a sealed envelope. 'Here we are, sir.'

Fergus slit it. The sheet of paper inside contained but two words. 'Mickey Mouse,' he read.

'Definitely an American operation,' Allack commented.

'Easy to remember. Tell the men, Sergeant Sullivan, that the password is Mickey Mouse. And then tell them to mount up.' He shook hands with Moon. 'Thanks for the ride, Lieutenant.'

'Sorry it was so bumpy,' Moon replied. 'Mind you shoot straight, sir.'

Fergus left the bridge and stood on the upper deck for a moment. Below him A Squadron were climbing into their tanks, slapping their hands together – it might have been June but it was extremely chilly – and attempting to chaff each other. He looked left and right, to the other LSTs, where B and C Squadrons would also be getting ready, watched the troopers filing down the ladders to the tank deck, waved at Hartley, who waved back. Then he looked ahead, and felt a slight constriction of the stomach. He could see the beach quite clearly now; it was only a mile away. Thus he could see the bodies dotting it, the shell and mine craters. He could see, too, various wrecked landing craft, lying on their sides half filled with water. And with men. Yet the firing in front of him was dying down, at least coming out to sea. Obviously the infantry had made their lodgement.

He climbed in beside Mather, remained standing in the open cupola hatch while he looked back up at Moon; he couldn't see forward because the landing ramp hid the view. The minutes ticked by, and the day grew steadily brighter and warmer. He listened to the noise of men shouting and screaming, mines exploding, bullets

285

whining . . . inside the well of the LST seemed an entirely different world, of peace and safety.

Then Moon gave him the signal. 'Start engines,' Fergus said into the wireless.

The tank engines roared and exhaust fumes clouded the air; the peace was over.

'Two hundred yards,' Moon shouted through his loudspeaker. 'Depths twelve feet.'

That would just cover the tank, Fergus thought.

'One hundred yards, depths six feet.'

Still sufficient to drown in, if trapped inside a tank.

'Fifty yards, depths four feet. Stand by. Stand . . .' there was a jarring bump from forward and Fergus was thrown so hard against the rim of the hatch that he lost his breath. Vaguely he was aware that the LST had slewed sideways, and then there was a tremendous explosion.

'Oh, Christ!' Mather muttered beneath him.

Fergus was again dazed, and recovered to a high-pitched screaming sound.

'Oh, God!' someone was shrieking. 'Oh, God! Help me, oh, God!'

Was there a woman on board? Fergus looked back at the bridge, and saw nothing but sea and other ships. He realized that when the LST had struck the underwater obstacle and slewed sideways, the stern had hit a mine. The resulting explosion had blown the stern right off, and half of the bridge as well, and the shrieking noise was Lieutenant Moon, who lay on the deck. But only half of him; there was nothing but a bloody mess below the waist. 'Oh, God!' he screamed again.

The mine had also done for several tanks, and presumably their crews. And the padre, who had been up there with the Lieutenant? Fergus couldn't tell, amidst the smoke and the noise – and there was nothing he could do about it, anyway.

He swallowed, and looked in front. Either the explosion or some gallant soul had released the ramp, and it was down; at an angle – the entire LST was at an angle – but still negotiable. He closed the hatch and sat beside Mather.

286

'Let's go. A Squadron will disembark,' he said into the wireless.

The driver engaged gear, and the tank rolled forward. It seemed to hesitate at the top of the ramp, and Fergus took a long breath. They had only poor Moon's word for it as to how deep the water was; the beach looked a surprisingly long way away for fifty yards. And floating immediately in front of them, past the end of the ramp, was the dead body of a soldier, on his face, head and legs down, body supported by his lifejacket, rump sticking up at the sky.

'Get this fucking thing moving,' Fergus bawled.

The tank shot forward, and the ramp went down beneath it. There was a whoosh of water, which rose to either side. But the ramp had struck bottom. The tank went into the water itself. For a moment Fergus's vision was obscured, as water flew past the observation slit like spray at sea, then the tank was on the beach.

And so were nearly all the others, as C Squadron and B Squadron also disembarked; their LSTs had fortunately survived the minefield. In front of them and to either side was a scene of frightening confusion. In the quite boisterous surf was a mixture of men and machines, dead and dying; quite a few of the landing craft seemed to have struck mines, and lay at grotesque angles, half submerged, while bodies surged to and fro on the tide. No one was paying them any attention. Jeeps raced up and down amidst clouds of sand while officers bellowed orders; red-capped military police carefully laid strips of white tape; wounded sat or lay around, bleeding and groaning while field stretcher-bearers tended those they could help; infantry toiled over the dunes as they made their way inland; and over all shells still exploded and occasional bullets whined. Fergus had thought the most horrendous scene he had ever witnessed was the beach at Dunkirk, but this was far worse. The only saving grace was that the aircraft which droned ceaselessly overhead were all on their side.

He looked back to see Allack standing in the cupola of Sullivan's tank and waving his beret. Thank God for that, he thought. But as the vehicle splashed ashore the Major gave a curious little pirouette, and fell right out of the hatch and into the water, his body rocked to and fro with all the others.

'Oh, shit,' Fergus said; they had become good friends.

'Well done, Westerns,' came the voice of Brigadier Manton over the wireless. 'Colonel Mackinder, take your tanks up that gully on your right. The enemy have been eliminated on this beach. Move inland as fast as possible, but keep in touch with Brigade. Good hunting.'

'Well done,' Fergus muttered. Presumably losing four tanks to a mine and the regimental adjutant to a sniper was good going, in the general scale of expected casualties. And the padre. Presumably he and Allack would be buried by somebody else, if they were found before they disintegrated. But if the enemy had been eliminated, who the hell had fired that shot?

'Westerns will advance,' he said.

Waved on by MPs, the tanks roared up the beach and into the gully, which might once have been a roadway. Now it was a shell-pitted strip of horror. The Germans defending this beach had not been 'eliminated' easily. There were dead British soldiers to either side, and some more wounded as well, gazing at their bleeding stumps of arms and legs with expressions of bewilderment. Medics moved about these too, and more MPs were attempting to organize a column of those who could move back to the dressing stations on the beach. To one side was the shattered remains of one of those fearsome bunkers they had been told about, great masses of reinforced concrete tossed about as if they had been clay; intermingled with the wreckage were greygreen figures, lying quietly.

'Do you read me, Sergeant Sullivan?' Fergus asked.

'Loud and clear, sir. Sorry about the Major. Took us by surprise, that did.'

'Close up,' Fergus told him.

The tank topped the rise and entered brilliant sunlight, blasting its way through the clouds. Fergus was quite blinded, and threw up the observation hatch. He thrust his

288

head out, and saw a sapper Captain and several of his men standing at the side of the road. 'Mickey Mouse,' the Captain said, and saluted.

For a moment Fergus thought the man had gone mad, then he remembered and saluted in turn. 'Mickey Mouse.'

'Bear to the left, if you will, sir,' the Captain said. 'We know that's clear.'

Fergus nodded. 'Regiment will bear left,' he said into the wireless.

They rolled away from the beach, and into the midst of columns of advancing infantrymen. It all seemed rather like manoeuvres, when they were free of the horror and turmoil of the landing. The sun rose steadily into the sky in front of them, apple trees made avenues to either side, and in the distance they saw the roofs of houses.

Houses meant Germans.

'It's called Le Hamel,' explained the infantry Colonel. 'Filled with Jerries. Can you give them a push? They have machine guns.'

Fergus had no idea where Brigade was, and he had no adjutant. But he could look over his shoulder and see the tanks of B and C Squadrons rumbling along the road behind him. 'Stand by,' he said into the wireless. 'Your chaps will have to mop up,' he told the infantryman.

'Happy to do so, old man,' was the reply.

The road debouched into an open space before the village, and machine-gun bullets began to spatter in the dust. Fergus sat down and closed the hatch. 'Full speed,' he said. 'And open fire.'

A Squadron blasted the houses in front of them with their seventy-fives; masonry and woodwork dissolved. French houses, Fergus thought. In Libya the houses had belonged to aliens; here the householders were allies. Hopefully they weren't in residence at the moment.

There was a flash of light from the left of them, and then another.

'Brewed, by God!' Mather said, looking at one of his command on fire. 'That's an anti-tank gun.'

'Kill the bugger,' Fergus snapped, and the gun turned to

smother the hidden weapon with fire. Most of the rest of the squadron also concentrated on it, and within seconds the eighty-eight was silenced. So was the firing from in front of them, save for the occasional snipe. The tanks had to form line to roll up the street and debouch into the square, before a hotel. Instantly they were surrounded by men, women, children, dogs and chickens, cheering and clapping; they seemed to emerge from every cellar and every doorway; presumably the families whose houses had been destroyed were amongst them – now they waved German helmets and discarded rifles; from the upstairs window of one house two young men pushed a dead German soldier, so that he fell into the street with scattered arms and legs. The crowd cheered more loudly.

Fergus threw back the hatch and looked out, and discovered a young woman climbing up the tank. She reached him before he could remonstrate, skirt and loose blouse flying in the wind, legs exposed, while her compatriots cheered some more, and threw her arms round his neck to kiss him on the mouth.

'I say,' he protested, and looked over his shoulder. The same thing was happening to Lieutenant Brereton in the following machine. Fergus disengaged himself and dropped back inside, and Mather took his place. Now there were several people sitting on the tank, and a large overspill of red wine began dripping through the hatch. Fergus thumbed the mike. 'Westerns to Brigade,' he said. 'Where are you chaps?'

'Brigade,' came the reply. 'Locate yourself.'

'Le Hamel,' Fergus said. 'And if we don't get out of here in a hurry, we're not going to.'

'Estimate strength of resistance,' the Brigade Major told him.

Red wine splashed off Fergus's head, and he also tasted cider. There was a loud squealing noise. 'Resistance estimated at several hundred barrels of plonk,' he said. 'Reinforced by ditto rough cider and a regiment of nubile young women, anxious to prove it.'

'Move through the village,' the Brigade Major said.

'Brigade is to either side of you. Assist in clearing *bocage* beyond. Headquarters will have cider in preference to red wine, but you may retain a sample of third resistance unit if practical.'

Everyone's hysterical, Fergus thought. Well, wasn't he? 'Keep moving,' he said into the wireless. 'Keep moving. Just for God's sake don't run anyone down, unless they're wearing grey.'

Mather dropped beside him. 'They're happy to see us,' he said.

'So they'll probably kiss Jerry if he happens to come back, as well,' Fergus said. 'Concentrate,' he told the driver. 'What the hell is *bocage*, anyway?'

'It's the name they give the country around here,' Mather explained. 'Rather like the south of England, only more so, if you follow me, sir. Patchwork fields, separated by hedgerows, and sunken lanes. I wouldn't have thought it was good tank country.'

Mather was absolutely right. The regiment moved out of the town on a good road, but soon found it blocked by self-propelled guns and by teeming thousands of soldiers, mostly support troops, who had by-passed the German resistance in Le Hamel. Orders drifted in over the radio in profuse confusion, but Fergus finally managed to raise Brigade again.

'Our objective is the village of Ryes,' Manton told him. 'Brigade will rendezvous there, and then move on Bayeux. That will cut the Caen-Carentan Road, and is our target for tonight. Move it.'

Mather was already looking at the map. 'Ryes,' he said. 'Heck, only a couple of miles away.'

It was only eleven in the morning, but breakfast seemed a long way in the past. And the road in front remained blocked. 'Down there,' Fergus said, pointing at a lane leading off which seemed reasonably empty.

The tank swung to the right and the regiment followed. Within minutes they were in a curving, narrow – they brushed the earth banks to either side – unsurfaced and

291

empty roadway. 'This is great,' Mather said. 'Just as long as we don't meet anyone coming the other way.'

Visibility was less than in fog; they could see nothing but the hedgerows to either side. Fergus climbed out of the hatchway and tried standing up, and still could see nothing; he nearly fell off.

'I say, sir, do be careful,' Mather requested, obviously having in mind that if the Colonel and the adjutant both went astray he might have to take command.

Fergus climbed back in, and studied his compass; the sun had gone back behind the clouds. They were travelling in a generally southerly direction, which was correct, according to the map; it had to be – behind the earthen banks even the wireless was muted.

'People,' remarked the driver, after another fifteen minutes.

'Halt,' Fergus said to his column, and raised the hatch again.

'Thank God you've come along,' said the infantry Major. 'Oh, ah, Mickey Mouse.'

'Quite,' Fergus agreed. 'You have a problem?'

'The bastards are dug in over there, with machine guns. Can't get at them.'

Fergus studied the nearest hedge, which was all he could see. Sticking out of it were several pairs of boots.

'First lot up, get it,' the Major complained. 'Our Colonel's one of those. You can't run through a hedge, you see, sir.'

Fergus nodded. 'We'll see what we can do. A Squadron,' he said into the wireless, 'will turn sharp left and flatten that hedge. And the next one. B Squadron will proceed along the lane and enfilade any enemy positions. C Squadron is in reserve. Wait for the command.' He popped his head out of the hatch again. 'Any idea of numbers?'

'Quite a few,' the Major said. 'Difficult to estimate, really. Every time we put our heads through that hedge, bingo, somebody's shot.'

'Quite,' Fergus said again. He didn't relish going into action on somebody else's reconnaissance, at least at this level, but there seemed nothing for it. 'Well, have your men ready to advance.' He sat beside Mather. 'A Squadron, move,' he said. 'B Squadron, move.'

The driver swung the wheel hard left and the tank slewed round and assaulted the bank. In the narrow lane it was necessary to jockey back and forth several times, and from the noise behind them the rest of the squadron were having similar problems. But at last the front went up and so did the gun, pointing at the sky. Branches waved in front of them, crackling and breaking, and machine-gun bullets bounced off the armour. Heat rose around the crew, and there was an outbreak of cursing. By God, Fergus thought, if Jerry has an anti-tank gun handy, he'll never have a better target. But at last the tracks gripped and the branches began to fall aside. In front of them was a small open field, then another hedgerow. And then another, and another, and another. One of them at least was spitting flame.

'Traverse left, ten degrees, range one hundred yards, fire,' Mather said.

The gun exploded, and part of the next hedgerow but one disintegrated. Grey-clad figures fell about. Now the whole squadron was over the rise and shooting, while B Squadron rumbled by to their right. A Squadron crossed the field, clanking and rumbling, guns firing, and mowed down the next hedgerow. Grey-clad figures stood around with their hands in the air.

'Are you there, Major?' Fergus said into the wireless.

'Right behind you, sir.'

At a safe distance. 'I have some custom for you,' Fergus said.

They heard a violent explosion, crossed the next field, and looked down on B Squadron, neatly in line on the lane, and stationary.

'What the hell is going on?' Fergus radioed to B Squadron.

'I think Captain Hartley has brewed, sir,' Lieutenant Cassidy told him.

'Oh, hell.' So there was an anti-tank gun, only it was aimed down the road instead of across the field. Because of course, if the lead tank went up on such a narrow roadway, the rest were stymied. They would all have to move across country. But brewed? Hartley? 'All right, Cassidy, take command,' Fergus said. 'Come up on to the field level. C Squadron, do the same and move forward. Remember that there must be an anti-tank gun up there.'

A Squadron advanced again, and with a mighty roaring of engines B Squadron joined them. They went in and out of hedgerows and were assailed by a sudden burst of fire which sent one of the Shermans sideways with its tracks shot off.

'There's the bugger,' Mather shouted. 'Traverse right, seven degrees, range four hundred yards, fire.'

The gun exploded.

'Full speed,' Fergus snapped.

This was difficult to achieve on the broken ground, but the tank wallowed forward, and looked down on the gun emplacement. Someone's shooting had been accurate, for the gun crew lay around their shattered weapon in the profusion of death. He looked back down the lane, and could see the burning remnants of Hartley's tank. But presumably, he thought, General Headquarters would continue to regard the casualties as quite light.

The regiment reached more open country just on lunch time, and Fergus called a halt. In a dip about three miles away he could see a church steeple which he took to be Ryes. 'We'll eat,' he told his men, and began searching the wireless for Brigade.

'Your position is admirable,' Manton told him. 'Any casualties?'

'I have fifty-three tanks ready for duty,' Fergus said. 'So I seem to have lost seven. But four went up with the LST. One I know is brewed. One was left in a field a mile back but I estimate is repairable. And one just seems to have gone astray. I know my adjutant is dead as well as the padre.'

'The padre? That's bad luck.' Manton's tone suggested he considered it damned carelessness. 'How is your fuel situation?'

'About another hour.'

'That should do it,' Manton assured him. 'My position is two miles to your left, so we are looking at the same village. Reconnaissance suggests it may be held in force, so we will eat before advancing. Infantry support is also on its way. Stand by.'

Fergus climbed out of the tank to stretch his legs with Mather and the lieutenants. The rest of the regiment had closed up by now, and Captain Smithie and Lieutenant Cassidy joined them. 'We have a battle waiting for us, gentlemen,' Fergus told them. 'Eat, drink and be merry.'

The sun had by now disappeared beneath huge clouds sweeping in from the sea, although it remained quite warm. But now it started to rain, a steady, remorseless downpour which got everywhere. The regiment might again have been in a world all of its own. The troopers finished their soggy meal and climbed back into their soggy tanks, where their soggier bodies created clouds of steam. Overhead aircraft were still roaring, and there were a series of sharp explosions from in front of them; presumably Ryes was being liberated.

'I don't see how they can see what they're doing,' Mather remarked. 'Let's hope they don't drop anything short.'

Fergus thought that was extremely possible.

'Vehicles approaching from behind,' Smithie warned. C Squadron was parked nearest to the road.

'Start up and turn,' Fergus told him. 'Squadron alert.' He raised the hatch to look out, water pounding on his beret and trickling down his neck, and gazed at the rest of the brigade.

'Brigade will advance,' Manton said. 'To the south.'

'I'm glad he said that,' Mather remarked. 'That must be where Jerry is.'

But Jerry wasn't; he had pulled out of Ryes. Unfortunately, the fuel situation was now acute, and the brigade soon ground to a halt again. 'Here we stay,' Manton told them. 'We'll try for Bayeux tomorrow.'

That night, huddled in the still teeming rain, feeling the field in which they were parked slowly turning into a bog, they listened to reports of a German counter-attack, with armour, on the Canadians to their left, and cursed at their inability to do anything about it. But the attack was driven off, and next morning the rain had stopped, although there was still a lot of cloud about, and by the comments on the wireless the roads were worse than ever. But sufficient fuel got through to replenish the tanks, and that afternoon they rolled into Bayeux, where they were greeted by the Sixth Airborne Division, who had been holding the town for nearly forty-eight hours. The paratroopers were glad to be relieved, but the people of Bayeux were not as enthusiastic as those nearer the coast. They did not enjoy having had their little town knocked about, and they were displeased with the peremptory attitude of the Free French officers who accompanied the British and assumed command.

'I wonder if there'll be time to look at the tapestry?' Mather asked.

There was; having reached the vital road, the orders were to consolidate their holdings and wait for reinforcements. Next day the remainder of the division was landed, and the following afternoon their support trucks arrived, Sergeant-Major Manly-Smith himself driving the ACV.

'Am I glad to see you, Sergeant-Major,' Fergus said. And remarkably he was. He needed his mechanics and he needed more ammunition and he needed more food, but it was the sight of Bert, big and coarse and cheery, that he needed most.

'Is the padre with you, after all, sir?' Bert asked. 'I couldn't find him anywhere on the beach.'

'I don't think there's a lot of him to be found, Bert,' Fergus said. 'Poor old Johnny Long.' He was just contemplating the letter he would have to write to Long's old widowed mother, with the weak heart. 'Major Allack bought it as well, and a lot of other good chaps.'

'But we're winning, sir,' Bert pointed out. He was a pragmatist.

On Saturday they were informed that Montgomery

himself had come ashore and established his headquarters. By Monday the 12th more than three hundred thousand men and fifty thousand vehicles had been landed, and the Americans were breaking out towards Carentan.

During all this time the Germans were hardly conspicuous. They could not move by day, as the Allied air forces continued to roam the skies, quite unopposed by any enemy aircraft, shooting at anything which trembled on the wrong side of the front. And as the British armour had fuelling problems, the German situation had to be desperate.

But they were still going to fight. On Tuesday, a week after the landings, one of the division's supply columns, twenty-five vehicles long, was pounced upon by a single Tiger tank. Alarm calls went out, and the regiment was one of those that raced to the rescue; when they got there, they found nothing but the burnt-out trucks and the dead and dying men.

'You know something,' Fergus told his officers. 'This war isn't going to be over all that quickly.'

The British continued to mark time, turning out for an inspection by King George himself, while the Americans swung to their right to complete the capture of the Cotentin Peninsula and the seaport of Cherbourg. This was now becoming vital, as the entire strategic plan, and the main reason for the British hold-up, was lack of logistical support. The weather, instead of improving, merely got worse, and although with great ingenuity the Engineers created the two artificial harbours – Mulberrys, they were called – by sinking ships off selected beaches to create breakwaters, while equally ingeniously, fuel was being piped across the Channel by an undersea line – Pluto – there was still not enough getting ashore to supply both armies at the same time, and a tremendous storm, which began to blow on the 19th, completely wrecked the American Mulberry and badly damaged the British, making the situation still more acute.

By then however the Americans were investing Cherbourg, and although the garrison refused to surrender, the town was eventually carried by assault. While the siege was still going on, the British were at last able to resume their advance, on Caen.

Here too the resistance was fierce, and although the regiment, fed up with kicking their heels in the rain, and watching the bog in which they were parked turning into a vast cesspool, were delighted at the prospect of action, they soon realized they were in for a hard slog. Fergus had by now promoted Smithie to adjutant, and given Cassidy and Withers brevet rank of captain. His tanks were fighting fit and fully fuelled, and his men ready to go.

This was just as well, because the Germans had now committed a considerable portion of their armour, as the attack on Caen had been intended to make them do, and the Westerns soon found themselves in the midst of a mêlée quite as furious as anything they had experienced in the desert. Except that this wasn't the desert. It was a series of once green fields which had been churned into huge mud baths, and were liquefied almost every day by renewed showers of rain, in between which a really hot sun brought out the flies to go buzzing around the many burned-out tanks, grotesque monsters already turning to rust, the green-faced cadavers which had once been their crews grinning idly at the passing clouds.

'Funny, I never thought of the desert as clean until now,' Mather remarked.

The battle raged for ten days, in which time no one ever left his tank except under the direst emergency, such as a serious natural call; empty shell cases were fine as urinals, but couldn't really cope with solid stuff. Then it was necessary to seek a convenient shell hole, but when several of his men failed to return, Fergus felt compelled to issue orders that as constipation was preferable to death, such expeditions were only to be undertaken at night.

The fuel trucks and support columns had the hardest time, as they were continually being shot up, but as usual RSM Manly-Smith coped with tireless energy and efficiency. Yet it was the longest and grimmest ten days the regiment had ever known. The battle raged back and forth outside the city, the Germans counter-attacking whenever the British stopped to replenish, and the British surging forward again, but gaining very little ground. Fergus kept reminding himself that this was all part of the plan, that taking Caen was not the goal, only the forcing of Rommel to commit his armour so that the Americans could break out, and this he had done – but it was a depressing battle for that reason: there seemed no overall tactical concept other than to find Germans and shoot at them.

Yet furiously as the Germans fought, the odds against them were too great. On 29 June the Americans finally took Cherbourg – although the harbour was so badly damaged it would not be usable for several weeks – and were ready for their break-out. Still the panzers hung on in front of Caen, and a week later Montgomery ordered a full-scale aerial blitz on the city. The troopers watched from their cupolas as four hundred and fifty Halifax and Lancaster bombers delivered two thousand tons of bombs on to the German defences – but not all found their target.

'There ain't going to be much left of that lot,' Bert commented. He had, as usual at night, brought the support trucks up to the edge of the battlefield.

There wasn't. The Germans held out for another week, before pulling back. Fergus rolled up the top of a slight slope and finally looked down on the city, and recalled tales his father had told him of Flanders in the last war. It was difficult to discover a single house standing, although, with the careless uncertainty of warfare, there was a forest of single walls rising out of immense piles of rubble.

'No place for tanks,' Mather remarked.

Fergus agreed with him. But he wanted to stretch his legs. He left Smithie in command – they were down to thirty-six vehicles, now, until their replacements came along – and with the new padre, Captain Wint, who had only just arrived and was dead keen, made his way down the slope. They were saluted and directed by the ubiquitous redcaps, who had already taken control of all the roads in or out of the stricken city, and entered the suburbs, where they came upon a group of Canadian soldiers burying one of their number.

'You want to watch it, sir,' remarked the sergeant. 'The place is full of snipers.'

Fergus nodded, and he and Wint made their way through the rubbled streets, keeping close to such walls as remained standing. After the furious battles of the previous month it was strangely quiet, a silence broken every few minutes by a shot or a shout, or the rumble of falling masonry.

'Fairly gives one the creeps,' Wint commented.

They discovered they were not alone. Out of the wreckage arose children, gaunt skeletons of little boys and girls, clothes torn and dirty, who stared at them from huge shadowed eyes.

'How's your French?' Fergus asked.

'Non-existent, I'm afraid.'

'Bonjour,' Fergus said, grinning at them.

'Please, sir,' said one little girl in English. 'Have you any chocolate?'

She held a smaller sister by the hand. Fergus wondered when last they had eaten anything at all.

'I'm afraid not,' he said.

'I have.' Wint had a sweet tooth, and now from the pocket of his battledress he took an unopened Cadbury's bar, and held it out.

The girl hesitated.

'Take it,' Wint said. 'All of it.'

She drew a deep breath, as if summoning up all her courage, then snatched the bar and ran into the rubble, her sister chasing behind her. Several of the other children ran as well.

'I wonder how much of it she'll get,' Fergus mused.

They came across a church, relatively undamaged – only half a wall and part of the roof had been blown away – that was being used as a hospital, found nuns and priests assisting the army doctors who were doing what they could. There were wounded civilians in here, some of them suffering from hideous injuries. But Fergus was used to hideous injuries. What disturbed him was that the church had also been used as a receptacle for the sick from more exposed hospitals. Somehow it seemed unreasonable that a man dying of tuberculosis should be lying next to a woman dying because her leg had been blown off.

'You know what,' he said to Wint. 'Let's get the hell out of here.' Because they were the strong and the living, if only temporarily.

'I'll stay a while,' the padre said. 'Might be able to help.'

'Yes,' Fergus said, and made his way back through the rubble.

It was a relief to be back with the tanks, even if the stench of the unburied dead lay across these fields too. But these were men, and had been men, who had died with weapons in their hands, suddenly, and unexpectedly. To dwindle, slowly, was not a fate he wanted to experience.

'Ah, sir,' Smithie said when he clambered into the ACV he would again be able to use as a home; Waterman had a kettle on, and was buttering biscuits. Fergus wondered where on earth he had got the butter from, but being Waterman he had probably stolen it, so it was better not to ask. 'There was an MP here looking for you.'

'Got me at last, have they? What did he want?'

'Seems his captain had a message for you. Something about asking you to help identify someone they found in the Gestapo cells in the city.'

'That involves me?'

'Well, yes, sir. Apparently one of the people there used your name, as a sort of reference.'

Fergus frowned at him. 'My name? A prisoner of the Gestapo?'

'Yes. I have it written down here. This woman claims to have been a British agent – she's French of course – who was parachuted in to France back in 1942, and was picked up by the Gestapo fairly quickly. She says she was actually employed by your father, Sir Murdoch. Well, of course, if this were true, she would be entitled to special treatment and back pay and God alone knows what else, but naturally she has no proof. The MP captain pointed this out, and also told her that confirmation of her story would be difficult, because Sir Murdoch is a prisoner of war in Germany. So then she told the captain that she also knew Sir Murdoch's son, Major Fergus Mackinder. Bit out of date with her ranking, what? Anyway, he was wondering if you could spare the time to go along and at least identify her.'

Fergus sat down. 'What is her name?' he asked, his throat suddenly dryer than even when he had been in the hospital.

'Ah . . .' Smithie consulted his notebook. 'I don't know if I've spelt it right. Monique . . . Monique Deschards.'

12
Yugoslavia, 1944

With a deep-throated 'oorah' the partisans arose from their concealment in the trees and rushed down the slope. The German forces beneath them were still recovering from the smothering mortar fire to which they had been subjected, and perhaps they had not expected to be confronted by quite so many foes. But Tito commanded at least brigade strength now, and was very well equipped; the partisans could control events, at least outside of the major towns and fortified strongholds. Yet these towns and strongholds still had to be supplied, and however powerful the relief columns, they were subject to overwhelming attacks by determined men and women, resolutely led. As now.

Murdoch glanced at Tito, who stood beside him on the hillside, watching the fighting in the valley. He had directed the whole operation personally, using only the single girl radio operator who knelt behind him. He had a team of these, every one devoted to her leader, ready at any moment to die for him. But then, every man in the army was equally devoted.

And himself? Murdoch had now lived and fought with this man for better than a year. That was longer than he had expected to spend in Yugoslavia, but he had no intention of calling it a day until the Germans had been liquidated or driven out. With perhaps the exception of General Paul von Reger; but to his great relief Paul had been transferred to a command in Germany. Perhaps he would, after all, survive the war, and make something of his life; certainly he could not be held responsible for Edmunds's death.

For the rest, Murdoch preferred the idea of liquidation – at least where the Gestapo were concerned. Every time he squeezed his trigger, he did it for Edmunds.

But he did not often squeeze his trigger, nowadays. He had been reverted to his more natural role, that of commanding general, by the marshal. He didn't command either, nowadays, of course. He advised, from time to time. And he organized the drops of arms and ammunition and radios and medicine and everything an army needs to sustain it in the field – except food: the guerillas lived off their own.

And he moved at Tito's side. He realized he was more than just a mascot. Tito knew a great deal about him, as he knew a great deal about everything, and to have a very famous soldier, holder of the Victoria Cross and a multitude of other decorations, as well as the experience necessary to obtain such trinkets, fighting beside him gave him an increased sense of power.

He was a surprising man, as Murdoch had discovered during their evening chats around the fire. He had fought with the Austro-Hungarian armies during the Great War, unwillingly, as he had been a conscript. But he did not regret those years. 'They taught me a great deal,' he told Murdoch. 'Not about command. I was a private soldier. But one cannot command unless one knows about the private soldier, his hopes and fears, his sufferings and his little ways. Is that not true?'

'Very true.'

'But you were never a private soldier.'

'Our system is not actually geared to it. Although there have been commanders who have risen from the ranks. But every officer must know his men.'

'Oh, yes,' Tito agreed. 'This was the fault of the Austrians. They did not know, and they cared nothing for their men. They led us into battle without even knowing our names. This was at company level. So we cared nothing for them. When the Russians flooded through Galicia in 1916 and my unit was surrounded, we surrendered. Why should we fight for men who cared nothing for us, for a government that cared nothing for us either?'

'So that's how you went to Russia,' Murdoch mused.

'Oh, indeed.' Tito grinned. 'When the Bolsheviks

released me from that prison camp, and said go home, I said, "No, I would rather stay here with you. I have nothing to go home for." So I stayed. I once shook hands with Trotsky. This is not something I should tell Generalissimo Stalin, eh? Not now. But I shook hands with Stalin also . . . when Trotsky was technically his superior.

'I fought in the Russian Civil War. That was a war. Compared with it, this is nothing. We killed everyone we did not like the look of, and the Whites killed everyone they did not like the look of either. Those whom we left alive died of starvation. It is a good thing there are so many Russians, eh? But there too I learned a lot. About survival, and about leadership.'

'But you did, eventually, return home.'

'Of course. A man must do that. And was imprisoned as a Communist agitator. There is a welcome, eh? So when I left prison I returned to Moscow. And went to school. I had never been to school before, beyond learning to read and write. Now I went to the Lenin School in Moscow. Think of it, I was nearly forty and I was receiving an education for the first time. When I returned to Yugoslavia, I was made General Secretary of the Communist Party.' He grinned again. 'This time I avoided arrest, eh?'

'I have been told that you were in Spain,' Murdoch said.

'No. I never fought for the Republicans. But I spent that war in Paris, helping to organize their supplies. That was very instructive.' He glanced at Murdoch. 'So was Paris.'

Murdoch could believe that: the Marshal, willing to share the utmost privation with his men, was equally prepared to enjoy himself whenever the opportunity arose – they were at that moment drinking good brandy which Murdoch had had dropped by the RAF.

'And then, this,' Tito said thoughtfully.

'Which is also instructive,' Murdoch suggested.

'Less so than the others. Now I am putting all my previous instruction to use. Do you think I am doing so successfully?'

'Very successfully. When the war is over you will be a hero to your people.'

A curious look had crossed Tito's face. 'I am already a hero to my people. When the war is over, supposing I survive it, I would like to be a great deal more.'

Here was that dangerous ground hinted at by Colonel Kostitch. Poor old Kostitch. Murdoch saw little of him nowadays, had not seen him at all since Markham had come across to join him with the Communists, although he knew the Colonel was still fighting away to the north. As, presumably, was Mikhailovitch.

'I am sure your government will give you a senior post,' he said carefully. 'They may even make you a general.'

'A general!' Tito gave a shout of laughter. 'I already am a marshal. As for this government of which you speak, which government will it be? Those feeble kings and princes who did their best to lose our country?'

'It will be the policy of the Allies, I have no doubt,' Murdoch said, speaking more carefully yet, 'to restore the status quo ante bellum wherever possible. At least until things settle down and it is possible to hold plebiscites and proper elections so that the people can decide who and what they really want.'

'Plebiscites, elections,' Tito mused. 'How ordered you English are. But then,' he added with a smile, 'there are no mountains, as high as these, in England. Your characters are different.'

With that, he had ended that particular conversation.

Leaving Murdoch with a great deal to think about. But that Tito was going to be a force in Yugoslav politics after the war was certain. As long as he did not contemplate using force to achieve his ambitions. Perhaps, Murdoch thought, my most important role will come after the shooting has stopped.

And now his strange friend had gained another victory. 'They will mop up,' Tito said, putting his binoculars away. 'Let us make a move.'

Because after every little battle, it was necessary to move headquarters as quickly as possible, before the Junkers arrived overhead. That was the true measure of the partisans' success, the true indication of how long a road still lay in front of them, until the Allies could spare them aircraft of their own.

They climbed the slopes and found their way through the valleys. Murdoch had done this so often now that it was second nature to him – and to his body; only sometimes at night, when it was raining or very cold, did his joints ache, and an unutterable weariness creep over him.

The women and reserves were waiting for them, and here were no bearded and filthy bandits such as Murdoch had encountered in Kostitch's camp. The partisans wore khaki uniforms, even the women, and every one was armed. Tito's current mistress was a dark-haired woman, in her middle thirties, of whom he seemed very fond, although there had been others before her.

'Oh, yes,' Tito told his people. 'A victory. Now we must move.'

'There is a message for you, Marshal,' said one of the girl telegraphers.

Tito took the sheet of paper, studied it, and gave a grin. 'The mountain does indeed come to Mahomet, every so often,' he observed to Murdoch. 'This is from Moscow.'

'Moscow?' Murdoch's brain began to race.

'Indeed,' Tito said. 'They have decided to recognize me as the leader of the Yugoslav partisans. Is that not nice of them?'

'I'm not sure General Mikhailovitch will appreciate that decision,' Murdoch said.

'I am sure you are right. It is, of course, only worth as much as the paper on which it is printed, at this moment. But Moscow has also decided to send a mission.' He grinned. 'I suspect they have learned of your presence here, and feel that they too should be represented, even if they cannot quite equal you, Sir Murdoch. They wish me to make the arrangements.' Another grin. 'How will you enjoy sharing your sleeping bag with a real Communist, General?'

'That depends on the Communist, Marshal,' Murdoch replied.

But he felt it was something which had to be passed on,

and he and Markham, a silent, brooding man since the loss of Edmunds, carefully coded a message for dispatch that evening. 'This may seem irrelevant now,' Murdoch wrote, 'but may assume great importance after the war. Until instructions are received, I will maintain every friendly contact with the Russians.'

London replied a fortnight later, to say that he had made the correct decision, and that he was to continue in his policy. To add to the strength of his position, however, London was also sending out another mission, to join Markham and himself: the reply added, cryptically, that the new mission would bring special instructions for Sir Murdoch Mackinder, personally. Murdoch could guess what they would be.

'We are to become a regular League of Nations,' Tito said jovially. He did not seem upset by the imminent arrival of a clutch of 'experts' to tell him what he was doing wrong – he had no doubt at all of his own ability.

The English mission actually arrived first, a good dozen men, headed by a Brigadier, who landed at a hastily constructed airstrip high in the mountains. 'I'm afraid my orders are to place you on this plane and send you back, Sir Murdoch,' Brigadier MacLean said, after shaking hands.

'Have you a warrant for my arrest?' Murdoch inquired.

'Well, of course not, sir. Everyone recognizes that you have done a grand job here. But I do have written orders from the Prime Minister himself.'

'Which I intend to ignore. I'm not in the habit of abandoning a job until it is finished. I also have some personal business to complete.'

'Yes, sir,' MacLean said, and looked extremely embarrassed. 'I imagine the PM foresaw what your probable reaction might be. I have therefore been given other written orders, instructing me to take command of the British Mission, and everyone connected with it. This actually does give me the right to arrest you, and put you on that plane.'

'It won't make your welcome from Tito very warm.'

MacLean sighed. 'If you remain here, sir, it will be as a

civilian observer, under my command. My orders are perfectly clear about that.'

'Yes, sir!' Murdoch acknowledged.

MacLean gazed at him for several seconds, then held out his hand. 'I'm actually damned glad you're staying, Sir Murdoch. But you must realize that from here on, everything must be done in my name and under my authority.'

'So am I, glad to be staying, Fitzroy,' Murdoch said, and squeezed his fingers.

MacLean had brought with him a personal letter from Churchill to Tito, the promise of ever greater logistical support, and a present, a terrier named Tigger.

'Tigger,' Tito said, as he cradled the little dog in his arms. 'What does this mean, Tigger?'

'Well,' MacLean said, and looked at Murdoch.

'It's a diminutive for Tiger, I suppose,' Murdoch said. 'It comes from a children's story, which is a classic in England, about a small boy and his bear.'

'And his tigger,' Tito suggested.

'Oh, quite.'

'He will go with me everywhere,' Tito decided.

He was less content with the second half of the letter, which urged, logically enough, that were he to cooperate more closely with General Mikhailovitch and the Chetniks, he would accomplish more and bring the day of victory ever closer.

'Your Mr Churchill has never been to Yugoslavia,' he said. 'Why should he have? We are an artificial nation, Sir Murdoch, General MacLean. In 1919, when they were putting the world to rights, as they thought, the United States, Great Britain, France and Italy took various remnants of the Austro-Hungarian Empire and pressed them together, as a child might do with several different-coloured pieces of Plasticine, and said, this will be a nation. The nucleus was Serbia. The various additives were Montenegro, Croatia, Bosnia, the Banat . . . these are different people, hurled together and told to be of one nationality: Yugoslavia.'

'So were England, Ireland, Scotland and Wales,' Murdoch pointed out. 'At various times, to become the United Kingdom.'

'Quite,' Tito agreed. 'And they continued to fight each other for more than a hundred years after the Union. Indeed, they continue to fight each other still, and will again, when the war is over. I only wish to make the point that Mikhailovitch and I are presently bound by one concern, to beat the Germans. At least, I am bound by that concern. As regards Mikhailovitch, I sometimes wonder. In any event, I do not believe that we would fight well side by side.' He gave one of his grins. 'I would have to be looking, from side to side, too much of the time.'

'That is going to be quite a problem, when the shooting stops,' Murdoch confided to MacLean when they were alone. 'To stop it from starting again, from side to side.'

'Yes,' the Brigadier agreed. 'Anyway, I think we may have scored a point with little Tigger. The Marshal seems awfully fond of him.'

'Let's see what the Russians have to offer him,' Murdoch decided. 'Before we celebrate.'

'It is my great pleasure and honour,' announced General Sherepkin, 'to present you, Marshal, on behalf of General-issimo Stalin, the Order of Victory.'

He snapped his fingers, and one of his aides stepped forward with a large jewel case, from which the General took a huge ruby star, studded with diamonds. This he proceeded to drape around Tito's neck.

'Oh, hell,' MacLean muttered.

Sherepkin then proceeded to kiss Tito on each cheek.

'You didn't do that either,' Murdoch pointed out.

But the General was beating a hasty retreat as Tigger snapped at his ankles.

'He is a capitalist dog,' Tito explained.

The General frowned. He was obviously a very sober man.

With a very serious purpose. The dozen or so members of the British mission were swamped by the thirty-odd

310

Russians who had descended upon the partisans. There were colonels and captains, wireless operators and weapons experts and, needless to say, commissars come to instruct the partisans in the ways of the faithful – 'We have a problem on our hands,' MacLean muttered – and even some females, all wearing uniform. These were all introduced both to Tito and to the British officers, and Murdoch suddenly realized just how big a problem they did have – or at least, himself.

'Sir Murdoch,' said Yasmin Bogoljubova. 'I have anticipated this moment for six years.'

She was now Colonel Yasmin Bogoljubova, and wore a green skirt and blouse, with brass buttons and epaulettes revealing her rank, which also indicated that she was a Commissar of the Communist Party. Her beret was also green, and also carried her badge of rank; she had cut her silky black hair and it was all but concealed. Her boots were black and knee length, and she wore a belt from which hung a revolver holster. She seemed a far cry from the slightly hysterical and somewhat emaciated girl who had crept into his London flat and tried to murder him in 1938; she looked trim and fit and as darkly beautiful as ever. But she was the same girl. Only now she was a woman.

'I didn't know you knew any Russians,' MacLean remarked when the introductions were over.

'I've met a lot of odd people in my time,' Murdoch agreed. 'And that young woman is only half Russian, anyway. The other half is Pathan.'

'That's an interesting combination. How on earth did it come about?'

'Well basically because her Pathan mother married a Russian,' Murdoch suggested. 'Her mother was a Mahsud princess who caused a great deal of trouble on the North West Frontier once upon a time.'

'I see. And you met her when you served up there.'

'Yes,' Murdoch said. 'I hanged her.'

MacLean's head turned, sharply. 'You hanged . . . a Mahsud princess?'

'For the mutilation and murder of some of my men, yes.'

'Good Lord! Then this girl . . .'

'She tried to do me once before,' Murdoch said.

'We'll have to tell Tito. Have her sent back.'

'I don't think we will do that,' Murdoch said. 'I am no believer in coincidences.'

'They do happen.'

'Not very often. No, Brigadier, Tito remarked, when he heard the Russians were sending a mission, that they must have found out I was here. This girl was sent.'

'To murder you? My God, we can't have that. I can still arrange for you to be flown out, you know.'

'I'd prefer to stay and find out just what she has in mind,' Murdoch said.

MacLean scratched his head. 'Well, I'm going to detail one of my people to keep an eye on her, night and day.'

'I intend to do that myself,' Murdoch told him.

Murdoch knew she would seek him out, as soon as there was an opportunity – and whatever her purpose. That afternoon he walked away from the caves where the headquarters was currently situated, down the slope and into the trees. It was late spring, and the weather was perfect; this high up it was not even very hot, and there was a whisper of breeze to sough through the pines.

He went down the hill some hundred feet to where he knew there was a little stream, fed from the mountain spring where the camp drew their water. The stream was about three feet wide, and he waded across, found a suitable tree, and sat down, with his back to the camp itself. He was out of sight of it anyway, and behind this wide tree he was totally concealed from anyone on the far side of the stream; he did not suppose there could be a more private place in all Yugoslavia. He hadn't looked back once, since leaving the camp, but he did not suppose he would have very long to wait. He took his service revolver from his holster and laid it on the ground beside him, after checking the chambers. But whether he would have to use it depended on her. It would be bad for business, of course. He regarded Tito almost as a friend, now, but yet the Marshal was a supporter of the Moscow regime rather than Westminster, and to have one of his Russian guests gunned down would probably upset him. Thus it would have to be a clear-cut case of self-defence.

But what would he feel about doing it? If he felt no regrets for having executed Chand Bibi, who was about the coldest-hearted killer he had ever encountered, he had always felt some pity for her daughter, whose entire life had been confounded by her mother's sudden death. It was difficult to be sure why he felt that way. Part had been the natural pity of any thinking human being for a child, suddenly and brutally orphaned at the age of nine – and Yasmin had actually seen her mother dangling from the rope. But it was salutary to remind himself that had he not caught up with Chand Bibi and destroyed her army in the last of his famous cavalry charges, Yasmin would have grown up in the Mahsud nation and the Mahsud way. She would have learned that the British were her hereditary enemies, and that the most famous deed she could accomplish for her people would be to sit on the chest of a wounded British soldier, and having sliced away his genitals, then slowly and carefully remove his nose and lips and ears before poking out his eyes.

She had been saved that. But might it not be bred in her heart and mind? And in any event, had she really been taught a lot different, in Russia? Not on the evidence of 1938.

Yet he had not killed her then. Of course, she had, in his terms, been innocent then. She had tricked her way into his apartment when he was alone there, produced a pistol and told him she was going to shoot him. How naïve could one be, when confronting a man with thirty-eight years' experience of killing people, without being killed himself? She had wanted to savour her moment of triumphal revenge, and had wound up disarmed and a prisoner. Yet the gun had been hers, and she was the intruder. Had he, as he so easily could have done, turned it on her and

313

announced that it had gone off during the struggle, no one would have doubted him for a moment.

Instead, he had handed her over to the police for deportation. He had not expected ever to see her again That he had done so had to be her decision, and not a trick of Fate. He could only wait to find out what had inspired that decision.

The rustle of the water submerged all other sounds, yet he knew when she was there. A lifetime of soldiering caused the hair on the back of his neck to prickle, the adrenalin to start flowing into his arteries, long before she appeared, some ten yards to his right, her boots and the hem of her skirt wet from where she had waded the stream. And she had not yet seen him, looked first to her right, and only then to her left. By then he had picked up the revolver.

She inhaled, sharply, an attractive gesture. 'Are there enemies in these hills, Sir Murdoch?' Her English contained only a trace of accent.

'One tends to be careful,' Murdoch replied.

She came towards him. 'Do you walk in the woods every afternoon?'

'No.'

'That is what the women in the camp told me.' She stood above him. 'So I assumed there had to be a reason.'

'I thought you might like a little chat,' Murdoch said. 'And tried to make it easy for you.'

'You are a true gentleman,' she acknowledged. 'And this chat was to end with my execution?' She pointed at the revolver, which lay on his lap – his finger was still on the trigger.

'I was interested to know whether you considered we still have some unfinished business.'

'Indeed we have, Sir Murdoch. We have to beat the Germans. Is that not why you are here?'

'So tell me why *you* are here. I imagine you can fight the Germans just as enthusiastically, and far more effectively, on the Russian front.'

'I am a Commissar in the Russian Army. I go where I am sent, to fight.'

'And the fact that you knew I was here had nothing to do with where you were sent?'

Yaskin regarded him for several seconds, then she suddenly stretched. 'It is warm. Much warmer than I had expected.'

'It will be much colder come January. If you are still here.'

'Of course I will still be here, Sir Murdoch. Unless, perhaps, Germany has surrendered by then.' She smiled at him. 'Or you have shot me.'

She stepped away from him, and round the tree. He stood up, moving slowly and carefully, back still pressed against the trunk, and waited. When she did not reappear, he stepped round the tree himself, revolver held in both hands. But he slowly lowered it as he watched her, feeling somewhat embarrassed.

Yasmin had discarded belt and beret, and was sitting down to pull off her boots. Her back was to him, but she had no doubt he was there. In many ways they were well matched, he thought.

But perhaps that was being optimistic, because having discarded her boots, she now pulled up her skirt and rolled down her stockings; he could hardly compare his legs with those smoothly sheened limbs. Then she stood up, and removed her blouse; she wore no brassiere. He watched, becaused she obviously intended him to, as she slid her skirt and drawers past her knees and stepped out of them. He had thought Annaliese von Reger the most perfectly formed human creature on God's earth, except for her mother. He had thought Monique Deschards comparable only to Jennifer Manly-Smith as the most compelling of all God's female creations. And he had thought his wife the most lovable of all women, and still did think so. But here was the most earthily desirable of women, a tremble of muscle at thigh and shoulder and even affecting the heavy breasts; with her hair cut short there was no distraction from the effect of her powerful body.

He had thought that about her mother too – and Chand Bibi's hair had always been long.

315

She stepped into the water and sank to her knees, giving a little shudder as she did so. 'It is so cold,' she said. 'And so refreshing. Why do you not join me, Sir Murdoch?'

'Sudden cold is bad for the rheumatism,' he said.

She looked over her shoulder. 'I do not believe you suffer from rheumatism. You move like a young man.'

'Only in some directions.'

She gave a tinkle of laughter. 'I must find out in which they are.'

Murdoch picked up her holster, extracted the pistol, and pocketed the magazine.

'I have others, at the camp,' she said.

'I'm sure you do,' he agreed. He holstered his own gun, went through her clothing, found the long, slim-bladed knife sheathed on the inside of her skirt.

'I never knew you were interested in women's underwear,' she said, facing him as she scooped water over her shoulders, idly.

'I am interested in everything about you, Yasmin,' he said, and tossed the knife several feet away. Then he sat down, facing her. 'Now I can enjoy you.'

She stood up. Water dripped from shoulder and armpit and nipple and pubic bush. 'I want you to enjoy me, Sir Murdoch.'

'I am doing so,' he said. 'But I will bet I am not doing so half as much as Sergeant Ferris, my bodyguard, just up the hill over there.'

He thought her angry squeal as she had dropped back into the water represented a victory of sorts: she really was a far more moral creature than Annaliese von Reger. That night as they sat around their camp fire and drank the vodka the Russians had also brought with them in large quantities she merely glowered at him.

'I would say she's definitely bearing a grudge,' MacLean confided.

'This is a recent one,' Murdoch told him.

Sherepkin had a great deal to say. 'Generalissimo Stalin feels that now is the time for a big push,' he said. 'He is

316

confident that with a concerted effort here, in the direction of Sarajevo, you will tie up a great number of German forces. And with the great Russian armies battering at the Germans in the east, and the British and the Americans fighting in the west, the defeat of the Hitlerites will be brought that much closer.'

Tito listened, nodding sagely, and as the evening wore on and the vodka level sank in the bottles, Sherepkin grew ever more expansive. By the time he was carried to his sleeping bag he was talking about the fall of Sarajevo. Tito, who could drink any man under the table, also went to bed, but next morning he sat beside Murdoch to shave in the crisp morning air.

'What do you think?' Tito asked.

'You will be outgunned, and outnumbered,' Murdoch told him. 'Even now. Chipping away as you are doing is the best way to occupy the Germans in Yugoslavia. It is a matter of pure mathematics. You have perhaps five thousand men at your disposal, and Mikhailovitch may have five thousand more. Ten thousand men. And what is the German occupying force? Two hundred thousand men? You are doing far more effective work by just being here, than you could ever do by getting your force destroyed, even if your people were to take two Germans for every one of them, because at the end of it they would still be able to afford to withdraw a hundred and fifty thousand for service elsewhere.'

'I have never heard of war estimated in such terms before,' Tito said thoughtfully. 'Have you never led your men into battle against overwhelming odds? I know you have. I have read of your deeds.'

Murdoch smiled. 'On at least one occasion I didn't have much choice, because I was surrounded and had to fight or die. On the others, I was required to make tactical sacrifices to aid the army as a whole.'

'Well, that is what we must do. This war involves everyone. We are only a small part of it. But the General-issimo has ordered me to carry out an offensive here in Yugoslavia, and I will do so.'

'The decision must be yours,' Murdoch agreed.

'But you do not agree with it.'

'No, I do not.'

Tito wiped his chin, and slapped Murdoch on the shoulder. 'Then you do not have to take part in it.'

Murdoch grinned at him. 'How will I know what you need replacing, afterwards?' he asked.

For the next fortnight everyone was too busy for Murdoch ever to see Yasmin more than in passing. No doubt she remained angry with him. No doubt she had come to Yugoslavia to murder him. But it was not possible while they were surrounded with so much hustle and bustle, and while one of MacLean's men was always at his shoulder. So no doubt her milk was curdling, he supposed – if women like Yasmin Bogoljubova had any milk.

Meanwhile, elaborate plans were laid. Tito, on the insistence of Sherepkin, sent messengers to Mikhailovitch and to all the small guerilla commanders, such as Kostitch, calling on them to join with his people in the grand offensive. Meetings were held, at which Tito and Mikhailovitch sat opposite each other, and discussed the forces they would bring into the field and the areas in which they would operate. They even discussed tactical plans. But neither would combine with the other.

'It would, of course, be far more effective if your several forces were to be thoroughly integrated,' Murdoch told Tito.

The Marshal shook his head. 'That can never be, with Mikhailovitch.'

'The man is not to be trusted,' Sherepkin growled. 'We know this, in Moscow.'

'With respect, Sir Murdoch,' MacLean decided, 'I would like you to remain at base camp and monitor events from there. I will accompany the Marshal in the field.' He met Murdoch's gaze. 'You did agree to accept my command, sir. And frankly, you are not expendable. While I am sure your influence on events will be much greater than mine, should things go astray.'

Murdoch had to agree he was right. But it was none-theless galling to watch the men, and the women, for Tito had armed every woman able and willing to fight, march off down the hillside to take up their positions. He simply had to remember, he kept telling himself, that he was now a very senior soldier indeed. Montgomery did not get involved in the thick of the fighting, and neither did Eisenhower – which of course was the reason why they were still commanding armies and he was relegated to this side show – illegally.

At least Yasmin accompanied the Russians. He could relax somewhat. Perhaps she would get her head shot off. He sent his bodyguard off with MacLean.

The army melted away, and the hillside was utterly quiet. Only a few hundred women, some guards, the goats and cattle, and the dog Tigger were left. They might have been a community of farmers, minding their own business. Under the guidance of their patriarch, Murdoch thought irritably.

It was impossible to know what was happening down there in the valleys and beyond the lake, because Tito had decreed radio silence; each man in his command knew what he was required to do, and hopefully further orders would not be necessary. At the appointed hour the faint rumble of gunfire came up into the hills, and through binoculars Murdoch could make out smoke rising into the still air. That had to be an outlying engagement.

Two days later the planes came. One of the women was on spotting duty, and she hurried down to the encampment to warn of the approach. 'Avione!' she shouted. 'Avione!'

Murdoch levelled his glasses, made out a squadron of Junkers 87s, flying low, looking – he hustled everyone into the caves, which formed a network through the mountain-side, remained himself near the entrance with a dozen men. The dive bombers flew on, past them, and then suddenly turned back. Someone had spotted something . . . or perhaps they had just been told to bomb wherever they saw water – the one essential of life the guerillas could not conceal.

The planes screamed down at the mountain with that so familiar wail, and the bombs fell from their undercarriages. The mountain shook and columns of earth and rock and water hurled themselves into the sky.

'They know we are here,' said the senior remaining partisan, Colonel Ivkov, watching the explosions coming closer.

'No,' Murdoch said. 'They are guessing. And they cannot destroy the water. No matter how they block it or dam it, it will re-emerge somewhere else.'

But the partisans were getting restless, gripping their rifles the more tightly, staring out of the aperture, until one leapt to his feet, gun to his shoulder, and fired. Instantly another followed his example, and then all twelve of them were blazing away.

'Damnation,' Murdoch muttered.

The rifle bullets were doing no damage, but the men had been seen, and now one of the Junkers was flying straight at the cave mouth.

'Back,' Murdoch snapped. 'Fall back.' There was another, smaller exit lower down the hill which could be used if this one became totally blocked. 'Back.'

The men hesitated, and Murdoch looked past them at the deadly egg dropping from beneath the aircraft's wheels.

Then there was nothing at all.

Murdoch was aware less of pain than of a crushed feeling, which left him exhausted. His nostrils were clear, because he could breathe, yet he inhaled dirt and dust to suggest that they had recently been blocked. And memory was a kaleidoscope of movement, up and down, jolting and uncomfortable, as if he had been slowly rolling down to hell. But he looked at blue sky, so bright it hurt his eyes.

He heard voices, and tried to turn his head. This was painful, and he decided it would be better to turn his whole body. But that was impossible.

He lay still, and considered his situation. He was bandaged, in several places, and cocooned in his sleeping bag. He was also naked. And very thirsty.

He opened his mouth, drew a long breath, and called 'Hello.'

He heard feet, and then the brightness of the sky was obscured. He was looking at Yasmin Bogoljubova. Desperately he tried to move his arm, to find his revolver. But his revolver had gone with his clothes; as his bodyguard had gone with MacLean.

'You must not be restless,' Yasmin told him.

Murdoch licked his lips. She too seemed to be unarmed – she was not wearing her pistol. But he remembered the knife beneath her skirt. On the other hand, she looked tired rather than aggressive, or even mocking, as on so many occasions. She even looked concerned.

'I am very thirsty,' he said.

'I will fetch water.'

She came back a few minutes later with an enamel mug, knelt beside him, and raised his head, held the mug to his lips. Water trickled down his throat.

'What are you doing here?' he asked.

'At the moment, looking after you.'

'Should you not be fighting?'

She pulled a face, and took the cup away. 'Are you hungry?'

Murdoch realized that he was, very hungry.

'You should eat,' Yasmin told him. 'You have not eaten for several days.'

'Several days?'

She frowned at him. 'Try not to be excited. Yes. You have been semi-conscious, unable to move, for three days, since my return, and you were out for the day before that, too. Do you not remember? The cave fell in on you.'

'Then how the hell did I survive?'

'The women dug you out. You were lucky, in that sense. Most of the men with you were killed outright. You were even luckier in that you did not break anything serious, merely got a bad bump on the head. How is your head?'

'It hurts,' Murdoch said, realizing that it did.

'And you were even luckier that I returned the following day,' Yasmin told him. 'The women did not know what to do with you.'

'But you did.'

'Of course. I am trained as a nurse, amongst other things. I realized at once that you were suffering from severe concussion, and also from the effects of being buried alive. I had you bathed and bandaged and placed in your sleeping bag. And I fed you medicine.'

'You, did all that, Yasmin?'

Her smile was twisted. 'Why not? You could be my commanding officer, now. I do not know, for certain. I will fetch food.'

Again he tried to move, to look after her, but gave it up after a few seconds. And by then she was back, with a bowl of gruel. She sat beside him, raised his head to rest on her lap, and began to feed him. 'Do you realize there are thirteen separate scars on your body? I counted them. That was before the various cuts and bruises caused by the falling rock. You are a very tough old man, Sir Murdoch.'

'So I've been told. Why did you come back so quickly? What happened to the offensive?'

'It was a disaster.'

His turn to frown at her. 'A disaster?'

'Oh, yes. The Germans knew we were coming.'

'They could not have done so.'

'Then they are clairvoyant. Every position we assaulted was ready for us. Our people were shot to pieces.'

'Brigadier MacLean?'

'I do not know.'

'Tito?'

'I do not know about him, either. The Germans counter-attacked, with panzers, and we were scattered. General Sherepkin is dead, together with all of our people.'

Well, Murdoch thought, the whole hare-brained scheme was his idea, anyway.

'What of Mikhailovitch?' he asked.

'When we realized we were beaten, we contacted his command by radio, and were told that they too could make no headway. By then the Germans were in our midst. Marshal Tito told us to scatter and make for the emergency rendezvous. So I did that. As I say, I do not know what happened to the Marshal and your General.'

'My God,' Murdoch muttered. 'They are probably at the rendezvous. We must get there as quickly as possible.'

'We are already at the rendezvous,' Yasmin told him.

'Already? But . . .'

'We could not stay at the cave. Those caves. So we moved here. That is why you are so thoroughly strapped up. We have carried you, for two days.'

His frown deepened as he gazed at her. 'But you did not come straight here. You went to the old camp first. Why did you do that?'

She smiled at him, and laid his head back on the sleeping bag; the gruel was finished. 'I went there to find you. Sherepkin is dead. So are all my comrades. Tito has disappeared. It is probable that he too is dead. Your Brigadier MacLean has gone with him. All our unit commanders are dead or missing. So it is very likely that you will now have to be our commanding officer.' She stood up, and looked down at him. As he looked up at her, past the faintly swaying hem of her skirt. 'You will have to tell me what to do.'

Murdoch first of all had her take the bandages off. His uniform was apparently cut to pieces, and its destruction had been completed by Yasmin as she had extracted him from it. He wondered what thoughts had coursed through her mind at that moment – because at that moment she had, for the first time in her life, truly had him at her mercy. But she had kept him alive. Because of some ingrained sense of duty, that beating the Nazis was more important than any personal feelings? Or for some other quite unthinkable reason?

'I saved your ribbons,' she told him, showing him the strip of cloth she had cut away from the breast of his tunic. 'There are so many of them. Did you get one for killing my mother?'

'Not exactly,' he said. It was the first time since their

reunion that she had mentioned the pit that lay between them.

'Well, if you lead us to victory against the Nazis, perhaps I will be able to obtain the Order of Victory for you. Would you not like that?'

'I might. You would have to find out if my government would let me accept it.'

'But of course they will. Your government and mine are friends, are they not?' She studied him as she spoke.

'Oh, indeed,' he agreed.

She had obtained some clothes for him, the khaki uniform worn by the partisans, and she stitched the ribbons on to the blouse. But she would not let him get dressed. 'You are not strong enough yet,' she told him. 'You need rest.'

'How can I command lying on my back in a sleeping bag?'

She smiled. 'There is not very much to command, at this moment, Sir Murdoch. I can handle it. We must wait and see how many people eventually find their way back to us.'

She was right, of course; as far as he could make out hardly two hundred people had so far assembled at the rendezvous, and more than half of these were women and children. While she was equally right that she could handle the situation, for she had posted guards, organized a cooking and washing roster, and had sent men out to gather food. If it was surprising that hard-bitten guerillas of more than thirty should so willingly take orders from a girl of twenty-four, the men were also trained Communists, which meant that they obeyed commissars, of whatever age or sex.

But he remained anxious to be up and doing, especially as more and more men arrived, all looking battle weary and fatigued. 'It was terrible,' said Colonel Vidmar, who was so far the senior survivor. 'It was a massacre. Our cause has been set back ten years.'

'Give me those clothes,' Murdoch told Yasmin next morning. 'I am as fit as a fiddle.'

324

'We shall find out,' she said. 'This morning I shall bathe you.'

'You will not.'

'How else will I know if you are really well?'

'You can tell by bathing me?'

'Of course. Here is the water.'

Four young women stood around him with full buckets.

'I begin to take your point,' Murdoch said.

Yasmin smiled, and removed her tunic; the girls took off their blouses; brassieres had never reached the mountains of Montenegro. 'Now we shall see,' she said.

He discovered that he was not as fit as a fiddle after all.

'Of course, you are an old man,' Yasmin said sympathetically.

'Not that old,' Murdoch growled.

'How long is it since you had sex?'

'A long time. Two years. But that was by force of circumstances, rather than choice.' Which was not altogether true.

'Then perhaps you are atrophied,' she said. She and the girls inserted him back into the sleeping bag. 'You have done enough,' she told her helpers. 'Go about your duty.'

They seemed reluctant to leave but, like the men, obeyed the commissar.

'What are you going to do now?' Murdoch asked in some alarm; she was taking off her boots.

Her skirt and drawers followed them to the ground. 'A man without sex is only half a man,' she said. 'If you are going to lead us you must be a whole man.'

He decided she was right. He had been foolish. Lee had never expected him to be faithful to her, physically, during their long separations; she knew better than most the emotional stresses of combat, and even more, command. And a man without sex *was* only half a man. He was going to need all his confidence and all his energy to make something of this mess: to have a body as sensual as Yasmin's sliding into the sleeping bag against him brought back both in full measure.

As she discovered with her fingers. 'I was being pessimistic,' she said. 'But you must take your time. I want you to make love to me as you did to my mother.'

'I never made love to your mother,' Murdoch told her. 'She made love to me, once.'

'Then I am luckier than she,' Yasmin said, and lay on top of him, moving to and fro so that her breasts swept across his face while his penis was imprisoned between her legs. 'Or am I the one making love, now as well?'

'No,' Murdoch said, and held her face still to kiss her on the lips.

He was just old enough to be her grandfather, if he had married very young. And there was a world of hatred between them, which he had no doubt was only temporarily allayed by their extraordinary situation. Yet perhaps those things made her the more sweet.

Even if the more confusing.

'I thought you came here to kill me,' he said into her hair as she lay in the crook of his arm.

'Perhaps I did. I am not sure. I only know that when I heard you were here, I wanted to be here too.'

'Because you hated me.'

'I do not know that any more, either. I told you, this is not a time for hating anyone – except the Germans. But it is also a time for living, while we can, because we do not know when we will die. Is that not true?'

'Amen,' he agreed.

She joined him again that night, and proved to her own satisfaction that he was entirely well again. 'Tomorrow you will take command,' she said.

But they were awakened just before dawn by excited shouting. Murdoch sat up to watch MacLean and Markham coming towards him. 'Well, glory be,' he said. 'I thought you were dead.'

'And we thought . . . are you all right?' MacLean asked, peering at him in the gloom. Then he saw Yasmin's head. 'Yes, I suppose you are. But I thought . . .'

'So did I,' Murdoch agreed.

'Then you won't be needing Sergeant Ferris at your back all the time.'

'He hasn't been around much lately, so I have had to make my own arrangements.' Murdoch got out of the bag and dressed himself. 'Where is Tito?'

'I am here.' The Marshal had Tigger cradled in his arms, and looked tired, as well as dirty. And very grim. 'You have heard what happened?'

'Yes,' Murdoch said.

'So you are pleased to have been proved right.'

'No,' Murdoch said.

Tito sighed, and sat down; one of the women brought him a glass of wine. 'It should have been a great success. But the Germans knew we were coming, and where we were coming, and even in what strength.'

'You mean we were betrayed.'

'I do not see what else can have happened. If I knew . . .' he gazed at the remnants of his army.

'Well, we shall have to start all over again,' Murdoch said.

'We cannot, until we have discovered who the traitor is, and rooted him out. Or them. Or we will simply be betrayed again.'

Once again he looked over his people. Yasmin emerged from the sleeping bag and dressed herself, then sat next to Murdoch. 'It is a frightening situation,' she said.

'Are you the only survivor of your group?' Tito asked.

'The only one. They knew we were coming too,' she said.

'Mikhailovitch,' Colonel Vidmar growled.

Tito's head turned sharply.

'What makes you say that?' MacLean asked.

'Because I had to flee to his people before I could get back here,' Vidmar told them. 'I did not then know the true extent of the disaster; I only knew that my forces had been wiped out. Mikhailovitch never attacked at all, beyond a demonstration. Then he pulled his men back into the mountains.'

'He never attacked?' Tito asked.

Vidmar shook his head.

'It doesn't make sense,' MacLean said. 'Surely he wants the Germans out of Yugoslavia as much as anyone? And surely he realizes that they have lost the war and must go? Why would he want to help them prolong this agony?'

'Oh, he wants the Germans out of Yugoslavia as much as anyone, Brigadier,' Tito agreed. 'And he knows they have lost the war. He is concerned with what happens afterwards. Who will rule Yugoslavia? General Mikhailovitch and his Chetniks? Or Marshal Tito and his Communists. It would make his ambition much easier to realize, if before leaving the Germans were to destroy the Communists, is that not so?'

'Good God!' MacLean said, and looked at Murdoch. 'Do you accept that, sir?'

Murdoch remembered how, after he had returned from Mikhailovitch's headquarters, nearly two years ago, when Mikhailovitch had realized they were not going to work together, Colonel Kostitch's camp had suffered a surprise attack and nearly been wiped out.

Tito watched his expression. 'Yes,' he said. 'You had better report what has happened to London, Sir Murdoch. Ask them from me how long they are going to continue supporting such a man. Tell them that the time has come to make a decision, between us.'

'You have no proof, as yet,' Murdoch said. 'It is purely circumstantial. And you are prescribing a recipe for civil war. I would prefer to be more sure of the situation, Marshal, before I plunge Yugoslavia into yet more horror.'

Tito gazed at him for a moment, then gave one of his grins. 'Then we will get proof. And until then, we will share nothing with Mikhailovitch. Not even our thoughts.'

13
France, 1944

The military policeman had come on a motorcycle, and Fergus accepted a lift back into the city as a pillion passenger; he was not prepared to wait for any more suitable transport.

He did not want to have the time to think, to wonder . . . Monique had been in the hands of the Gestapo for very nearly two years. He did not want to have to consider what that might mean, what she might look like. He just wanted to see her again, because she was alive.

The MP threaded his way in and out of rubble and people with great expertise. There were more people now, emerging from the cellars beneath their ruined homes as they realized that the fighting had actually stopped for good, as far as they were concerned, and that the Germans had actually gone, for good.

They were people with much to remember, and much to avenge. Even the MP had to stop when they reached one square, because of the crowd blocking the streets. They were watching an act of vengeance: three young women, stripped to their underwear and with their hands tied behind their backs, were being forced to kneel on the pitted ground while their hair was shorn. They wept, as the men performing the act twisted their heads to and fro, and women stooped in front of them to spit in their faces, and little boys poked at them with sticks.

'Can you not stop this?' Fergus asked.

'Seems they slept with the Germans, sir,' the MP replied.

'But even so . . . you should stop it.'

There was a group of policemen on the far side of the square, watching what was happening.

'Surely those fellows could break it up?'

329

'We're under orders not to interfere, sir. Unless it comes to a lynching. These people have a lot on their minds.'

A way was cleared, and the motorbike continued on, the crowd pausing in its labours long enough to cheer the British officer. Fergus had a vision of Annaliese being treated like that, her magnificent hair being cut away to the sound of obscene laughter . . . because, had Annaliese been French, she would have slept with the best available going, and that had to be the occupying forces.

The motorbike turned down a side street and arrived before a rather ordinary-looking building, less damaged than some others although the roof was gone. Here too there was a crowd of French men and women, staring and muttering. There were two MPs guarding the doors, and as the bike stopped they opened them to allow a woman out.

Fergus's heart leapt, and then sagged. This was an old woman. But who was to say that Monique Deschards was not now an old woman?

But this woman had been expected by the crowd. She paused on the street, blinking in the light, moving slowly and stiffly – she was very thin. Then several people ran forward, to embrace her and weep with her. Fergus heard the word 'Mama!' repeated time and again.

They waited for the little knot of people to move down the street, then the MP took Fergus up to the door. 'Colonel Mackinder to see Captain Lamming,' he told the sergeant who appeared; Fergus gathered that they were keeping the building firmly sealed.

The sergeant nodded, and allowed them in. Fergus found himself in a very typical police charge room, with a desk, filing cabinet and various chairs; there was no one present now, however, except the MPs. 'All very civilized here, sir,' the sergeant said. 'If you'll come up.'

There was a short flight of stairs to his right. Fergus followed him up and was shown into a comfortable office, again containing desk and filing cabinet, and with a carpet on the floor. Here the window had been shattered by a shell blast, but the mess had been cleared up and the room was otherwise undamaged. The only occupant was a rather

330

young MP captain, who hastily stood and saluted. 'Lamming, sir. Very good of you to come down.'

Fergus shook hands. 'Anything I can do to help.' He was going to let no one know how excited he was.

'Well, sir . . . oh, please sit down.' He gestured at the only other chair in the room. The sergeant withdrew, closing the door behind him. 'It's a grim business. The Gestapo pulled out with the rest of their army. In fact, I rather suspect they led the rush. They were in such a hurry they didn't empty their cells, either by execution or by opening the doors. So we found a good dozen people in here.'

'I saw one leaving, just now,' Fergus said.

'Madame Robert. She is the first we have been able to release.'

'The first?' Fergus was astonished.

'Well, you see, sir, it's not quite as simple as merely opening a cell door. We are processing these people as quickly as we can, but we simply have to make sure who they are. Nearly all of them claim to have been members of the resistance, but none of them can prove it. Where they can name friends or relatives still living in Caen or nearby, who may be able to vouch for them, that should be all right. But of course finding these friends or relatives in the chaos out there is proving difficult. Madame Robert was fortunate; her son actually came here asking if she was still inside.'

'Aren't you being a little unkind?' Fergus asked. 'These people must have suffered God knows what torments in this building, and you are keeping them here that much longer simply because they can't identify themselves?'

'With respect, sir, the Gestapo may be a pretty unpleasant police force, but it is still a police force. It is possible that some of the people here are criminals rather than resistance fighters. Of course they would claim to have belonged to the maquis, but the authorities aren't going to thank me for turning, for example, a wanted murderer or sex offender loose.'

331

'Hm,' Fergus said. 'I suppose you have a point. So what has this Madame Deschards been claiming?'

'Well, sir, as I told your adjutant, this woman has made the most extravagant claim of all. She isn't satisfied with claiming to be a maquis. She says she is, or was, actually a British agent, and when asked to name her control in England, she named your father. Well, sir, that made me suspicious, because of course Sir Murdoch Mackinder is a prisoner of war in Germany. On the other hand, she does claim to have been dropped into France before Sir Murdoch disappeared, but then, she could have picked up his name anywhere – or even been given it by her German so-called captors.'

'You think Monique Deschards is a spy?' Fergus asked incredulously. But why was he incredulous? Had he not once considered that possibility himself?

'We have to take everything into account, sir. It would not be the first time the Germans have left behind an agent. I mean, think of it. Suppose I accepted her story and returned her to England. She says she was selected by Sir Murdoch personally. But Sir Murdoch isn't there. Yet would she have access, however temporarily, to one of our most secret establishments while her true identity was sorted out.'

'Yes,' Fergus said. 'How do I come into it?'

'Well, sir, when I told her that Sir Murdoch was unfortunately unavailable to confirm her story, while she mentioned one or two other names in England, she also added that she knew Sir Murdoch's son. She called you Major Mackinder, to be sure, but she did know the name of your regiment, the Royal Western Dragoon Guards, and seeing that I was aware you were in the vicinity . . .'

'Yes,' Fergus said. 'She did know the name of my regiment. And I was a major when we met.'

'You mean you do know the lady, sir? That would be a great relief. Would you be prepared to identify her as the Monique Deschards you knew?'

'Yes,' Fergus said. Oh, yes, he thought.

★

'I'm afraid she's been rather knocked about,' Captain Lamming explained as he led Fergus down the stairs.

'Then how can you imagine she is a double agent?'

'Ah, well, sir, the Gestapo would have knocked her about in that case, wouldn't they? To make it look right.'

Fergus made no reply to that, and Lamming was ushering him through a doorway at the rear of the outer office, into a corridor which ended in a flight of stairs. The corridor was narrow, damp, and had no windows; it was illuminated by a series of naked electric bulbs. It stank of disinfectant. Along one wall there was a series of very stout wooden handles, some six feet from the floor and projecting about eight inches.

'Really a sort of, abandon hope all ye who enter here, atmosphere,' Lamming remarked. 'This is the first Gestapo headquarters I have actually been in. Well, we were given some idea of what to expect before the invasion, but frankly . . . I hope you have a strong stomach, sir.'

'I am about to find out,' Fergus said. Monique had spent two years in here?

'After being arrested, and presumably charged,' Lamming explained, 'the suspects were first of all brought into this corridor to be searched. They stood with their legs apart and their hands up, grasping those handles, and their heads against the wall. If they moved during the search they were beaten. As you can imagine, this gave the policemen considerable opportunity for misbehaviour, especially where women were concerned.'

Misbehaviour, Fergus thought. Monique would have stood here, to be raped.

Lamming led him down the steps, into a fair-sized room. At the far end there was a desk, and facing the desk, occupying the entire rest of the area, were two rows of backless benches.

'They apparently call this the tram,' Lamming explained. 'After arrest and charging, and having been searched, upstairs, the suspect was brought down here to await interrogation. He, or she, was told to sit down on one of the benches, facing the officer behind the desk. They had to keep absolutely still, until called for. They sometimes sat there for forty-eight hours.'

Fergus gazed at the benches in consternation. 'Forty-eight hours? No one can sit bolt upright for forty-eight hours. No one could possibly sit down for that long. I mean, what about natural calls?'

'It didn't pay to have one, sir,' Lamming said. 'There were always guards in the room, armed with rubber truncheons. Anyone moving so much as an inch was hit with a truncheon. If the suspect fell off the bench, he, or she, was beaten until he resumed his seat. It was all part of a softening up process. Really rather dreadful, I suppose. Do you know, we have poured gallons of disinfectant down here, and the Germans used it liberally as well, but you can still smell the stench.'

'Yes,' Fergus said. How long had Monique sat here?

Lamming led him across the room and opened a door on the far side. 'Now here is where the real unpleasantness began,' he said.

Fergus followed him into another corridor, damper than the one at street level. Immediately facing him, an open door gave access to another office. Then to his right the corridor stretched past several iron doors, each with a peephole in it. Most of these doors were also open; each was guarded by an MP, and from inside the cells there came the sounds of voices, some speaking in low, well-modulated tones, others shouting, some weeping.

'They are of course being interrogated now by our people, or discussing the situation with various padres,' Lamming told him. 'Somewhat different to what happened when the Gestapo were here.' He pointed along the corridor, to the only article of furniture to be seen. It was a plain table, on which sat a large wireless set. 'That used to be turned up to full volume when someone was being questioned in this office,' Lamming said. 'So the people on the street wouldn't hear the shrieks of the suspects. But of course, everyone soon worked out that when the wireless was playing at full blast, some poor devil was suffering.' He stood aside to allow Fergus into the office, and Fergus obliged. He wanted to know what Monique had suffered.

'Almost medieval, really,' Lamming suggested.

Fergus gazed at the desk and its comfortable chair, and then at a stool set in the middle of the room facing it. The stool was some four feet high, bolted to the floor, and was shaped rather like a horse's saddle, save that there was no middle except for two iron bars about six inches apart. Surrounding it, set into the floor, were four iron rings.

'The suspect was made to sit on that horse,' Lamming explained, 'and his, or her, feet were secured to two of those rings. Their arms were carried above their heads and secured to those rings in the ceiling.'

Fergus looked up, and was dazzled by the ubiquitous naked electricity; he wasn't sure that wasn't the most unpleasant aspect of the place – presumably the lights were never switched off.

'This left them absolutely helpless,' Lamming continued. 'Of course by now their clothing had been removed. In that position, their, ah, thighs separated by the two bars on which they were sitting, they were subjected to a great deal of abuse.' He pointed to the wall, where several instruments were hanging, and touched them with his swagger stick. 'The whip, of course. Very primitive. Salt solution. Very primitive, and rather lengthy. Cigarette ends were used as well, of course. Mere pinpricks, you might say. These are the things they liked best.' His stick touched what looked rather like small jump leads for a car battery. 'These crocodile clips were attached to various, ah, convenient parts of the body, and then the wire plugged into that hand-powered generator over there. When the interrogator cranked the handle, an electric current passed along the wire. By using both alligator clips, it was possible to pass the current into the suspect's body at one place, and out at the other. This is really quite excruciatingly painful, and the great thing about it is that the amount of current can be accurately controlled. Turning the handle slowly, you see, sir, produces just a trickle of electricity, enough to, shall we say, stimulate the suspect. Turning the handle faster increases the flow. By turning it at full speed, even

335

death could be induced. But the Gestapo were experts at the art of interrogation. Still are, I suppose.'

The art of interrogation, Fergus thought. Monique would have sat on that saddle, while those electrodes were attached to her nipples or thrust between her legs . . . 'What is your profession in civil life, Captain?' he asked.

'Profession, sir? I'm a policeman.'

'Ah,' Fergus said. 'Now would you mind taking me to Madame Deschards?'

'Oh, yes, sir, of course. I just thought you might like to see how the other half lives, as it were.'

'I found it fascinating,' Fergus acknowledged, choosing his words with care. 'I don't suppose you . . . I mean, we, ever use methods like that to interrogate our suspected spies?'

'Good heavens, sir, what a suggestion,' Lamming protested.

'But we do get the answers, presumably.'

'Oh, indeed, sir,' Lamming said. 'We do get the answers.' He had dropped his voice as they walked down the corridor. Fergus could not stop himself from glancing to his left as they did so, to see the shattered wrecks of human beings sitting on the narrow iron cots, pouring out their hearts to the various MP sergeants and officers who sat beside them.

Suddenly he wanted to turn and run. He felt as if he could not breathe, was being choked to death by the stench of disinfectant, just as his ears were being pounded by the sound of people screaming in agony and of a radio playing music at full volume.

He didn't want to see Monique. Not if she had been reduced to a wreck.

'This is the cell, sir,' Lamming whispered.

'Is she alone?'

'Yes, sir. In view of her claim . . . well, we still have agents behind the German lines. I couldn't risk allowing her to mix with any of the other inmates. Or even my men.'

'Quite,' Fergus said.

'You don't have to go in, sir. You can see through the peephole.'

Fergus stepped up to the judas window, took a long breath, and put his eye to the aperture. He gazed at a cell, devoid of furniture save for an iron cot and a latrine bucket. The latrine bucket was presently empty, to his relief. On the bed there was a horsehair mattress but no clothes. And on the mattress there lay a woman, wearing a dressing gown. She appeared to be asleep, as her eyes were closed, but she lay on her back with her hands clasped beneath her head, and her face was clearly visible – needless to say there was a naked bulb dangling above her head. She did not present quite the horrifying picture Fergus had feared. Her hair had been cut short . . . or rather, he realized, it had once been shaved, like those women in the street, and was still in the process of growing back. The legs emerging from the hem of the dressing gown were thinner than he remembered, but still revealed firm flesh and muscle, and the dressing gown rose and fell from still very definite mounds at her breasts. The face had suffered most, he supposed, but even that wasn't the gaunt mask of yellow skin, tightly stretched from bone to bone, that he had expected to see. It too had lost weight, and wore a less confident, more bitter, expression than he recalled, but it was pleasantly suntanned and with a touch of colour in the cheeks. And she breathed, slowly and regularly. He could remember that face smiling and laughing. As she would smile and laugh again, now. Relief flooded through his system almost like a physical dose. She might have been raped a hundred times, and beaten a hundred times, and subjected to the most humiliating tortures and treatment evil men could devise – he still wanted to go in there and take her in his arms.

'As I said, sir she's had a rough time,' Lamming said. 'We're doing what we can, of course. We've given her food and milk, and she's been examined by a doctor.'

'And you still think she could be a double agent?'

'Well, sir, everything is possible. The doctor says that she is basically quite fit. Suffering from malnutrition, of course, but only slightly, as you see; more a severe dietary deficiency than an actual lack of food. And while there is

337

some evidence of physical mistreatment, much of it took place a good while ago. There are only a few recent injuries.'

'Doesn't all of that fit her story of being arrested two years ago?'

'Yes, sir. But what has happened to her since then? Look at her skin. It is not the dead white one would have expected to find in someone locked up all of this time. That woman has been out in the open air, quite recently and over a considerable period.'

'Have you tried asking *her* what has happened to her all of this time?'

'Only superficially, sir. It is usually a waste of time interrogating a suspect until one is in possession of all the facts known about her, or him.'

'I would prefer it if you did not refer to her as a suspect,' Fergus told him.

'Oh, quite, sir. Just a manner of speaking. What I would like you to tell me, sir, is . . . is she really Monique Deschards?'

'Yes,' Fergus said. 'She is.'

'There's a relief. And she did work for your father?'

'I'm afraid I have no idea.'

'Ah. That rather puts us back to square one.'

'Not necessarily. I would like to speak with her.'

Lamming frowned. 'Are you sure that's wise, sir? Rather tips our hand, as it were. I mean, obviously I didn't tell her you were in the vicinity.'

'Captain Lamming,' Fergus said. 'I have not the slightest fear that Madame Deschards is a German spy, or indeed is anything other than she claims to be. She is a very old friend, and I would like to speak with her.'

'Well, sir, if you insist . . .'

'I do insist. And I wish to be alone. With no one peering through this ghastly contraption, either.'

Lamming looked hurt. 'As you wish, sir. Ten minutes do you?'

'When I am finished, I will come and tell you,' Fergus said.

★

338

Fergus opened the door, slowly and carefully; yet he could not avoid a faint squeak, and Monique's eyelids quivered. It squeaked again when he closed it behind him, and this time her eyes opened, and she sat up, seeming to curl herself in a ball as she did so, careless of exposing her legs as she tried to cram herself against the wall behind the bed. 'Don't,' she whispered in French. 'Please . . .' She stared at him, but at his uniform rather than his face. 'I am sorry,' she said in English. 'One forgets. And then remembers.'

'I can imagine,' Fergus said.

Monique looked at his face for the first time. 'Oh, my God!' she whispered.

He took a step closer, and she seemed to shrink away from him. His brain had gone blank – he had no idea what one should say at a moment like this.

'They wanted you identified, you see,' he said.

Monique was desperately gathering the dressing gown around her.

'Now that I have done so, they are going to let you go,' he told her.

'They do not believe me,' Monique said. 'I have seen this in their faces.'

'Well . . .' Fergus stood above her. How he longed to take her in his arms. 'They find it difficult to accept that you could have been taken by the Gestapo two years ago, and not executed, or sent to a camp, or . . .'

'I have been in a camp,' she said in a low voice.

'Would you like to tell me about it?'

Monique licked her lips.

Fergus sat on the end of the cot. 'May I?'

'I am your prisoner,' she said.

'You are nobody's prisoner, Monique. It is just necessary to tell me what happened, and you will be released.'

'Where is Sir Murdoch?' she asked. 'They told me he could not come to see me, but I know they are lying. Bring him to me, and I will speak with him.'

'I'm afraid they were telling you the truth. Dad went off to do a bit of cloak and dagger himself, and is still there.'

She frowned at him. 'He's not dead?'

'Oh, no. But he won't be back until after the war, and that could still be some time off.'

Monique gazed at him for several seconds. Then she said, 'I did not expect to see you. I did not ask to see you.'

'You mentioned my name to the captain.'

'I want to get out of here. That is all I want to do.'

'And I have come to help you do that, Monique.'

'Why?'

'Because . . . because of a great many things. But principally, I think, one night in Cairo.'

She stared at him. 'You are married?' she asked.

'Why, no.'

'Why not?'

'Well . . . I haven't really had the time. And . . .' but now was not the time.

She sighed. 'And now you wish to know about me. It should not be you, Fergus.'

'I think it should, because I will believe you. And Monique, I have inspected this place. You do not have to go into any details.'

She shuddered. 'They brought me here when I was arrested. It was a raid, on the house where I was staying. They smashed down the doors and shot at everything that moved. I had no time to reach either my gun or my tablets.' She sighed. 'I do not know if I would have taken them. I was too young. Life was too sweet.'

'I am glad you did not take the tablets,' Fergus said. 'Having found you.'

She gave him another quick glance, and once again seemed to recoil against the wall. 'I wished I had, when they brought me here. You say you have seen . . .'

'Yes,' he said.

'But you have never felt! It is more than the humiliation of being searched, of having their fingers . . .' she sighed. 'Or of sitting in the tram, hour after hour . . . it is the fear. When they have hurt you, time and again, so badly, your whole being is concentrated on not being hurt again. And you know, no matter what you do, how hard you try, that you are *going* to be hurt again, as badly as they choose.'

340

She hugged herself, and he said nothing. Because there was nothing to say. She would tell him what she wished. Far more important, she would tell herself what she wished. That way would lie the essential dividing line between madness and sanity, for the rest of her life.

'They kept me here for a week, and I wished I could die every second of those days. But I denied everything. Over and over again. I denied everything.'

'And therefore betrayed nothing. You are a very brave woman, Monique.'

'I screamed,' she said. 'I screamed so much I lost my voice. And I begged them to stop. When one begs, one humiliates even one's tormentors. So they became tired of playing with me and sent me away.'

'To a camp?'

'A camp,' she said. 'Yes.' She turned over her arm to show him the blue numbers on her flesh.

'Good God! They branded you?'

'It is their way of keeping track of their prisoners. There are so many people in those camps. They have no names, only numbers.'

'And you survived there.'

'Yes,' she said. 'I survived there.'

'And quite well, from the look of things. We have heard some unpleasant stories about those camps. It is a great relief to know that they aren't true.'

She gazed at him. 'They are true, Fergus.'

'But . . .'

'There, too, was constant humiliation. I do not speak of being shaved, every hair removed from my body – to prevent my infestation with lice, you understand. Or beaten at the whim of any guard. But a woman who is young, and reasonably good-looking, is treated better than the rest. Because she is a woman, and the Gestapo are also men.'

Now her eyes seemed to be impaling him. 'My God!' he muttered. Then she *had* been raped by a hundred men. No, a thousand.

'For two years I had nothing to do but sun myself, eat,

and lie on my back,' Monique said, her voice toneless. 'And then . . . it seems they arrested someone here in Caen, only a few days ago, and he mentioned my name. So they brought me back here to confront this man. I think they were going to shoot us both. But then the bombers came, and I think they forgot about the prisoners. We were left alone, until the British broke in.'

'Thank God for that,' he said. 'Monique . . . when you leave here, where will you go? I mean, obviously you will have to spend some time in hospital, until you are quite well again. And then, if I confirm your story, you will technically still be in my father's employ . . .'

'They cannot send me into German territory again. They cannot.'

'They will not. But they will wish to know all that you have suffered, people you have met, names and places . . .'

'I will tell them that. But I will not work for them again. Not even for your father, Fergus.'

'I understand that. And when they have questioned you, they will probably give you extended leave of absence until you can be discharged.' He smiled at her. 'They also owe you two years' salary. There will be quite a lot of money, waiting for you, in London. Have you any money?'

'I haven't needed money, for two years.'

He had hoped for a responding smile. 'Well, you won't have to worry about that,' he said. 'But afterwards . . . when they give you your leave . . . are your parents still in Cairo?'

'I do not know. I presume so.'

'I will try to find out, and then arrange for you to go there.'

'No,' she said. 'I do not want to go to my parents.'

'Ah. Well . . .' he took a long breath. 'Would you like to go to my home, in England?'

'Why should I go there?'

'Well . . . you would be safe there, and you could regain your health there. My mother would be delighted to look after you. And then, when the fighting is finished, I . . . well . . .' her eyes were like steel shutters, trying to block

342

the flow of words. Because she knew that he did not know if they would be true: she had spent two years in a Gestapo brothel.

'You are very kind,' she said. 'But if I start to accept pity, I will have no more life. Besides, why should you be kind to me, and not all of the others?'

'It is not pity,' Fergus said. 'Or even kindness. I . . .' once again he was looking into her eyes.

'You do not believe what I have told you,' she said.

'I do. Of course I do.'

'Then you do not understand it. I have been a whore, Fergus. For the Gestapo.'

'Yes, I understand that. But . . .'

'But you do not care!' Suddenly her voice gained strength. 'At this moment, you do not care. You remember how once we had a good time together, and you think such a time will come again. It can never come again,' she shouted. 'Never! If any man ever touches me again I will scratch out his eyes.'

'Are you all right, sir?' Lamming called through the peephole.

'Go away, Captain, there's a good fellow,' Fergus said.

Monique's shoulders sagged, and her voice dropped. 'I am sorry. You were trying to help me. I am sorry.' She raised her head. 'I cannot be your mistress, Fergus.'

'I . . . ah . . . I wasn't actually thinking of that.'

'I cannot be your wife, either. You must understand that. I cannot be anything, except what I am.'

He stood up. 'I think you need time. Where will you go?'

'Are the Germans really defeated?'

'They are in the process of being defeated. They are certainly being driven out of France.'

'Then I will go to Paris. When it is liberated.'

'Paris?'

'I have friends there. I even own an apartment. My husband and I lived in Paris before the war.' Almost she smiled. 'We were married in Paris.'

'You *had* friends there, Monique. You *had* an apartment. Do you think you will still find them, after four years.'

'I will find something.'

'Yes,' he said. 'If, when I have the opportunity, I were to come to Paris, would you care to see me?'

'You have been very kind,' she said.

'Then will you give me the address?' He took his notebook and pencil from his breast pocket, held it out.

She hesitated, then took it and wrote the address, handed the book back.

'Then I will say au revoir, instead of goodbye,' Fergus said.

'Yes,' she agreed. 'Au revoir.'

Fergus wasn't sure whether he wanted to burst into song or not. She was alive, and he had found her. She had been hurt, and misused, thus she was bitter. But surely she would get over that. And he would find her again. Even if the Paris apartment had been destroyed, he would find her again. And love her again? He did not think he had stopped doing that, from the moment of their first meeting. No matter how many men she had been forced to service.

But before he could do that, it was necessary to win the war. He wrote out a full statement of what Monique had told him for Captain Lamming, requested her immediate transfer to hospital for a thorough checkup before she was released, and then rejoined the regiment.

At the end of July the Americans broke through the German defences in front of Avranches, and sweeping east and south on a broad front were in Rennes in Brittany on 3 August. Two days later the British, also moving east, recaptured Villars-Bocage, from which their advanced units had been driven before the battle for Caen. By now Eisenhower had arrived in Normandy, and had taken over supreme command of the Allied forces, with the result that Montgomery's strategic plan was immediately jettisoned. Instead of a direct thrust to Paris, leaving the German armies south of the Seine cut off and helpless, followed by a drive on a narrow front for the Rhine, the Supreme Commander elected to advance on a broad front right across France. That this decision chose to ignore any logistical

344

problems seemed obvious to every soldier, but Eisenhower would have his way; the two American armies were removed from Montgomery's command and made into a single Army Group Twelve, under the orders of General Bradley.

Of course the Germans could not hope to stop such an immense force as was now advancing on them, but they, and the inevitable waits for the arrival of sufficient fuel to enable the tanks and trucks to continue moving, could certainly delay it. Thus the day following the capture of Villars-Bocage the panzers launched a counter-attack on the First Canadian Army outside Caen. The regiment was called to action, but long before they reached the scene the Germans had been blasted by rocket-firing Typhoons, and the panzers had melted away. Meanwhile the Americans, sweeping through Brittany and thence to the south, had taken Brest and Lorient and St Nazaire, famous names – but places which were bound to fall anyway, while in the East the Russians were already at the Vistula, although they were delaying crossing the river while the Polish Home Army fought it out with the Germans in Warsaw.

This looming situation, with the probability that, at the present rate and direction of the two advances, the Russians could be at the Rhine from the East, having 'liberated' all of Europe east of Switzerland while the Allies were still messing about in France, appeared to worry the British commanders and politicians far more than it did the Americans. Eisenhower and his chief, Roosevelt, regarded the Russians as their most powerful allies in the fight against Hitler, and were concerned solely with killing and capturing every German soldier they could discover; postwar arrangements would be taken care of by the United Nations Organization, in an atmosphere of fellowship and good will. The British, with their vastly greater experience of European history and politics, knew that where the Russian armies penetrated, they would carry their political commissars with them and they would take care that only those prepared to obey orders from Moscow would survive to form postwar governments, as indeed they were blatantly doing in Poland, as they sat across the river and watched the Home Army, which was violently anti-Communist, being systematically liquidated by the German troops, while doing absolutely nothing to help them – they would not even let the Allies use Russian-held airfields as staging posts to fly in supplies to the beleaguered Poles. It therefore seemed logical to British minds that wherever possible, the penetration and liberation of occupied countries should be accomplished by Allied troops, or Great Britain could find herself looking across the Channel at a Communist Europe.

The Americans regarded this as merely an aspect of British imperialism, and came close to saying so in public: obviously, they suggested, England was looking forward to dominating the Continent following the defeat of Germany, and was therefore jealous of the looming Russian rival.

Montgomery was not the sort of man to criticize his superiors, at least to his own inferiors, but when he paid a visit to the regiment, which was temporarily bogged down for lack of fuel, Fergus could tell he was deeply concerned, and totally fed-up with events in the south, where the Americans had landed yet another army, the Seventh, on the Riviera, about as far removed from any critical centres of fighting as could be imagined.

Meanwhile the advance continued, slowly. On 17 August the British and Canadians took Falaise while the Americans surged through Dreux, Chartres and Orleans. This left the Germans with no option but to retreat through the Falaise Gap, a narrow salient, in which their crowded forces presented the Allied air forces with the perfect target: the enemy were cut to pieces by repeated sorties. Feeling that their hour had at last arrived, the French Underground now staged a rising in Paris. Unlike what was happening in Warsaw, the Allies were not going to let a massacre happen here, and five days later the capital fell, troops of General de Gaulle's Free French Army being, appropriately, the first to enter the city.

Now once more Montgomery reiterated his plea to be allowed to launch an all-out drive for the Rhine and North Germany, the objective being to get to Berlin before the

Russians – Eisenhower refused. Montgomery's disappointment was hardly diminished by his being promoted Field Marshal at the beginning of September.

The advance plugged on throughout the autumn. The British proved what could be accomplished by smashing through three hundred and sixty kilometres in four days to reach Brussels on the fifth anniversary of the declaration of war, 3 September. Fergus rode in his lead tank through cheering crowds, and drank champagne from the necks of the bottles that were thrust at him and his exhilarated men.

'Good to be back, eh, sir?' asked RSM Manly-Smith. 'When you remember the last time.'

'Yes,' Fergus agreed. He remembered the last time only too well, as in the spring of 1940 the British and French armies, suddenly abandoned by their Belgian allies, had fallen back on the coast. How long ago that seemed, and it was only four and a half years. But they had been different men, then. The regiment had been composed almost entirely of veterans who had been in India, the officers as well. Ian had been the adjutant, soon to become colonel, and Bert had been a very youthful corporal. And Dad had, literally, dropped out of the sky as he escaped from Holland, and had taken command in that glorious mêlée with the German armour.

But then had come the disaster of Dunkirk. And now, out of all those who had once trodden this way, only himself and Bert remained, at least still wearing this uniform. Two men, bound together by a link stronger even than comradeship, even if they were not both aware of it. But Annaliese's time must be very close, now. He would have to tell Bert the true situation then. And now, with Monique so strangely returned into his life, he did not think he would find any difficulty in doing that.

And if there were only two veterans of Dunkirk, he yet commanded a regiment of veterans, who had fought their way right across France. That was a thought to make the heart swell.

★

347

There was no time to stop and enjoy the pleasures of Brussels, for the Germans were in full retreat and the drive was ordered to continue. Antwerp was reached the next day, and they entered eastern Holland – the islands and river mouths being by-passed for the time being owing to the danger of the armour becoming bogged down as the Germans opened the dykes – to continue their dash for the Rhine. Thus it was the Americans who first crossed the German border, just north of Trier.

The passage of the Rhine now began to occupy the thoughts of every commander, especially as the many mouths of that great river had each to be negotiated, and the enemy defence was clearly hardening up. Montgomery's dream remained that gallop across the North German plain, before winter set in, and with this in mind he planned to force the Rhine in Holland, inside of the Dutch water defences, but outside of the Fatherland itself. The key question was how to cross the river in strength; obviously the Germans were not going to leave any bridges intact when the Allies got too close. A plan was therefore formed to seize three of them by a coup de main carried out by the First Allied Airborne Army, which was to be dropped in the Arnhem-Nijmegen area, seize the vital bridges, and hold on there until the main armies could come to them. It was a bold concept, and had it worked, the idea of a drive across North Germany might also have come off, despite all. Unfortunately, unknown to the planners, the Germans had a panzer division in the area, recuperating, and this, and reinforcements, were hurled into the battle. Resistance stiffened in front of Arnhem, and the Allies were unable to penetrate and link up with the paratroopers. After a week of bloody and bitter fighting, the remnants of the Airborne Army were pulled out; some seven thousand men of the British division did not come back.

The push for the Rhine continued for some weeks. The main part was taken by the Americans besieging Aachen, for which the Germans fought with the utmost tenacity; it did not surrender until 21 October. Meanwhile news had filtered through of Rommel's death. He had been badly wounded when Allied fighters had strafed his command car in Normandy, and had been recovering at his home in Germany. Now he appeared to have suffered a relapse which he did not survive. It was not until after the war that the true story emerged, that he had been forced to commit suicide because of his implication in the Hitler assassination plot during the summer.

Fergus was far more interested in the news, received the day Aachen fell, that in Yugoslavia, Tito's partisans had linked up with the advancing Russians and had captured Belgrade. He had heard nothing of his father now for some time, did not even know if he was still alive – but Father would always survive. And now, it seemed, he had triumphed again.

With the Germans still fighting with the utmost desperation on the west bank of the Rhine, determined to keep the Allies from reaching that true boundary of the Fatherland, and the weather now definitely showing signs of breaking, the British were diverted at last into cleaning up Holland. This was really not the country for tanks, and for the regiment it was a matter of waiting and watching, in increasingly unpleasant conditions, as the rain poured down and turned even the best of roads into quagmires.

This was the final straw as regards the concept of reaching the Rhine, galloping across North Germany, and finishing the war by Christmas, and the Allies went into winter quarters, rather as their forefathers had done in previous centuries, in this same part of Europe; it was a salutary thought that the only European war in which fighting had gone on the year round had been the Great War.

The regiment was encamped just outside the village of Bassenge, actually in Belgium, although equidistant between Liege in the south, and Maastricht, close to the German border, in the north, and only a few miles west of the River Meuse, which formed a boundary between the British and US armies to the south. The vicinity of the two large towns was convenient from the point of view of overnight passes to keep the troopers contented. Here they could only wait for the weather to improve, when the river could perhaps be challenged, and the advance resumed. No one expected this to be a problem, militarily. The Allied advanced units, mainly Americans, had already crossed the river without meeting much German opposition; the retreating enemy had apparently been so demoralized they had not even blown the bridges. Thus once the ground became firm enough for armour the drive for the Rhine could continue.

For Fergus it was also a case of waiting for news from England. This finally arrived in the last week of November, and when he read his mother's letter, Fergus knew that the moment he had both feared and anticipated for several months could no longer be delayed. He sent for the Sergeant-Major.

Obviously he had to proceed with some caution. 'You know, Sergeant-Major,' he said, 'why don't you apply for a commission? I'm damned sure you'd get one. I mean, you're Ralph Manly-Smith's son, you're a veteran soldier, you're a sergeant-major, and you're only twenty-two years old. You could wind up a brigadier.'

'Me, sir? I'm happy where I am,' Bert said.

He was an odd fellow, Fergus thought, not for the first time. It was almost as if he didn't want to be an officer just because his father had been one.

'Well,' he said, 'the decision must be yours, of course. But . . . you might wish to change your mind. I want to have a chat with you, Bert. This is not about army business, and it is therefore between two men, not between the colonel and the sergeant-major. Take a seat.'

Bert gazed at him for several seconds before obeying. Hastily he took off his beret and rested it on his knee. Certainly he had an idea what was coming: Fergus almost thought he could see his mind racing.

'Mrs Mackinder, Annaliese,' Fergus said, 'has just had a baby.' He tapped the letter on his desk. 'The news arrived yesterday.'

Bert gazed at him.

350

'Your baby, Bert. Your son.'

'Sir . . .'

'It is your baby. It certainly isn't mine. And you were last in Somerset in February. Nine months ago.'

Bert began to twist the beret, while his face glowed, and his entire large body seemed to shrivel.

'Do you love her, Bert?' Fergus asked.

Bert raised his head. 'Love her, sir. Why . . .'

'Yes, or no, Bert.'

Bert swallowed. 'Yes, sir. I asked her to marry me, sir. But she wouldn't. I feel like shit, sir. It just happened. You know what she's like.'

'I only found out what she's like just before the invasion,' Fergus told him.

'You've known all that time, sir?'

'Yes. It didn't seem appropriate to speak of it before. But now . . . I am not going to marry her, Bert. She knows this. I think it would be the decent thing for you to marry her instead.'

'She'll never do it, sir.'

'She will, if you become an officer.'

Bert considered that.

'There is also the point that if you put in for a commission, they would probably send you home for a spell. You could see the boy. And Annaliese.'

'She doesn't love me, sir.'

'She's the mother of your child, Bert. I think she could well fall in love with you, if you handle it right. She obviously likes *making* love to you.'

'Yes, sir,' Bert said, and gulped again.

'I'd like you to consider what I've said, Bert. I also think that you should write her.'

'Me, sir?'

'Yes. I think she would like to hear from you. Oh, by the way, I would like to adopt my brother's son, if that is all right with you.'

'With me, sir?'

'I've already told Annaliese,' Fergus said. 'You make a decision, Bert.'

351

*

It was remarkable how much better Fergus felt after that chat, what a weight he felt lifted from his shoulders. He was especially pleased with the calm way Bert had taken it. Perhaps he should have done it long before; he had had a touch of moral cowardice there. On the other hand, the calmness on both sides had been at least partly due to the fact that he had no longer felt any personal anger about what had happened. So perhaps the wait had been necessary, after all. And now it was up to Bert – and Annaliese. His concern was to find Monique again, just as soon as he could. Supposing the war was ever going to end. Because the weather just got worse, and was suddenly accompanied by a very sharp fall in the temperature. Fergus awoke on the morning of Sunday, 10 December, to find his entire command covered in white, and when later on that day Manton arrived, the Brigadier also took a gloomy view of the situation.

'It's going to be a long winter, Fergus,' he told him. 'Everyone is just plain tired and fed up. You can let your men take it a bit easier.'

'Agreed, sir. But the Germans are only a few miles away, over there.'

'They are even more tired and fed up than we are,' Manton asserted. 'There's no point in keeping our people on constant alert until there's a thaw. But Monty wants to have a word.'

Next morning Fergus drove west to GHQ, a long and hazardous journey on the slippery roads, and was entertained to dinner. 'You have been a colonel the devil of a long time,' Montgomery told him. 'I think it's time you moved up. Manton is moving up to take division; I'd like you to have the brigade.'

Fergus didn't know what to say.

'I know you've served with the Westerns throughout your career,' the Field Marshal went on. 'But you know armoured fighting, and you know the commanders in the other regiments. Congratulations. Who do you recommend for colonel of the regiment?'

352

'Well, Jim Smithie, sir. He's next in seniority. He's been my adjutant since poor Johnny Allack bought it on the beach.'

'And as adjutant?'

'Ronnie Mather. They're both good men.'

'Good. Inform Smithie that he will take command of the Westerns, as from tomorrow. And move Mather up as well. Oh, and you can take some leave. I'm sure you need it. Have three days in Paris, and enjoy yourself. You'll take over the brigade a week today, Monday, the 18th.'

Fergus didn't know whether he was standing on his head or his heels. Next morning he returned to Bassenge, his jeep slithering and sliding on the icy roads, and called an officers' meeting. The opposition they had encountered since Caen had been so slight that they had not suffered a single casualty from lieutenant up, and he had got to know these men really well. 'So there it is,' he told them. 'I'm being booted upstairs.'

'Oh, best congratulations, sir,' Mather said. 'There's no one could possibly deserve it more.'

Smithie was overwhelmed. 'I'll try to look after the regiment for you, sir,' he promised. 'Until the next Mackinder comes along.'

'That will be some time in the future,' Fergus told him, thinking of little four-year-old Ian.

The Sergeant-Major was dumbfounded. 'I never thought you'd be leaving us, sir,' he said.

'Had to happen,' Fergus told him. 'Have you written Annaliese?'

'Well, yes, sir, I have. But I haven't had a reply.'

'Early days, Bert. You'll get your reply for Christmas.'

Then he could sit back and savour his good fortune. He was to be a brigadier. He was only thirty-four years old, so he could claim to have his foot at last firmly on the ladder of command; Dad, for all his fame, had not become a brigadier until thirty-six. It was a future to which he had always looked, without, in the hurly-burly of the war, ever considering it in practical terms. There was the war, and there was After the War – if one survived that long. Time enough to consider After the War when it finally arrived, and that was going to take a little while longer.

But he was going to command the brigade, if ever they could have a proper armoured battle again. He felt not the least bit afraid of that. He was Murdoch Mackinder's son, and he did not lack the family confidence.

At least in military matters. He was aware of feeling distinctly nervous as he neared Paris. He left Maastricht in the weekly dispatch truck driven by Sergeant Sullivan before it was dawn on Thursday the 14th, taking the road which ran beside the Meuse, through Liège and then Namur. The skies were leaden, and it was snowing lightly, and as this area formed the border between the British and American armies, the roads were already bad; they were clogged with traffic, as Christmas fare was slowly taken up to the front – the doughboys were not going to be asked to go without their pudding and turkey, even in the midst of a war. Thus the journey took several hours longer than he had anticipated, and was a broken and not entirely teetotal affair, as every American unit with whom they became bogged down seemed to be getting ready to celebrate Christmas several days early.

Certainly there was hardly an indication that the Germans were indeed only twenty-odd miles away, still clinging to that famous and all-important river. 'I guess they'll be pulling back across it for good, when the weather improves,' opined an American Colonel with whom Fergus shared a mid-morning coffee well laced with brandy. 'Those guys know they're licked. Why should they want to stay around and get flattened?'

Fergus was reminded, apart from the weather, of the periods in between battles in North Africa, when the troops had sunbathed and the war had seemed a very long way away; the situation here in the Ardennes appeared even more similar because of the way the American forces were spread out, each unit clinging resolutely to its own little village, or farm, where there was some warmth to be found. In North Africa, those periods of non-war had been apt to end with dramatic and brutal suddenness, especially where

354

Rommel was concerned. Presumably this one would also, when the first thaw came, but at least there was no longer a Rommel to trouble them.

It was well into an early December dusk when the truck finally rolled through the suburbs of Paris. Fergus had given Sullivan the address Monique had written down, but his knowledge of the city was limited, so they homed on the Arc de Triomphe, and there consulted a taxi driver. It was really quite remarkable how quickly the city had returned to normal. It had only been liberated a few months previously, and the war was still very much on -- presumably there were blackout restrictions in force - yet the Champs Elysées was a ribbon of light and a mass of people, wrapped up against the cold, but either peering into shop windows as they made their Christmas preparations or sitting at boulevard cafés drinking their coffee and aperitifs.

The city was remarkably undamaged, as well. The Allied air forces had spared it as much as possible, and the German commander, General von Choltitz, had disobeyed Hitler's orders to destroy it before surrendering. Once again, Fergus thought, four years might never have been, and it could have been his only previous visit here, at Christmas 1939, when, the regiment again stationed only a few miles to the north, they had been awaiting the explosion which would shake the world.

Monique must have been living here in 1939, before her husband had been killed and the Germans had flooded across her country. As she was here now. The taxi driver would have given them the necessary directions, but Sullivan had other places to call, so Fergus said goodbye, agreed to meet the sergeant at that same spot at seven o'clock on Sunday morning, and took the taxi instead. He was too excited to delay a moment longer.

It was only when he had paid off the cab, and was standing on the ice-covered pavement looking at the darkened apartment building, that he realized that he really had no idea whether or not Monique was, actually, in Paris. She had only been found in July. Not quite five months ago. She might still be at a debriefing centre in England. If only Dad were here, he would have been able to find out.

But as he had come all this way . . . he rang the bell, holding his parcel against himself.

'Who is there?' asked the concierge.

'A British officer,' Fergus said in his best French. 'I am looking for a Madame Monique Deschards.'

'Is she expecting you?'

His heart leapt: she was here. 'I think so.'

'You will have to come up, Monsieur. There is no telephone yet, you understand. And no elevator.'

The door creaked in, and she peered at him, a woman who was not as old as she appeared; she would have been in Paris throughout the occupation, Fergus realized.

He stepped inside, and the door closed. There was no immediate difference in temperature, although a single electric light bulb glowed. What memories that must have brought back to Monique, he thought.

'And no heating, either,' the concierge said, climbing the uncarpeted stairs in front of him.

Fergus made no reply to that; he was not interested in heating at that moment. 'But the building is undamaged,' he ventured.

'Undamaged! Ha!'

There seemed no answer to that either, so he waited while they climbed two more flights.

'Madame Deschards has only just returned,' the concierge said, chattily.

'Ah,' Fergus said.

'No more than a week.' They paused on a landing, and she rapped on a door with her knuckles. 'Madame?' the concierge called. 'Madame? There is a gentleman here to see you. Well, an English soldier.' She seemed to have changed her mind about the description.

'A soldier? Just a moment.'

They waited, while Fergus tried to keep his breathing under control, then the door opened. Monique again wore a dressing gown, but this was for warmth, over a dark blue shirt and slacks, clearly hastily pulled on; thick socks were tucked into heavy carpet slippers. Her hair had grown a little since last he had seen her, and was tousled; she thrust the fingers of one hand through it as if trying to straighten it. She wore no make-up.

She stared at him for a moment, and her mouth formed a little O.

'The bad penny always turns up,' Fergus said, in English.

'You know him?' asked the concierge, in French.

'Oui. Yes,' Monique said, speaking both languages at once.

'Bang on the floor if you need me,' the concierge said, and shuffled back down the stairs.

'She's quite a card,' Fergus remarked.

'Yes.' Monique drew a long breath, and stepped back. 'You'd better come in.'

Fergus stepped into a neat little apartment, surprisingly well furnished. He stood in the middle of the lounge/diner, looked at heaps of books.

Monique shrugged. 'I only got back a week ago.'

'So the concierge told me. I'm a lucky fellow. How was the apartment?'

'Exactly as I left it. Can you believe it? That concierge is a treasure. So I have been putting things right. I packed up all my books, you see. Now I have taken them out again . . . it is strange to be home, after so long.'

'And so much,' Fergus said without thinking, and could have bitten his tongue.

'Yes,' she said. 'Would you like a drink?'

'Would you?' He took out the bottle of brandy he had bought from the NAAFI before leaving GHQ. 'Coals to Newcastle, I suppose.'

'Not really. Good brandy is very expensive in Paris. Everything is very expensive, in Paris.'

'But you're managing?'

'So far.' She opened a cupboard and took out two goblets. 'You were right; they owed me a lot of money in London. Two years' pay. I am quite wealthy, for the moment.'

'You're looking well,' he said.

She held out the glasses, and he poured. As he took his, their fingers touched, for a moment.

'I love you,' he said.

She gazed at him, and then sipped her drink. 'Here's to a merry Christmas,' she said. 'Is it going to be a merry Christmas?'

'I hope so. For both of us. Will you marry me?'

She drank some more brandy. 'Would you like something to eat? I have some crêpes . . .'

'I'd like to take you out to dinner.'

'That is very kind of you.' She looked down at herself. 'I will have to change. Will you excuse me?'

'Of course.'

'Have a seat . . .' she hesitated. 'No,' she decided. 'Come into the bedroom.'

'Are you sure?'

'I am sure you are a gentleman, Fergus.'

Hesitantly he followed her into the bedroom. A very feminine bedroom, but with a double bed. It smelt of the perfume he remembered from Cairo.

'Sit down in here instead,' Monique suggested.

Carefully Fergus sat on the end of the bed.

Monique took off her dressing gown, and then the rest of her clothes. She undressed with a total naturalness, without a hint of coquetry. He knew that she wanted him to look at her, and he wanted to do that; surprisingly, there were very few scars, beyond a few tiny dark patches which might have been flat moles, and if she was thinner than he remembered, she actually looked very fit.

When she was naked, she came and stood in front of him. 'Those are burns, caused by cigarettes,' she explained.

His head jerked. The dark spots were clustered around her nipples and, as she raised one leg, on the inside of her thighs.

'There is not much else visible,' she said. 'The rest are inside.'

'Monique . . .'

'You must know these things,' she said seriously, turning

358

away and going into the bathroom. When she returned, she began to dress again, sitting down to roll on nylon stockings, and then adding white lace underwear, while he gazed at her. He had never actually known such intimacy with a woman before. He had watched them undress, but never dress. She was trying to establish a mood. But was the mood for him, or for herself? 'I treated myself, in England,' she said. 'They gave me a whole clutch of clothing coupons, and I had all of that money.' She clipped her brassiere. 'Do you know that they are talking about giving me a medal?' She looked at the row on his breast. 'I wonder what colour it will be.'

She opened the wardrobe and took out a black dress. 'I think this is the most appropriate. It is also made of wool. Do you know that this dress has hung here for four years? It has a smell of mothballs about it. Will that upset you?'

'No,' he said. 'Will you marry me?'

She held out her brandy goblet; it was empty. 'Would you give me another drink?'

He took the glass into the lounge, poured. She followed him, stood beside him to take the drink. 'I have grey in my hair, now.'

'Join the club.'

'Will you kiss me?'

He kissed her, resting his hands lightly on her arms. 'Oh, my darling girl,' he said. 'I thought you didn't want to be touched.'

'And you still asked me to marry you?'

'I was happy to wait. I have waited for four years.'

'In which time you have only seen me three times. This is the third time.'

'I thought of you, all the time. I went looking for you, in Cairo, but you had already gone to England.'

'I should have stayed, but I did not know you would ever come back. Did you know I had gone to work for your father?'

'No, I didn't.'

'He knows I had met you,' she said. 'I told him. He was a fine old gentleman.'

'Still is, I hope.'

'Oh, I hope so. Do you know, I think he fancied me himself.'

'I can imagine he did. He must have been very upset when he learned you had been taken.' And only a few weeks later, Fergus realized, he went off to Yugoslavia, without telling a soul. He must have been *very* upset. 'He will be delighted to have you as a daughter-in-law.'

'Yes,' she said. She finished her drink, put down the glass, and then began unbuttoning her dress. 'Do not let's go out to dinner, after all. Stay here with me.'

'Are you sure, Monique?'

'No,' she said. 'I wish to *be* sure. And only you can do that for me. And Fergus . . . if I weep a little, forgive me.'

He wanted to sing and dance and shout, as he made his way through frozen streets to the pick-up point for the dispatch truck. It was early in the morning of Sunday, 17 December, and Monique was still in bed. Apart from a brief shopping expedition on Friday morning, they had spent most of the two days in bed. For one thing, it had been the only warm place in the apartment, and for another, they had had so much to do.

So much to do. Not just with fingers and lips and genitals. So much to do with thoughts, as well. They had not spoken a great deal, and Monique had, as she had warned, wept a little. But soon she had laughed, as well. He did not suppose she had laughed in two years. But this was Monique, restored to life, and love, and laughter. Monique Mackinder, as she would become, as soon as the last German had surrendered. A woman who had suffered the torment of the damned, and had yet been determined to survive. A woman to treasure.

He slapped his gloved hands together, and watched the truck come round the corner, sliding sideways towards him. It stopped a few feet away, and Sullivan threw open the door.

'Not too fast, Sergeant,' Fergus told him. 'I want to stay in one piece.'

360

'That may not be easy, sir.' The sergeant was very excited. 'All officers and men are to report to their units just as rapidly as possible. The Germans have launched a massive attack in the Ardennes, sir. They're ripping the Yanks apart up there. All hell has broken loose.'

Fergus leapt in beside him. 'So get me to the regiment, Sergeant. On the double.'

14
Yugoslavia, 1944

Tito's offensive might have been premature, but nothing could stop the steady advance of the Russian armies. In April they had burst through the Ukraine and stood on the borders of Rumania, which had indeed led to their command to the partisans to distract the German forces further to the south, and in the summer, having re-taken the Crimea, they drove into Poland. Their August decision to stand before the Vistula and let the Home Army fight it out with the Germans did not disturb the Yugoslav partisans. 'The Poles are all fascists,' growled Colonel Vidmar. 'Just like Mikhailovitch and his creatures.' No one seemed to find it sinister that the Russians had not yet materialized in the Balkans either, as promised; their communiqués spoke of increased resistance in the Carpathians. Tito and his men were concerned only with Mikhailovitch's alleged treachery.

The growing antagonism between the two halves of the Yugoslav resistance was a disturbing aspect of the situation for Murdoch and MacLean. Tito had no proof that Mikhailovitch had betrayed him: he was merely certain that he had. More to the point, however, it was convenient for him to *be* certain of it. The shape of postwar Yugoslavia was occupying an ever larger place in his thoughts, and any means of denigrating his rival amongst the people at large – and the Allied Powers – was to be exploited. But as far as Murdoch was concerned, although he too had his doubts about the Chetnik leader, they were both his allies, and would continue to be until he was otherwise ordered.

The dropping of supplies to Mikhailovitch's people annoyed Tito, however, and after conferring with the new

Russian mission which soon arrived, he came to see Murdoch.

'I think I know you well enough now, Sir Murdoch,' he said, 'to be able to speak to you as man to man.'

'Of course,' Murdoch agreed, feeling a sinking sensation in his stomach.

'I know you are concerned that my country may well be fighting a civil war when the Germans have surrendered,' Tito said. 'And I share your concern. It is therefore necessary to make sure of the situation now. You must tell London and Washington the facts, and have them instruct the Chetniks to place themselves unreservedly under my command. Now.'

Obviously he was repeating what he had been told to say by the Russians. 'And what are the facts, Tito?' Murdoch asked.

'That Mikhailovitch is trying to have my people destroyed by the Germans, so that he can take over the country.'

'And is that not what you intend to do?'

Tito gazed at him, and then grinned. 'When the time comes, we will hold democratic elections, Murdoch.'

'I will inform London of that,' Murdoch said. 'But suppose Mikhailovitch also intends to hold elections?'

'If he does, they will not be honest. London must choose, Murdoch. And it must be now.'

Murdoch considered. 'And what if they choose Mikhailovitch? Will you accept such a decision?'

'I am supported by Moscow,' Tito reminded him. 'They cannot choose Mikhailovitch.'

'I suppose we don't have any choice,' Murdoch told MacLean. 'All we can hope to do is prevent a massacre.'

The message went off, and the Russian advance went on. The 'liberation' of Rumania was finally achieved by mid-September, whereupon Bulgaria promptly changed sides and declared for Russia. That Yugoslavia would be next on the list was obvious, and now the long-awaited reply from London arrived.

'Well,' MacLean said when it had been decoded. 'That is most definitely it.'

Murdoch took the sheet of paper and read:

> Your instructions are to inform General Mikhailovitch that it is the joint decision of the governments of Great Britain and the United States that they can no longer support the Chetnik armies, either politically or logistically, unless they are immediately totally integrated with the forces of Marshal Tito. It is the decision of the Allied Governments that this united force will be under the command of Marshal Tito.
>
> Should General Mikhailovitch concur in this decision, you are required to act as Allied liaison officer between the two groups to ensure that the unification of the Yugoslav Army proceeds in a satisfactory manner. Should General Mikhailovitch refuse to accept the determination of the Allies, with which the Soviet Union is associated, then it will be necessary to have his forces disarmed and placed under restraint as soon as is convenient and until such time as a properly constituted Yugoslav government can deal with the matter. Such disarmament should be accompanied by as little bloodshed as possible.
>
> This communication is to be shown to Marshal Tito.

'With as little bloodshed as possible,' Murdoch commented. 'There's a tall order. Fitzroy, we have just been instructed to condemn a good many men to death.'

'Pretty ghastly,' MacLean said. 'Well, we had better have a word with the Boss.'

Tito was in high good humour even before he was shown the Allied message. 'The Germans are pulling out of Greece,' he told them. 'Into Yugoslavia. I have just been instructed to launch another offensive before their Army Group F can be re-established on our soil. And this time, my friends, we will be cooperating, not with the Chetniks, but with the Red Army itself. They are about to cross the border.'

364

'Well, hallelujah,' Murdoch said. 'It looks like this got here just in time.'

MacLean gave Tito the paper. The Marshal read it and slapped his thigh. 'I had no doubt of it. Are you going to put these facts to Mikhailovitch?'

'We have been ordered to do so.'

'It would be best simply to round them up, now. We must have the matter cleared up before we begin our attack.'

'You mean, start a civil war even before you have defeated the Germans. That would be disastrous. And wasteful. There is every possibility that once he reads this telegram Mikhailovitch may decide there is nothing else he can do but place his men under you.'

'I will believe that when I see it,' Tito grunted.

'Nonetheless, it is something we must hope will happen. I'll leave right away.'

'Now, wait a moment,' MacLean protested.

'It's the obvious way to handle it,' Murdoch told him. 'I know Mikhailovitch. If anyone can talk him into doing the sensible thing, I can. And with respect, Fitzroy, I can pull more rank than you.'

'Um,' MacLean said unhappily. 'You can't cross the mountains alone.'

'I'll take Markham. I would also like to take with me, Marshal Tito, your personal guarantee of the safety of Mikhailovitch and his men when they come in to surrender.'

Tito nodded. 'Every man who turns in his weapon will be granted safe conduct, providing he does so by the end of this month; I repeat, this matter must be cleared up before we start our offensive in October. Any man who is prepared to fight loyally with my people may even retain his weapon. This does not apply to Mikhailovitch and his principal officers, of course. They have too much to answer for.'

'They must not be executed without a proper trial,' Murdoch insisted.

Tito grinned. 'They will have a proper trial, Murdoch. I give you my word.'

'But not the word of his Russian masters,' MacLean muttered when they returned to their encampment.

'You do not wish Captain Markham,' Yasmin decided. 'You will take me instead.'

'Why should I do that?' Murdoch asked.

'There are several reasons. There should be a Russian observer at your discussion with Mikhailovitch. I am a better cook than Markham. And you can sleep with me, and not him. I am your woman, am I not, my Murdoch?'

He had no doubt that her anxiety to remain at his side was at least partly because she was not regarded with total favour by the head of the new Russian mission, General Sukhomin – or by his staff. In the constantly suspicious world of the Communist hierarchy, presumably the fact that she alone had survived the destruction of her comrades was a matter for investigation. Sukhomin had held a long private interview with her, from which she had emerged looking distinctly shaken; she had told Murdoch that the General had wished to send her home, but she had protested on the grounds that she was a necessary liaison officer for the British – she begged him to endorse her claim.

Murdoch had supported her, for a multitude of reasons. He had grown to need her. A man had to have a woman, even a man who had seen better days. In fact, she had made him very happy in the months since nursing him back to health. In the turmoil of re-creating a partisan army after the disaster of the spring he had not been prepared to look ahead to the problems of peace, except in so far as they affected his job in hand. As Yasmin certainly appeared to be a dedicated Communist, he had always presumed when the shooting stopped she would go her own way. He hoped that; if necessary he was prepared to vouch for her loyalty and integrity to Stalin himself. Quite apart from the possible complications of her remaining around, he had actually grown to like Yasmin Bogoljubova the person rather than merely enjoy Yasmin Bogoljubova the woman. And it was difficult to believe that she still harboured thoughts of avenging her mother – she had proved such a perfect mistress. He supposed he was one of the most fortunate men in the world.

And she would undoubtedly be useful for more than cooking or warming his sleeping bag; she was as competent a guerilla as any of Tito's men. But he wasn't at all sure of the reception he was going to get from Mikhailovitch. 'I'll take both of you,' he said.

She pouted, but accepted his decision. They left the next morning, walking down the slope away from the partisan headquarters, and finding their way amidst the many encampments that had sprung up on the lower slopes and in the valleys. Despite his recent defeat, Tito did not lack for support and more men were coming in every day as news of the Russian victories was received, and carefully disseminated. Thus presumably he would win an election after the war by a large margin. However sad that might be for the youthful exiled king, Murdoch fervently hoped that would be so: only by possessing an unchallengeable mandate from the Yugoslav people could Tito ever deal fairly with his political opponents – and even that had ultimately to depend on the will of his Russian masters, because that they would be his masters, now, seemed certain.

'You are pensive, my Murdoch,' Yasmin remarked that evening, after they had left the partisan army behind and had descended into the largely deserted valley by the lake; they camped at the side of the water, after having carefully inspected the banks through their glasses for any signs of German patrols.

'I foresee a lot of trouble for this fair land,' he said.

'It has already had a lot of trouble.'

'Quite. And it will have more, after the war, before it finds peace with security.'

'There will be peace with security,' she asserted. 'We will see to that.'

'We being the Red Army.'

'It is the most powerful factor in Eastern Europe,' she said seriously.

'And suppose not all the people in the Balkans wish to live under the "security" of the Red Army?'

'They will wish it. They have no alternatives.'

'You mean that you commissars will make sure that they have no alternatives, is that not right?'

She gazed at him for several seconds. 'Do you suppose that England and America will interfere?'

Murdoch sighed. 'No, worse luck. I don't think they will. They will be too pleased to have stopped fighting the Germans to wish to start fighting the Russians.'

'Then we have nothing to quarrel over.'

He could not help but probe. 'What will you do after the war is over?'

'I would prefer not to consider that until the war *is* over.'

'You are not afraid you will be in trouble?'

She gazed at him. 'Why should I be in trouble, my Murdoch? For sleeping with you? I have enjoyed that.'

Almost he supposed she was using a past tense. But then she finished her coffee, and spread the sleeping bag. 'We have a long day's walk tomorrow. Come to bed.' Markham had already turned in.

She was more than usually loving. He concluded that she was more nervous than she pretended.

Next day they continued on their way, and that afternoon were stopped by two Chetnik scouts. These took charge of them, camped with them that night, and early on the third morning they were brought before Mikhailovitch.

'My people told me you were coming, General Mackinder,' Mikhailovitch said. 'Had you not come, I would have had to send to you. We put in for a drop a month ago, but it has not been made, and your people will not acknowledge our signals. What has happened?'

'I think we should sit down and talk about it,' Murdoch said.

Mikhailovitch glanced at Yasmin, then indicated the house where he kept his headquarters. His camp suggested much more of a military establishment than did Tito's; instead of scattered groups living in caves there were orderly rows of huts and tents; but there were less of the Chetniks, and they were less ebullient, less confident, in their demeanour.

Murdoch, Yasmin and Markham were given goat stew to eat and whisky to drink, and then they sat around his conference table with his officers – while armed guards stood at the doors.

'You do not suppose he will attempt treachery?' Yasmin whispered.

'It would be very foolish of him to do so,' Murdoch said. 'Just remember that you volunteered to come.'

'What have you got to tell me?' Mikhailovitch asked. 'Not that Tito is planning another offensive, I hope.'

'I have received a communication from the British Government which I have been instructed to place before you,' Murdoch told him, and gave him a copy of the message.

Mikhailovitch read it. He did not change expression, but his ears glowed when he raised his head. 'This is the darkest treachery.'

'It was a decision which had to be made, one way or the other,' Murdoch explained. 'You may regret that the decision is against you, but it may well be possible for you to reverse it, at the polls, after the war.'

'The polls,' Mikhailovitch said disgustedly. 'Do you really suppose there are going to be any polls, after the war? This country, the entire Balkans, will be ruled by Russia.'

'There are polls, even in Russia, General,' Yasmin told him.

'Oh, indeed,' Mikhailovitch said grimly. 'And anyone who does not vote for the official Communist candidate is sent to a labour camp. Are your governments really going to permit this to happen throughout Eastern Europe, General Mackinder?'

'I do not know what my Government is going to do, General,' Murdoch said. 'I have been given an order, and that order I have carried out. I must now ask for your answer.'

'You expect my men to fight under Tito's command? They will never do that.'

'Then I must ask you to lay down your weapons and cease operations against the Germans. Marshal Tito will send instructions as to where you should conduct your men.'

'My men will never surrender to Tito, either,' Mikhailovitch said.

'I would ask you to reconsider that decision, General,' Murdoch said. 'The Marshal has given safe conduct to every man who surrenders to him by the end of this month. After that, you will be considered as outlaws, and hunted down. That would be a very foolish thing for you to risk.'

'My people would prefer to be outlaws than to live as slaves of the Communists.'

'At least you must give them the choice, surely,' Markham put in.

'I am their commanding officer. I give the orders. I do not offer choices.'

'Then I am very sorry, for you and your men,' Murdoch said.

'This guarantee of safety, does it apply to my officers and myself?'

'Personal safety, yes. I'm afraid the Marshal has some reservations regarding your dealings with the Germans.'

'Dealing with the Germans?' Mikhailovitch shouted. 'I do not deal with the Germans. That is a foul calumny.'

'In particular,' Murdoch continued patiently, 'the Marshal is concerned about your failure to support him during the spring offensive, and he is determined that you shall explain your conduct before a court of law. However, he has given his word that it will be a fair trial.'

'You are naïve,' Mikhailovitch told him.

Murdoch sighed. 'It would be better to stand trial than to be slaughtered.'

'I disagree with you. We have not been slaughtered by the Germans. They have been trying for three years to do that. It will take Tito a hundred years to slaughter us, and soon we will have the people behind us.'

'We are wasting our time,' Yasmin said. 'The sooner we return to the Marshal the better.'

'Why should the shooting not start now?' remarked one of Mikhailovitch's aides, a saturnine man named Vabitsch. 'These people have just declared themselves our enemies. That woman is a Russian commissar. If there is any shooting to be done, let us begin with them. Her, certainly.'

Markham and Yasmin both looked at Murdoch. Who looked at Mikhailovitch. 'I would hope that you will not contemplate anything so foolish, General,' he said. 'You are taking a very irrational decision in any event. Were you to murder three representatives of the Allied Powers, then every man's hand would be against you, and even if you were to win your fight with Tito you would yet be brought down, and condemned.'

Mikhailovitch chewed his lip.

'We are already condemned,' declared Colonel Vabitsch. 'We have been betrayed, and sentenced to death. Make no mistake about that. Now we need the time to organize ourselves. Until these people return to him, Tito will not know what our answer is. Therefore they should not return at all. This is war to the death now, General. Tito must be classed with the Germans. And so must all who support him.'

Mikhailovitch slapped the table. 'We have been allies. Now we are to be enemies, General Mackinder. The choice has been yours. But I will not murder you. Come to me at the head of the Communists, with arms in your hands, and I will kill you. Now leave my people. I give you safe conduct. But you must go now.'

'I am glad to be away from there,' Yasmin confided as they climbed back into the hills. 'I felt that we were in a den of thieves.'

'I can understand their feelings,' Murdoch said. 'They were our friends.'

'And now they are our enemies. These things happen.'

'They should not. You're probably more used to them in Russia than we are.'

371

'They happen all the time. Once I was your enemy. I think I must have been your bitterest enemy. Even you, Murdoch. Now, am I not your friend?'

'I don't know that, for sure,' Murdoch said. 'Are you? Or would you still obey an order, say from Moscow, to kill me?'

'Would you not obey an order to kill me?' she countered.

They gazed at each other, and she smiled. 'We are two of a kind, Murdoch. Fighting animals. I wish I had known you in your prime.'

'I don't think we would have got on very well,' Murdoch told her.

He decided against camping by the lake this time, stayed in the hills. The going was harder, but they were all concerned about possible Chetniks who might not take Mikhailovitch's ruling – and that evening they realized they were being followed.

'Seven men, I think, sir,' Markham said, having studied the hillside below them very carefully with his glasses.

'Yes,' Yasmin said, kneeling beside him. 'Seven. What are you going to do, Murdoch? We need to rest. *You* need to rest.'

'Yes,' he agreed. 'I'm the problem. At the same time, I think I'm the one they're the least likely to kill. You're in the most danger, Yasmin. So you and Markham press on another couple of miles. I'll make camp here.'

'No,' she said. 'I will stay here with you.'

'Now look here, Yasmin . . .'

'I am not in your army, so you cannot give me orders,' she pointed out. 'Send Captain Markham on, to report to Tito. I will stay. If anyone is going to kill you, it is going to be me.'

Murdoch wished she wouldn't say things like that.

'Well, sir,' Markham said, ignoring their exchange. 'If the lady is staying I think I should too.'

Murdoch considered. 'No,' he decided. 'You must go on, Percy. Someone must return to tell Tito that Mikhailovitch has definitely refused his terms. In any event, that really takes away their reason for killing us, except out of anger;

we may well be able to negotiate. We'll camp here, and you'll leave as soon as it is dark.

'I really do wish you would go with him,' he told Yasmin, as she cooked their evening meal, while Markham watched the hills behind them.

'My business is to remain here,' she said.

Almost as if Moscow had now determined she would be his bodyguard, he thought. 'Then we'll have to take turns at keeping watch. Check your weapons.'

He took the first two hours himself. At eleven Markham, having shaken hands, crawled away into the darkness. Murdoch woke Yasmin at midnight. It was a crisp, clear autumnal night, still quite warm, and with a full moon. She peered around her as she crawled out of the sleeping bag. 'Are they close?'

'There is nothing to be seen or heard at all,' he assured her.

'Perhaps we were mistaken.'

'There were seven men following us,' he said. 'We weren't mistaken about that.'

He got into the bag, warm and smelling of her scent, and closed his eyes, but did not immediately sleep. No doubt it was the sense of being in imminent, private danger. This was the strangest situation he had ever found himself in, far away from drill and spit and polish and saluting, with no men to command – and no men to worry about, either. Yet fighting a most savage war. Which was about to become more savage? He very much feared it was. But he had been sent here to fight Germans, men like Roebel – thank God Paul was no longer around – not Chetniks.

Yet he was also here to obey his orders.

He became aware of movement, kept his eyes closed with an effort. Yasmin was bending over him, peering at him. He waited, while a deadly chill crept through his system. 'If anyone is going to kill you, it will be me,' she had said. But that was impossible. Not this girl with whom he had shared so much. Not the woman who had nursed him back to health . . . he listened to the stealthy slither of her knife being drawn from its sheath.

'I am sorry, my Murdoch,' she said softly. 'But this was always what had to happen.'

She had, as usual, talked too much. Murdoch's muscles were tensed, and with a single convulsive movement he sent himself and the sleeping bag rolling away from her. The knife struck the earth where he had been, and she whipped it up again with an exclamation in Russian, reaching after him. But by then he was already out of the bag, and his revolver was drawn.

She glared at him in the moonlight, breath hissing in a mixture of chagrin and fear; she had dropped the knife and her hand hovered close to the holster on her belt. 'You have more lives than a cat,' she said.

'Tell me why?' he asked. 'Not still Chand Bibi?' He had to find a reason, as well as the will, to kill her.

She shrugged. 'Perhaps that makes it easier. But I am obeying orders. We agreed that we would always do that, my Murdoch.'

'From Moscow?'

'Of course.'

'But why? Why did you not kill me four months ago, when I was helpless?'

'I had no orders to do so, then. General Sukhomin brought the orders.'

'And you are that much of a mindless robot?'

'I obey orders, my Murdoch. Do you not always do the same?'

Still they stared at each other; she was waiting for the slightest lapse in his concentration, to draw her pistol. And he was willing her to try: he was not sure he could execute her as well in cold blood.

'Then tell me why Moscow wishes me dead,' he said.

'You are against us.'

'I am still fighting beside you.'

'That is an act of policy. You are still against us. And you are Tito's friend. He listens to you at least as much as he did to General Sherepkin, or as he will to General Sukhomin. He will wish to have you as his adviser after the war. He has said this.'

'And your masters will have no one interfering with their plans for Eastern Europe,' Murdoch said. 'I cannot tell you how sorry I am, Yasmin. I had thought . . . but no matter. Drop your holster belt, and I will spare your life.'

'And take me back, your prisoner?' Her lip curled. 'You will not do that, my Murdoch. You will not even kill me. You are an old man, who has fallen for a young girl. What does the adage say? There is no fool like an old fool?'

'Do not push your luck, Yasmin,' Murdoch said. 'I gave you your life once. And you helped me back to health, once. We are quits. Drop that belt, or I will kill you.'

'Come and take it from me, my Murdoch,' she invited.

Murdoch shot her through the heart.

He left her lying on the hillside, knelt beside her for some time as he waited to see what reaction might be aroused by the sound of the shot winging through the hills, but there was none. It wanted still an hour and a half to dawn, as he again picked his way over the wooded slopes, up and down. He was aware of being more tired than ever before in his life. Sixty-three was a little much for this kind of thing, no matter how fit one might be. But it would soon be over, now, and then he would be going home . . . for the last time, this time.

The black had turned to grey when he heard the clicks, from in front of him. He dropped to his knees, wondering why he bothered. But there was still everything to live for, for him. Providing he could also forget a great deal.

'You are surrounded and outnumbered, General Mackinder,' Colonel Vabitsch called. 'If you open fire you will be killed.'

Murdoch waited.

'We have got your man, the Captain,' Vabitsch said. 'He is already dead, because he would not surrender.'

Murdoch sighed.

'As you killed your woman,' Vabitsch said. 'We heard the shot. She deserved to die. She was a Communist. But you are still our enemy. Here is your friend's body.'

Murdoch stared up the slope, and watched Markham's

body rolling down it; the cord which had strangled him was still round his neck – that was why he had heard no shots. He realized that he had to think very quickly. Vabitsch and his men must have kept going all the night, and thus had got ahead of him. The Colonel's voice had come from higher up the hillside, and it was likely that he had concentrated his men there. Below him the trees and bracken clustered more thickly, but that increased shelter was a good way away. Yet it was the only hope of survival.

'I will count to ten, General,' Vabitsch said. 'Then my men will open fire.'

Murdoch took a long breath, and prepared to hurl himself down the slope.

'Your time is up, General,' Vabitsch shouted.

Murdoch sent a burst of automatic fire up the hill, then commenced to roll. Bullets sang above his head and kicked the earth, and he came to rest behind a boulder, still some distance from the thicker underbrush. But he was still alive.

Just. Vabitsch's men were still firing, and the hillside was a hail of bullets. Flat on his face, Murdoch looked down, tensed himself for another desperate roll, and saw men on the slopes below him as well, and these numbered some twenty. The newcomers were not at the moment joining in the gunfight, but were studying the hill through binoculars. His heart gave a sudden surge; even at a distance he could make out the stocky figure of Colonel Kostitch.

'Well, glory be, the US cavalry,' he muttered.

Vabitsch had ordered his men to cease fire, and the echoes drifted through the hills.

Murdoch took another long breath. 'Colonel Kostitch!' he bellowed. 'General Mackinder. I need . . .'

There was another burst of firing from above him, and he felt a numbing sensation in his leg. 'Oh Christ,' he growled. Blood was oozing out of a gash in his trousers, but at least it was not pulsing. He ripped the material and found the wound. 'Not too bad,' he said to himself. 'No bones or arteries involved.' He fumbled in his haversack for his first-aid kit, began to wrap the torn flesh in the bandage roll. 'I'll survive.'

The great survivor, he thought. That is what they should call me. He realized he was quite light-headed.

But he was going to survive. Because from down the hill orders were being shouted, and Kostitch's men were shooting as well now, at the men up the hill.

Vabitsch again called for a cease fire. 'Why are you shooting at my men, Colonel Kostitch?' he shouted.

'That is General Mackinder,' Kostitch replied.

'I require your protection, Colonel,' Murdoch shouted.

'You have it, General,' Kostitch said. 'Vabitsch, the General is under my protection.'

'You do not understand, Kostitch,' Vabitsch said. 'Your friend the General has sold us out to the Communists. He has come here to tell us this.'

'The General is under my protection,' Kostitch said again. 'We are comrades in arms.'

He had continued to advance up the hill while he spoke, and Murdoch knew he was safe.

'You are a fool,' Vabitsch said, and took his men off.

Kostitch's men buried Markham on the hillside, looking at the western sky. It was probably, Murdoch thought, the place the captain would most like to lie for ever, in the same soil as Private Edmunds. But that he should have been killed by Chetniks was a suggestion of the tragedy that lay ahead.

Kostitch listened gravely to what he had to say. 'I could never support a Communist government in Yugoslavia,' he said. 'Not even one led by Tito. He has proved himself a great soldier, but as a dictator he will be ruled by Stalin. I could never accept that.'

'He has promised that he will be his own man,' Murdoch said. 'And I will do my best to see that he is.' If only to spite Moscow, he thought.

'I am sure you will, General. As he may wish to remain independent. But many a man has supposed he could work with Stalin, and found out differently. You wait. Even your Churchill and your Roosevelt will discover the same thing.'

'We must hope things will change,' Murdoch said. 'So what are you going to do?'

'Fight the Germans,' Kostitch said. 'They slaughtered my family, in 1941. My wife, my daughters, my mother, and my son. Do you remember that Fräulein my people captured, when you fought with us? How we left her?'

'Yes,' Murdoch said.

'That is how I found my wife and daughters. I will fight the Germans, and I will worry about what happens, after. You tell Marshal Tito this.'

'Will you fight under his command?'

'Of course. He is a marshal, I am only a colonel. I will place my people under his command, until the Germans are defeated. Then we will oppose him. Tell him this also.'

'I will do that,' Murdoch said, and shook hands. 'I owe you my life. I give you my personal guarantee of safety. I am sure Marshal Tito will endorse it.'

'To have fought beside you has been a privilege, General,' Kostitch said. 'I would like to do so again, once more, before I die.'

Kostitch and his men took Murdoch back to their own encampment, which was only a few miles away, and a day's march from Tito's outposts. They made a stretcher for him, as he had lost a lot of blood and, now that the shock had worn off, his leg was extremely painful; Kostitch had antibiotics, however, dropped by the RAF, and was able both to dress the wound and then bandage him securely. 'You will be all right,' he said. 'You have been wounded before, eh?'

'Occasionally,' Murdoch told him. They had left the encampment immediately, Murdoch still, to his great embarrassment, being carried on his stretcher, and now sat around the camp fire and inhaled the mixture of wood smoke and crisp night air, and drank brandy. 'But I think I'm getting a little old for it.'

'Age is in the mind,' Kostitch smiled. 'Oh, the body catches up with one, eventually. But a youthful mind will resist that longer than one which thinks in old terms. You are not yet old, Sir Murdoch. Not the way you clamber up and down these hills.'

'You tell my legs and back that,' Murdoch said. 'Even without holes in them.'

'They will be better when they have rested. What I do find strange is that you wish to support the Communist cause. This is sad.'

'I am obeying the orders of my Government.' Murdoch told him.

'Then *they* are supporting the Communists, which is even sadder.'

'I think they are trying to accept the facts of life,' Murdoch suggested. 'They know that there is nothing they can do to prevent the Red Army from taking control of Yugoslavia. It is therefore necessary to remain friends with them until arrangements can be made for proper elections.'

'That will never happen, my friend. Do you not remember what I told you when Tito's people first came to us? We may regain our bodies from the Germans. But we will never regain our souls from the Reds.'

'But you said you will fight under Tito.'

'And I will do that. Until the war is over. Which side will you be on then, Sir Murdoch?'

'Yours, Colonel. By that, I mean the side of an independent Yugoslavia, free to choose her own form of government.'

'Because you owe me your life?'

'Because I think you are right about the Reds.'

Kostitch grinned. 'You have restored my faith in human nature. But I will give you a piece of advice, my friend: do not have any faith in the nature of a Communist. Not even Marshal Tito.'

Next morning Kostitch himself insisted upon accompanying Murdoch and the four stretcher-bearers for the last part of the journey. He also took with him two other men. They had been on their way for three hours, and knew they were within the territory controlled by the Communists, when they were stopped by a challenge.

'Is that you, Colonel Kostitch?' shouted Colonel Vidmar.

'It is I,' Kostitch replied.

'Throw down your weapons. Tell your men to do likewise.'

Kostitch inspected the tumbled rocks in front of him; to their right there was a defile which led past them. It was the route he had intended to take, and it was impossible to tell how many men were hidden in the rocks. He looked at Murdoch.

'The Colonel is escorting me, Colonel Vidmar,' Murdoch said. 'The Colonel also wishes to speak with Marshal Tito. There is no need for him to disarm himself. He has accepted the new situation.'

'Has Mikhailovitch?' Vidmar asked, still speaking from concealment.

'I'm afraid not. I will make a full report to the Marshal.'

'He awaits it,' Vidmar said. 'Very well, you may retain your weapons, Colonel Kostitch, but my men will carry General Mackinder. You will walk in front of us. Pass through the defile.'

Murdoch looked at Kostitch.

The Colonel shrugged. 'We had better do what he says, or we will be here all day. He is obviously afraid of us, probably because he has only one or two men with him. Convince him that we mean him no harm.'

Murdoch hesitated, then nodded. The stretcher-bearers laid him on the ground.

'Proceed down the defile, Colonel Kostitch,' Vidmar commanded. 'And keep your men under control.'

'My men are always under control,' Kostitch said.

Murdoch watched Kostitch and his six men move away. 'This is very unnecessary, Colonel Vidmar,' he protested, sitting up. 'Colonel Kostitch has indicated his willingness to serve under the Marshal.'

'He fights with Mikhailovitch,' Vidmar retorted, and in the same breath shouted, 'Down, General.'

Murdoch obeyed instinctively, hurling himself to the ground, but continuing to look up the slope as he did so, and gasping with horror and disgust as he saw the muzzles of the machine guns protruding through the rocks.

Kostitch saw them too, and shouted, and again, as he saw, not half a dozen men, but over a hundred lining the rocks. He drew his pistol, but the machine guns were already chattering and the rifles exploding. Murdoch turned his head to watch the Chetniks falling about, blood flying from their shattered bodies. Kostitch had been the first to die, cut to pieces by the machine-gun streams.

The firing ceased; only the echoes bounced off the hilltops. Slowly Murdoch pushed himself back to a sitting position, looking at the dead men.

Vidmar came down the slope to join him. 'A clean job,' he remarked. 'I must thank you for cooperating, General.'

'Cooperating?' Murdoch shouted. 'You have just committed murder, Colonel. And I will see that the world knows of it.'

'I was doing my duty,' the Colonel said stiffly. 'They were our enemies.'

'He was right,' Tito said. 'They were our enemies. Kostitch, at any rate.'

'He was an honest man who was coming here to offer his services to you,' Murdoch said. 'He was coming in good faith. He had only the previous day rescued me from men who would have murdered me.'

'As they murdered Captain Markham and Colonel Bogoljubova,' Tito observed.

'Yes,' Murdoch agreed. There was no point in telling anyone the truth about Yasmin's death. If he refused to do so for long enough, he might forget the truth himself.

'Then you agree that they are our natural enemies.'

'Some of them. Kostitch was not. He opposed Mikhailovitch's people to help me, Tito. And you had given me authority to guarantee those men's lives. This is a foul business.'

Tito stared at him. He had never seen Murdoch so angry before. 'I doubt you understand, even now, the issues at stake here, my old friend.'

'You must take me for a fool. I will ask you one question,

Marshal: did you give Vidmar orders that the Chetniks were to be shot on sight?'

Tito did not lower his gaze. 'No,' he said. 'I did not give him that order. I told him to exercise the utmost caution in approaching any of Mikhailovitch's people, for fear of treachery.'

'Then he entirely exceeded his instructions. I wish him court martialled.'

'He is one of my most able commanders,' Tito protested.

'He is a cold-blooded murderer.'

'So is every professional soldier. So are you, Sir Murdoch. Oh, we may commit our murders in the name of our religion, our country, our loved ones. That does not alter the fact.'

A cold-blooded murderer, Murdoch thought. Or murderess. Yes, Tito was right. They were all cold-blooded murderers. But yet had Vidmar forced him to betray a friend. And besides, he was tired. Old and tired.

'Come, my friend,' Tito said, as jovially as he could. 'These things happen, in time of war. We cannot let them upset us. In a week's time we will start our offensive. We are going to take Belgrade. What do you think of that? It will be our greatest victory. Nothing will stand in our way after that. I am told your wound is not a serious one. Will you not ride with me, in triumph, into Belgrade?'

And watch more murders, Murdoch thought. Why, I had even planned one of my own: Roebel of the Gestapo. But he was all done murdering.

Then was he going to walk away from here, from all the work he had done, all the effort he had made? Moscow was afraid of the influence he might have on Tito. But they were wrong. He knew now that no one was going to have any influence on Tito. Perhaps not even Moscow. Certainly not Murdoch Mackinder.

'I'm afraid I cannot,' he said. 'I have been ordered to return home, by my Government.'

15
The Ardennes, 1944

The truck nearly overturned several times in the first few miles. Then they ran into very heavy traffic, all heading west.

'What the hell is going on?' Fergus demanded of an American Major, supervising what seemed like a massive withdrawal at a crossroads where all traffic had ground to a halt.

'The Krauts are through on a big front,' the Major said. 'We can't stop them. The orders are to pull out.'

Fergus found it incredible that the German Army, beaten and battered for more than two consecutive years now, in both the east and the west, would yet have the morale, much less the men and materiel, to launch an 'unstoppable' counter-attack.

'Well,' he said. 'Do you reckon you could clear a way for me to get through?'

'Where are you headed?' the Major wanted to know.

'I'm trying to rejoin my regiment.' There was no time to explain that he was actually a brigadier – he hadn't had the time to change his badges yet.

'Which regiment?'

The Major was being unduly suspicious, but Fergus remained patient. 'The Royal Western Dragoon Guards, of the Seventh Armoured Division of the British Army,' he said. 'We were camped outside Maastricht.'

'Maastricht? Shit, the Germans probably have there by now.'

Fergus began to feel agitated. 'Then will you clear a space for me to get through, for Christ's sake!'

'Okay, buddy. Okay. It's your funeral.'

The Major gave orders, MPs stopped various lines of

traffic, and the truck squeezed through and proceeded north. Fergus thumbed the wireless receiver but the air was a complete jumble of panic-stricken voices. While the roads remained jammed with vehicles and now too there was more sinister evidence of trouble to the east: combat troops began to appear, dazed and frightened, some even without their weapons.

'Looks like real trouble,' Sullivan said.

'Yes,' Fergus agreed. But how the hell had it happened?

The skies remained leaden and there were occasional flurries of snow; the roads, however, were so crammed with traffic that there was no chance for ice to form. Fergus could hear the roar of guns to the east, but was concerned mainly with regaining Brigade – it would be a hell of a thing to be given a command and have it destroyed before he even took over. He could hear the drone of aircraft, but they were above the clouds and it was impossible to tell whether they were Allied or German. Equally would it be impossible for the planes to tell what was happening beneath them, at least to the point of doing any accurate bombing.

They stopped for a bite of lunch at noon – Sullivan having come armed with sandwiches and coffee – while retreating Americans still continued to flood round them. Rumours were wild, estimates as to how far the Germans had reached being catastrophic. They shouted at the command truck as they passed.

'Tanks, man, great big panzers!'

'Must be a whole army of them.'

'Paratroopers. Man, they been dropping all over the place.'

'And are those guys moving!'

Paratroopers, out of total cloud cover?

Others grumbled about diversions and various roads being closed. 'Goddamn MPs think they own the fucking world,' one of them said.

'Was there any suggestion of this when you left the regiment, Sergeant?' Fergus asked.

'It was quiet as the grave, sir,' Sullivan said. 'What do you think can have happened?'

'I think that we had better get a move on,' Fergus told him.

The traffic thinned as they crossed the border into Belgium, and suddenly they raced up an empty road signposted to Philippeville . . . and a mile further skidded on a corner: Sullivan lost control, and the truck went over on its side. Fergus saw the accident coming and he braced himself, but even so as the truck went on to its right he fell on top of the sergeant, who was knocked unconscious. Fergus clambered out of the upper door, and looked around him. He was bruised and had a few minor cuts caused by glass splinters, but was otherwise unhurt; Sullivan was both bleeding and pinned.

The road remained empty for a few minutes, then he heard the sound of an engine, and out of the afternoon murk emerged an American MP's jeep, containing a corporal and a captain. 'Thank God!' Fergus said, jumping down. 'There's an injured man in that truck. I need help to get him out.'

The Captain stepped out of the jeep. 'You shouldn't be on this road at all, Colonel.' He spoke with a rather flat, nasal accent. 'It's closed.'

'Closed? What for?'

The Captain glanced at his corporal. 'Headquarters staff will be moving along here from Bastogne, sir. Seems the Germans are making a deep penetration.'

Fergus frowned at him. Bastogne was some sixty miles east of Philippeville. That was a long way for a headquarters staff to be clearing the way for their retreat: that sounded more like an absolute rout.

'Well,' he said. 'They'll take a good while to get here. You fellows give me a hand with my driver.'

Once again the captain and the corporal exchanged glances, and the corporal got out from behind the wheel. Fergus was aware of a curious prickling sensation behind the ears. The two men were immaculately dressed as American soldiers, they spoke with American accents . . . 'Heil Hitler!' he snapped.

385

Both men instinctively came to attention, realized what they had done, and reached for their sidearms. But Fergus was ahead of them, had drawn his service revolver. He fired six times. The first bullet was wild, the second struck the captain in the shoulder as he drew his own pistol, the third went past him and hit the corporal in the face, the fourth struck the corporal in the chest as Fergus got the gun under control, the fifth missed and the last slammed into the captain's skull as he groped for his Luger with his other hand.

The sounds of the shots drifted away into the afternoon, and Fergus found that he was panting. He reloaded, made sure both the 'MPs' were dead, then climbed back on to the truck and lowered himself into the cab. But Sergeant Sullivan was also dead; he must have died within seconds of the accident.

Fergus climbed back out, got behind the wheel of the jeep, turned it, and raced to the north.

Philippeville was a chaotic mass of support staff packing up, trucks waiting to be loaded, and people in a panic. Some civilians were already attempting to stream to the west, further adding to the confusion on the roads. Others stood around gaping at the American soldiers who down to this morning they had regarded as invincible liberators.

Fergus fought his way through behind a blaring horn, turned right for Dinant and then left for Namur, intending to skirt the western side of the big flap. Even so progress was dreadfully slow, and the reports of disaster in the east grew with each village. He managed to wheedle some petrol out of a dump master just north of Namur, but by now it was growing dark, he had not eaten since his early sandwich lunch, and he had little hope of finding his command at night.

But the next heavy conglomeration of traffic he drove into, almost literally, because the trucks were using no lights, turned out to be a British infantry regiment.

'Where are you heading?' he asked the Lieutenant-Colonel.

'We've been ordered to fall back on Brussels, don't you know.'

'On Brussels? My God! Whose orders were those?'

'GHQ, of course.'

'They were from your Brigadier, personally?'

'No. They were in writing, brought by an MP lieutenant.'

Fergus snapped his fingers. 'They were forged.'

'Oh, really, old man. They were quite pukka. I have the order here.'

They studied the sheet of paper by the light of a torch. It certainly looked genuine, had all the official seals, and had been signed by the brigade major.

'I still think it's a forgery,' Fergus said. He just could not imagine Montgomery ordering such a precipitate or far-reaching retreat – or any subordinate officer doing so without first checking with the Field Marshal. 'I have an idea there are a whole hell of a lot of Germans behind our lines, dressed as British and American MPs, dislocating traffic, and carrying false orders.'

'My dear fellow,' the infantry Colonel remarked. 'You must have had a damned good leave.'

Fergus saw no point in quarrelling. 'Anyway, I'm trying to find my brigade,' he said. 'My regiment is the Royal Westerns.'

'An,' the Colonel said.

'You've seen them?'

'Well, no, I haven't. But earlier this afternoon, just before dusk, we did mingle briefly with First Fifty-Third Lancers. Aren't they brigaded with you?'

'Yes. Thank God for that. Where are they?'

'They were about five miles north of here.'

'And presumably they too were heading for Brussels.'

'Well, of course, old man. That's where we're to concentrate.'

Fergus nodded. 'I won't see you there.' He got into his jeep and roared into the night.

The German plans, and the way they were being carried

387

out, were becoming more sinister with every minute. Fergus had never known such a devious operation – nor one whose deviousness was proving so successful. He felt himself sweating with anxiety, despite the cold.

The roads grew even more clogged in the darkness, with men cursing and swearing against the lone jeep going the wrong way. But Fergus fought on, although now he was dropping with fatigue, and he was rewarded just before midnight, when he came across a line of tanks, proceeding slowly west.

'Where is Colonel Harding?' he demanded.

'With the ACV, sir, trying to raise Brigade,' the Lieutenant said.

Fergus got to Harding ten minutes later. 'Fergus!' the lancer commander shouted. 'What in the name of God are you doing here? Your chaps haven't been shot up?'

'I have no idea,' Fergus said. 'I am trying to find them. But what the hell are you doing *here*?'

'We've been told to pull out.'

'Don't tell me,' Fergus said. 'They were written orders, brought to you by an MP lieutenant.'

'That's right. I suppose you got the same.'

'Billy, I will bet my last penny that that MP lieutenant was a German.' He told Harding of his experience south of Philippeville.

'Holly hell!' Harding commented. 'If that's true . . . oh, Jesus Christ.'

'Exactly,' Fergus agreed. 'Now, you were trying to raise Brigade. Why?'

'To ask permission to call it off for tonight. My men are dog tired, and this road is so goddamned choked we might as well pull out and wait until dawn.'

'Right. Only you're not pulling out to wait. You're pulling out to turn round and go back.'

'Go back? Now, really, Fergus, my men . . .'

'May be tired, but we have a lot to do. You may have heard a rumour that I now have Brigade, Billy.'

'Well, yes. Best congratulations, old man. But you don't take command until tomorrow.'

388

'Tomorrow is in half an hour. I am taking command right this minute, Billy. Give me your notebook and a map.'

Harding hesitated, then handed over the book. Fergus studied the map and then wrote very carefully: 'Brigade will concentrate on Bassenge north of Liège.' He signed it.

'Bassenge? But Fergus, the enemy already have Eupen. And Malmedy. There are rumours of nine thousand Americans having been captured. Liège is being evacuated. They could be across the river and in Bassenge right now.'

'Then we'll throw them back out,' Fergus told him. 'I have given you an order, Billy. I wish that order carried out.'

'Yes, sir.' Harding grinned. 'You know, you could lose the brigade before you even take command of it.'

'That thought had crossed my mind,' Fergus agreed. 'In which case I'll sell you my first used car. Now let's get these tanks turned around. Your men can sleep as they move, taking turns at driving.'

He ate, then snatched a couple of hours' sleep in Harding's ACV; worried as he was about the whereabouts of the regiment, he knew he could do nothing more without some rest. He left orders that attempts were to continue to raise Brigade and Division by radio, but the air continued to be clogged. So were the roads, and progress against the tide of terrified humanity was slow. But Fergus was awakened at dawn with the glad news that Brigade was at last on the air.

'Conant, here, Brigadier,' the Major said.

'Is General Manton with you?'

'No, sir. General Manton went off to Division on Friday. I was told to hold the fort until you took over.'

'I have taken over,' Fergus told him. 'Where are you?'

'We're just outside Walschoutem, sir. I know our orders were to be further west by this time, but frankly, we haven't been able to make the progress anticipated.'

Walschoutem was a village some fifteen miles north-east of Namur, and the same distance west of Bassenge. It was thus now some five miles north-east of the lancers.

'Who have you got with you?'

389

'Macalee's hussars.'

'Where are the Westerns?'

'I'm afraid they're still further back, sir. I left them to form the rearguard. I don't suppose they're more than five miles this side of Bassenge by now.'

'Hallelujah!' Fergus shouted. 'Have they reported any enemy activity north or west of the river?'

'Not as yet, sir.'

'All right, Conant. Turn yourself round and make for Bassenge.'

'For Bassenge, sir? But we only evacuated it yesterday morning.'

'So now we're going to reoccupy it. Move it, Conant. Try to contact Division and tell them that I am concentrating the Brigade on Bassenge, and will attempt to counter-attack the enemy by means of the bridge at Vise. Then get through to the Westerns and tell them to stay put, and to expect me for lunch.'

'Yes, sir.' Conant sounded a little dazed.

'How the hell are you going to reach the dragoons for lunch?' Harding asked him. 'On these roads?'

Fergus pointed at the farmhouse about half a mile away; a quick inspection through his binoculars had established that the farmer had so far not evacuated; there was smoke coming out of the chimney. 'Don't let's ever forget that we really were once a cavalry regiment, Billy,' he said.

He put out a call for volunteers who could ride, thinking what a strange message to be sending to cavalrymen, and got six men. They sloshed through the snow to the farmhouse, and found, as Fergus had surmised, that the family had determined to sit it out, and that there were actually four horses still in the stable. The farmer was willing to rent three, and provided saddles and harnesses; in ten minutes Fergus and two of the troopers were mounted. 'Tell Colonel Harding I hope to see him in Bassenge by tonight,' he told the others, and led his escort across the field.

Progress was slow where the snow was heavy, but it was

much quicker than on the road; even at a walk the horses were capable of making more speed than a bumper to bumper truck. But soon Fergus took to the road himself, able to thread his mount in and out of the blocked vehicles. He and his escort attracted a good deal of comment, the general opinion seeming to be that he was mad. As the cold began to strike through his greatcoat, he wondered if he wasn't.

Most of the troops and the refugees seemed to be obsessed only with getting out of the path of the German juggernaut, but in the middle of the afternoon Fergus encountered an American Major commanding a with-drawing infantry battalion, who seemed to be keeping his head, and showed a good deal of interest when he dis-covered that Fergus was reconcentrating in the face of the enemy onslaught.

'Fucking awful show,' he remarked. 'You seriously going to try to stop them, sir?'

'You're damn right,' Fergus told him. 'We know they haven't crossed the river yet. That means they're advancing on a very narrow front, and relying on the effect of surprise. That has to leave their lines of communication vulnerable. Now tell me about the bridges over the river.'

'Well, we have engineers standing by to blow them the moment the Germans appear.'

'But they're still intact.'

'Sure, at the moment. We need them for withdrawing our people.'

'That includes the one at Vise?'

'As far as I know. But according to the last report I had, that's well back behind the panzers' present position. Luckily they're moving west all the time, and not north.'

'That's the point. That's where they're going to be thin on the ground. So that's where I'm going to hit them.'

'Gee, I sure wish I was coming with you,' the Major said. 'But we got orders to pull back twenty miles.'

'I think you should ignore those orders,' Fergus suggested. 'I could do with some infantry support. Your fellows have bazookas, haven't they?'

'Sure we have, but hell . . . you trying to get me cashiered?'

'We'll be cashiered together, if we fail, Major. But maybe they'll pat us on the back if we succeed?'

'That would sure be something.' He brooded for a few seconds. Then he said, 'Okay, you're on, Colonel. It'll take a little while to get these trucks turned around.'

'Then start now. I'm afraid I don't know your name.'

'Schmidt, sir.'

'Schmidt?'

Major Schmidt grinned. 'I was actually born in Milwaukee, sir.'

'If you say so, Major. My name is Mackinder.'

'Say, I've read about you.'

'No,' Fergus corrected him. 'You have probably read about my father. There's just one more thing: have you got any dynamite?'

'I reckon so. We have our own engineer squad.'

'Lend it to me.'

'Lend it?'

Fergus grinned. 'Call it lend lease, Major Schmidt.'

'You gonna take it on that horse? What the hell for?'

'Major, right now I don't know who's actually on our side or not. I propose to be able to handle any situation which may crop up.'

The dynamite was fetched, and carefully packed in a saddlebag. Fergus shook hands. 'I'll see you in Bassenge, Major, just as quickly as possible.'

He was accumulating himself a small division, he thought. Mackinder's last charge. It would certainly be that if he acted without orders and got himself chopped up.

It was half past one that afternoon when he and his two lancers rode their exhausted horses into the midst of the Royal Western Dragoon Guards.

'There is one hell of a flap going on,' Smithie told him. 'I was never so happy as when I received your orders to stand fast. What the devil is happening?'

Fergus sat at the area map in his old ACV. 'So far as I can

392

make out, the enemy are launching an all-out drive south-west from the vicinity of Cologne. They have definitely taken Eupen, followed by Malmedy. That indicates a south-westerly direction. Now, they must have an object-ive; they simply do not have the men or the materiel to take on the entire combined Allied armies in a pitched battle. But if you follow the line of their advance, a pattern begins to develop. You have pulled back five miles from the river. Has the bridge at Vise been blown yet?'

'I don't think so. A sapper party turned up just as we were leaving, and said they had orders to blow the bridge the moment the Germans approached. But I think we would have heard the bang if they had.'

'Correct. None of the other bridges this side of Namur have had to be blown either, yet. That means the Germans are sticking to the south of the Meuse, just. Now why are they doing that? It has to be because the river is the dividing line between the British and American forces. They know that at that point there will be some lack of clarity in command. And they've been proved right. They have also planned, and are carrying out, the most disruptive fifth-column work I have ever heard of. Now, my guess is that they are driving straight for Namur, the hinge of the two Allied groups as it were. Their idea is that the Yanks will fall away to the south-west, and the British will naturally recoil to the north-west. If they swing up towards Antwerp, after getting across at Namur, they could split the two halves of the Allied army right open, and perhaps hope to defeat each one in detail.'

'Can they possibly do that, sir?' Mather asked. All the squadron commanders had by now accumulated.

'I doubt it. But if they're allowed to try hard enough they could keep the war going for one hell of a long time yet. It's all working out for them, right now. But let's think about it logically. Firstly they are creating a big salient, relying on the withdrawal of all our forces to protect their flanks until their reserves can secure them. Secondly, they have to have a large reserve available, to throw at whichever wing of our forces they intend to roll up. We can't do anything about the south and the Americans, but we sure as hell can do something about up here. If we cross at Vise and strike south, we'll not only cut the German line of communications, but we'll possibly check the advance of their second strike. So that's our target. I've ordered the entire brigade to re-concentrate on Massenge by tonight, and I also have some hopes of at least one American infantry regiment joining us. I want every one of you to understand that we are taking on what could be vastly superior enemy forces, and that I am acting without orders. I am trying to contact General Manton, however, and I am sure he will support our intentions, hopefully with the rest of the division. For the time being, however, we are on our own. Are you with me?'

'Yes, sir!' they chorused.

'Right. So now I want the regiment to head back to Bassenge as quickly as possible. There we'll prepare our crossing. But I also want a reconnaissance sent out towards the Vise bridge.'

'Yes, sir!' Smithie said, and gave the necessary orders.

The roads east were now clear; as Conant had said, the regiment had formed the rearguard, and there was nothing left between them and the river. Yet it took time for the tanks and trucks to be turned round and headed the other way, and it was already close to dusk when they once more rolled into Bassenge. But Bassenge was also deserted save for a few stray dogs which set up a mournful wailing as the tanks clanked into the village square.

'I have Division, sir,' said the telegrapher.

Murdoch took the handset.

'Report your position,' came the command.

'Royal Western Dragoons are in Bassenge,' Fergus said. 'Brigade will concentrate here tonight, and I will attempt to cross the Meuse tomorrow morning and attack the German right.'

'Have you orders to do that?' The Staff Major was clearly astonished.

'I have received no orders to do anything.'

'Well, really, I say, Brigadier . . .'

'Is Major-General Manton with you?'

'Why, yes, sir.'

'Let me speak with him.'

Manton came on the air. 'I was told your people were out of there, Fergus.'

'Did you give that order, sir?'

'No, I did not. I was in Brussels on Friday. I came back here yesterday to find everyone moving west. Apparently on orders from GHQ. I've tried to contact Monty, but he's in high-level conference. You say you're concentrating on Bassenge. Are the bridges still intact?'

'I'm trying to ascertain that now,' Fergus said. 'But I'll get across somewhere.'

'I would prefer it if you held on for a while. Complete your concentration, but take no further action unless the bridge at Vise is actually attacked. If you cross in brigade strength you are likely to be chopped up. On the other hand, Jerry has to widen his salient some time, and it's most likely that he will attempt to do so to the north, in which case you will be in the right place to stop him; he's far more likely to make his crossing at Vise than risk getting his armour bogged down in Liège or Maastricht. So your first business is to prevent any German irruption north or west of the Meuse. I'm going to try to get support up to you. But I'm not promising anything for twenty-four hours, given the state of the roads. Now Fergus, I want you to remember that you're up against some fanatics, from what we can gather; reports have been coming in that SS detachments have been shooting American prisoners.'

'Just so long as you're coming,' Fergus told him.

The troop which had gone out on reconnaissance came back just on dark.

'Not a thing, sir,' said Lieutenant Charters. 'Not a soul in sight on the south bank. And the sappers say there's been no movement either.'

Fergus frowned at him. 'Not even the sounds of movement?'

'No, sir.'

'But the bridge is still intact?'

'Yes, sir.'

'Did you tell the sappers we were coming?'

'Yes, sir. They didn't look too happy.'

'I imagine they're just longing to blow that bridge,' Smithie suggested.

'I wish to hell I knew what was going on south of the river,' Fergus growled. 'And now we've been ordered to stay here. Damnation. I want a patrol up there all night, Jimmy.'

'It'll be there,' Smithie promised.

Fergus went off to see if the three horses, which had walked patiently along with the tanks on the return march, had been looked after, and found them in the care of the Sergeant-Major.

'Some foul-up,' Bert commented.

'A gambler's throw,' Fergus assured him. 'In a week's time this will be history. Have you heard from Annaliese yet?'

'No, sir.'

'Well, I imagine the mails have been snarled up by this little mess. What about your application for a commission?'

'Nothing there yet, either, sir.'

'It'll be along. I suspect you have a long career ahead of you. And a successful one.'

Bert grinned. 'If we survive this one, sir.'

'Oh, indeed. That goes for all of us.'

He climbed into his old bunk in the tiny sleeping cabin of the ACV, which Smithie had willingly evacuated. He was dog tired. He wanted nothing more than to sleep for a week. But at the same time he was feeling the exhilaration of impending battle, on top of the exhilaration of having held Monique in his arms. As he was going to do for the rest of his life. When he had nipped this little German plan in the bud.

He was awakened just before dawn by an apologetic Trooper Waterman. 'Division is on the air, sir.'

Fergus hurried into the back of the vehicle, where the telegrapher was hunched over his set.

'This is General Manton,' the General said. 'You'll be pleased to know, Fergus, that Monty has been appointed commander of all Allied forces north of the "bulge", as they're calling it. He has the First and Ninth US armies under him, as well as our own people.'

'Hallelujah,' Fergus said. 'Now at last we may get something done.'

'You bet. You'll also be pleased to know that he entirely approves your action. You anticipated his own dispositions, in fact, to come in on the German lines of communication. He is therefore concentrating on you just as rapidly as he can. Is your brigade with you, yet?'

Fergus looked at Smithie, who had just got into the truck. The Colonel shook his head. 'Nothing.'

'Not yet, sir,' Fergus said.

'Well, see if you can hurry them up. Your orders are to hold that bridge. Maintain it intact as long as you can, but should German armour commence to cross it in such force that you cannot stop them, it is to be blown. We can always make another.'

'Yes, sir,' Fergus said. He let the General off the air, then thumbed the mike again. 'Conant,' he said. 'Conant, where the devil are you?'

'Ten miles away, sir. It's not been possible to make any quicker time. These roads are so chopped about they're damn near impossible even for tanks.'

Fergus knew he was right. 'Well, keep coming as fast as you can,' he told him. 'Any word from Colonel Harding?'

'I'm right behind the hussars, sir,' Harding replied.

'Major Schmidt?'

'Behind your lancers, Brigadier.'

'That's fine. Keep coming.'

'Brigade,' said an urgent voice. 'Brigade. B Troop, A Squadron, calling Brigade.'

'That's our reccy unit,' Smithie said.

'Come in, B Troop, this is Brigade.'

'Enemy armour approaching the Vise bridge, sir. In strength.'

'Estimate the strength.'

'At least a division, sir, but it could be more.'

'That's it,' Fergus said. 'We can't stop them with just the regiment. Tell the sappers to blow, Lieutenant.'

'The sappers aren't here, sir,' the Lieutenant said.

'Say again?'

'There's no one about at all, sir.'

'Oh, Jesus Christ,' Smithie commented.

'He isn't here, either,' Fergus said.

'But how . . .'

'They've done us again. Those weren't our sappers at all. They were Jerries dressed up. They were there to *protect* the bridge just in case any genuine sappers turned up. God damn. I had a feeling about that. Thank God I did something about it. Tell your men to start up, Jimmy. We have to get down to that bridge.'

'You said we couldn't stop them with one regiment?'

'We don't have any choice. Lieutenant Masters, I want you to stay put.'

'You want me to try to destroy the bridge with gunfire, sir?'

'You won't do that, with a seventy-five millimetre, and you'll just give your position away. No, Lieutenant, I want you to hold on, and if the enemy armour starts to cross before we can get to you, stop them.'

There was a moment's silence, then Masters said, 'Yes, sir.'

'Good man,' Fergus said. 'Shouldn't be too long. Brigade out.' Fergus replaced the handset and looked at Smithie.

'You've just told him to commit suicide,' the Colonel said.

'Yes,' Fergus said. 'So let's get down there to pick up the pieces.' He summoned Bert. 'I want you on this one, Sergeant-Major,' he said. 'Have you any experience with dynamite?'

'A little, sir.'

Fergus gave him the saddlebag. 'You'll ride with Colonel Smithie and me.'

Bert gazed at him. 'You want me to blow the bridge, sir?'

'Somebody has to do it, Bert. I'll be there with you.'

The engines were started, the carbon dioxide fumes rising and hanging on the still, cold air, and then the tanks rolled out of the village and down the road, behind a screening troop.

'Report, B Troop,' Fergus said.

'Cripes, sir, there must be hundreds of them. And there is artillery and infantry support.'

'Are they at the bridge yet?'

'Perhaps half a mile, sir.'

'Have they seen you?'

'No, sir. We are in a dip.'

'Well, good shooting, Lieutenant. We're on our way.'

'Come on,' Smithie said. 'Come on.'

The tanks were moving as fast as they could along the icy road; there was nothing to be gained by attempting to go across country, because there was no telling how thick the ice was and when the vehicles would become completely bogged down. At least the Germans would be having the same problem.

They heard gunfire from in front of them.

'There goes Masters,' Smithie growled. 'That boy had promise.'

'He'll get a medal, no matter what happens,' Fergus promised.

The firing flared in violence for several minutes, then died away again.

'Whatever happens,' Fergus repeated.

They were very close now. B Troop of C Squadron moved forward with its five tanks as an advance guard, rolling up the slight rise that separated them from the river, while the remainder of the regiment formed column of squadrons behind it, leaving the road and advancing on a front of fifteen tanks. Now Lieutenant Porter's voice came over the wireless, distinctly anxious. 'There is enemy armour across the bridge, sir.'

'Any sign of Lieutenant Masters?'

Porter's voice seemed to have a catch in it. 'There's a lot of burning stuff down there, sir.'

Fergus thumbed the mike again. 'Westerns,' he said. 'This is Brigadier Mackinder. I would like you to join me in the regimental prayer.' He waited for a moment, while the tanks slowly rolled up the hillside. Then he said, 'May the great God of battle, who has guided the fate of this famous regiment on many a hard-fought field, and never failed to lead it to distinction, grant that on this day, faced as we are with a host of enemies of our King and our Country, every man will do his duty, so that should we fail in our ordained task, it will yet be said of us, they were the Royal Western Dragoon Guards, who fought and died according to the ancient valour of their regiment and their blood.'

As he finished, the regiment topped the hill, and looked down on the scene beneath them. 'Gentlemen,' he said. 'There is your enemy.'

As Porter had said, the Germans were still crossing the bridge; their armour was strung out for a considerable distance south of the river. Accompanying them were truckloads of infantry, and self-propelled artillery. With anti-tank guns – though these were not yet in position. But the immediate problem was the force already on the west bank; Fergus's quick estimate was that there could hardly be less than two hundred tanks already across.

He had stumbled on a hornet's nest. But hadn't that been what he was looking for?

And Masters had gone out fighting. If the position of the British troop was marked by burning tanks, there were also three German panzers in the river, into which they had clearly been pushed by those behind after they had been brewed by the British seventy-fives.

He glanced at Smithie. 'Tell them to go, Colonel,' he said.

'The regiment will advance,' Smithie said into the wireless. 'Open fire.'

'The bridge,' Fergus told him. 'The bridge.'

The tanks rolled down the slope, firing as they did so.

The first panzers in front of them dissolved in a mass of flaming steel and dying men, and they were racing at the German concentration. Guns boomed and men shouted; the wireless crackled with orders.

'The bridge!' Fergus shouted again.

In front, behind, and to either side was a blaze of gunfire. He glanced over his shoulder and saw Bert, clutching his dynamite in his arms. The Sergeant-Major gave him a grin.

Smithie was snapping orders. 'Traverse right, range one hundred yards, fire. Traverse left, range seventy-five yards, fire.'

The gun swung to and fro and exploded time and again, and the interior of the tank filled with smoke and fumes. They coughed and choked, but in front of them the opposition fell to either side before the fury of their assault. Tank tracks flew apart, trucks exploded and burst into flame, foot soldiers scurried for shelter. Snow flew into the air, mingled with black dirt and blood. And the bridge was in front of them, still filled with tanks.

'Form a leaguer,' Fergus snapped into the wireless. 'All remaining tanks form a leaguer. Sergeant-Major, earn yourself a medal.'

For they were at the bridge, and the belching seventy-five had stopped another tank in its tracks, thirty feet from the west bank. Once again those behind were crowding it, attempting to push it into the swift-flowing water, but there were minutes to spare.

The driver brought the tank round in a tight circle, and Bert threw open the hatch. He had never lacked courage, Fergus remembered. Out he leapt, the sticks of precious dynamite clutched to his chest. One bullet in there and no part of him would ever be found. But fortune favoured the brave, and he slithered down the bank beneath the steel struts.

Fergus had time to look around him, because, amazingly, the firing had stopped, although the echoes still reverberated from the low clouds. Some thirty-five tanks had burst through the German force and were now hastily wheeling into position to his left and right, guarding the bridgehead. Behind them was a torn mass of burning metal and men, for they had inflicted at least as many casualties as they had suffered. But there were still well over a hundred and fifty German tanks on the west side of the river, and these were now regrouping.

'That was well executed, Brigadier Mackinder,' said a new voice, speaking English with only a trace of accent. 'In keeping with your name. But now your regiment is quite surrounded. The only course open to you, in order to avoid needless bloodshed, is to surrender.'

'Who the hell is that?' Fergus demanded.

'I am Major-General Paul von Reger,' the voice said. 'Commanding this division.'

'Von Reger? Good God!'

'Yes,' Paul said. 'As we are by way of being related, Brigadier, I would not like to see you needlessly killed. Lay down your arms. There is nothing dishonourable in surrendering when confronted with such odds.'

'Related, sir?' Smithie whispered.

'He's my fucking brother-in-law,' Fergus growled.

'Good heavens! Small world, isn't it? But . . . what are we going to do, sir?'

'Not a damn thing, until we hear from the Sergeant-Major.' Obviously Reger had not seen Bert leaving the tank; certainly he seemed to have no concept that the idea behind the dragoons' suicidal charge was to blow the bridge. Annaliese's brother, he thought. There was a turn-up for the book. He wondered what Paul von Reger would say if he knew that he had *two* near relatives with the regiment.

'I must have your answer, General Mackinder,' Paul said. 'I will give you five more seconds.'

'It's been fun,' Smithie muttered.

Bang-bang on the side of the tank. 'Let's get the hell out of here, sir,' Bert Manly-Smith shouted, dropping into their midst.

Amazingly, he appeared quite unhurt; even his beret was at its usual cocky angle.

'Regiment will advance,' Fergus said into the wireless. 'And open fire.'

402

Engines roared, and the tanks started to move back towards the German armour. Fergus thrust his head through the hatch and looked back, just in time to see the stricken tank on the bridge plunging into the river. The German column started to move again.

'You are a fool, Mackinder,' Paul von Reger said. 'You . . .' his voice was lost in the roar from behind them. Once again Fergus looked back. Bert hadn't been able to do a very professional job; only the very northern supports of the bridge had been blown, but some twenty-five feet of the span had collapsed down the river bank, taking with it the leading tank. No doubt the German engineers would have it functional again in a couple of hours – but a couple of hours was surely all he needed.

'You are a man of great resource, Brigadier,' Reger said. 'I will wish you goodbye.' He then gave several rapid orders in German, but as he did so another voice cut across his.

'Regiment will deploy and advance,' it said.

'Harding!' Fergus shouted.

'Regiment will deploy and advance,' repeated Macalee of the hussars.

'Hoorah!' Smithie bellowed.

'Get out of those trucks,' Major Schmidt was saying. 'Bazooka squad to the front. Let's get us some Krauts.'

The dragoons were already in the thick of the mêlée with the Tigers, but the Germans had also heard the voices behind them. And now there came yet another.

'We are in contact, Brigadier Mackinder,' General Manton said. 'Division is deploying now. Just hold them for half an hour, Fergus.'

'We can do that,' Fergus shouted above the din of the exploding seventy-five. He heard Reger bellowing more orders in German, presumably warning his tanks which were still on the bridge to pull back before they became sitting targets for the divisional artillery. His own force was now scattered, as the hussars and the lancers tore into them from behind. The noise was terrific, and the screaming of the engines, the reports of the guns, the constant chatter in both English and German over the radio had a dazing effect, just as the swirling mud and flying snow obscured visibility.

But the noise was diminishing. Fergus listened to Reger again, shouting, his voice this time higher.

'We've brewed him,' Smithie said.

Fergus threw open the hatch and looked out, saw men jumping from a burning Tiger a few hundred yards away. The battle was now definitely dying down. 'Get over there,' he said. 'I want that fellow.'

Paul von Reger had lost his cap and his uniform was torn and blackened with smoke. He was fortunate to have escaped the burning, exploding tank, and his eyes were dull as he watched the destruction of the remnants of his advanced brigade; those who thought to escape over the hill were met by the American infantry and their bazookas.

'The fortunes of war,' he said, and held out his Luger pistol, butt first.

'The fortunes of war,' Fergus agreed. 'Keep your sidearm, General.'

He escorted his captive to the ACV which had now appeared on the scene with the rest of the support vehicles. The battle was over, and won; the remainder of the German armour was hastily pulling back off the bridge, and the brigade was emplaced on the ridge overlooking it; there would be no repairing the damage until division came up, and then it would be British sappers who would do the job, to allow British armour to cross.

'Tea, gentlemen.' Waterman was offering, and Padre Wint was also there. Smithie was making a list of casualties.

'It seems odd,' Fergus remarked, 'that we have never met. You know both my father and mother, and my late brother, I believe.'

It was even odder, he thought, how unlike Annaliese this man was, at least in appearance. He had dark hair and his features were far stronger than his sister's. In fact, they reminded Fergus of someone, although for the life of him he couldn't think who.

'Yes,' Reger said, and sipped his tea.

'Well . . .' Fergus didn't know what to say. 'Your sister

is well, I believe. She's. . . .' he changed his mind. One couldn't really tell a prisoner of war that his sister had just given birth to an illegitimate child.

'That is good to know,' Reger said.

'Yes. Well . . . it won't succeed, you know. Your push. It was a crazy idea.'

'Yes,' Reger said. 'It was the Fuehrer's idea.'

'Ah. Well, if you don't mind my saying so, he's no military genius. If he'd stayed on the defensive, husbanded his resources, especially his panzers, he might have kept things going for a while. But now we are counter-attacking, your people are going to be wiped out. How many panzer divisions did you throw in?'

'Three,' Paul said. 'The last three.'

'Good Lord! Well . . . that's about it, I would say.'

'Yes,' Paul said. 'He has led us to utter disaster. The Fuehrer.'

Fergus had nothing to say to that.

'It has been good to meet you at last,' Paul said. He finished his tea, stood up, and saluted – the old Wehrmacht salute.

Hastily Fergus did the same.

'And now . . . I wonder if I might be permitted to be alone for a little while?' Reger asked. 'I have a letter to write.'

'Of course, my dear fellow. Use my sleeping cabin.' He opened the door for him.

'This is a remarkable vehicle,' Paul commented.

'Oh, just a working caravan,' Fergus explained. 'Very convenient.'

'I'm sure it is,' Reger said.

Fergus closed the door on him.

'Strange fellow,' Wint commented. 'Could almost be British.'

'Yes. His mother was Dutch, as I understand it. Come along, Padre, let's go and inspect the troops.'

They spent the next hour with the men, examining the tanks, talking with the wounded. 'I am certainly going to recommend you for one of these, Sergeant-Major,' Fergus said, tapping the crimson ribbon on his breast.

'Me, sir?' Bert was astonished. 'What have I done?'

'Behaved with a courage over and above the call of duty.'

'Never had a scratch, sir. Since that brew-up in Libya, no Jerry has come near me.'

'Let's hope it stays that way. Joey all right?'

'Oh, yes, sir. We Manly-Smiths are indes . . .'

They both turned, as did the padre, at the sound of the muffled explosion.

'Jesus Christ!' Fergus said. 'With respect, Padre; that came from the ACV.'

They ran through the snow, encountered an ashen-faced Waterman. 'That Jerry General, sir,' he gasped. 'He's shot himself. In your cabin.' That apparently was what was most upsetting him.

Fergus leapt into the truck. The door to his sleeping cabin was ajar, and he gazed at Paul von Reger. The General had put his pistol muzzle into his mouth and pulled the trigger. There was blood everywhere, but he must have died instantly.

'I'll have it cleaned up in a jiffy, sir,' Waterman promised.

Fergus bent over the dead man, took the envelope from his left hand, frowned at it. Paul had indeed written a letter. And it was addressed to Lieutenant-General Sir Murdoch Mackinder.

The war in Europe was to last another four months, but the German offensive in the Ardennes was Hitler's last throw. As Fergus had told Reger, those seven divisions, three of them armoured, might have held the line of the Rhine for a considerable time. But once Montgomery's counter-offensive was aided by clearing skies, which allowed the Allied air forces to see what was going on beneath them, the German forces in the 'bulge' were blasted out of existence.

By the middle of January, just a month after the so highly organized counter-offensive had begun, it was all over, and some hundred and twenty thousand German soldiers were dead, wounded, or prisoners, together with six hundred tanks. The Americans had actually lost more tanks, most of them in the first few panic-stricken days, but personnel deaths were less than ten thousand: British losses were minimal.

A week later the Allies were advancing again. By the end of the month they were at the Rhine, and although German resistance once again stiffened, at the beginning of March the bridge at Remagen was captured intact, and the invasion of the German heartland could begin.

By then the brigade had had a lot more hard fighting in the Reichswald, but they were with Montgomery's Twenty-first Army Group when it in turn forced the Rhine at Wesel, and crashed on into North Germany.

Here the brigade was pulled out for rest and recuperation, which was badly needed after four months of continuous action. And here, at the beginning of April, Bert received orders to return to England to commence training as an officer.

'Well, I'll be damned, sir,' he said to Fergus. 'I had thought I'd see the end of this lot.'

'The way the Germans are crumbling, I don't think you'll make it back in time,' Fergus told him. 'You're also to receive that medal, remember.'

'Hell, sir, I shan't know what to say.'

'I'm sure you'll think of something, Bert. And you'll also be getting leave to go down to Somerset.'

'Yes, sir.' Bert looked even more embarrassed about that, but Fergus did not doubt that he would think of something to say there too.

He had written his mother and Annaliese to tell them of the death of Paul, but he had not forwarded Paul's letter; it remained in his briefcase: he rather felt that Dad might appreciate having it delivered personally.

Next morning he was shaving, and listening to the roar of support trucks arriving – they would provide the transport for Bert's drive back to Antwerp – when Waterman stammered, 'I beg your pardon, sir, but . . . the General is here.'

Waterman was a dragoon, so there could be no doubt about who he was speaking about. Fergus hastily rubbed a towel over his face and dashed into the rear of his ACV, to stare at his father.

'You took some catching up with,' Murdoch said. He wore uniform and looked as fit as ever, but there was less than the usual good humour in his face.

Fergus saluted and then grasped his hand. 'Where on earth have you sprung from?'

'England.'

'When last I heard you were in Yugoslavia.'

'I got back in November.'

'In November? Good Lord! And you never let me know.'

'Well, I had been wounded . . .'

'Not again. Oh, Dad, whatever did Mom say?'

At last Murdoch smiled. 'She wasn't very pleased. But I think she was pleased to have me back. She sends her best love.'

'And . . ?'

'Well,' Murdoch said, sitting down, and obviously choosing his words with great care. 'Churchill didn't want word of my return to leak out.'

'I'm surprised he didn't lock you up. I know he had it in mind.'

Murdoch's face at last relaxed into a grin. 'He seems to think I did quite a good job. I'm to get the Order of Merit.'

'Oh, Dad! Best congratulations.'

'Thanks. This visit is also top secret. I simply had to come, however.'

'And it's great to see you. How was Yugoslavia?'

'Yugoslavia,' Murdoch said, 'was grim. And is going to get grimmer, regardless of when the Germans call it a day. But I imagine that goes for several places in Europe.'

Fergus realized that his father was definitely not in a good mood. 'You, ah . . . know about the situation at home.'

'Yes,' Murdoch said. 'Is Bert around?'

'I imagine so. He's leaving today, for England. He's going to be an officer. Can you imagine that? We both felt he'd do better with Annaliese as an officer.'

'Yes,' Murdoch said. 'I'd like a word with him.'

Fergus frowned. 'You're not going to lay into him, I

hope. He really has behaved very well, except for, well . . . the beginning, I suppose. And he's going to get the VC for destroying that bridge under enemy fire.'

'I am delighted,' Murdoch said. 'I am very proud of him. I am very proud of all of you. But I'm afraid that I have to speak with him. And you.'

'Oh. Waterman, find the Sergeant-Major for me, will you? On the double, there's a good chap.'

'I gather you, and the regiment, have been covering yourselves with glory, as usual,' Murdoch remarked.

'We happened to be there. You wouldn't care to tell me what's on your mind?'

'I'd rather tell you just once,' Murdoch said. 'Ah, Sergeant-Major, good to see you.'

Bert was panting with exertion as he climbed into the truck and saluted. 'And to see you, sir!'

Murdoch shook hands. 'I'd like you to sit down, Bert.'

Bert glanced at Fergus, and received a quick nod. Cautiously he lowered himself on to the bench seat that ran along the side of the ACV.

Murdoch sat opposite him. 'You haven't seen your son yet, Bert, have you?'

Again Bert gave Fergus an anxious glance. 'Not yet, sir. I hope to do so this coming week.'

'Well, I can tell you that he is a fine healthy babe. He's at Broad Acres. Being looked after by Lady Mackinder.'

'Yes, sir,' Bert said. 'That's very kind of her ladyship, sir.'

Fergus was slightly quicker on the uptake. 'Where is Annaliese?' he asked.

Murdoch took a long breath. 'Annaliese is dead.'

Both the younger men stared at him in consternation.

'She went up to London a fortnight ago. Neither Lady Mackinder nor I knew anything about it until after she had left. Apparently she just walked out of the house in the middle of the night, and walked into Bath as well. She left a note. It said that she simply had to let off some steam after being cooped up at Broad Acres for nearly a year. I suspect the news of Paul's death had something to do with her mood. Well, I chased behind her, but there wasn't really any hope of catching or finding her, so I returned home. It wasn't until four days ago that we received word that her body had been found and identified, as the widow of the late Colonel Ian Mackinder.'

'But . . . how?' Fergus asked.

Bert was apparently incapable of speech.

'She was the victim of a V-2 rocket. Would you believe that it must have been one of the very last to fall on London? There hasn't been one since 29th March.'

'Good Lord!' Fergus said. 'Poor Liese. I am so terribly sorry, Bert.'

'Yes,' Murdoch said.

Bert sighed, his shoulders hunched. 'I don't think it was meant to be, sir.' The shoulders squared. 'The boy . . . he is my son, sir.'

'Of course he is, Bert,' Murdoch agreed. 'But, do you think you can cope?'

'He is my son, sir,' Bert repeated. 'And I am going to be an officer.'

'Yes,' Murdoch said. 'You are.' He stood up, held out his hand. 'Lady Mackinder will be very glad to see you, Bert.'

'Thank you, sir.' Bert saluted, then went down the ladder.

'He took it very well,' Murdoch said.

'I think, in fact, that he never actually loved Annaliese,' Fergus said. 'However much he wanted her. It was her misfortune, to be wanted but not loved. But I'd like him to have the boy. I'd like to think of him going to Sandhurst. The boy.'

'He will,' Murdoch said. 'But you . . . you haven't said what you feel about Annaliese.'

'Roughly the same as Bert.'

'Hm. You're thirty-five. It's a shame you aren't married.'

'I will be, very shortly.'

Murdoch raised his eyebrows. 'Anyone I know?'

Fergus grinned. 'As a matter of fact, yes. A woman named Monique Deschards.'

'Monique . . . Good God. I thought she was dead.'

Fergus told him how he had found her, and again in Paris.

Murdoch squeezed his hand. 'I am absolutely delighted. And I know your mother will be too. Oh, I am so pleased. Well, aren't you going to let me inspect your brigade, even if I am retired?'

'Of course. But there is something I must give you, first.' He handed over Paul's letter.

Murdoch frowned as he slit the envelope, read the contents. Then he crumpled it into a ball. 'Did he die well?'

'He fell on his sword, in a manner of speaking, in the best tradition of defeated and disillusioned commanders. At least he never knew about Annaliese.'

'Did he say anything before he shot himself?'

'No. Should he have?'

'He was your brother.'

'My . . .' Fergus's jaw dropped.

'Yes. I had an affair with his mother, way back during the Boer War, and he was the result. Oh, Lee knows about it. Always has done. There didn't seem much point in telling any of you, when you were kids. And then, when Paul became a Nazi, there seemed even less point.'

'Good Lord! And he never said a word. Oh, Dad, I am most terribly sorry.'

'I said, he did become a dyed in the wool Nazi,' Murdoch reminded him. 'And at least he died well.'

'But, if he was my brother, then Annaliese . . .'

'No, she is pure Reger. Or I couldn't have let her marry Ian. Or you.'

'I thought his face was familiar . . . my God, he looked like you,' Fergus said.

'Yes, he did. Well . . . it's all over and done with now. My God, forty-five years I have been mixed up with that family. And he was the very last. I'm glad he died like a gentleman.'

'Paul wasn't the last von Reger, Dad.'

Murdoch raised his head.

'There's little Ian.' Fergus smiled. 'But he's the last Mackinder, too. That little chap has quite a heritage to live up to.'

411

Epilogue
1985

That was no longer true, Murdoch thought, as he glanced at Brigadier Ian Mackinder, and from him to young Murdoch, seated opposite him at the bottom of the centre leg, face animated as he talked with his subaltern friends. Amongst whom was Ralph Manly-Smith, Bert's grandson. Like Bert, his son Albert had got moving young, as regards both marriage and children.

They would be re-fighting the battles of the past, because they had seen none of their own; they were too young even to have been in the Falklands. Should he pray to God that they never *would* fight a battle of their own? Or would that be to negate man's natural state?

The noise of conversation and clinking glasses rose around him, almost like the din of battle. He heard little of it, beamed benevolently when someone addressed him; his hearing was getting a little weak, certainly in a large gathering. Besides, these regimental dinners always filled him with so much nostalgia.

He had so much to remember.

South Africa! The Modder River. Murdoch Mackinder and Bert Yeald, a very young second lieutenant and a very young corporal, leading a fording party, without orders, into the Boer position. The story of his life, presumably.

Margriet Voorlandt!

Somaliland, surrounded by the Mad Mullah's warriors, and leading his squadron in a famous charge! Sergeant-Major Yeald had been at his side then too.

The Curragh, and the hideous spectre of an army mutiny!

Mons and Le Cateau, fighting the swarming Germans tooth and nail!

Mesopotamia, and Chand Bibi!

Amiens, and riding into battle beside the first tanks!

Meeting Hitler in the Landsberg!

The North West Frontier, and the final confrontation with the Mahsuds!

Jennifer Manly-Smith!

Dunkirk, and that last glorious tank battle in which he had been involved! And the death of Ian.

And then, the triumphs of the Hitler War. Fergus's triumphs. But out of the war had come, for all its tragedies, much solid happiness. If his apprehensions for the Balkans, and indeed all of Europe – apprehensions which had been shared by Churchill, but not, unfortunately, by Roosevelt – had been proved only too accurate, and they had had to live through a generation of fear, those days at last seemed to be ending; he had at least been right about Tito, who had very soon thrown off the Russian yoke, regardless of the risk involved.

While domestically, his life had bloomed in retirement. There had been so much to enjoy. Fergus and Monique; if they had never been able to have children following her horrific experiences, they had been very happy, and Fergus had got his KCMG. Young Ian, who had grown into the so competent soldier beside him. The glorious return of Harry, not after all killed, but a prisoner of the Japanese for four years; he had thrown that aside with the spirit of a true Mackinder to become a best-selling novelist. Bert and his son. Bert hadn't quite made brigadier, but he had died a colonel. Ralph and Jennie would have been proud.

And Lee and himself, and Broad Acres. They had trodden a long and sometimes tortuous path together. But she had forgiven all his twists and turns, and they had had a so happy old age together. Since her death, five years ago, he had tended to live more and more in the past.

More and more, he thought. As he grew more and more tired. It was way past his bed time, and his resident nurse would be having kittens. But he did not want to go home. Here he was in the heart of his true family, the regiment, for whom, he knew, he remained the one and only General.

'Gentlemen,' Brigadier Ian *Mackinder said, standing. 'Pray rise for the loyal toast.' He waited while the officers stood, and then raised his glass. 'Gentlemen, the Queen!'

Only then did he meet his son's eyes. Murdoch was staring up the table, an expression of horror on his face. Ian looked down, at Sir Murdoch. The general had not risen. And now everyone was staring with equal consternation.

'Oh, my God!' Fergus bent over his father, put his hand on his breast, his ear to his nostrils.

'Sergeant-Major, fetch a doctor,' someone called.

Fergus straightened. 'The General is dead,' he announced.

The company stared at him.

Fergus took a long breath, then picked up his glass. 'Gentlemen, I give you the greatest fighting soldier this army has ever possessed, Sir Murdoch Mackinder.'

'Sir Murdoch Mackinder,' they said.

Sir Murdoch Mackinder, Lieutenant Murdoch Mackinder thought. Now I do have a great deal to remember. And live up to.

I shall not fail him.

4330